P9-CEQ-887

ON
MYSTIC
LAKE

Other books by Kristin Hannah

HOME AGAIN

WAITING FOR THE MOON

WHEN LIGHTNING STRIKES

IF YOU BELIEVE

THE ENCHANTMENT

A HANDFUL OF HEAVEN

ONCE IN EVERY LIFE

KRISTIN HANNAH

ON MYSTIC LAKE

Crown Publishers, Inc.
New York

Published by Crown Publishers, Inc., 201 East 50th Street, New York, New York 10022. Member of the Crown Publishing Group.

Random House, Inc. New York, Toronto, London, Sydney, Auckland
www.randomhouse.com

CROWN and colophon are trademarks of Crown Publishers, Inc.

Design by Nancy Kenmore

Printed in the United States of America

Library of Congress Cataloging-in-Publication Data

Hannah, Kristin.
    On mystic lake / Kristin Hannah. — 1st ed.
    I. Title.
  PS3558.A4763047   1999
  813'.54—dc21   98-26448
                                          CIP

ISBN 0-609-60249-7

10   9   8   7   6   5   4   3   2   1

First Edition

To Barbara Kurek.

My mother couldn't have chosen a better

godmother for me . . .

To the men in my life, Benjamin and Tucker . . .

And in memory of my mother, Sharon Goodno John.

I hope they have bookstores in Heaven, Mom.

ACKNOWLEDGMENTS

Some books are battles. Others are wars. To my generals—Ann Patty, Jane Berkey, and Linda Grey—thanks for always demanding my very best; to Stephanie Tade, thanks for believing in this book from the very beginning; to Elisa Wares and the wonderful team at Ballantine Books, thanks for your continued support and encouragement along the way; to my comrades—Megan Chance, Jill Marie Landis, Jill Barnett, Penelope Williamson, and Susan Wiggs—thanks for always being there, for listening and laughing and everything in between; and to my guardian angel, my *über*-agent, mentor, and friend, Andrea Cirillo, thanks for everything.

PART ONE

*The true voyage of self-discovery
lies not in seeking new landscapes
but in having new eyes.*

MARCEL PROUST

CHAPTER 1

Rain fell like tiny silver teardrops from the tired sky. Somewhere behind a bank of clouds lay the sun, too weak to cast a shadow on the ground below.

It was March, the doldrums of the year, still and quiet and gray, but the wind had already begun to warm, bringing with it the promise of spring. Trees that only last week had been naked and brittle seemed to have grown six inches over the span of a single, moonless night, and sometimes, if the sunlight hit a limb just so, you could see the red bud of new life stirring at the tips of the crackly brown bark. Any day, the hills behind Malibu would blossom, and for a few short weeks this would be the prettiest place on Earth.

Like the plants and animals, the children of Southern California sensed the coming of the sun. They had begun to dream of ice cream and popsicles and last year's cutoffs. Even determined city dwellers, who lived in glass and concrete high-rises in places with pretentious names like Century City, found themselves veering into the nursery aisles of their local supermarkets. Small, potted geraniums began appearing in the metal shopping carts, alongside the sun-dried tomatoes and the bottles of Evian water.

For nineteen years, Annie Colwater had awaited spring with the breathless anticipation of a young girl at her first dance. She ordered bulbs from distant lands and shopped for hand-painted ceramic pots to hold her favorite annuals.

But now, all she felt was dread, and a vague, formless panic. After today, nothing in her well-ordered life would remain the same, and she was not a woman who liked the sharp, jagged edges of change. She preferred things to run smoothly, down the middle of the road. That was where she felt safest—in the center of the ordinary, with her family gathered close around her.

Wife.

Mother.

These were the roles that defined her, that gave her life meaning. It was what she'd always been, and now, as she warily approached her fortieth birthday, it was all she could remember ever wanting to be. She had gotten married right after college and been pregnant within that same year. Her husband and daughter were her anchors; without Blake and Natalie, she had often thought that she might float out to sea, a ship without captain or destination.

But what did a mother do when her only child left home?

She shifted uneasily in the front seat of the Cadillac. The clothes she'd chosen with such care this morning, navy wool pants and a pale rose silk blouse, felt wrong. Usually she could take refuge in fashionable camouflage, by pretending to be a woman she wasn't. Designer clothes and carefully applied makeup could make her *look* like the high-powered corporate wife she was supposed to be. But not today. Today, the waist-length brown hair she'd drawn back from her face in a chignon—the way her husband liked it, the way she always wore it—was giving her a headache.

She drummed her manicured fingernails on the armrest and glanced at Blake, who was settled comfortably in the driver's seat. He looked completely relaxed, as if this were a normal afternoon instead of the day their seventeen-year-old daughter was leaving for London.

It was childish to be so scared, she knew that, but knowing didn't ease the pain. When Natalie had first told them that she wanted to graduate early and spend her last quarter in London, Annie had been proud of her daughter's independence. It was the sort of thing that seniors at the expensive prep school often did, and precisely the sophisticated sort of adventure Annie had wanted for her daughter.

Annie herself would never have had the courage for so bold a move—not at seventeen, not even now at thirty-nine. Travel had always intimidated her. Although she loved seeing new places and meeting new people, she always felt an underlying discomfort when she left home.

She knew this weakness was a remnant of her youth, a normal by-product of the tragedy that had tainted her childhood, but understanding her fear didn't alleviate it. On every family vacation, Annie had suffered from nightmares—dark, twisted visions in which she was alone in a foreign land without money or direction. Lost, she wandered through unfamiliar streets, searching for the family that was her safety net, until, finally, sobbing in her sleep, she awoke. Then, she would curl into her husband's sleeping body and, at last, relax.

She had been proud of her daughter's independence and courage in choosing to go all the way to England by herself, but she hadn't realized how hard it would be to watch Natalie leave. They'd been like best friends, she and her daughter, ever since Natalie had emerged from the angry, sullen rubble of the early teen years. They'd had hard times, sure, and fights and hurt feelings, and they'd each said things that shouldn't have been said, but all that had only made their bond stronger. They were a unit, the "girls" in a household where the only man worked eighty hours a week and sometimes went whole days without remembering to smile.

She stared out the car window. The concrete-encrusted canyons of downtown Los Angeles were a blur of high-rise buildings, graffiti, and neon lights that left streaking reflections in the misty rain. They were getting closer and closer to the airport.

She reached for her husband, touched the pale blue cashmere of his sleeve. "Let's fly to London with Nana and get her settled with her host family. I know—"

"*Mom,*" Natalie said sharply from the backseat. "Get real. It would be, like, *so* humiliating for you to show up."

Annie drew her hand back and plucked a tiny lint ball from her expensive wool pants. "It was just an idea," she said softly. "Your dad has been trying to get me to England for ages. I thought . . . maybe we could go now."

Blake gave her a quick look, one she couldn't quite read. "I haven't mentioned England in years." Then he muttered something about the traffic and slammed his hand on the horn.

"I guess you won't miss the California traffic," Annie said into the awkward silence that followed.

In the backseat, Natalie laughed. "No way. Sally Pritchart—you remember her, Mom, she went to London last year—anyway, Sally said it was way cool. Not like California, where you need a car to go anywhere. In London, all you do is get on the Underground." She poked her blond head into the opening between the two front seats. "Did you take the Underground when you were in London last year, Dad?"

Blake slammed on the horn again. With an irritated sigh, he flicked on his turn signal and jerked the car into the fast lane. "Huh? What was that?"

Natalie sighed. "Nothing."

Annie squeezed Blake's shoulder in a gentle reminder. These were precious moments—the last they'd see their daughter for months—and, as usual, he was missing them. She started to say something to fill the silence, something to keep from thinking about the loneliness of a house without Natalie, but then she saw the sign, LAX, and she couldn't say anything at all.

Blake pulled onto the exit ramp and drove into the dark silence of the underground parking lot, killing the engine. For a long moment, they all sat there. Annie waited for him to say something fatherly and important, something to mark the occasion. He was so good with words, but he merely opened his door.

As always, Annie followed his lead. She got out of the car and stood beside her door, twirling her sunglasses in her cold, cold fingers. She looked down at Natalie's luggage—a single gray duffle bag and a green canvas Eddie Bauer backpack.

She worried that it wasn't enough, that it was too unwieldy . . . she worried about everything. Her daughter looked so young suddenly, her tall, thin body swamped by a baggy denim dress that stopped an inch above her scuffed black combat boots. Two metal clips held her long, silver-blond hair away from her pale face. Three silver earrings formed a curved ladder up her left ear.

Annie wanted to manufacture a conversation—toss out bits of advice about money and passports and the importance of always being in a group of kids—but she couldn't do it.

Blake walked on ahead, carrying the two lonely pieces of luggage, as Natalie and Annie followed silently in his wake. She wished he'd slow down and walk with them, but she didn't say anything—just in case Natalie hadn't noticed that her dad seemed to be in a rush. At the ticket counter, he handled everything, and then the three of them headed for the international terminal.

At the gate, Annie clung to her navy handbag as if it were a shield. Alone, she walked to the huge, dirty window. For a split second, she saw herself reflected in the glass, a thin, flawlessly dressed housewife standing by herself.

"Don't be so quiet, Mom. I can't take it." The words contained a tiny wobble of anxiety that only a mother would hear.

Annie forced a laugh. "Usually you guys are begging me to keep quiet. And it's not like I can't think of a million things to say right now. Why, just yesterday I was looking at your baby picture, and I thought—"

"I love you, too, Mom," Natalie whispered.

Annie grabbed her daughter's hand and held on. She didn't dare turn toward Natalie, afraid that her heartache would show. It was definitely not the image she wanted her child to carry like a bit of too-heavy baggage onto the plane.

Blake came up beside them. "I wish you had let us get you first-class tickets. It's such a long flight, and the food in coach is horrible. Christ, you'll probably have to assemble your own beef pot pie."

Natalie laughed. "Like you would know about the food in coach, Dad."

Blake grinned. "Well, it's certainly more comfortable."

"This isn't about comfort," Natalie answered. "It's about *adventure*."

"Ah, adventure," Annie said, finding her voice at last. She wondered how it felt to have such big dreams, and once again she was envious of her daughter's independence. Natalie was always so sure of who she was and what she wanted.

A voice boomed over the loudspeaker. "We will now begin boarding flight three-five-seven, with service to London."

"I'm going to miss you guys," Natalie said softly. She glanced at the plane, chewing nervously on her thumbnail.

Annie placed a hand on Natalie's soft cheek, trying to memorize everything about this moment, the tiny mole beside her daughter's left earlobe, the exact hue of her straight blond hair and blue eyes, the cinnamon sprinkling of freckles across her nose.

Annie wanted to implant it all into her memory so she could pull it out like a treasured photograph over the next three months. "Remember, we'll call every Monday—seven o'clock your time. You're going to have a great time, Nana."

Blake opened his arms. "Give your old dad a hug."

Natalie hurled herself into her father's arms.

Too soon, the voice came over the loudspeaker, announcing the boarding of Natalie's row.

Annie gave Natalie one last long, desperate hug—not nearly long enough—then, slowly, she drew back. Blinking away tears, she watched Natalie give her ticket to the woman at the doorway, and then, with a last, hurried wave, her daughter disappeared into the jetway.

"She'll be fine, Annie."

She stared at the empty doorway. "I know."

One tear, that's how long it took. One tear, sliding down Annie's face, and her daughter was gone.

Annie stood there long after the plane had left, long after the white trail of exhaust had melted into the somber sky. She could feel Blake beside her. She wished he'd take her hand or squeeze her shoulder or pull her into his arms—any of the things he would have done five years ago.

She turned. In his eyes, she saw her own reflection, and the misty mirror of their life together. She'd first kissed him when she was eighteen years old—almost Natalie's age—and there'd never been another man for her in all the years since.

His handsome face was as serious as she'd ever seen it. "Ah, Annie . . ." His voice was a cracked whisper of breath. "What will you do now?"

She was in danger of crumbling, right here in this sterile, crowded airport. "Take me home, Blake," she whispered unevenly. She wanted her things around her now, all the reminders of who she was.

"Of course." He grabbed her hand and led her through the terminal and into the garage. Wordlessly, they got into the Cadillac and slammed the doors shut. The air-conditioning came on instantly.

As the car hurtled down one freeway after another, Annie felt exhausted. She leaned heavily in her seat and stared out the window at this city that had never become her city, although she and Blake had moved here right after college. It was a sprawling labyrinth of a town, where gorgeous, elaborately appointed dowager buildings were demolished daily by a few well-placed charges, where men and women with no appreciation for art or beauty or constancy set fire to fuses that blasted tons of sculptured marble and glass into piles of smoking, belching rubble. In this city of angels, too few noticed the loss of one more landmark. Before the collapsed building had even cooled, developers swarmed City Hall, climbing over one another like black ants for permits and easements. Within months, a sleek, glass-faced child of a building would rise higher and higher into the smoggy brown sky, so high that Annie often wondered if these builders thought they could access heaven with their leveraged millions.

She was seized by a fierce, unexpected longing to return home. Not to the crowded, affluent beauty of Malibu, but to the moist green landscape of her youth, that wild part of western Washington State where mushrooms grew to the size of dinner plates and water rushed in silver threads along every roadside, where fat, glossy raccoons came out in the light of a full moon and drank from mud puddles in the middle of the road. To Mystic—where the only skyscrapers were Douglas firs that had been growing since the American Revolution. It had been almost ten years since she'd been back. Perhaps she could finally talk Blake into a trip now that they were no longer tethered to Southern California by Natalie's school schedule.

"What do you think about planning a trip to Mystic?" she asked her husband.

He didn't look at her, didn't respond to her question, and it made her feel stupid and small. She pulled at the large diamond stud in her ear and stared outside. "I was thinking about joining the Club. God knows I'll have more time on my hands now. You're always saying I don't get out of the house enough. Aerobics would be fun, don't you think?"

"I haven't said that in years."

"Oh. Well . . . there's always tennis. I used to love tennis. Remember when we used to play doubles?"

He turned off the freeway and eased onto the twisting, traffic-clogged Pacific Coast Highway. At the gated entrance to their road, he waved to the guard and passed into the Colony, the beachfront jewel of Malibu. Rain beaded the windshield and blurred the world for a split second, before the wipers swept the water away.

At their house, he slowed, inching down the brick-paved driveway. He stopped in front of the garage.

Annie glanced at him. It was odd that he hadn't pulled into the garage. Odd that he hadn't even hit the door's remote control. Odder still that he'd left the car running. He hated to leave the Cadillac out in the rain. . . .

He's not himself.

The realization sanded the hard edges from her anxiety, reminded her that she wasn't as alone as she felt. Her high-powered, ultra-competent husband was as fragile as she was right now.

They would do it together, she and Blake. They would get each other through this day, and all the empty-nest days and nights to come. They had been a family before Natalie, and they would be one again, just the two of them. It might even be fun, like the old days when they had been best friends and partners and lovers . . . the days when they went out dancing and didn't come home until the sun was peeking up from the horizon.

She twisted around to face him, and brushed a lock of hair from his eyes. "I love you. We'll get each other through this."

He didn't answer.

She hadn't really expected him to, but still the awkward silence stung. She tucked the disappointment away and opened the car door.

Tiny shards of rain slipped through the opening, mottling her sleeve. "It's going to be a lonely spring. Maybe we should talk to Lupita about planning a barbecue. We haven't had an old-fashioned beach party in years. It'd be good for us. God knows it's going to be weird walking around the house without—"

"Annie," he said her name so sharply that she bit her tongue in the middle of her sentence.

He turned to her, and she saw that there were tears in his eyes.

She leaned over and touched his cheek in a fleeting, tender caress. "I'm going to miss her, too."

He looked away and sighed heavily. "You don't understand. I want a divorce."

CHAPTER 2

"I meant to wait to tell you . . . at least until next week. But the thought of coming home tonight . . ." Blake shook his head and let the sentence trail off.

Very slowly, Annie closed the car door. Rain hit the windshield and ran in streaks down the windows, obscuring the world outside the car.

She couldn't have heard right. Frowning, she reached for him. "What are you talking about . . ."

He lurched against the window, as if her touch—the touch he'd known for so long—were now repugnant.

It all became real suddenly, with that gesture he wouldn't allow. Her husband was asking for a divorce. She drew back her hand and found that it was trembling.

"I should have done this a long time ago, Annie. I'm not happy. I haven't been happy with you in years."

The shock of it was unlike anything she'd ever experienced. It was everywhere, spreading through her in wave after numbing wave. Her voice was tangled deep, deep inside of her, and she couldn't find the frayed start of it.

"I can't believe I'm saying this," he said softly, and she heard the choked-up thickness of his breathing. "I'm seeing someone else . . . another woman."

She stared at him, her mouth hanging open. He was having an *affair*. The word sank through her, hurting all the way to the bone. A thousand tiny details slipped into place: dinners he'd missed, trips he'd taken to exotic locations, the new silk boxer shorts he'd started wearing, the switch in colognes from Polo to Calvin Klein after all these years, the love they made so rarely . . .

How had she been so blind? She *must* have known. Deep inside, in some primitive feminine core, she must have known what was happening and chosen to ignore it.

She turned to him, wanting to touch him so badly it was a physical ache. For half her life, she'd touched him whenever she wanted, and now he had taken that right away. "We can get over an affair. . . ." Her voice was feeble, not her voice at all. "Couples do it all the time. I mean . . . it'll take me some time to forgive you, time to learn to trust, but—"

"I don't want your forgiveness."

This couldn't be happening. Not to her. Not to *them*. She heard the words and felt the pain, but it all had a dizzying sense of unreality about it. "But we have so much. We have *history*. We have Natalie. We can work this out, maybe try counseling. I know we've had problems, but we can get through it."

"I don't want to try, Annie. I want out."

"But *I* don't." Her voice spiked into a high, plaintive whine. "We're a *family*. You can't throw twenty years away. . . ." She couldn't find the words she needed. It terrified her, the sudden silence she found in her own soul; she was afraid there were words that could save her, save them, and she couldn't find them. "Please, *please* don't do this. . . ."

He didn't say anything for a long time—long enough for her to find a strand of hope and weave it into solid fabric. *He'll change his mind. He'll realize we're a family and say it was just a midlife crisis. He'll—*

"I'm in love with her."

Annie's stomach started a slow, agonized crumbling.

Love? How could he be in love with someone else? Love took time and effort. It was a million tiny moments stacked one atop another to make something tangible. That declaration—love—and everything it meant diminished her. She felt as if she were a tiny, disappearing person, a million miles away from the man she'd always loved. "How long?"

"Almost a year."

She felt the first hot sting of tears. A year in which everything between them had been a lie. Everything. "Who is she?"

"Suzannah James. The firm's new junior partner."

Suzannah James—one of the two dozen guests at Blake's birthday party last weekend. The thin young woman in the turquoise dress who'd hung on Blake's every word. The one he'd danced with to "A Kiss to Build a Dream On."

Tears stung Annie's eyes, turned everything into a blur. "But after the party, we made love. . . ."

Had he been imagining Suzannah's face in the darkness? Was that why he'd clicked off the bedroom lights before he touched her? A tiny, whimpering moan escaped her. She couldn't hold it all inside. "Blake, please . . ."

He looked helpless, a little lost himself, and in the moment of vulnerability, he was Blake again, her husband. Not this ice-cold man who wouldn't meet her gaze. "I love her, Annie. Please don't make me say it again."

The sour remains of his confession tainted the air, left her with nothing to breathe. *I love her, Annie.*

She wrenched the car door open and stumbled blindly down the brick walkway to her house. Rain hit her face and mingled with her tears. At the door, she pulled the keys from her handbag, but her hand was shaking so badly she couldn't find the lock on the first try. Then the key slipped into the slot and clicked hard.

She lurched inside and slammed the door shut behind her.

Annie finished her second glass of wine and poured a third. Usually two glasses of chardonnay left her giddy and reeling and trying to remember song lyrics from her youth, but tonight it wasn't helping.

She walked dully through her house, trying to figure out what she'd done that was so wrong, how she'd failed.

If only she knew that, maybe then she could make it all right again. She'd spent the past twenty years putting her family's needs first, and yet somehow she had failed, and her failure had left her alone, wandering around this too-big house, missing a daughter who was gone and a husband who was in love with someone else.

Somewhere along the way, she'd forgotten what she should have remembered. It was a lesson she'd learned early in life—one she'd thought she knew well. People left, and if you loved too deeply, too fiercely, their swift and sudden absence could chill you to the soul.

She climbed into her bed and burrowed under the covers, but when she realized that she was on "her" side of the bed, she felt as if she'd been slapped. The wine backed up into her throat, tasting sour enough that she thought she would vomit. She stared up at the ceiling, blinking back tears. With each ragged breath, she felt herself getting smaller and smaller.

What was she supposed to do now? It had been so long since she'd been anything but *we*. She didn't even know if there was an *I* inside of her anymore. Beside her, the bedside clock ticked and ticked . . . and she wept.

The phone rang.

Annie woke on the first ring, her heart pounding. It was him, calling to say it was all a mistake, that he was sorry, that he'd always loved her. But when she picked up the phone, it was Natalie, laughing. "Hey, Mom, I made it."

Her daughter's voice brought the heartache rushing back.

Annie sat up in bed, running a weak hand through her tangled hair. "Hi, honey. I can't believe you're there already." Her voice was thin and unsteady. She took a deep breath, trying to collect herself. "So, how was your flight?"

Natalie launched into a monologue that lasted for a steady fifteen minutes. Annie heard about the plane trip, the airport, about the strangeness of the London Underground, and the way the houses were all connected together—like, San Francisco, you know, Mom—

" . . . Mom?"

Annie realized with a start that she'd lapsed into silence. She'd been listening to Natalie—she truly had—but some silly, pointless turn in the conversation had made her think of Blake, of the car that wasn't in the garage and the body that wasn't beside her in bed.

God, is that how it's going to be from now on?

"Mom?"

Annie squeezed her eyes shut, a feeble attempt to escape. There was a white, static roar of sound in her head. "I . . . I'm right here, Natalie. I'm sorry. You were telling me about your host family."

"Are you all right, Mom?"

Tears leaked down Annie's cheeks. She didn't bother to wipe them away. "I'm fine. How about you?"

A pause crackled through the lines. "I miss you guys."

Annie heard loneliness in her daughter's voice and it took all of her self-control not to whisper into the phone, *Come home, Nana. We'll be lonely together.*

"Trust me, Nana, you'll make friends. In no time at all, you'll be having so much fun that you won't be sitting by the phone waiting for your old mom to call. June fifteenth will come much too quickly."

"Hey, Mom, you sound kinda shaky. Are you going to be okay while I'm gone?"

Annie laughed; it was a nervous, fluttery sound. "Of course I will. Don't you dare worry about me."

"Okay." The word was spoken so softly Annie had to strain to hear it. "Before I start crying, I better talk to Daddy."

Annie flinched. "Dad's not here right now."

"Oh."

"He loves you, though. He told me to tell you that."

"Yeah, of course he does. So, you'll call Monday?"

"Like clockwork."

"I love you, Mom."

Annie felt tears flood her throat again, squeezing until she could hardly talk. She suppressed a fierce urge to warn Natalie about the world, to tell her to watch out for lives that fall apart on a rainy spring day without warning. "Be careful, Natalie. Love you."

"Love you."

And the phone went dead.

Annie placed the handset back on the base and crawled out of bed, stumbling blindly into her bathroom. The lights came on like something out of an Oliver Stone movie. She stared in horror at her reflection. She was still wearing her clothes from the airport, and they were wrinkled into something she didn't recognize. Her hair was stuck so tightly to her head it looked as if she'd used Elmer's glue as conditioner.

She slammed her fist onto the light switch. In the blessed darkness, she stripped down to her bra and panties and left the wrinkled clothes in a heap on the tile floor. Feeling tired and old and swollen, she walked out of the bathroom and crawled back into bed.

She could smell him in the fabric of the sheets. Only it wasn't him. Blake—her Blake—had always worn Polo. She'd given him the cologne for Christmas every year; it came already wrapped for the holiday in a green gift box at Nordstrom. She'd given it to him every year and he'd worn it every day . . . until Calvin Klein and Suzannah changed everything.

Annie's best friend showed up bright and early the next morning, pounding on the front door, yelling, "Open up in there, goddamn it, or I'll call the fire department."

Annie slipped into Blake's black silk bathrobe and stumbled tiredly toward the front door. She felt like hell from the wine she'd drunk last night, and it took considerable effort simply to open the door. The expensive stone tiles felt icy cold beneath her bare feet.

Terri Spencer stood in the doorway, wearing a baggy pair of faded denim overalls. Her thick, curly nimbus of black hair was hidden by a wild scarlet scarf. Bold gold hoops hung from her ears. She looked exactly like the gypsy she played on a daytime soap. Terri crossed her arms, cocked one ample hip, and eyed Annie. "You look like shit."

Annie sighed. Of course Terri had heard. No matter how much of a free spirit her friend claimed to be, her current husband was a dyed-in-the-wool lawyer. And lawyers gossiped. "You've heard."

"I had to hear it from Frank. You could have called me yourself."

Annie ran a trembling hand through her tangled hair. They had been friends forever, she and Terri. Practically sisters. But even with all they'd been through together, all the ups and downs they'd weathered,

Annie didn't know how to begin. She was used to taking care of Terri, with her wild, over-the-top actress lifestyle and her steady stream of divorces and marriages. Annie was used to taking care of everyone. Except Annie. "I meant to call, but it's been . . . difficult."

Terri curled a plump arm around Annie's shoulder and propelled her to the overstuffed sofa in the living room. Then she went from window to window, whipping open the white silk curtains. The twenty-foot-tall, wall-to-wall windows framed a sea and sky so blue it stung the eyes, and left Annie with nowhere to hide.

When Terri was through, she sat down beside Annie on the sofa. "Now," she said softly. "What the fuck happened?"

Annie wished she could smile—it was what Terri wanted, why she'd used the vulgarity—but Annie couldn't respond. Saying it out loud would make it too real. She sagged forward, burying her puffy face in her hands. "Oh, God . . ."

Terri took Annie in her arms and held her tightly, rocking back and forth, smoothing the dirty hair from her sticky cheeks. It felt good to be held and comforted, to know that she wasn't as alone as she felt.

"You'll get through it," Terri said at last. "Right now, you think you won't, but you will. I promise. Blake's an asshole, anyway. You'll be better off without him."

Annie drew back and looked at her friend through a blur of stinging tears. "I don't . . . want to be without him."

"Of course you don't. I only meant . . ."

"I know what you meant. You meant that it will get easier. Like I'd trust your opinion on this. You change husbands more often than I change underwear."

Terri's thick black eyebrows winged upward. "Score one for the housewife. Look Annie, I know I'm harsh and pessimistic, and that's why my marriages fail, but remember what I used to be like? Remember in college?"

Annie remembered, even though she wished she didn't. Terri used to be a sweet little Pollyanna; that's why they'd become best friends. Terri had stayed innocent until the day her first husband, Rom, had come home and told her he was having an affair with their accountant's daughter. Terri had had twenty-four hours' notice, and then *wham!* the checking account was gone, the savings had been mysteriously "spent," and the medical practice they'd built together had been sold to a buddy for one dollar.

Annie had been with Terri constantly back then, drinking wine in the middle of the day, even smoking pot on a few occasions. It had made Blake insane. *What are you doing still hanging around that cheap wanna-be, anyway?* he used to say. *You have dozens of more acceptable friends.* It had been one of the few times Annie had stood up to Blake.

"You stayed with me every day," Terri said softly, slipping her hand into Annie's and squeezing gently. "You got me through it, and I'm going to be here for you. Whenever you need me. Twenty-four hours a day."

"I didn't know how much it hurt. . . . It feels like , , ," The humiliating tears burned again. She wished she could stop them, but it was impossible.

"Like your insides are bleeding away . . . like nothing will ever make you happy again? I know."

Annie closed her eyes. Terri's understanding was almost more than she could bear. She didn't want her friend to know so much; not *Terri,* who'd never held a marriage together for more than a few years and couldn't even commit to owning a pet. It was terrifying to think that this was . . . ordinary. As if the loss of twenty years was nothing at all, just another divorce in a country that saw a million breakups a year.

"Look, kiddo, I hate to bring this up, but I have to. Blake's a hotshot attorney. You need to protect yourself."

It was bruising advice, the kind that made a woman want to curl up into a tiny, broken ball. Annie tried to smile. "Blake's not like that."

"Oh, really. You need to ask yourself how well you know him."

Annie couldn't deal with this now. It was enough to realize that the past year had been a lie; she couldn't fathom the possibility that Blake had become a complete stranger. She stared at Terri, hoping her friend could understand. "You're asking me to be someone I'm not, Terri. I mean, to walk into a bank and clean out the money, *our* money. It's so . . . final. And it makes this about things . . . just things. I can't do it to

Blake. I can't do it to *me*. I know it's naive—stupid, even—to trust him, but he's been my best friend for more than half my life."

"Some friend."

Annie touched her friend's plump hand. "I love you for worrying about me, Terri. Really, I do, but I'm not ready for this advice. I hope . . ." Her voice fell to a whisper. She felt hopelessly naive when she looked into Terri's sad, knowing eyes. "I still hope I don't need it, I guess."

Terri forced a bright smile. "Maybe you're right. Maybe it's just a midlife crisis and he'll get over it."

They spent the next few hours talking. Time and again, Annie pulled a memory or an anecdote out of the black hat of her marriage and tossed it out, as if *talking* about her life, remembering it, would bring him home.

Terri listened and smiled and held her, but she didn't offer any more real-world advice—and Annie was thankful. Sometime around noon they ordered a large lamb sausage pizza from Granita's, and they sat on the deck and ate the whole thing. As the sun finally set across the blue Pacific, Annie knew that Terri would have to go soon.

Annie turned to her best friend. Finally, she asked the question that had been hovering for the better part of the afternoon. "What if he doesn't come back, Terri?" She said it so quietly that, for a moment, she thought the words were buried in the distant sound of the surf.

"What if he doesn't?"

Annie looked away. "I can't imagine my life without him. What will I do? Where will I go?"

"You'll go home," Terri said. "If I'd had a dad as cool as Hank, I would have gone home in an instant."

Home. It struck her for the first time that the word was as fragile as bone china. "Home is with Blake."

"Ah, Annie," Terri sighed, squeezing her hand. "Not anymore."

Two days later, he called.

His voice was the sweetest sound she'd ever heard. "Blake . . ."

"I need to see you."

She swallowed hard, felt the sudden sting of tears. *Thank you, God. I knew he'd come back.* "Now?"

"No. My schedule's kind of tight this morning. As soon as I can break free."

For the first time in days, Annie could breathe.

When Blake stared at the soaring white angles of the house, he felt an unexpected pang of loss. It was so beautiful, this home of theirs, so stunningly contemporary. A real showpiece on a street where teardowns routinely cost five million dollars and nothing was too expensive.

Annie had conceived, created, and designed this place. She'd taken the view—sea and sand and sky—and translated it into a home that seemed to have grown out of the hillside. She'd chosen every tile, every fixture; all through the house were incongruous little items of whimsy— an angel here, a gargoyle there, a ratty old macrame plant hanger in the corner of a room with thousand-dollar-a-square-foot wooden paneling, a family photo in a homemade shell frame. There was no place inside that didn't reflect her bubbling, slightly off-center personality.

He tried to remember what it had felt like to love her, but he couldn't anymore.

He'd been sleeping with other women for ten years, seducing them and bedding them and forgetting them. He'd traveled with them, spent the night with them, and through it all, Annie had been at home, baking recipes from *Gourmet* magazine and picking out paint chips and tile samples and driving Natalie to and from school. He'd thought sooner or later she'd notice that he'd fallen out of love with her, but she was so damn trusting. She always believed the best of everyone, and when she loved, it was body and soul, forever.

He sighed, suddenly feeling tired. It was turning forty that had changed his outlook, made him realize that he didn't want to be locked in a loveless marriage anymore.

Before the gray had moved its ugly fingers into his hair and lines had settled beneath his blue eyes, he thought he had it all—a glamorous career, a beautiful wife, a loving daughter, and all the freedom he needed.

He traveled with his college buddies twice a year, went on fishing trips to remote islands with pretty beaches and prettier women; he played basketball two nights a week and closed the local bar down on Friday nights. Unlike most of his friends, he'd always had a wife who understood, who stayed at home. The perfect wife and mother—everything that he thought he wanted.

Then he met Suzannah. What had begun as just another sexual conquest rolled into the most unexpected thing of all: love.

For the first time in years, he felt young and alive. They made love everywhere, all times of the day and night. Suzannah never cared what the neighbors thought or worried about a sleeping child in the next room. She was wild and unpredictable, and she was smart—unlike Annie, who thought the PTA was as vital to world order as the EEC.

He walked slowly down to the front door. Before he could even reach for the bell, the hand-carved rosewood door opened.

She stood in the doorway, her hands clasped nervously at her waist. A creamy silk dress clung to her body, and he couldn't help noticing that she'd lost weight in the past few days—and God knew she couldn't afford it.

Her small, heart-shaped face was pale, alarmingly so, and her eyes, usually as bright and green as shamrocks, were dull and bloodshot. She'd pulled her long hair into a tight ponytail that accentuated the sharp lines of her cheekbones and made her lips look swollen. Her earrings didn't match; she was wearing one diamond and one pearl, and somehow that little incongruity brought home the stinging pain of his betrayal.

"Blake . . ." He heard the thin lilt of hope in her voice, and realized suddenly what she must have thought when he called this morning.

Shit. How could he have been so stupid?

She backed away from the door, smoothing a nonexistent wrinkle from her dress. "Come in, come in. You . . ." She looked away quickly, but not before he saw her bite down on her lower lip—the nervous habit she'd had since she was young. He thought she was going to say something, but at the last minute she turned and led the way down the hallway and out onto the huge, multitiered deck that overlooked the Colony's quiet patch of Malibu beach.

Christ, he wished he hadn't come. He didn't need to see her pain in sharp relief, in the way she kept smoothing her dress and jabbing at her hair.

She crossed to the table, where a pitcher of lemonade—his favorite—and two crystal glasses sat on an elegant silver tray. "Natalie's settling in well. I've only talked to her once—and I was going to call again, but . . . well . . . it's been hard. I thought she might hear something in my voice. And, of course, she'll ask for you. Maybe later . . . while you're here . . . we could call again."

"I shouldn't have come." He said it more sharply than he intended, but he couldn't stand to hear the tremor in her voice anymore.

Her hand jerked. Lemonade splashed over the rim of the glass and puddled on the gray stone table. She didn't turn to him, and he was glad. He didn't want to see her face.

"Why did you?"

Something in her voice—resignation, maybe, or pain—caught him off guard. Tears burned behind his eyes; he couldn't believe this was *hurting*. He reached into his pocket and pulled out the interim settlement papers he'd drafted. Wordlessly, he leaned over her shoulder and dropped them on the table. An edge of the envelope landed in the spilled lemonade. A dark, bubbling splotch began to form.

He couldn't seem to draw his eyes from the stain. "Those are the papers, Annie. . . ."

She didn't move, didn't answer, just stood there with her back to him.

She looked pathetic, with her shoulders hunched and her fingers curled around the table's edge. He didn't need to see her face to know what she was feeling. He could see the tears falling, one after another, splashing on the stone like tiny drops of rain.

CHAPTER 3

"I can't believe you're doing this." Annie hadn't meant to say anything, but the words formed themselves. When he didn't answer, she turned toward him. Sadly, after almost twenty years of marriage, she couldn't bear to meet his eyes. "Why?"

That's what she really wanted to understand. She'd always put her family's needs above her own, always done everything she could to make her loved ones feel safe and happy. It had started long before she met Blake, in her childhood. Her mother had died when Annie was very young, and she'd learned how to seal her own grief in airtight compartments stored far from her heart. Unable to comprehend her loss, she'd focused on her grieving father. It had become, over the years, her defining characteristic. Annie the caretaker, the giver of love. But now her husband didn't want her love anymore, didn't want to be a part of the family she'd created and cared for.

"Let's not rehash it again," he said with a heavy sigh.

The words were like a slap. She snapped her head up and looked at him. "Rehash it? Are you *joking*?"

He looked sad and tired. "When did you ever know me to joke?" He shoved a hand through his perfectly cut hair. "I didn't think about what you'd . . . infer from my phone call this morning. I'm sorry."

Infer. A cold, legal word that seemed to separate them even more.

He moved toward her, but was careful not to get too close. "I'll take care of you. That's what I came to say. You don't have to worry about money or anything else. I'll take good care of you and Natalie. I promise."

She stared at him in disbelief. "February nineteenth. You remember that date, Blake?"

His million-dollar tan faded to a waxen gray. "Now, Annalise—"

"Don't you 'now, Annalise' me. February nineteenth. Our wedding day. You remember that day, Blake? You said—you *vowed*—to love me till death parted us. You promised to take care of me on that day, too."

"That was a long time ago."

"You think a promise like that has an expiration date, like a carton of milk? God . . ."

"I've changed, Annie. Hell, we've been together more than twenty years; we've both changed. I think you'll be happier without me. I really do. You can focus on all those hobbies you never had time for. You know . . ." He looked acutely out of his depth. "Like that calligraphy stuff. And writing those little stories. And painting."

She wanted to tell him to get the hell out, but the words tangled with memories in her head, and it all hurt so badly.

He came up beside her, his footsteps clipped and harsh on the stone flooring. "I've drafted a tentative settlement. It's more than generous."

"I won't make it that easy for you."

"What?"

She could tell by his voice that she'd surprised him, and it was no wonder. Their years together had taught him to expect no protest from Annie about anything. She looked up at him. "I said, I won't make it easy for you, Blake. Not this time."

"You can't stop a divorce in California." He said it softly, in his lawyer's voice.

"I know the law, Blake. Did you forget that I worked beside you for years, building the law firm with you? Or do you only remember the hours *you* put in at the office?" She moved toward him, careful not to touch him. "If you were a client, what advice would you give?"

He tugged at his starched collar. "This isn't relevant."

"You'd tell yourself to wait, spend some 'cooling off' time. You'd recommend a trial separation. I've *heard* you say it." The words tripped her up in sadness. "Jesus, Blake, won't you even give us that chance?"

"Annalise—"

She kept tears at bay one trembling breath at a time. Everything hung on the thread of this moment. "Promise me we'll wait until June—when Natalie gets home. We'll talk again . . . see where we are after a few months apart. I gave you twenty years, Blake. You can give me three months."

She felt the seconds tick by, slicing tiny nicks across her soul. She could hear the even, measured cant of his breathing, the lullaby that had eased her into sleep for more than half her life.

"All right."

The relief was overwhelming. "What are we going to tell Natalie?"

"Christ, Annie, it's not like she's going to have a heart attack. Most of her friends' parents are divorced. That's half of our goddamn problem, all you ever think about is Natalie. Tell her the truth."

Annie felt her first spark of true anger. "Don't you dare make this about motherhood, Blake. You're leaving me because you're a selfish prick."

"A selfish prick who's in love with someone else."

The words cut as deeply as he intended them to. Tears burned behind her eyes, blurred her vision, but she'd be damned if she'd let them fall. She should have known better than to fight with him—she had no practice, and hurtful words were his profession. "So you say."

"Fine," he said in a clipped, even voice, and she knew by the tone of it that this conversation was over. "What do you want to tell Natalie and when?"

This was the one answer she had. She might be a complete failure as a wife and lover, but she knew how to take care of her daughter. "Nothing for now. I don't want to ruin this trip for her. We'll tell her . . . whatever we need to . . . when she gets home."

"Fine."

"Fine."

"I'll send someone over tomorrow to pick up a few of my things. I'll have the Cadillac returned on Monday."

Things. That's what it came down to after all these years. The bits and pieces that were their life—his toothbrush, her hot rollers, his album collection, her jewelry—became just things to be divided up and packed in separate suitcases.

He picked up the envelope from the table and held it out to her. "Open it."

"Why? So I can see how generous you've been with *our* money?"

"Annie—"

She waved a hand. "I don't care who owns what."

He frowned. "Be sensible, Annie."

She looked at him sharply. "That's what my dad said to me when I told him I wanted to marry a skinny, dirt-poor, twenty-year-old kid. *Be sensible, Annie. There's no rush. You're young.* But I'm not young anymore, am I, Blake?"

"Annie, please . . ."

"Please what—please don't make this hard on you?"

"Look at the papers, Annie."

She moved closer, stared up at him through her tears. "There's only one asset I want, Blake." Her throat closed up and it became hard to speak. "My heart. I want it back in one piece. Have you given me that in your precious papers?"

He rolled his eyes. "I should have expected this from you. Fine. I'll be living at Suzannah's house if there's an emergency." He pulled out a pen and wrote on a scrap of paper from his wallet. "Here's the number."

She wouldn't take the piece of paper from him. He let go and it fluttered to the floor.

Annie lay perfectly still in her king-size bed, listening to the familiar sound of her own breathing, the steady rhythm of her own heart. She wanted to pick up the phone and call Terri, but she'd already leaned on her best friend too much. They'd talked daily, for hours and hours, as if talking could ease Annie's heartache, and when their conversations ended, Annie felt more alone than ever.

The last week had passed in a blur, seven endless days since her husband had told her he was in love with someone else. Each lonely night and empty day seemed to hack another bit of her away. Soon, she'd be too small for anyone to notice at all.

Sometimes, when she awoke, she was screaming, and the nightmare was always the same. She was in a dark room, staring into a gilt-edged mirror—only there was no reflection in the glass.

Throwing back the covers, she climbed out of bed and went to her walk-in closet. She yanked open her lingerie drawer and pulled out a big gray box. Clasping the box to her chest, she moved woodenly back to the bed. A lifetime's collection of photographs and mementos lay at her fingertips, all the favorite pictures she'd snapped and saved over the years. She went through them slowly, savoring each one. At the bottom of the box, she found a small bronze compass, a long-ago gift from her father. There was no inscription on it, but she still remembered the day he'd given it to her, and the words he'd said: *I know you feel lost now, but it won't last forever, and this will make sure that you can always find your way home again . . . where I'll always be waiting.*

She clutched the bit of metal in one hand, wondering when and why she'd ever taken it off. Very slowly, she slipped it around her neck again, then she turned to the photographs, beginning with the black and white ones, the Kodak trail of her own childhood. Small, dog-eared photos with the date stamped in black across the top. There were dozens of her alone, a few of her with her daddy. And one of her with her mother.

One.

She could remember the day it was taken; she and her mom had been making Christmas cookies. There was flour everywhere, on the counter, on Annie's face, on the floor. Her dad had come in from work and laughed at them. *Good God, Sarah, you're making enough for an army. There's just the three of us. . . .*

Only a few months later, there were only two of them. A quiet, grieving man and his even quieter little girl.

Annie traced the smooth surface of the print with her fingertip. She'd missed her mother so often over the years—at high school graduation, on her wedding day, on the day Natalie was born—but never as much as she missed her now. *I need you, Mom,* she thought for the millionth time. *I need you to tell me that everything will be all right. . . .*

She replaced the treasured photograph in the box and picked up a colored one that showed Annie holding a tiny, blotchy-faced newborn wrapped in a pink blanket. And there was Blake, looking young and handsome and proud, his big hand curled protectively around his baby girl. She went through dozens more pictures, following Natalie's life from infant to high school senior, from graham crackers to mascara.

Natalie's whole life lay in this box. There were countless pictures of a smiling, blue-eyed blond girl, standing alongside a succession of stuffed animals and bicycles and family pets. Somewhere along the way, Blake had stopped appearing in the family photos. How was it that Annie had never noticed that before?

But Blake wasn't who she was really looking for.

She was looking for Annie. The truth sank through her, twisting and hurting, but she couldn't give up. Somewhere in this box that held the tangible memories of her life, she had to find herself. She went through print after print, tossing aside one after another.

There were almost no pictures of her. Like most mothers, she was always behind the camera, and when she thought she looked tired, or fat, or thin, or ugly . . . she ripped the photo in half and ditched it.

Now, it was as if she'd never been there at all. As if she'd never really existed.

The thought scared her so badly, she lurched out of bed, shoving the photographs aside with a sweep of her hand. As she passed the French doors, she caught sight of a disheveled, desperate-looking middle-aged woman in her husband's bathrobe. It was pathetic what she was becoming. Even more pathetic than what she'd been before.

How dare he do this to her? Take twenty years of her life and then discard her like a sweater that no longer fit.

She strode to the closet, ripping his clothes from their expensive hangers and shoving them in the garbage. Then she went to his study, his precious study. Wrenching the desk drawer open, she yanked everything out.

In the back of one drawer, she found dozens of recent charge slips for flowers and hotel rooms and lingerie.

Her anger turned into an honest-to-God fury. She threw it all—charge slips, bills, appointment reminders, the checkbook register—in a huge cardboard box. On it, in big bold letters, she wrote his name and office address. In smaller letters, she wrote: *I did this for twenty years. Now it's your turn.*

Breathing hard, feeling better than she had in days, she looked around at her perfect, empty house.

What would she do now? Where would she go? She touched the compass at her throat and she knew.

Perhaps she'd known all along.

She'd go back to the girl she'd seen in those rare black and white photos . . . back to where she was someone besides Blake's wife and Natalie's mother.

PART TWO

In the midst of winter,
I finally learned that there was in me
an invincible summer.

ALBERT CAMUS

CHAPTER 4

After hours of flying and driving, Annie was finally steering her rental car across the long floating bridge that connected the Olympic Peninsula to the rest of Washington State. On one side of the bridge, the waves were in a white-tipped frenzy; on the other side, the water was as calm and silvery as a newly minted coin. She rolled down the window and flicked off the air conditioner. Sweet, misty air swept into the car, swirling tiny tendrils of hair across her face.

Mile by mile, the landscape rolled into the vivid greens and blues of her childhood world. She turned off the modern freeway and onto the two-lane road that led away from the shore. Under a purplish layer of fog, the peninsula lay hidden, a pork chop of land ringed by towering, snow-capped mountains on one side and wild, windswept beaches on the other. It was a primitive place, untouched by the hustle and bustle of modern life. Old-growth forests were draped in skeins of silvery moss, and craggy coastlines were sheltered from the raging surf by a towering curtain of rock. At the heart of the peninsula was the Olympic National Park, almost a million acres of no-man's-land, ruled by Mother Nature and the myths of the Native Americans who had lived here long before the white pioneers.

As she neared her hometown, the forests became dense and dark, covered still in the early spring by a shimmering, opalescent mist that concealed the serrated tips of the trees. It was the time of year when the forests were still hibernating, and night fell before the last school bell had rung. No sane person ventured off the main road until early summer; legends were told and retold of children who did and were never seen again, of Sasquatches who roamed the thickets of this wood at night, snatching up unsuspecting tourists. For here, in the deepest reaches of the rain forest, the weather could change faster than a teenage girl's mind; it could turn from sunshine to snow in a heartbeat, leaving nothing but a blood red rainbow that wept into ebony at the edges.

It was an ancient land, a place where giant red cedar trees grew three hundred feet into the sky and fell into utter silence, to die and reseed among their own, where time was marked by tides and tree rings and salmon runs.

When Annie finally reached the town of Mystic, she slowed her speed, soaking in the familiar sights. It was a small logging community, carved by early, idealistic pioneers from the great Quinault rain forest. Main Street ran for only six blocks. She didn't have to reach its end to know that at Elm Street the rutted asphalt gave way to a puddled, pockmarked gravel road.

Downtown wore the shabby, forgotten look of a white-haired old man left out in the rain. A single, tired stoplight guided nonexistent traffic past the huddled group of brick- and wood-fronted stores. Fifteen years ago, Mystic had been a booming town supported by fishing and logging, but the intervening years had obviously been hard ones that had driven merchants to more lucrative communities and left in their wake several vacant storefronts.

Rusted pickup trucks were parked at an angle behind thirty-year-old meters; only a few people in faded overalls and heavy winter overcoats could be seen on the sidewalks.

The stores that were left had down-home names: The I of the Needle fabric shop, the Holey Moses Doughnut counter, the Kiddie Corner consignment clothing store, Dwayne's Lanes bowling alley, Eve's Leaves dress emporium, Vittorio's Italian Ristorante. Each window displayed a placard that read THIS ESTABLISHMENT SUPPORTED BY LOGGING—a resentful reminder to distant politicians, living in pillared homes in faraway cities, that logging was the lifeblood of this region.

It was an exhausted little logging town, but to Annie, whose eyes had grown accustomed to steel and concrete and glass, it was gorgeous. The sky now was gray, but she could remember how it looked without the cover of clouds. Here, in Mystic, the sky started deep in the palm of God's hand and unfurled as far as the eye could see. It was a grand land of sublime landscapes, with air that smelled of pine needles and mist and rain.

So unlike Southern California.

The thought came unwanted, a stinging little reminder that she was a thirty-nine-year-old woman, perched on the edge of an unwanted divorce. That she was coming home because she had nowhere else to go.

She tried not to think about Blake or Natalie or that big, empty house perched precariously above the beach. Instead, she remembered the things she didn't mind leaving behind—the heat that always gave her a headache, the cancer she could feel lurking in the invisible rays of the sun, the smog that stung her eyes and burned her throat. The "bad air" days when you were advised to stay indoors, the mud slides and fires that took out whole neighborhoods in a single afternoon.

Annie had roots in this county that went deep and spread far. Her grandfather had come here almost seventy years ago, a block-jawed German with an appetite for freedom and a willingness to use a saw. He had carved a good living from the land and raised his only son, Hank, to do the same. Annie was the first Bourne in two generations to leave this soil, and the first to get a college education.

She followed Elm Street out of town. On both sides of the road, the land had been cut into bite-size pieces. Modular homes huddled on squares of grass, behind yards cluttered with broken-down cars and washing machines that had seen better days. Everywhere she looked, Annie saw the evidence of logging: trucks, chainsaws, and signs about the spotted owl.

The road began its slow, winding crawl up the hillside, thrusting deeper and deeper into the forests. One by one, the houses receded, giving way to trees. Miles and miles of scrawny, new-growth trees huddled behind signs that read: CLEARCUT 1992. REPLANTED 1993. There was a new sign every quarter mile or so; only the dates were different.

Finally, she reached the turnoff to the gravel road that meandered through fifteen acres of old-growth timber.

As a child, this woodland had been her playground. She had spent countless hours climbing through the dewy salal bushes and over crumbling nurse logs, in search of treasures: a white mushroom that grew only by the light of a red moon, a newborn fawn awaiting its mother's return, a gelatinous cache of frog's eggs hidden in the bogs.

At last, she came to the two-story clapboard farmhouse in which she'd grown up. It looked exactly as she remembered: a gabled, fifty-year-old structure painted a pale pearl gray with white trim. A white-washed porch ringed the whole house, and baskets of winter-spindly geraniums hung from every post. Smoke spiraled up from the brick chimney and merged into the low-slung layer of gray fog overhead.

Behind it, a battalion of ancient trees protected a secret, fern-lined pond. Moss furred the tree trunks and hung in lacy shawls from one branch to another. The lawn melted down toward the silvery ribbon of a salmon stream. She knew that if she walked across the grass, it would squish between her toes, and this time of year, the stream would sound like an old man snoring in his sleep.

She maneuvered the rented Mustang to the parking area behind the woodshed and shut off the engine. Grabbing her purse, she walked up to the front door.

Only a moment after she rang the bell, her father opened the door.

The great Hank Bourne—all six feet three inches and 220 pounds of him—stood there for a second, staring at his daughter with disbelieving eyes. Then a smile started, buried deep in his silvery-white mustache and beard.

"Annie," he whispered in that scratchy, barrel-chested voice of his.

His arms opened for a hug, and she launched herself forward, burying her face in the velvety folds of his neck. He smelled of woodsmoke and Irish Spring soap and of the butterscotch hard candies he always kept in the breast pocket of his work shirt. Of her childhood.

Annie let herself be carried away by the comfort of her father's embrace. At last, she drew back, unable to look at him, knowing he'd see the tears in her eyes. "Hi, Dad."

"Annie," he said again, only this time she heard the question he didn't ask.

She forced herself to meet his probing gaze. He looked good for his sixty-seven years. His eyes were still as bright and curious as a young man's, even tucked as they were in folds of ruddy pink skin. The tragedies he'd endured appeared only occasionally and quickly retreated—a shadow that crossed his wrinkled face when a stoplight turned red on a rainy day, or when the heartless sound of an ambulance's siren cut through the fog.

He tucked a scarred hand—cut long ago by the unforgiving blades at the lumber mill—into the bib of his faded denim overalls. "You alone, Annie?"

She flinched. The question contained layers and layers. There were so many ways to answer.

He looked at her so intensely she felt uncomfortable, as if he were seeing into her soul, into that big house on the Pacific Ocean where her husband had said, *I don't love you, Annie.*

"Natalie left for London," she said weakly.

"I know. I've been waiting for you to call with the address. I thought I'd send her something."

"She's staying with a family called Roberson. It's raining every day, cats and dogs from what I und—"

"What's going on, Annie Virginia?"

She swallowed the rest of her sentence on a gulp of breath. There was nowhere now to go except forward. "He . . . he left me, Dad."

He looked hopelessly confused. "What?"

She wanted to laugh and pretend it was nothing, that she was plenty strong enough to deal with this, but she felt like a kid again, tongue-tied and lost.

"What happened?" he asked softly.

She shrugged. "It's an old story. He's forty . . . and she's twenty-eight."

Hank's lean, wrinkled face fell. "Oh, honey . . ." She saw him search for words, and saw the sadness fill his eyes when he came up empty. He moved toward her, pressed a dry-skinned palm against her face. For a heartbeat, the past came forward, slid into the present; she knew they were both remembering another day, long ago, when Hank

37

had told his seven-year-old daughter that there'd been an accident . . . that Mommy had gone to Heaven. . . .

She's gone, honey. She won't be coming back.

In the silence that followed, Hank hugged his daughter. She laid her cheek against the comforting flannel of his plaid work shirt. She wanted to ask him for some words of advice, some comforting thought to take to her lonely bedroom and curl up into, but they'd never had that kind of relationship. Hank had never been comfortable handing out fatherly wisdom. "He'll be back," he said quietly. "Men can be pretty damn stupid. But Blake will realize what he's done, and he'll be back, begging for a second chance."

"I want to believe that, Dad."

Hank smiled, apparently bolstered by the effect of his words. "Trust me, Annie. That man loves you. I knew it the first time I saw him. You were too young to get married, I knew, but you were a sensible girl, and I said to myself, now *there's* a boy who's going to take care of my daughter. He'll be back. Now, how about if we settle you into your old bedroom and then bring out the old chessboard?"

"That'd be perfect."

Hank reached out and grabbed her hand. Together they walked through the sparsely decorated living room and up the rickety stairs that led to the second floor.

At Annie's old bedroom, Hank turned the knob and pushed the door open. The room was a wash of yellow-gold wallpaper lit by the last lavender rays of the fading sun; it was a young girl's floral print, chosen by a loving mother a lifetime ago, and never changed. Neither Annie nor Hank had ever considered peeling the paper off, not even when Annie had outgrown it. A spindly white iron double bed dominated the room, its surface piled high with yellow and white quilts. Beside a narrow double-hung window sat a twig rocker, the one her father had made for her on her thirteenth birthday. *You're a woman now,* he'd said, *you'll be wanting a woman's chair.*

She had spent much of her youth in that chair, gazing out at the endless night, clipping photographs of celebrities from a *Teen Beat* magazine, writing gushy fan letters to Bobby Sherman and David Cassidy, dreaming of the man she would someday wed.

He'll be back. She wrapped Hank's words around her, letting them become a shield against the other, darker thoughts. She wanted desperately to believe her dad was right.

Because if he was wrong, if Blake didn't come back, Annie had no idea who she was or where she belonged.

CHAPTER 5

The night had passed in fitful waves. On several occasions, Annie woke with a start, the remnant of a sob floating in the darkness around her, the sheets coiled about her legs, damp and sour smelling. She'd spent the past four days wandering around this old farmhouse like a lost spirit, feeling restless and bruised. She rarely ventured far from the phone.

I made a mistake, Annie. I'm sorry; I love you. If you come home to me I'll never see Suzannah again. She waited for the call all day, and then, at night, she collapsed into a troubled sleep and dreamed about it again.

She knew she should do something, but she had no idea what. All her life she'd taken care of people, she'd used her life to create a perfect setting for Blake's and Natalie's lives, and now, alone, she was lost.

Go back to sleep. That was it. She'd burrow under the down comforter again and sleep. . . .

There was a knock at her door. "I'll be out in a while," she mumbled, reaching for her pillow.

The door swung open. Hank stood in the opening. He was wearing a red and blue plaid flannel shirt and a pair of bleached, stained denim overalls—the makeshift uniform he'd worn to the lumber mill for almost forty years. He was holding a tray full of food. Disapproval etched his face, narrowed his eyes. He carefully set down the tray and crossed the room. "You look like hell."

Stupidly, she burst into tears. She knew it was true. She was thin and ugly and dirty—and no one, including Blake, would ever want her again. The thought made her sick to her stomach. She clamped a hand over her mouth and raced to the bathroom. It was humiliating to know that her father could hear her retching, but she couldn't help it. Afterward, she brushed her teeth and moved shakily back into her room.

The worry in Hank's eyes cut like a knife.

"That's it," he said, clapping his hands together. "You're going in to see the doctor. Get your clothes."

The thought of going out, of *leaving,* filled her with horror. "I can't. People will . . ." She didn't even know what she was afraid of. She only knew that in this room, here in her little girl's bed, she felt safe.

"I can still throw you over my shoulder, kiddo. Either get dressed or go into town in those pajamas. It's up to you. But you're going to town."

She wanted to argue, but she knew her father was right, and frankly, it felt good to be taken care of. "Okay, okay." She made her way slowly into the bathroom and re-dressed in the same rumpled clothes she'd worn on her trip up here. Putting her hair up was way too much for her; instead, she finger-combed it and covered her bloodshot, baggy eyes with sunglasses. "Let's go."

Annie stared out the half-open window of her dad's Ford pickup. Behind her head, the empty gun rack clattered against the glass.

He maneuvered the vehicle expertly between the potholes in the road and pulled up in front of a squat, brick building. A handpainted sign read MYSTIC MEDICAL CLINIC. DR. GERALD BURTON, FAMILY PRACTITIONER.

Annie smiled. She hadn't thought about old Doc Burton in years. He had delivered Annie into the world and seen her through almost two decades of colds and ear infections and childhood accidents. He was as much a part of her youth as braces, proms, and skinny-dips in Lake Crescent.

Hank clicked off the engine. The old Ford sputtered, coughed, and fell silent. "It seems odd to be bringing you back here. I'm suddenly afraid I missed a booster shot and they won't let you start school."

Annie smiled. "Maybe Doc Burton will give me a grape sucker if I'm good."

Hank turned to her. "You were always good, Annalise. Don't you forget it."

His words brought it swelling back inside her, sent her falling back into that big house by the sea where her husband had told her he loved another woman. Before the sadness could get a good hold, she squared her shoulders and opened her door. "I'll meet you at . . ." She glanced around, wondering what was still around.

"The riverpark. You used to love it down there."

"The riverpark," she said, recalling all the evenings she had spent down at the bank, crawling through the mud, looking for fish eggs and dragonflies. With a nod, she climbed down out of the truck, hitched her bag over her shoulder, and strode up the concrete steps to the clinic's front door.

Inside, a blue-haired old lady looked up at her. Her name tag read, HI! I'M MADGE. "Hello. May I help you?"

Annie suddenly felt conspicuous in her rumpled clothes, with her hair hanging limp and lifeless around her face. Thank God the sunglasses hid her eyes. "I'm Annie Colwater. I'd like to see Doctor Burton. I think my father made an appointment."

"He sure did, darlin'. Have a seat. Doc'll see you in a jif."

After she filled out the insurance forms, Annie took a seat in the waiting room, flipping idly through the newest issue of *People* magazine. She hadn't waited more than fifteen minutes when Dr. Burton rounded the corner and strolled into the waiting room. The ten years she'd been gone showed in the folds of red skin along his neck and in the amount of hair he'd lost, but he was still old Doc Burton, the only man in all of Mystic who religiously wore a tie to work.

"Well, Annie Bourne, as I live and breathe."

She grinned up at the old man. "It's been a long time."

"So it has. Come, come." He slipped an arm around her shoulder and led her into the nearest examining room. She hopped up onto the paper-covered table and crossed her feet at the ankles.

He sat in a flecked, yellow plastic chair opposite her, eyeing her. Coke-bottle-thick glasses magnified his eyes to the size of dinner plates. She wondered how many years ago he'd started to lose his vision. "You don't look so hot."

She managed a smile. Apparently his vision wasn't all that lost. "That's why I'm here. Hank said I look like hell—he figured it must be a disease."

He let out a horsey laugh and opened a manila folder, poising a pen on the blank page. "Sounds like Hank. Last time I saw him he had a migraine—and he was sure it was a brain tumor. So, what's going on with you?"

She found it hard to begin. "I haven't been sleeping well . . . headaches . . . sick to my stomach . . . that sort of thing."

"Any chance you could be pregnant?"

She should have been prepared for the question. If she'd been ready, it wouldn't have hurt so much. But it had been years since any doctor had asked the sensitive question. Her own doctors knew the answer too well. "No chance."

"Any hot flashes, irregular periods?"

She shrugged. "My periods have always been irregular. In the last year, I've skipped a couple of months completely. Frankly, it's not something I worry about—missing a period. And yes, my own gynecologist has warned me that menopause could be just around the corner."

"I don't know . . . you're a little young for that. . . ."

She smiled. "Bless you."

He closed the chart, laid it gently across his lap, then looked up at her again. "Is there something going on in your life that would lead to depression?"

Depression.

One word to describe a mountain of pain. One word to steal the sunlight from a person's soul and leave them stranded in a cold, gray landscape, alone and searching for something they couldn't even name.

"Maybe."

"Would you like to talk about it?"

She looked at the old man. The gentle understanding in his rheumy eyes took her down a long and winding road, and at the end of it, she was twelve years old again, the first girl in her class to menstruate. Hank hadn't known what to say, so he'd bundled her up, taken her to Doc Burton, and let the doctor handle her fear.

Tears stung her eyes and slipped unchecked down her cheeks. "My husband and I recently separated. I haven't been . . . handling it very well."

Slowly, he pulled his glasses off, laid them on top of his papers, and tiredly rubbed the bridge of his beaked nose. "I'm sorry, Annie. I see too much of this, I'm afraid. It happens in little ole Mystic as often as it does in the big city. Of course you're blue—and depression could certainly explain sleeplessness, lack of appetite, nausea. Any number of symptoms. I could prescribe some Valium, maybe start you on Prozac. Something to take the edge off until you come out on the other side."

She wanted to ask him if he'd known a woman who came out on the other side . . . or one whose husband had changed his mind . . . but they were such intimate and revealing questions, so she remained silent.

He slipped the glasses back onto his nose and peered at her. "This is a time when you want to take dang good care of yourself, Annie. Depression isn't a thing to trifle with. And if it all gives you too many sleepless nights, you come on back around. I'll give you a prescription."

"Pills to take the place of a lover?" She forced a grim smile. "Those must be some drugs. Maybe I'll just take a handful now."

He didn't smile. "Handful isn't a word I like to hear, and sarcasm doesn't sit pretty on a lady's tongue, missy. Now, how long are you sticking around?"

She felt a wash of shame, as if she were ten years old again. "Sorry. I have to go . . . home in mid-June." *Unless Blake calls.* She shivered inwardly at the thought. "I guess I'll be here until then."

"Mid-June, huh? Okay, I want to see you on June first. No matter what. I'll set you up with an appointment, okay?"

It felt good to have someone care about her progress. "Okay. I'm sure I'll be better by then."

He walked Annie out of the clinic. Patting her shoulder, he reminded her again to take care of herself, then he turned and disappeared back down the hallway.

Annie felt better as she left the clinic and headed across town to the park. The crisp spring air rejuvenated her, and the sky was so blue and bright she had to put her sunglasses back on. It was one of those rare early spring days that held all the promise of summer. She passed a huge chainsaw-cut statue of a Roosevelt elk and wound through the park, kicking through the last black winter leaves that clung to the dewy grass

She found Hank sitting on the same wooden bench that had always been alongside the river. She sat down beside him.

He handed her a Styrofoam cup of steaming hot coffee. "Bet you haven't had a decent cup of coffee since high school."

She curled her fingers around the warm cup. "I *do* have a latte machine, Dad."

They sipped their coffees in silence. Annie listened to the comforting, familiar sound of the rushing water.

He pulled a croissant out of a paper sack and handed it to her. Her stomach rebelled at the thought of eating, and she waved it away.

"What did the doc say?" Hank asked.

"Big surprise . . . I'm depressed."

"Are you pissed off yet?"

"Last night I pictured Blake being eaten by piranhas—that seems angry, don't you think?" He didn't answer, just stared at her until, more softly, she said, "I was for a while, but now, I'm too . . . empty to be angry." She felt tears rise and she couldn't stop them. Humiliated, she looked away. "He thinks I'm nothing, Dad. He expects me to live off alimony and be . . . nothing."

"What do you think?"

"I think he's right." She squeezed her eyes shut. "Give me some advice, Dad. Some words of wisdom."

"Life sucks."

She laughed in spite of herself. It was exactly what she would have expected him to say, and even though it didn't help, the familiarity of it was comforting. "Thanks a lot, Dad. I ask for wisdom and you give me bumper stickers."

"How do you think people come up with bumper stickers?" He patted her hand. "Everything is going to work out, Annie. Blake loves

45

you; he'll come around. But you can't keep spending all your time in that bed. You need to get out. Do something. Find something to keep you busy until Blake gets his head out of his ass."

"Or hers."

"Nice comment from my little girl. Here's one for you," he said with a smile. "When life gives you lemons, make lemonade."

She pictured the pitcher of lemonade she'd made for Blake, and then the big splotch of it that had bled across the settlement papers. "I don't like lemonade."

His look turned serious. "Annie Virginia, I think you don't know what you like, and it's about time you found out."

She knew he was right. She couldn't go on the way she had been, waiting for a phone call that wasn't going to come, crying constantly.

"You've got to take some risks, honey."

"I take risks. I don't floss every day, and sometimes I mix floral and plaids. Once I wore white shoes *after* Labor Day."

"I mean—"

Annie laughed—the first real, honest-to-God laugh since the shit hit the fan. "Haircut."

"What?"

"Blake always liked my hair long."

Hank grinned. "Well, well. I guess you're a little angry after all. That's a good sign."

Lurlene's Fluff-n-Stuff was not the kind of salon Annie usually patronized. It was an old-fashioned, small-town beauty parlor housed in a Pepto Bismol–pink Victorian with glossy white gingerbread trim. A porch wrapped around the front of the house, offering shade to three pink wicker rocking chairs.

Annie parked beneath a hot pink sign that read: PARKING RESERVED FOR LURLENE'S CUSTOMERS ONLY. VIOLATORS WILL BE SUBJECT TO A CUT AND PERM. As she followed a walkway of heart-shaped cement stones up to the front porch, a tinny rendition of "It's a Small World" seeped from a single black speaker by the door.

She stopped, suddenly afraid. She'd had long hair forever. What was she thinking—that a pair of scissors could recapture her youth? *Calm down, Annie.* She took a deep breath, draining away everything except what she needed to take a single step forward, to walk up those steps and get a haircut.

She had almost reached the top step when the front door whooshed open and a woman appeared. She had to be at least six feet tall, with a pile of Lucille Ball red hair that pooched up to the doorway. Someone had poured her statuesque body into a pair of sparkly red spandex pants (either that, or it was a coat of glitter paint). A tight-fitting angora sweater in a black and white zebra print strained across breasts the size of the Alps. A huge zebra earring dangled from each ear.

The woman moved—an excited little shiver rippled along her whole body, right down to the gold Barbie-doll mules that encased her canoe-size feet. "You must be Annie Colwater. . . ." She pronounced it *Colwatah* in a Southern drawl as thick and sweet as corn syrup. "Why, darlin', I been waitin' on you! Your daddy said you wanted a make-over—why, I couldn't believe my ears. A makeover in *Mystic!*" She bounded down the creaking steps like a Rose Bowl float. "I'm Lurlene, sweetie. Big as a moose, you're thinkin', but with twice the fashion sense. Now, sugah, you come on in. You've come to the right place. I'll treat you like a queen." She patted Annie and took hold of her arm, leading her up the steps and into a bright, white and pink room with a few wicker-framed mirrors. Pink gingham curtains shielded the view and a pink hook rug covered the hardwood floor.

"Pink is my color," Lurlene said proudly, her drawl spinning the sentence into *pink is mah colah.* "The twin shades of cotton candy and summer glow are designed to make you feel special and safe. I read that in a magazine, and ain't it just the God's truth?" She led Annie past two other customers, both older women with their gray hair twined on tiny multicolored rods.

Lurlene kept up a steady chatter as she washed Annie's hair. *Oh, Lordie, I ain't seen this much hair since my Disco Barbie doll.* After she'd clamped a fuschia plastic cape around Annie's shoulders and settled her into a comfortable chair in front of the mirror, Lurlene peered over

Annie's shoulder. "You sure you want this cut? Most women'd give their husband's left nut for hair like this."

Annie refused to give in to the flutter of nerves that had settled somewhere in the region of her stomach. No more halfways. Not anymore. "Cut it off," she said evenly.

"Of *course* you're sure," Lurlene said with a toothy grin. "Somethin' shoulder length, maybe—"

"All of it."

Lurlene's painted mouth dropped open. "Off? As in . . . *off?*"

Annie nodded.

Lurlene recovered quickly. "Why, darlin', you're gonna be my crownin' achievement."

Annie tried not to think about what she'd done. One look at her own chalky, drawn face in the mirror, with her hair slicked back from her thin face, was enough to make her slam her eyes shut . . . and keep them shut.

She felt a tug on her hair, then a snip of steel blades, and a whoosh of hair fell to the floor.

Snip, whoosh, snip, whoosh.

"I shore was surprised when your daddy called. I've heard stories about you for years. Kathy Johnson—you recall her? Well, Kath and I went to beauty school together. 'Course Kath never actually finished— something about the scissors bothered her—but we got to be best friends. She told me tons o' stories about when y'all were kids. I reckon you'n Kathy were wild and crazy."

Kathy Johnson.

It was a name Annie hadn't heard in years. *Kathy and Annie, friends 4-ever. 2 good 2 be true.* That's what they'd written in each other's yearbook, what they'd promised as the end of high school neared.

Annie had always meant to keep the friendship up, to stay in touch, but somehow she never had. Like so many childhood friendships, it had dwindled to nothing. Christmas cards for a few years, and then even that had stopped. Annie hadn't heard from Kathy in years. The separation had started before high school was over, when Nick proposed to Kathy.

Nick.

Annie could still remember the day she'd first seen him. Junior English. He'd walked in arrogantly, his blue eyes challenging everyone in the room. He was wearing ragged Levi's and an overwashed white T-shirt, with a pack of cigarettes rolled up in his sleeve. He wasn't like anyone she'd ever seen before, with his wild, too-long black hair and don't-mess-with-me attitude. Annie had fallen in love on the spot; so had every other girl in the room, including her best friend, Kathy.

But it was Kathy he had chosen, and with that choice, Annie had tasted the first salty wounds of a broken heart.

She smiled at the memory, faded and distant as it was. Maybe she'd go see them, try to kick-start the old camaraderie—God knew it would be nice to have a friend right about now. If nothing else, they could laugh about the old days. "How are Nick and Kathy?"

The scissors abruptly stopped clipping. "You ain't heard?"

"About what?"

Lurlene leaned down in a cloud of rose-scented perfume. "Kathy died about eight months ago."

Annie opened her eyes. A pale, chalky woman with hacked-off hair stared back at her from the oval mirror. She slammed her eyes shut again. When she found her voice, it was thin and soft. "What—"

"I been helpin' out as much as I can—baby-sittin' an' such, but that child of his, Isabella, well . . . she just ain't right in the head anymore. Got herself kicked out of school yesterday. Can you imagine that? A six-year-old gettin' kicked outta school? Just what're they thinkin', I ask you? They all know about her mama. You'd think a little pity'd be in order. Nick's been lookin' for a nanny, but he finds fault with everyone I send him."

"How did it happen?" Annie's voice was a whisper.

"Just called her into the principal's office and said, kiddo you're outta school." Lurlene made a tsking sound. "That child don't need to get rejected again. What she *needs* is a daddy. 'Course a rabbit's a better parent than he is right now—and they eat their young. I wish I could do more for 'em, but Buddy—that's my husband—he says he raised his kids, all five of 'em, with his ex-wife, Eartha—you know her? She lives down around Forks. Anyway, Buddy don't want to go through *that* again, not marryin' Eartha, I mean, but raisin' kids. And I've never had kids, what do I know about it? I mean, I can give her a durn fine cut and perm, and even paint her little nails, but I don't know about much else. I don't mind watchin' her after school—she's actually quite a help around the place—but she scares me, if the truth be told, what with her problems and all."

It was all coming at Annie so fast. She couldn't make herself really comprehend it. *Kathy.*

How could Kathy be dead? Only yesterday they'd been best friends, playing together in the schoolyard at recess in elementary school, giggling about boys in junior high, and double dating in high school. They had been friends in the way that only girls can be—they wore each other's clothes and slept at each other's houses and told each other every little secret. They promised to always stay friends.

But they hadn't taken the time and energy to stay in touch when their lives went down separate roads . . . and now Kathy was gone. Annie hadn't *meant* to forget Kathy. But she had, and that's what mattered now. She had gone to Stanford, met Blake, and exchanged the past for a future.

"Nicky's fallin' apart, pure and simple," Lurlene said, snapping a big bubble of gum. "Him and Kathy bought the old Beauregard house on Mystic Lake—"

The Beauregard house. An image of it came to Annie, wrapped up in the tissue-thin paper of bittersweet memories. "I know it. But you still haven't told me how Kath—"

The hair dryer blasted to life, drowning out Annie's question. She thought she heard Lurlene still talking, but she couldn't make out the words. Then, after a few minutes, the dryer clicked off. Lurlene set the scissors down with a hard click on the white porcelain tile counter.

"Lordie, you do look fine," Lurlene squeezed her on the shoulder. "Open your eyes, honey, and take yourself a peek."

Annie opened her eyes and saw a stranger in the mirror. Her brown hair was so short there was no curl left. The pixie cut emphasized her drawn, pale skin, and made her green eyes look haunted and too large for the fine-boned features of her face. Without lipstick, her unsmiling mouth was a colorless white line. She looked like Kate Moss at fifty—after a lawn-mower attack. "Oh, my God . . ."

Lurlene nodded at her in the mirror, grinning like one of those dogs that sit in the back windows of cars. "You look just like that young gal that nabbed Warren Beatty. You know who I mean—the one from *The American President*."

"Annette Bening," said one of the ladies across the room.

Lurlene reached for her camera, a disposable. "I gotta get me a picture of this. I'll send it in to *Modern Do* magazine. I'll win that trip to Reno for sure." She hunkered down in front of Annie. "Smile."

Before Annie could think, Lurlene popped the photo and straightened, chewing on the scarlet tip of her acrylic nail. "I'll bet there ain't a hundred women in the world who can do justice to that haircut, honey, but you're one of them."

All Annie wanted was to get out of this room without crying. *It'll be all right. It'll grow back,* she told herself, but all she could think about was Blake, and what he would say about what she'd done when—*if*—he came back to her. Shakily, she reached for her handbag. "How much do I owe you?"

"Nothin', honey. We've all had bad weeks."

Annie turned to Lurlene. In the woman's heavily mascaraed eyes, there was real, honest-to-God understanding.

If she hadn't felt so sick, Annie might have managed a smile. "Thanks, Lurlene. Maybe I can return the favor sometime."

Lurlene's painted face cracked into a toothy grin. "Why, honey, this here's Mystic. You hang around long enough and a favor's gonna come beggin'." She bent down and grabbed a big green fishing tackle box from the corner. It hit the tile counter with a clatter and the lid snapped open. Inside was enough makeup to turn Robin Williams into Courtney Love. Lurlene grinned. "Now, are you ready for your makeover?"

Annie gasped. She could picture it—her face with more color than a Benjamin Moore paint wheel. "N-No thanks, I'm in a rush." She popped to her feet and backed away from the chair.

"But, but—I was gonna make you look like—"

Annie mumbled a hurried thank you and ran for the door. She escaped into her rented Mustang and cranked up the engine, barreling out of the driveway in a spray of gravel and a cloud of smoke. She made it almost a mile before she felt the sting of tears.

It wasn't until almost fifteen minutes later, as she drove past the corner of the World-of-Wonders putt-putt golf course, with her hands white-knuckled around the steering wheel and tears leaking down her cheeks, that she remembered the question that had been left unanswered.

What had happened to Kathy?

Annie drove around Mystic, down the rain-rutted back roads, up the bare, harvested hills, until the tears on her cheeks had dried to thin silver streaks. She knew she had to put on a happy face when she saw her dad. Finally, when she'd regained some measure of self-control, she went home.

Hank was seated in one of the old butter-yellow chairs beside the fireplace. A book of crossword puzzles lay open on his lap. At her entrance he looked up. The smile on his face fell faster than a cake when the oven door was slammed. "Holy hamhock," he said slowly.

Annie couldn't help laughing. "I've been cast in *G.I. Jane,* the sequel."

Hank's laugh started slowly, gathering strength. "It looks . . . good, honey."

"Good? I wanted to look younger, but I didn't want to look like an *infant.*"

Hank got to his feet and opened his arms. The magazine fell to the floor in a flutter of paper. "Come here, honey."

Annie walked into his embrace and let him hug her. When he drew back, he reached into his breast pocket and pulled out a small, wrapped piece of candy. Butterscotch. He'd always thought those candies would help Annie through the dark times. He'd given her one when her mom died. *Here, honey, have a piece of candy.* For years afterward, whenever she smelled butterscotch, she looked around, expecting to see Hank.

Smiling, she took the candy and unwrapped it, popping it in her mouth. It rolled around on her tongue, tasting of sweetness and memories.

He touched her cheek. "Real beauty is on the inside."

"That's something women say to each other, Dad. Trust me, men don't believe it."

Hank gave her a crooked grin. "I believe it, and last time I looked, I'm a man. And I think your haircut is stunning. It'll just take a little getting used to."

"Well, I *feel* like a new woman, and that's what I wanted."

"Of course it is." He patted her shoulder. "Now, how about a rousing game of Scrabble?"

Annie nodded and let him lead the way. He pulled the Scrabble box out from the armoire in the corner of the living room, where it had probably been sitting since the last time they'd played—twenty years ago. He dusted off the box and set out the board on the coffee table.

Annie stared at her seven smooth wooden squares, trying to come up with a word to start the game. "So, Dad, you didn't tell me about Kathy Johnson."

He didn't look up. "Didn't I? I thought I wrote you about it. Or maybe I told you when I was down for Christmas?"

"No."

He shrugged, and she could tell that he wasn't going to look up. "Oh, well. I guess you know now. That Lurlene's the mouth that roared in Mystic. Sorry you had to find out about it that way."

Annie could tell that Hank was uncomfortable. He kept pulling at his collar, though it wasn't even buttoned to his neck, and he was staring at his letters as if they were the original ten commandments. He was not the kind of man who liked to discuss death. Anyone's. But certainly not the untimely death of a woman he'd watched grow up.

Annie let the subject rest. Forcing a thin smile, she plucked up four letters and started the game. Anything she wanted to know about Kathy's death, or her life, would have to come from somewhere else.

CHAPTER 6

Nick Delacroix stood in his front yard in the pouring rain, staring down at the limp, sagging, half-dead cherry tree he'd planted last year. Slowly, he fell to his knees in the muddy grass and bowed his head.

He hadn't cried at his wife's funeral, or yesterday when his daughter had been kicked out of school, but he had the strangest goddamn urge to cry now—and over this stupid little tree that wouldn't grow. He pushed to his feet and then turned away from the tree, walking tiredly back up to the house.

But when he was safely inside, with the door slammed shut behind him, he couldn't forget about that damned tree.

It was all because of yesterday; it had been a bad day—and in the past eight months he'd had enough of them to know.

His Izzy had been kicked out of school.

At the thought, the anger came crawling through him again. When the anger faded, all he had left was shame.

Yesterday, his Izzy had stood in the principal's office, her brown eyes flooded with tears, her full, little girl's lips quivering. Her pink dress was stained and torn, and he'd known with a sinking feeling that it had been like that when she'd put it on. Her long black hair—once her pride and joy—was a tangled bird's nest because no mother's hand had combed through it.

He'd wondered fleetingly, absurdly, what had happened to all those pretty ribbons she'd once had.

We can't have her in school anymore, Mr. Delacroix. Surely you see that?

Izzy had stood there, motionless. She hadn't spoken—but then, she hadn't spoken in months. That was one of the reasons they'd expelled her . . . that and the disappearing. A few months ago, she'd started to believe she was disappearing, one tiny finger at a time. Now she wore a small black glove on her left hand—the hand she could no longer see or use. Recently she'd begun to use her right hand awkwardly, as if she believed some of those fingers were "gone" now, too.

She hadn't looked up, hadn't met Nick's eyes, but a single tear had streaked down her cheek. He'd watched the tear fall, hit her dress, and disappear in a tiny gray blotch.

He'd wanted to say something, but he had no idea how to comfort a child who'd lost her mother. Then, like always, his inability to help his daughter had made him angry. It had started him thinking that he needed a drink—just one to calm his nerves. And all the while, she had stood there, too quiet and still for a six-year-old, staring at him with a sad, grown-up disappointment.

He picked his way through the living room, stepping over containers from last night's takeout. A lonely housefly buzzed lazily above the scraps. It sounded like the roar of a lawn mower.

He glanced down at his watch, blinking until his vision cleared. Eight-thirty.

Shit. He was late to pick up Izzy. Again.

The thought of facing her, letting her down again, seeing that tiny black glove . . .

Maybe if he had a little drink. Just a short one—

The phone rang. He knew even before he answered that it was Lurlene, wondering where he was. "Heya, Lurl," he drawled, leaning tiredly against the wall. "I know, I know, I'm late. I was just leaving."

"No hurry, Nicky. Buddy's out with the boys tonight—and before you jump down my throat, Izzy's fine."

He released a sigh, unaware until this moment that he'd tensed up. "You don't care that I'm late, and Izzy is fine. So, what's up?"

Her voice fell to a stage whisper. "Actually, I was callin' with an interestin' bit o' gossip."

"Good God, Lurl. I don't give a shit—"

"I met an old friend of yours today—you care about *that* don'tcha? And I have to say, she ain't nuthin' like I expected her to be. Why, to hear you and Kath—oops! I didn't mean to mention her, sorry—anyway, she was just as sweet as cream butter. I wouldn't even have known she was rich. She was that everyday. Like Miss Sissy Spacek. I saw her on *Oprah* the other day and you woulda thought that lady was no differ'nt'n you or me."

Nick tried to keep up with the conversation, but it was spiraling beyond his control. "Sissy Spacek was in your salon today? Is that the point?"

Lurlene's musical laugh skipped up and down the scales. "You silly, of *course* not. This is Mystic, not Aspen. I'm talkin' about Annie Bourne. She's back in town, visitin' her daddy."

Nick couldn't have heard right. "Annie Bourne is back in town?"

Lurlene babbled on about haircuts and cashmere sweaters and diamonds the size of grapes. Nick couldn't keep his focus. *Annie Bourne.*

He mumbled something—he had no idea what—and hung up.

Jesus, Annie Bourne. She hadn't been home in years; he knew that because Kathy had waited futilely for phone calls from her old best friend.

Picking his way through the debris in his living room, he went to the fireplace and grabbed a picture off of the mantel. It was one he'd seen daily but hadn't really looked at in years. A bit faded, the colors sucked away by time and sunlight, it was of the three of them, taken in the last rosy days of the summer before their senior year. Annie and Kathy and Nick. The gruesome threesome.

He was in the middle, with an arm around each girl. He looked young and carefree and happy—a different boy from the one who'd lived in a cramped, dirty car only a few months before. In that perfect summer, when he'd first tasted the rain-sweet elixir called normal life, he'd finally understood what it meant to have friends, to *be* a friend.

And he had fallen in love.

The photograph had been taken in the late afternoon, when the sky was a deep and unbroken blue. They'd spent the day at the lake, shrieking and laughing as they dove off the cliffs into the water. It was the day he'd first understood it would have to come to an end, the day he realized that sooner or later, he'd have to choose between the two girls he loved.

There had never been any doubt about who he would choose. Annie had already applied to Stanford, and with her grades and test scores, everyone knew she'd be accepted. She was on her way in the world. Not Kathy. Kathy was a quiet, small-town girl given to blue moods . . . a girl who needed desperately to be loved and cared for.

He still remembered what he'd told Annie that day. After the life he'd lived with his mother, he knew what he wanted: respect and stability. He wanted to make a difference in people's lives, to be part of a legal system that cared about the death of a lonely young woman who lived in her car.

He'd told Annie that he dreamed of becoming a policeman in Mystic.

Oh, no, Nicky, she had whispered, rolling over on the blanket to stare into his face. *You can do better than that. If you like the law, think big . . . big . . . you could be a supreme court justice, maybe a senator.*

It had hurt him, those words, the quiet, unintentional indictment of his dreams. *I don't want to be a supreme court justice.*

She'd laughed, that soft, trilling laugh that always made his heart ache with longing. *You've got to think bigger, Nicky-boy. You don't know what you want yet. Once you start college—*

No college for me, smart girl. I won't be getting a scholarship like you.

He'd seen it dawn in her eyes, slowly, the realization that he didn't want what she wanted, and that he wouldn't reach that far. He didn't have the courage to dream big dreams. All he wanted was to help people and to be needed. It was all he'd ever known, all he was good at.

But Annie hadn't understood. How could she? She didn't know the gutters he'd crawled through in his life.

Oh, was all she'd said, but there'd been a wealth of newfound awareness in the word, a tiny unsteadiness in her voice that he'd never heard before. After that, they had lain side by side on the scratchy green blanket, staring up at the clouds, their bodies an infinitesimal distance apart.

It was so simple to him back then. He loved Annie . . . but Kathy needed him, and her need was a powerful draw.

He'd asked Kathy to marry him just a few months before gradua-tion, but it didn't matter by then, because Annie had known he would. They tried, after the engagement, to keep their friendship together, but inevitably they'd begun to drift apart. It had become Nick-and-Kathy, with Annie a bystander. By the time Annie left for college, amid a shower of promises to keep in touch, Nick had known there would be no lifelong friendship, no gruesome threesome anymore.

By the time he got back from Lurlene's, it was almost nine-thirty. Well past a six-year-old's bedtime, but Nick didn't have the heart to put her right to bed.

Izzy sat cross-legged on the floor in front of the cold, black fire-place. It had always been her favorite spot in this house; at least, it had been in the old days when there was always a fire crackling behind her, always a wave of gentle heat caressing her back. She was holding her rag doll, Miss Jemmie, in one arm—the best she could do since she'd begun "disappearing." The silence in the room was overwhelming, as pervasive as the dust that clung to the furniture.

It shredded Nick into helpless pieces. He kept trying to start a con-versation with his daughter, but all his efforts fell into the black well of Izzy's silent world.

"I'm sorry about what happened at school, Izzy-bear," he said awkwardly.

She looked up, her brown eyes painfully dry and too big for the milky pallor of her tiny face.

The words were wrong; he knew that instantly. He wasn't just sorry about what had happened at school. He was sorry about all of it. The death, the life, and all the years of distance and disappointment that had led them to this pitiful place in their lives. Mostly, he was sorry that he was such a failure, that he had no idea where to go from here.

He got up slowly and went to the window. A glimmer of moon-light skated across the black surface of Mystic Lake, and a dim bulb on the porch cast a yellow net across the twin rocking chairs that hadn't been used in months. Rain fell in silver streaks from the roofline, clattering on the wooden steps.

He knew that Izzy was watching him warily, waiting and worrying about what he would do next. Sadly, he knew how that felt, to wait with bated breath to see what a parent would do next. He knew how it twisted your insides into a knot and left you with barely enough oxygen to draw a decent breath.

He closed his eyes. The memory came to him softly, unintentionally, encoded in the percussive symphony of the rain, the plunking sound of water hitting wood. It reminded him of a day long ago, when a similar rain had hammered the rusty hood of his mother's old Impala . . .

He was fifteen years old, a tall, quiet boy with too many secrets, standing on the street corner, waiting for his mother to pick him up from school. The kids moved past him in a laughing, talking centipede of blue jeans and backpacks and psychedelic T-shirts. He watched enviously as they boarded the yellow buses that waited along the curb.

At last, the buses drove away, chugging smoke, changing gears, heading for neighborhoods Nick had never seen, and the school yard fell silent. The gray sky wept. Cars rushed down the street in a screeching, rain-smeared blur. None of the drivers noticed a thin, black-haired boy in ragged, holey jeans and a white T-shirt.

He had been so damned cold; he remembered that most of all. There was no money for a winter coat, and so his flesh was puckered and his hands were shaking.

Come on, Mom. That was the prayer he'd offered again and again, but without any real hope.

He hated to wait for his mother. As he stood there, alone, his chin tucked into his chest for warmth, he was consumed by doubt. How drunk would she be? Would it be a kind, gentle day where she remembered that she loved him? Or a dark, nasty day where the booze turned her into a shrieking, stumbling madwoman who hated her only child with a vengeance? Dark days were the norm now; all his mother could think about was how much she'd lost. She wailed that welfare checks didn't cover gin and bemoaned the fact that they'd been reduced to living in their car—a swallow away from homelessness.

He could always read her mood immediately. A pale, dirty face that never smiled and watery, unfocused eyes meant that she'd found her way to a full bottle. Even though he went through the car every day, searching for booze like other kids searched for Easter eggs, he knew he couldn't stop her from drinking.

He rocked from foot to foot, trying to manufacture some body heat, but the rain hammered him, slid in icy, squiggly streaks down his back. *Come on, Mom.*

She never came that day. Or the next. He'd wandered around the dark, dangerous parts of Seattle all night, and finally, he'd fallen asleep in the garbage-strewn doorway of a tumbledown Chinese restaurant. In the morning, he'd rinsed out his mouth and grabbed a discarded bag of fortune cookies from a Dumpster, then made his way to school.

The police had come for him at noon, two unsmiling men in blue uniforms who told him that his mother had been stabbed. They didn't say what she'd been doing at the time of the crime, but Nick knew. She'd been trying to sell her thin, unwashed body for the price of a fifth of gin. The policemen told Nick that there were no suspects, and he hadn't been surprised. No one except Nick had cared about her when she was alive; no one was going to care that another scrawny, homeless drunk, turned old before her time by booze and betrayal, had been murdered.

Nick buried the memory in the black, soggy ground of his disappointments. He wished he could forget it, but of course, the past was close now. It had been breathing down his neck ever since Kathy's death.

With a tired sigh, he turned and faced his utterly silent child. "Time for bed," he said softly, trying to forget, too, that in the old days—not so long ago—she would have mounted a formal protest at the thought of going to bed without any "family time."

But now, she got to her feet, held her doll in the two "visible" fingers on her right hand, and walked away from him. Without a single backward glance, she began the long, slow climb to the second floor. Several of the steps creaked beneath her feather weight, and every sound hit Nick like a blow. What in the hell was he going to do now that Izzy was out of school? She had nowhere to go and no one to take care of her. He couldn't stay home from work with her, and Lurlene had her own life.

What in the hell was he going to do?

Twice during the night, Annie awoke from her solitary bed and paced the room. Kathy's death had reminded her how precious time was, how fleeting. How sometimes life snipped the edges off your good intentions and left you with no second chance to say what really mattered.

She didn't want to think about her husband—*I love her, Annie*—but the thoughts were always there, gathered in the air around her, crackling like heat lightning in the darkness of her room. She stared at her face in the mirror, studying the haircut, trying to figure out who she was and where she belonged. She stared at herself so long, the image changed and twisted and turned gray, and she was lost in the blurry reflection of a woman she'd never known.

Without Blake, she had no one who'd witnessed the past twenty years of her life. No one but Hank who could remember what she'd been like at twenty-five or thirty, no one with whom to share her lost dreams.

Stop it.

She glanced at the clock beside the bed. It was six o'clock in the morning. She sat down on the edge of the bed, grabbed the phone, and dialed Natalie's number, but her daughter was already gone for the day. Then she took a chance on Terri.

Terri answered on the fifth ring. "This better be important," she growled.

Annie laughed. "Sorry, it's just me. Is it too early?"

"No, no. I love getting up before God. Is everything okay?"

Annie didn't know if things would ever be okay again, but that answer was getting stale. "I'm getting by."

"Judging by the hour, I'd say you weren't sleeping well."

"Not much."

"Yeah, I pretty much paced and cried for the first three months after Rom-the-shit-heel left me. You need to find something to do."

"I'm in Mystic; the choices are a bit limited. I suppose I could try my hand at beer-can art. That's a big seller up here. Or maybe I can learn to hunt with a bow and arrow and then stuff my own kills."

"It's good to hear you laugh."

"It beats crying."

"Seriously, Annie. You need to find something to do. Something that gets you out of your bed—or into someone else's. Try shopping. Go buy some new clothes. Something that changes your look."

Annie rubbed her shorn hair. "Oh, I've changed my looks all right. I look like Rush Limbaugh on Phen-fen."

They talked for another half hour, and when she hung up, Annie felt, if not stronger, then at least better. She roused herself from her bed and took a long, hot shower.

Dressing in a white cashmere, boat-necked sweater and winter-white wool slacks, she went downstairs and cooked Hank a big breakfast of scrambled eggs, orange juice, pancakes, and turkey bacon. It wasn't long before the aroma drew her dad downstairs.

He walked into the kitchen, tightening the gray cotton belt around his ankle-length robe. He scratched his scruffy white beard and stared at her. "You're up. Are you out of bed for long, or just roving until the headache starts again?"

The perceptiveness of the question reminded Annie that her father had known tragedy and had more than a waltzing acquaintance with depression himself. She pulled some china plates from the old oak break-front in the corner and quickly set two places at the breakfast table. "I'm moving on with my life, Dad. Starting now. Starting here. Sit down."

He pulled out a chair. It made a grating sound on the worn yellow linoleum. "I'm not sure feeding a man is a big leap forward."

She gave him a crooked grin and took a seat across from him. "Actually, I thought I'd go shopping."

He plucked up a mouthful of egg in his blunt-edged fingers. "In Mystic? Unless you're looking for the ideal steel-head lure, I don't know how much luck you'll have."

Annie stared down at her eggs. She wanted to eat—she really did—but the sight of the food made her faintly nauseous. She hoped her dad didn't notice. "I thought I'd start by getting a few books. This seems like a good time to catch up on my reading. Hell, I could get through *Moby-Dick* in my spare time. And the clothes I brought won't work up here."

"Yeah, white's not a very practical color up here in mudland." He poured a blot of ketchup alongside his eggs and peppered everything. Reaching for his fork, he glanced across the table at Annie. She could tell that he was doing his best not to grin. "Good for you, Annie Virginia." Then, softer, "Good for you."

Mystic dozed beneath a bright spring sun. The town was full of activity today, with farmers and housewives and fishermen scurrying up and down the concrete sidewalks, in a hurry to get their errands done while the clouds were slim and spread out beneath a pale blue sky. Everyone knew that those same clouds could suddenly bunch together like school-yard bullies, releasing a torrent of rain so vicious that even a full-grown eagle couldn't take flight.

Annie strolled down Main Street, peeking into the various stores, a couple of times pushing through a half-open door. Invariably a bell tinkled overhead and a voice called out, *Hiya miss. Fine day, isn't it?* At the Bagels and Beans coffee shop, she ordered a double tall mocha latte, and she sipped it as she moved down the street.

She passed stores that sold trinkets for tourists, hardware, fabric, and fishing tackle. But there wasn't a single bookstore. At the H & P Drugstore, she picked up the latest Pat Conroy best-seller but couldn't find anything else that interested her. There wasn't much of a selection. It was too bad, because she needed a manual for the rest of her life.

At last, she found herself standing in front of Eve's Leaves Dress Emporium. A mannequin smiled down at her from the display window, wearing a bright yellow rain slicker and matching hat. Her awkwardly bent elbow held a sign that read: *Spring is in the air.* Multicolored silk flowers sprouted from watering cans at her booted feet, and a rake was slanted against one wall.

Annie pushed through the glass door. A tiny bell tinkled at her entrance.

Somewhere, a woman squealed. "It *can't* be!"

Annie looked around for the owner of the voice. Molly Block, her old high school English teacher, came barreling through the maze of rounders, her fleshy arms waving.

"Annie?" she said, grinning. "Annie Bourne, is that you?"

"It's me, Mrs. Block. How are you?"

Molly planted her hands on her wide hips. "Mrs. Block. Don't make me feel so old, Annie. Why, I was practically a *child* when I taught your class." She grinned again, and shoved the wire-rimmed glasses higher on her nose. "It's grand to see you again. Why, it's been years."

"It's good to see you, too, Molly."

"Whatever brings you up to our neck of the woods? I thought you married a hotshot lawyer and were living the good life in smoggy California."

Annie sighed. "Things change, I guess."

Molly cocked her head to the left and eyed Annie. "You look good; I'd kill to be able to wear that haircut, but I'd look like a helium balloon. That white cashmere won't last long in this country, though. One good rainstorm and you'll think you left the house wearin' a dead rabbit."

Annie laughed. "That's the truth."

Molly patted her shoulder. "Follow me."

An hour later, Annie stood in front of a full-length mirror. She was wearing a nineteen-dollar pair of jeans (who knew they still made jeans at that price?), cotton socks and tennis shoes, and a baggy UW sweatshirt in a utilitarian shade of gray.

The clothes made her feel like a new woman. She didn't look like the thirty-nine-year-old soon-to-be-ex-wife of a hotshot California lawyer; she looked like an ordinary small-town woman, maybe someone who had horses to feed and porches to paint. A woman with a life. For the first time, she almost liked the haircut.

"They suit you," Molly said, crossing her beefy arms and nodding. "You look like a teenager."

"In that case, I'll take everything."

While Molly was ringing up the purchases, she rambled on and on about life in Mystic, who was sleeping with whom, who'd gone bankrupt over the spotted owl fiasco, who was running for city council.

Annie glanced out the window. She listened vaguely to the small-town gossip, but she couldn't really concentrate. Lurlene's words kept coming back to her, circling, circling. *Kathy died eight months ago.* She turned back to Molly. "I heard . . . about Kathy Johnson . . . Delacroix."

Molly paused, her pudgy fingers plucking at a price tag. "It was a true shame, that. You all used to be awfully close in high school." She smiled sadly. "I remember the time you and Nick and Kathy put on that skit for the talent show—you all sang some silly song from *South Pacific.* Nicky wore that outrageous coconut bra, and halfway through the song you all were laughing so hard you couldn't finish."

"I remember," she said softly, wondering how it was she'd forgotten it until this very second. "How's Nick doing since . . . you know?" She couldn't bring herself to actually say the words.

Molly made a tsking sound and snipped the price tag from the jeans with a pair of scissors. "I don't know. He makes his rounds and does his job, I guess—you know he's a cop, right? Don't see him smile much anymore, and his daughter is in pretty bad shape, from what I hear. They could use a visit from an old friend, I'll bet."

After Annie paid for her new clothes, she thanked Molly for the help and carried her purchases out to the car. Then she sat in the driver's seat for a while, thinking, remembering.

She shouldn't go to him, not now, not spur-of-the-moment, she knew that. A thing like this needed to be thought out. You didn't just go barging into a strange man's life, and that's what he was: a stranger. She hadn't seen Nick in years.

Besides, she was broken and battered herself. What good could she be to a man who'd lost his wife?

But she was going to go to him. She had probably known from the second Lurlene mentioned his name that it was inevitable. It didn't matter that it didn't make sense; it didn't matter that he probably wouldn't remember her. What mattered was that he'd once been her best friend, and that his wife had once been her best friend. And that she had nowhere else to go.

It was approaching nightfall by the time Annie gathered the nerve to go see Nick. A winding brown ribbon of road led to the Beauregard house. Towering old-growth trees bracketed the road, their trunks obscured by runaway salal bushes. Every now and then, through the black fringe of forest, she could see a glittering silver reflection of the lake. The last few rays of gray sunlight fell like mist through the heavy, moss-draped branches.

It wasn't raining, but tiny droplets of dew began to form on the windshield. In this, the land of ten thousand waterfalls, the air was always heavy with moisture, and the lakes were the aquamarine hue of glacial ice. Some, like Mystic Lake, were so deep that in places the bottom had never been found, and so remote that sometimes, if you were lucky, you could find a pair of trumpeter swans stopping by on their migratory patterns. Here, tucked into the wild, soggy corner of this secret land, they knew they would be safe.

The road twisted and turned and finally ended in a big circular dirt driveway. Annie parked next to a police squad car, turned off the engine, and stared at the beautiful old house, built back at the turn of century, when woods were solid and details were hand-carved by master craftsmen who took pride in their work. In the distance, she could hear the roar of the mighty Quinault River, and she knew that this time of year it would be straining and gnawing at its bank, rushing swollen and headlong toward the faraway shores of the Pacific Ocean.

A pale yellow fog obscured half of the house, drifting on invisible currents of air from the lake. It crept eerily up the whitewashed porch steps and wound around the carved posts.

Annie remembered a night when this house had been spangled in starlight. It had been abandoned then; every broken window had held jagged bits of shadow and moonlight. She and Nick had ridden their bikes here, ditched them alongside the lake, and stared up at the big, broken house.

I'm gonna own this house someday, Nick had said, his hands shoved deeply in his pockets.

He'd turned to her, his handsome face cut into sharp angles by the glittering moonlight. She hadn't even seen the kiss coming, hadn't prepared for it, but when his lips had touched hers, as soft and tentative as the brush of a butterfly's wing, she'd started to cry.

He had drawn back, frowning. *Annie?*

She didn't know what was wrong, why she was crying. She'd felt foolish and desperately naive. It was her first kiss—and she'd ruined it.

After that, he'd turned away from her. For a long time, he'd stared at the lake, his arms crossed, his face unreadable. She'd gone up to him, but he'd pulled away, mumbled something about needing to get home. It was the first and last time he'd ever kissed her.

She brushed the memory aside and fixed her thoughts on the here and now.

Nick and Kathy had fixed up the old house—the windows were all in place, and sunshine-yellow paint coated everything. Hunter-green shutters bracketed each window, but still the whole place looked . . . untended.

Last year's geraniums and lobelia were still in the flower boxes, now a dead, crackly bunch of brown stalks. The grass was much too long and moss had begun to fur the brick walkway. A dirty cement birdbath lay on its side amid gargantuan rhododendrons.

And still it was one of the most beautiful places she'd ever seen. The new spring grass was as green as emeralds and as thick as chinchilla fur; it swept away from the building and rolled gently to the blue edge of the lake. Behind the house, swollen clouds hung suspended in a sky hammered to the color of polished steel.

Annie tucked her purse under her arm and slowly crossed the squishy wet lawn, climbing the white porch steps. At the oak door, she paused, then took a deep breath and knocked.

No answer.

She was just about to turn away when she heard the slow shuffling of feet. Suddenly the door swung open, and Nick was standing in front of her.

She would have recognized him anywhere. He was still tall, over six feet, but time had whittled the football star's muscles to a whipcord leanness. He wasn't wearing a shirt, and the dark, corrugated muscles of his stomach tapered down into a pair of bleached Levi's that were at least two sizes too big. He looked as tough and sinewy as old leather, with pale, lined skin stretched across hollowed-out cheeks. His hair was ragged and unkempt, and something—either time or grief—had sucked its color away, left it the silvery hue of a nickel when struck by the sun.

But it was his eyes—an eerie, swimming-pool blue—that caught and held her attention. His gaze flicked over her, a cop's look that missed no detail, not the brand-new tomboy haircut or the newly purchased small-town clothes. Certainly not the Buick-size diamond on her left hand. "Annie Bourne," he said softly, unsmiling. "Lurlene told me you were back in town."

An uncomfortable silence fell as she tried to figure out what to say. She shifted nervously from side to side. "I'm . . . sorry about Kathy."

He seemed to fade a little beneath the words. "Yeah," he answered. "So am I."

"I know how much you loved her."

He looked as if he were going to say something, and she waited, poised forward, but in the end he said nothing, just cocked his head and swung the door open wider.

She followed him into the house. It was dark—there were no lights on, no fire in the fireplace—and there was a faint musty smell in the air.

Something clicked. Brilliant white light erupted from a shadeless lamp; it was so bright that for a moment she couldn't see anything at all. Then her eyes adjusted.

The living room looked like someone had dropped a bomb on it. There was a scotch or whiskey bottle lying beside the sofa, a drop of booze puddled at its mouth; open pizza boxes littered the floor; clothes lay in heaps and on chairbacks. A crumpled blue policeman's shirt hung across the television screen.

"I don't seem to spend much time at home anymore," he said into the awkward silence. Reaching down, he grabbed a faded flannel shirt from the floor and put it on.

She waited for him to say something else, and when he didn't, she glanced around. The sprawling living room was floored in beautiful oak planks and dominated by a large brick fireplace, blackened by age and smoke. It looked as if there hadn't been a fire in the hearth in a long, long time. The few bits and pieces of furniture—a faded brown leather sofa, a tree-trunk end table, a morris chair—were scattered haphazardly around the room, all wearing tissue-thin coats of dust. A stone archway led into a formal dining room, where Annie could see an oval maple table and four scattered chairs, their seats cushioned by red and white gingham pads. She supposed that the closed green door led to the kitchen. To the left, an oak staircase hugged the brightly wallpapered wall and led to a darkened second floor.

Annie felt Nick's gaze on her. Nervously, she picked an invisible lint ball from her sleeve and searched for something to say. "I hear you have a daughter."

Slowly, he nodded. "Izzy. Isabella. She's six."

Annie clasped her hands together to keep from fidgeting. Her gaze landed on a photograph on the mantel. She picked her way through the rubble on the floor and touched the photo. "The gruesome threesome," she said, smiling. "I can't remember this one. . . ."

Lost in her own memories, Annie vaguely heard him pad out of the room. A moment later, he was back.

He came up behind her, so close she could feel the warmth of his breath on the back of her neck. "Would you like a drink?"

She turned away from the fireplace and found him directly behind her, holding a bottle of wine and two glasses. For a second, it startled her, then she remembered that they were grown-ups now, and offering a glass of wine was the polite way to entertain a guest. "A drink would be great. Where's your daughter? Can I meet her?"

An unreadable look passed through his eyes. "She's staying with Lurlene tonight. They're going to see some cartoon at the Rose theater with Buddy's granddaughters. Let's go sit by the lake." He grabbed a blanket from the sofa and led her out of the house. Together, not too close, they sat down on the blanket.

Annie sipped at the glass of wine Nick had poured for her. Twilight slipped quietly through the trees in blood-red streaks. A pale half moon rose slowly upward, spreading a blue-white veil across the navy-blue surface of the lake. Tiny, silvery peaks rippled against the shore, lapped against the pebbly ground. Memories sifted through the air, falling like rain to the ground around them. She remembered how easy it had once been with them, as they sat together at sporting events, watching Kathy cheerlead at the sidelines; how they'd all squeezed together in vinyl booths to eat greasy hamburgers and fries after the games. They'd known how to talk to each other then—about what, she couldn't recall—but once she'd believed she could tell him anything.

And now, all these years later, with the bumpy road of their separate lives between them, she couldn't think of how to weave a fabric of conversation from a single thread.

She sighed, sipping her wine. She was drinking more than she should, and faster, but it eased her awkwardness. A few stars came out, pinpricks of light peeking through the purple and red twilight sky.

She couldn't stand the silence anymore. "It's beautiful—"

"Nice stars—" They both spoke at the same time.

Annie laughed. "When in doubt, mention the weather or the view."

"We can do better than that," he said quietly. "Life's too damned short to spend it making small talk."

He turned to her, and she saw the network of lines that tugged at his blue eyes. He looked sad and tired and infinitely lonely. It was that, the loneliness, that made her feel like they were partners somehow, victims of a similar war. So, she put the small talk aside, forgot about plundering the shared mine of their teenage years, and plunged into intimacy. "How did Kathy die?"

He sucked down his glass of wine and poured another one. The glittering gold liquid crested at the rim of the glass and spilled over, splashing on his pant leg. "She killed herself."

CHAPTER 7

Annie stared at Nick, too stunned to respond. "I . . ." She couldn't say the pat, *I'm sorry*. The words were too hollow, almost obscenely expected. She gulped a huge swallow of wine.

Nick didn't seem to notice that she hadn't spoken—or maybe he was grateful for it. He stared out at the lake, sighing heavily. "Remember how moody she used to be? She was teetering on the edge of despair even then—her whole life—and none of us knew it. At least, *I* didn't know it . . . until it started to get bad. The older she got, the worse it became. Manic-depressive. That's the technical term. She started having episodes right after her twentieth birthday, just six months after her folks were killed in a car accident. Some days she was sweet as pie, then something would happen . . . she'd cry and lock herself in a closet. She wouldn't take her medication most of the time, said it made her feel like she was breathing through Jell-O." His voice cracked, and he took a huge, gulping swallow of wine. "One day, when I came home from work early, I found her standing in the bathroom, crying, knocking her head against the wall. She just turned to me, her face all smeared with tears and blood, and said, 'Hi honey. You want me to make you lunch?'

"I bought this place to make her happy, hoping maybe it would help her remember what life used to be like. I thought . . . if I could just give her a home, a safe place where we could raise our kids, everything would be okay. Christ, I just wanted to help her . . ."

His voice cracked again, and he took another drink of wine. "For a while, it worked. We poured our hearts and souls and savings into this

71

old mausoleum. Then Kathy got pregnant. For a while after Izzy was born, things were good. Kathy took her medication and tried . . . she tried so hard, but she couldn't handle a baby. She started to hate this place—the heating that barely worked, the plumbing that pinged. About a year ago, she gave up the medications again . . . and then everything went to hell."

He finished his second glass of wine and poured another. Shaking his head, he said softly, "And still, I didn't see it coming."

She didn't want to hear any more. "Nick, you don't—"

"One night I came home from work with a quart of butter brickle ice cream and a rented video and found her. She'd shot herself in the head . . . with my gun."

Annie's fingers spasmed around the stem of her glass. "You don't have to talk about her."

"I *want* to. No one else has asked." He closed his eyes, leaning back on his elbows. "Kathy was like the fairy tale—when she was good, she was very, very good, and when she was bad, you wanted to be in Nebraska."

Annie leaned back beside him, gazing up at the stars. The wine was making her dizzy, but she was glad; it blurred the hard edges of his words.

He gave her a tired smile. "One day she loved me with all her heart and soul, and the next day, she wouldn't even speak to me. It was worst at night; sometimes she'd kiss me, and other times she'd roll toward the wall. If I even touched her on those nights, she'd scream for me to get away. She started telling wild stories—that I beat her, that Izzy wasn't really her child, that I was an imposter who'd murdered her real husband in cold blood. It made *me* . . . crazy. The more she pulled away, the more I reached out. I knew I wasn't helping, but I couldn't seem to stop myself. I kept thinking that if I loved her enough, she'd be okay. Now that she's gone, all I can think about is how selfish I was, how stupid and naive. I should have listened to that doctor and hospitalized her. At least she'd be alive. . . ."

Without thinking, Annie reached for him, touched his face gently. "It's not your fault."

He gave her a bleak look. "When your wife blows her brains out in your bed, with your baby daughter just down the hall, believe me, *she* thinks it's your fault." He made a soft, muffled sound, like the whimpering of a beaten pup. "God, she must have hated me. . . ."

"You don't really believe that."

"No. Yes. Sometimes." His mouth trembled as he spoke. "And the worst part is—sometimes I hated her, too. I hated what she was doing to me and Izzy. She started to be more and more like my mother . . . and I knew, somewhere down inside, I knew I wasn't going to be able to save her. Maybe I stopped trying . . . I don't know."

His pain called out to her, and she couldn't turn away. She took him in her arms, stroking him as she would have soothed a child. "It's okay, Nick. . . ."

When he finally drew back and looked at her, his eyes were flooded with tears. "And there's Izzy. My . . . baby girl. She hasn't said a word in months . . . and now she thinks she's disappearing. At first it was just a finger on her left hand, then her thumb. When the hand went, she started wearing a black glove and stopped talking. I've noticed lately that she only uses two fingers on her right hand—so I guess she thinks that hand is disappearing, too. God knows what she'll do if . . ." He tried to smile. She could see the superhuman effort he was making simply to speak, but then he failed. She could see when the control slipped away from him, tearing away like a bit of damp tissue. "What can I do? My six-year-old daughter hid under her bed one night because she heard a noise. She wanted to go to her mommy and get a hug, but thank God, she didn't. Because her mommy had put a gun to her head and blown her brains out. If Izzy had walked down the hall that night, she would have seen bits and pieces of her mommy on the mirror, on the head-board, on the pillow. . . ." Tears streaked down his unshaven cheeks.

His grief sucked her under, mingled somewhere in the darkness with her own pain. She wanted to tell him that it would all be okay, that he would survive, but the words wouldn't come.

Nick gazed at her, and she knew he was seeing her through the blur of his tears. He touched her cheek, his hand slid down to coil around her neck and pulled her closer.

She knew that this moment would stay with her forever, long after she wanted to forget it. She would perhaps wonder later what had moved her so—was it the shimmering of the stars on the lake, or the way the mixture of moonlight and tears made his eyes look like pools of molten silver? Or the loneliness that lay deep, deep inside her, like a hard square of ice pressed to her broken heart.

She whispered his name softly; in the darkness it sounded like a plea, or a prayer.

The kiss she pressed to his lips was meant to comfort; of that she was sure, a gentle commiseration of understood heartache. But when their lips touched, soft and pliant and salty with teardrops, everything changed. The kiss turned hot and hungry and desperate. She was thinking of Blake, and she knew he was thinking of Kathy, but it didn't matter. What mattered was the heat of togetherness.

She fumbled with the buttons on his shirt and pressed her hands beneath the worn flannel as quickly as she could, sliding her open palms against the coarse wiry hairs on his chest. Her hands moved tentatively across his shoulder, down his naked back. Touching him felt secret and forbidden, dangerous, and it made her *want* . . .

With a groan, he wrenched his shirt off and tossed it aside. Annie's clothes came next. Her gray sweatshirt and bra sailed across the wet grass like flags of surrender.

Cool night air breezed across her bare skin. She closed her eyes, embarrassed by the intensity of her desire. His hands were everywhere, touching her, rubbing, stroking, squeezing, sliding down the curve of her back. In some distant part of her mind, she knew that she was getting carried away, that this was a bad idea, but it felt so good. No one had wanted her this badly for a long, long time. Maybe forever . . .

They became a wild, passionate tangle of naked limbs and searching mouths. Annie gave in to the aching pleasure of it all—the hard, calloused feel of his fingers on her face, her breasts, between her legs. He touched her in places and ways she'd never imagined, brought her body to a throbbing edge between pleasure and pain. Her breathing shattered into choppy, ragged waves, until she was gasping for air and aching for release. "Please, Nick . . ." she pleaded.

She clung to him, feeling the damp moisture of tears on her cheeks, and she didn't know if they were his or hers or a mingling of the two, and when he entered her, she had a dizzying, desperate moment when she thought she would scream. . . .

Her release was shattering. He clung to her, moaned, and when she felt his orgasm, she came again, sobbing his name, collapsing on his damp, hairy chest. He gathered her into his arms, stroking her hair, murmuring soft, soothing words against her ear. But her heart was pounding so hard and her pulse was roaring so loudly in her ears she had no idea what he said.

When Annie fell back to earth, amid a shower of stars, she landed with a thud. She lay naked beside Nick, her breathing ragged. Overhead, the sky was jet-black and sprinkled with starlight, and the night smelled of spilled wine and spent passion.

Very slowly, Nick pulled his hand away from hers. Without the warmth of his touch, her skin felt clammy and cold.

She grabbed one end of the blanket and pulled it across her naked breasts, sidling away from him. "Oh, my God," she whispered. "What have we done?"

He curled forward, burying his face in his hands.

She scouted through the wet grass and grabbed her shirt, pulling it toward her. She had to get out of here, now, before she fell apart. "This didn't happen," she said in a whispery, uncertain voice. "This did *not* happen."

He didn't look at her as he scooped up his clothes and hurriedly dressed. When he was armored again, he stood up and turned his back on her.

She was shaking and doing her best not to cry as she dressed. He was probably comparing her to Kathy, remembering how beautiful his wife had been, and wondering what the hell he'd done—having sex with a too-thin, too-old, too-short-haired woman who had let herself become such a nothing. . . .

Finally, she stood. She stared down at her own feet, wishing the ground would open up and swallow her. "I better get—" She'd been about to say *home,* but she didn't have a home any more than she had a husband there waiting for her. She swallowed thickly and changed her words. "Back to my dad's house. He'll be worried—"

At last, Nick turned to her. His face was lined and drawn, and the regret in his eyes hit her like a slap. God, she wanted to disappear. . . .

"I've never slept with anyone but Kathy," he said softly, not quite meeting her eyes.

"Oh," was all she could think of to say, but his quiet admission made her feel a little better. "This is a first for me, too."

"I guess the sexual revolution pretty much passed us by."

Another time it might have been funny. She nodded toward her car. "I guess I should get going."

Wordlessly, they headed back to the car. She was careful not to touch him, but all the way there, she kept thinking about his hands on her body, the fire he'd started deep inside her, in that place that had been cold and dead for so long. . . .

"So," he said into the awkward silence, "I guess Bobby Johnson was lying when he said he nailed you after the Sequim game?"

She stopped dead and turned to him, fighting the completely unexpected urge to laugh. "*Nailed* me?"

He shrugged, grinning. "He said it, not me."

"*Nailed* me?" She shook her head. "Bobby Johnson said that?"

"Don't worry—he said you were good. And he didn't even *imply* a blow job."

This time she did laugh, and some of her tension eased. They started walking again, across the wet grass, to her car. He opened the door for her, and it surprised her, that unexpected gesture of chivalry. No one had opened a car door for her in years.

"Annie?" He said her name softly.

She glanced up at him. "Yes?"

"Don't be sorry. Please."

She swallowed hard. For a few moments, Nick had made her feel beautiful and desirable. How could she feel sorry about that? She wanted to reach out for him again, anything to stave off the cold loneliness that would engulf her again the moment she climbed into her rented car and closed the door. "Lurlene told me you were looking for a nanny . . . for Isabella. I could watch her . . . during the day . . . if that would help you out. . . ."

He frowned. "Why would you do that for me?"

The question saddened her; it was full of mistrust and steeped in a lifetime's disappointments. "It would help *me* out, Nick. Really. Let me help you."

He stared at her a long time, that wary cop's look again. Then slowly, pointedly, he took hold of her hand and lifted it. In the pale moonlight, the three-carat diamond glittered with cold fire. "Don't you belong somewhere else?"

Now he would know what a failure she was, why she'd come running back to Mystic after all these years. "My husband and I have recently separated. . . ." She wanted to say more, tack a lighthearted excuse on the end of the glaring, ugly statement, but her throat closed up and tears stung her eyes.

He dropped her hand as if it had burned him. "Jesus, Annie. You shouldn't have let me act like such a whiny asshole, as if no one else in the world had a problem. You should have—"

"I *really* do not want to talk about it." She saw him flinch, and was immediately sorry for her tone of voice. "Sorry. But I think we've had enough shoulder-crying for one night."

He nodded, looking away for a minute. He stared at his house. "Izzy could use a friend right now. I'm sure as hell not doing her any good."

"It would help me out, too. I'm a little . . . lost right now. It would be nice to be needed."

"Okay," he said at last. "Lurlene could use a break from baby-sitting. She and Buddy wanted to go to Branson, and since Izzy's out of school . . ." He sighed. "I have to pick Izzy up from Lurlene's tomorrow. I could meet you at her house—she lives down in Raintree Estates—you remember where that is? Pink house with gnomes in the front yard. It's hard to miss."

"Sure. What time?"

"Say one o'clock? I can meet you there on my lunch break."

"Perfect." She stared up at him for another long minute, then turned and opened her car door. She climbed in, started the engine, and

77

slowly pulled away. The last thing she saw, out of her rearview mirror as she drove away, was Nick looking after her.

Long after she'd driven away, Nick remained on the edge of the lawn, staring down the darkened road. Slowly, he walked back into the house, letting the screen door bang shut behind him. He went to the fireplace and picked up the photograph of the three of them again. He looked at it for a long, long time, and then tiredly, he climbed the long, creaking staircase up to his old bedroom. Steeling himself, he opened the door. He moved cautiously inside, his eyes adjusting quickly to the gloom. He could make out the big, unmade bed, the clothes heaped everywhere. He could see the lamp that Kathy had ordered from Spiegel and the rocking chair he'd made when Izzy was born.

He grabbed a T-shirt from the floor, slammed the door behind him, and went down to his lonely couch, where he poured himself a stiff drink. He knew it was dangerous to use alcohol to ease his pain, and in the past months, he'd been reaching for that false comfort more and more.

Leaning back, he took a long, soothing drink. He finished that drink and poured another.

What he and Annie had done tonight didn't change a thing. He had to remember that. The life she'd stirred in him was ephemeral and fleeting. Soon, she'd be gone, and he'd be left alone again, a widower with a damaged child who had to find a way to get through the rest of his life.

There was a light on in the living room when Annie pulled up to her dad's house. She winced at the thought of confronting him now, at two o'clock in the morning, with her clothes all wrinkled and damp. God, she probably smelled like sex.

She climbed out of the car and headed into the house. As she'd expected, she found Hank in the living room, waiting up for her. A fire crackled cheerily in the fireplace, sending a velvet-yellow glow into the darkened room.

She closed the door quietly behind her.

Hank looked up from the book he was reading. "Well, well," he said, easing the bifocals from his eyes.

Annie self-consciously smoothed her wrinkled clothes and ran a hand through her too-short hair, hoping there was no grass stuck to her head. "You didn't need to wait up for me."

"Really?" He closed the book.

"There's no need to worry. I'm a hell of a long way from sixteen."

"Oh, I wasn't worried. Not after I called the police and the hospital."

Annie sat down on the leather chair beside the fireplace. "I'm sorry, Dad. I guess I'm not used to checking in. Blake never cared . . ." She bit back the sour confession and forced a thin smile. "I visited an old friend. I should have called."

"Yes, you should have. Who did you go see?"

"Nick Delacroix. You remember him?"

Hank's blunt fingers tapped a rhythm on the cover of the book, his eyes fixed on her face. "I should have expected you'd end up there. You three were as tight as shoelaces in high school. He's not doing so good, from what I hear."

Annie imagined that Nick was a delectable morsel for the town's gossips. "I'm going to help him out a little. Take care of his daughter while he's at work, that sort of thing. I think he needs a breather."

"Didn't you two have sort of a 'thing' in high school?" His gaze turned assessing. "Or are you planning to get back at Blake?"

"Of course not," she answered too quickly. "You told me I needed a project. Something to do until Blake wakes up."

"That man's trouble, Annie Virginia. He's drowning, and he could take you down with him."

Annie smiled gently. "Thanks for worrying about me, Dad. I love you for it. But I'm just going to baby-sit for him. That's all."

"That's all?" It wasn't a question.

"You told me I needed to find a project. What am I supposed to do—cure cancer? I'm a wife and mother. It's all I know. All I am." She leaned forward, ashamed that she couldn't tell him the whole truth— that she didn't know how to be this alone. So, she told him the next best thing. "I'm too old to lie to myself, Dad, and I'm too old to change, and if I don't do *something* I'm going to explode. This seems as good as anything. Nick and Izzy need my help."

"The person you need to help right now is you."

Her answering laugh was a weak, resigned little sound. "I've never been much good at that, now have I?"

CHAPTER 8

Annie threw back the covers and stumbled out of bed, the gauzy filaments of a nightmare wrapped around her. It was the same dream she used to have years ago, and she'd begun lately to have it again. She was trapped in a huge mansion, with hundreds of empty rooms everywhere, and she was searching desperately for a way out.

Her first thought when she woke was always *Blake?* But, of course, he wasn't beside her in bed. It was one of the many aspects of her new life to which she would have to become accustomed. There was no one to hold her after a nightmare.

It was getting harder and harder for her to believe that Blake would ever come back to her, and the loss of that transient hope made her feel as hollow as a reed sucked dry by the summer heat.

Tears stung her eyes. Last night she had broken her marriage vows for the first time in her life; she had shattered the faith she'd made with the only man she'd ever loved. And the hell of it was, he wouldn't care.

Nick was just getting ready to sign off for his lunch break when the call came in, a domestic disturbance on Old Mill Road.

The Weaver place.

With a sigh, Nick radioed the dispatcher and asked her to put a call in to Lurlene. He wouldn't make his meeting with Annie and Izzy.

Flicking on his siren and lights, he raced down the rutted strip of asphalt that led out of town. He followed Old Mill Road along the winding curves that sidled along the Simpson tree forest, over the concrete bridge above the choppy silver rapids of the Hoh River, and came at last to the driveway. A lopsided, dented mailbox, rusted to the color of Georgia mud, hung precariously from an arched piece of weathered driftwood. He turned cautiously down the road, a narrow, twisting swatch cut by hand from the dense black forest around it. Here, deep in the rain forest, no sunlight penetrated the trees; the foliage had a dark, sinister cast even in the middle of the day. At the end of the mud lane, a half-acre clearing butted up against a hillside of dense evergreen trees. Tucked into the back corner of the clearing a rickety mobile home squatted in the mud. Dogs yelped and barked at his entrance.

Nick radioed the dispatcher again, confirming his arrival, and then he hurried from the squad car. With one hand resting on the butt of his gun, he splashed through the puddles that pocked the driveway and charged up the wooden crates that served as the front steps. He was about to knock when he heard a scream from inside the trailer.

"Police!" he yelled as he pushed through the door. It swung inward and cracked on the wall. A shudder reverberated through the room. "Sally? Chuck?"

Outside, the dogs went wild. He could imagine them straining on their chains, snapping at one another in their desperation to attack the trespasser.

He peered through the gloomy interior. Avocado-colored shag carpeting, littered with beer cans and ashtrays, muffled the heavy sound of his boots as he moved forward. "Sally?"

A shriek answered him.

Nick ran through the dirty kitchen and shoved through the closed bedroom door.

Chuck had his wife pinned to the fake wood paneling. She was screaming beneath him, trying to protect her face. Nick grabbed Chuck by the back of the neck and hurled him sideways. The drunken man made an *oofing* sound of surprise and stumbled sideways, cracking into the corner of the pressboard bureau. Nick spun and grabbed him again, cuffing him.

Chuck blinked up at him, obviously trying to focus. "Goddamn it, Nicky," he whined in a low, slurred voice. "What in the fuck are you doing here? We was just havin' a argument. . . ."

Nick holstered a fierce, sudden urge to smash his fist into Chuck's fleshy face. "Stay here, goddamn it," he said instead, shoving Chuck so hard he crashed to the floor, taking a cheap Kmart lamp with him. The lightbulb splintered and left the tiny room in shadows.

Nick rested his hand on his baton as he cautiously made his way to Sally. She was leaning against the wall now, her torn, stained dress splattered with blood. A jagged cut marred her lower lip, and already a purplish bruise was seeping across her jaw.

He couldn't readily recall how many times he'd been here, how many times he'd stopped Chuck from killing his wife. It was a bad situation, this marriage, and had been long before Chuck got laid off at the mill, but since then, it had become a nightmare. Chuck spent all day at Zoe's Tavern, sucking down beers he couldn't afford and getting mad. By the time he crawled off his bar stool and made his stumbling way home, he was as mean as a junkyard dog, and when he pulled his broken-down pickup into his driveway, he was ready to do some serious damage. The only one around was his wife.

Nick touched Sally's shoulder.

She made a gasping sound and cringed. "Don't—"

"Sally, it's me. Nick Delacroix."

She slowly opened her eyes, and when she did, he saw the bottomless well of her despair, and her shame. She brought a shaking, bruised hand to her face and tried to push the blood-matted hair from her face. Tears welled in her blackened eyes and streaked down her battered cheeks. "Oh, Nick . . . Did the Robertses call you guys again?" She edged away from him and straightened, trying to look normal and in control. "It's nothing, really. Chuckie just had a bad day, is all. The paper company isn't looking for any employees. . . ."

Nick sighed. "You can't keep doing this, Sally. One of these days he's going to kill you."

She tried to smile. It was a wobbly, unbalanced failure, and it tore at Nick's heart. As always, Sally made him think of his mother, and all the excuses she'd made for alcohol over the years. "Oh, no, not my Chuckie. He gets a little frustrated, is all."

"I'm going to take Chuck in this time, Sally. I want you to make a complaint."

Chuck lurched from his place at the corner, stumbling into the bed. "She won't do that to me, willya honey? She knows I don't mean nothing by it. It's just that she makes me so damned mad sometimes. There wasn't nothin' in the whole house to eat when I got home. A man *needs* somethin' to eat, ain't that right, Nick?"

Sally glanced worriedly at her husband. "I'm sorry, Chuckie. I didn't expect you home s'early."

Defeat rounded Nick's shoulders and washed through him in a cold wave. "Let me help you, Sally," he said softly, leaning toward her.

She patted his forearm. "I don't need no help, Nick. But thanks for comin' by."

Nick stood there, staring down at her. She seemed to be shrinking before his eyes, losing weight. The ragged cut of her cotton dress was too big for her; it hung off her narrow shoulders and lay limply against her body. He knew as certainly as he knew his own name that one day he would answer one of these calls and Sally would be dead. "Sally—"

"Please, Nick," she said, her voice trembling, her eyes filling with tears. "Please, don't . . ."

Nick turned away from her. There was nothing he could do to help her. The realization caused an ache deep inside him, and left him wondering why in the hell he did this job. There was no success, or damned little of it. He couldn't do much of anything to Chuck unless Chuck killed his wife, and of course, then it would be too late.

He stepped over an upended laundry basket and took hold of Chuck's collar. "Come on, Chuck. You can sleep it off downtown."

He ignored Chuck's whining and refused to look at Sally again. He didn't need to. Sally would be following along behind them, whispering words of apology to the husband who'd broken her bones, promising to be "better" when he came home, vowing to have dinner on the table on time.

It didn't sicken Nick, her behavior. Unfortunately, he understood Sally. He had been like her in his youth, had followed his mother around like a hungry dog, begging for scraps of affection, taking whatever affection she would occasionally fling his way.

Yes, he understood too well why Sally stayed with Chuck. And he knew, too, that it would end badly for both of them. But there was nothing he could do to help them. Not a goddamn thing except to throw Chuck in jail to sleep off his drunk, and wait for the next domestic disturbance call on Old Mill Road.

Izzy Delacroix lay curled in a tight little ball on Lurlene's guest bed. The pillow didn't smell right—not the right smell at all. That was one of the things that made Izzy cry almost every night. Since her mommy went to Heaven, nothing smelled right, not the sheets or the pillows or Izzy's clothes.

Even Miss Jemmie didn't smell like she was s'posed to.

Izzy clutched the doll to her chest, stroking her pretty yellow hair with the two fingers she had left on her right hand, her thumb and pointy finger.

At first it had sorta scared her, when she'd figured out that she was disappearing. She'd started to reach for a crayon, and halfway there, she'd noticed that her pinky finger was sort of blurry and gray. The next day it was invisible. She had told her daddy and Lurlene, and she could tell by the way they looked at her that it scared them, too. And that icky doctor—it had made him look at her like she was a bug.

She stared at the two fingers that remained on her right hand. *It's goin' away, Mommy.*

She waited for an answer, but none came. Lots of times, she imagined her mommy was right beside her, and she could talk to her just by thinking the words.

She wished she could make it happen right now, but it only seemed to happen at special times—at the purply time between day and night.

She needed to talk to her mommy about what had happened the other day. It had been so bad. One minute, she'd been looking at the pictures in her book, and the next thing she knew, there was a scream inside her. She knew it wasn't good to scream in school—the other kids already thought she was stupid—and she'd tried really, really hard to keep her mouth shut. She'd clenched her hands into tight balls and squeezed her eyes shut so hard she'd seen stars in the darkness.

She had felt so scared and so lonely she couldn't breathe right. The scream had started as a little yelp that slipped out. She had clamped a hand over her mouth but it hadn't helped.

All the kids had stared at her, pointing and laughing.

And the scream had come out. Loud, louder, loudest. She'd clamped her hands over her ears so she couldn't hear it. She'd known she was crying, but she hadn't been able to stop that, either.

The teacher had grabbed Izzy's gloved hand, squeezing around all that nothingness. It had made Izzy scream harder that she couldn't feel anything.

"Oh, pumpkin, it's not invisible," Mrs. Brown had said softly; then she'd gently taken Izzy's other hand and led her down the hallway.

And the scream had gone on and on and on.

She had screamed all the way down the hall and into the principal's office. She had seen the way the grown-ups looked at her—like she was crazy—but she couldn't help herself. All she knew was that she was disappearing, one finger at a time, and no one seemed to care.

As quickly as the scream had come, it went away. It left her shaken and weird-feeling, standing in the middle of the principal's office, with everyone staring at her.

She had inched her way into the corner, wedged herself between a yucky green sofa and the window. The grown-ups' voices kept going, talking about her, whispering. . . .

Everyone cared about why she didn't talk anymore, that's all. That Dr. Schwaabe, all he cared about was why she didn't talk, and Izzy heard Lurlene and Buddy. They acted like she couldn't hear because she didn't talk. Lurlene called her "poor little thing" all the time—and every time she said it, Izzy remembered the bad thing, and she wished Lurlene would stop.

Then, like a knight out of one of Mommy's fairy tales, her daddy had walked into the principal's office. The grown-ups shut up instantly, moved aside.

He wouldn't have come to the school if she hadn't started screaming, and for a second, she was glad she'd screamed. Even if it made her a bad girl, she was glad to have her daddy here.

She wanted to throw herself in his arms, say, *Hi, Daddy,* in that voice she used to have, but he looked so sad she couldn't move.

He was so handsome; even since his hair had changed color after the bad thing, he was still the most handsome man in the world. She remembered what his laugh used to sound like, how it used to make her giggle right along with him. . . .

But he wasn't really her daddy anymore. He never read her stories at night anymore, and he didn't throw her up in his arms until she laughed. And sometimes at night his breath smelled all mediciney and he walked like one of her wobbly toys.

"Izzy?" He said her name softly, moving toward her.

For one heart-stopping minute, she thought he was going to touch her. She wormed her way out from the corner and baby-stepped his way. She leaned toward him, just a little teeny bit, but enough so maybe he'd see how much she needed him.

He gave a sharp sigh and turned back to face the grown-ups. "What's going on here, Bob?"

Izzy almost wished for the scream to come back, but all she felt was that stinging quiet, and when she looked down, another finger was gone. All she could see on her right hand was her thumb and pointy finger.

The grown-ups talked a bunch more, saying things that she wasn't listening to. Then Daddy went away, and Izzy went home with Lurlene. Again.

"Izzy, sweetheart, are you in there?"

She heard Lurlene's voice, coming through the closed bedroom door. "Come on out, Izzy. There's someone I want you to meet."

Izzy wanted to pretend she hadn't heard, but she knew there wasn't any point. She just hoped Lurlene wasn't going to give her another bath—she always used water that was way too cold and got soap in Izzy's eyes.

She sighed. *Miss Jemmie, we gotta go.*

She clutched the doll with her good arm and rolled out of bed. As she walked past the vanity, she caught a glimpse of herself in the mirror. A short, skinny girl with dirty black hair and one arm. Her eyes were still puffy from all that crying.

Mommy never let her look like this.

The bedroom door swung open. Lurlene stood in the opening, her big feet smacked together, her body bent at the waist. "Good morning, sweetheart." She reached out and tucked a tangled chunk of hair behind Izzy's ear.

Izzy stared up at her.

"Come on, pumpkin."

Wordlessly, Izzy followed her down the hallway.

Annie stood in the entryway of Lurlene and Buddy's triple-wide mobile home, on a patch of pink carpet.

Lurlene's husband, Buddy—*nice ta meetcha*—sat sprawled in a burgundy velour Barcalounger, with his feet elevated, a *Sports Illustrated* open on his chest, his right hand curled around a can of Miller. He was watching Annie carefully.

She shifted from foot to foot, trying not to think about the fact that she wasn't a psychiatrist, or that the child's trauma was a dark and bottomless well, or that Annie herself was lost.

She knew that love was important—maybe the *most* important thing—but she'd learned in the past weeks that it wasn't a magic elixir. Even Annie wasn't naive enough to believe that every problem could be solved by coating it in love. Some pain couldn't be assuaged, some traumas couldn't be overcome. She'd known that since the day her own mother had died.

"Nick ain't comin'. Did Lurlene tell you that?"

Annie frowned and glanced at Buddy. "Oh. No. I didn't know."

"He don't never show up when it matters." He took a long slug of beer, eyeing Annie above the can's dented rim. "You're taking on a hell of a job, you know. That Izzy's as unscrewed as a bum valve."

"Nick told me she hasn't spoken in a while, and about the . . . you know . . . disappearing fingers."

"That ain't the half of it. She's got the kind of pain that sucks innocent bystanders under and drowns 'em."

In other words: *you're out of your depth here, city girl.* Annie knew how she must appear to him, with her cheap jeans that still showed the manufacturer's creases and the tennis shoes that were as white as new fallen snow. She went to tuck a lock of hair behind her ear, but there was no hair there. Embarrassed, she forced a smile. "That rain yesterday hurried spring right along. Why, at my dad's house, the daffodils are busting out all over. I thought maybe—"

"Annie?"

It was Lurlene's voice this time. Annie slowly turned.

Lurlene appeared at the end of the hallway, clad in a neon-green sweater and a pair of skin-tight purple faux snakeskin leggings. She clashed with everything in the house.

A child hung close to her side, a small girl with big brown eyes and hair the color of night. She was wearing a too-small pink dress that had seen better days. Her thin legs stuck out from the hemline like twin beanpoles. Mismatched socks—one pink, one yellow—hugged her ankles and disappeared into a pair of dirty Beauty and the Beast tennis shoes.

A little girl. Not an assortment of psychological problems or a trauma victim or a disciplinary problem. Just a plain, ordinary little girl who missed her mother.

Annie smiled. Maybe she didn't know about traumatic muteness and how the doctors and books and specialists thought it should be treated. But she knew about being afraid, and she knew about mothers who disappeared one day and never came back.

Slowly, with her hand out, she moved toward the girl. "Hey, Izzy," she said softly.

Izzy didn't answer; Annie hadn't expected her to. She figured Izzy would talk in her own sweet time. Until then, Annie was just going to act as if everything were normal. And maybe, after what Izzy had been through, silence was the most normal thing in the world.

"I'm Annalise, but that's a mouthful, isn't it. You can call me Annie." She kneeled down in front of the little girl, staring into the biggest, saddest brown eyes she'd ever seen. "I was a good friend of your mommy's."

A response flickered in Izzy's eyes.

Annie took it as encouragement. "I met your mom on the first day of kindergarten." She smiled at Izzy, then stood and turned to Lurlene. "Is she ready to go?"

Lurlene shrugged, then whispered, "Who knows? Poor thing." She bent down. "You remember what we talked about. Miss Annie's goin' to be takin' care of you for a while, durin' your daddy's work hours. You be a good girl for her, y'hear?"

"She most certainly does *not* have to be a good girl," Annie said, winking at Izzy. "She can be whatever she wants."

Izzy's eyes widened.

"Oh." Lurlene pushed to her feet and smiled at Annie. "God bless you for doing this."

"Believe me, Lurlene, this is as much for me as anyone. See you later."

Annie looked down at Izzy. "Well, Izzy. Let's hit the road. I'm positively dying to see your bedroom. I'll bet you have all kinds of great toys. I *love* playing Barbies." She led the way to the car, settled Izzy in the front seat, and clicked the seat belt in place.

Izzy sat in the passenger seat, strapped tightly in place, her head tilted to one side like a baby bird's, her gaze fixed on the window.

Annie started the car and backed out of the driveway, steering carefully past a crowd of ceramic gnomes. She kept talking as she drove, all the way past the Quinault Indian reservation, past the roadside stalls that sold smoked salmon and fresh crabs, past a dozen empty fireworks stands. She talked about anything and everything—the importance of old-growth trees, the viability of mime as an art form, the best colors, her favorite movies, the Girl Scout camp she and Kathy had gone to and the s'mores they'd made at the fire—and through it all, Izzy stared and stared.

As Annie followed the winding lake road through towering trees, she felt as if she were going back in time. This rutted, gravel road, spackled now with bits of shade, seemed a direct route to yesterday. When they reached the end of the road, Annie found herself unable to move. She sat behind the wheel of the car and stared at the old Beauregard place. Nick's home, now.

I'm going to own this house someday.

It had sounded like a silly dream to Annie then, all those years ago, a bit of glass spun in a young man's hand. Something to say on a starlit night before he found the courage to lean down and kiss the girl at his side.

Now, of course, she saw the magic in it, and it cut a tiny wound in her heart. Had she even *had* a dream at that tender age? If so, she couldn't remember it.

She pulled into the gravel driveway and parked next to the woodpile. The house sat primly in the clearing before her. Sunlight, as pale and watery as old chicken broth, painted the tips of the lush green grass and illuminated the daffodil-yellow paint on the clapboard siding. It still looked forlorn and forgotten, this grande dame of a Victorian house. In places the paint was peeling. Some of the shingles had fallen from the gabled roof, and the rhododendrons were crying out to be cut back.

"I'll bet that used to be a fort," Annie said, spying the broken boards of a treehouse through the branches of a dormant alder. "Your mom and I used to have a girls-only for—"

Izzy's seat belt unhooked with a harsh click. The metal fastener cracked against the glass. She opened the door and ran toward the lake, skidding to a stop at a picket-fenced area beneath a huge, moss-furred old maple tree.

Annie followed Izzy across the squishy lawn and stood beside the child. Within the aged white fence lay a beautiful square of ground that wasn't nearly as wild and overgrown as everything else on the property. "This was your mom's garden," she said softly.

Izzy remained motionless, her head down.

"Gardens are very special places, aren't they? They aren't like people . . . their roots grow strong and deep into the soil, and if you're patient and you care and you keep working, they come back."

Izzy turned slowly, tilted her head, and looked up at Annie.

"We can save this garden, Izzy. Would you like that?"

Very slowly, Izzy reached forward. Her thumb and forefinger closed around the dead stem of a shasta daisy. She pulled so hard it came out by the roots.

Then she handed it to Annie.

That dried-up, hollowed-out old shoot with the squiggly, hairy root was the most beautiful thing Annie had ever seen.

CHAPTER 9

Izzy clutched Miss Jemmie under her arm; it was the best she could do without all her fingers. She lagged behind the pretty, short-haired lady.

She was glad to be home, but it wouldn't last long. The pretty lady would take one look at Daddy's mess in the house and that would be that. Grown-up girls didn't like dirty places.

"Come on, Izzy," the lady called out from the porch.

Izzy stared up at the front door. She wished her daddy would suddenly shove through that door and race down the creaky old porch steps like he used to, that he'd sweep Izzy into his big, strong arms and spin her around until she giggled, kissing that one tickly spot on her neck.

It wouldn't happen, though. Izzy knew that because she'd been having the same dream for months and months and it never came true.

She remembered the first time her daddy had brought them out here. That was when his hair was black as a crow's wing and he never came home smelling like the bad place.

That first time had been magic. He had smiled and laughed and held her in his arms. *Can't you just see it, Kath? We'll plant an orchard over there . . . and fill that porch with rocking chairs for summer nights . . . and we can have picnics on the grass. . . .* He'd kissed Izzy's cheek then. *Would you like that, Sunshine? A picnic with chicken and milkshakes and Jell-O salad?*

She'd said, *Oh, yes, Daddy,* but they'd never had a picnic, not on the lawn or anywhere else. . . .

The front door creaked open, and Izzy remembered that the lady was waiting for her. She trudged reluctantly up the porch steps. The lady—Annie; she had to remember that the lady's name was Annie—clicked on the lamp beside the sofa. Light landed in streaks on Daddy's mess. Bottles, pizza boxes, dirty clothes were lying everywhere.

"As Bette Davis would say, 'what a dump.' Your father certainly doesn't win the Felix Unger award."

Izzy winced. That was it. Back to Lurlene's for chipped beef on toast. . . .

But Annie didn't turn and walk away. Instead, she picked her way through the junk and flung open the curtains in a cloud of dust. Sunlight poured through the two big picture windows. "That's better," she said, glancing around. "I don't suppose you know where the brooms and dustpans are? A bulldozer? How about a blowtorch?"

Izzy's heart started beating rapidly, and something felt funny in her chest.

Annie winked at her. "I'll be right back." She hurried out of the living room and disappeared into the kitchen.

Izzy stood very still, barely breathing, listening to the rapid fluttering of her heart.

Annie came back into the living room carrying a black garbage bag, a broom, and a bucket of soapy water.

That strange feeling in Izzy's chest seemed to grow bigger and bigger, until she almost couldn't breathe. Slowly, she moved toward Annie, waiting for the lady to throw her hands up and say, *it's too goddamn much work, Nicky,* like her mommy used to.

But Annie didn't say that. Instead, she bent over and picked up the garbage, one piece at a time, shoving it into the black bag.

Cautiously, Izzy moved closer.

Annie didn't look at her. "It's just junk, Izzy. Nothing permanent. There's nothing done here that can't be undone. My daughter's room used to look like this all the time—and she was a perfectly lovely teenager." She kept talking, and with each unanswered sentence, Izzy felt herself relaxing. "Why, I remember this place when I was a little girl. Your mom and daddy and I used to peek in the windows at nighttime, and we'd make up stories about the people who used to live here. I always thought it was a beautiful, wealthy couple from back East, who walked around in tuxedos and evening gowns. Your dad, he thought it was once owned by gamblers who lost everything in a single hand of cards. And your mama—why, I can't recall what she used to think. Probably something romantic, though." She paused long enough to smile at Izzy. "Maybe when the weather warms up, we could have a picnic on the lawn. Would you like that?"

Izzy felt the weirdest urge to cry. She wanted to say, *We could have milkshakes and Jell-O salad,* but she didn't. She couldn't have, even if she'd really tried. Besides, it was just one of those things grown-ups promised even when they didn't mean it.

"In fact," Annie said, "we could have a mini-picnic today. When I get the living room cleaned up, we'll have cookies and juice outside— iced raisin cookies and Maui punch. That sounds good, don't you think? 'Yes, Annie, I think that would be terrrrrific.' That's my Tony the Tiger impression. Natalie—that's my daughter; she's almost a grown up now—she used to love Frosted Flakes. I'll bet you do, too."

Izzy bit back an unexpected smile. She liked the way Annie didn't wait for her to answer. It made Izzy feel like she wasn't so different, like not talking was as okay as talking.

Tiny step by tiny step, she inched sideways. When she reached the sofa, she sat down, ignoring the dust that poofed up around her. Bit by bit, the garbage disappeared, and after a while, it began to look like home.

Annie tapped lightly on Izzy's bedroom door. There was no answer. Finally, she pushed open the door and went inside. The room was small and dark, tucked under an overhang in the roofline. A charming dormer reached outward, capturing the last pink light of day behind pale, worn lace curtains. The walls were done in a beautiful lavender-striped paper, and a matching floral print covered the bed. A Winnie-the-Pooh lamp sat on a white bedside table.

Nick and Kathy had probably planned this room and saved for it, wanting to create the perfect place for their child. Annie could remember the dreams that came with pregnancy, and the endless details of hope. Much of it started with the nursery.

Annie didn't know much about manic-depression, or how it had twisted and changed Kathy, but she knew that Kathy had loved her daughter. Every item in this room had been lovingly chosen, from the Little Mermaid nightlight to the Peter Rabbit bookends.

She crossed the clothes-strewn wooden floor to the bed. Izzy's dainty profile made a beautiful cameo against a faded yellow Big Bird pillowcase. A fuzzy purple blanket was drawn taut across her shoulders and tucked gently beneath her chin. The doll—Miss Jemmie, Lurlene had said—was sprawled on the floor, her black button eyes staring up at the ceiling. Izzy's tiny, black-gloved hand lay like a stain on the lavender lace bedspread.

Annie hated to wake the sleeping girl, but she was a big believer in routine. Children needed to know where the limits were and what rules governed. She'd put Izzy down for a nap at two-thirty—and was surprised when she actually fell asleep. Now, at four o'clock, it was time to wake up.

She bent down and jostled the little girl's shoulder. "Wake up, sleepyhead."

Izzy made a tiny, mewling sound and snuggled deeper under the covers.

"Oh, no, you don't. Come on, Izzy."

One brown eye popped open. Izzy used two fingers on her right hand to push the covers back. Blinking and yawning, she sat up.

"I thought you'd like to take a bath before your daddy gets home." Annie smiled and held up the bag of treats she'd brought with her. "I got you some new clothes and a few surprises—Lurlene told me what sizes to get. Come on." She helped Izzy out of bed and led her to the bathroom, where she quickly ran some water into the tub.

Then she knelt in front of the child.

Izzy eyed her warily.

Annie looked down at Izzy's gloved hand. "Don't you just hate it when parts of you start disappearing? Now, hands up."

Izzy dutifully raised her right arm. Her left arm hung limply at her side, the black-gloved fingers completely slack.

Annie sat back on her heels. "How, exactly, do we undress the invisible parts? I guess, if I just peel your jammies back . . ." Slowly, she pulled the sleeve along the "invisible" arm. Then she reached for the glove.

Izzy made a choking sound and wrenched away from her.

"Oh, sorry. The glove can't come off?"

Izzy stared intently at a spot somewhere behind Annie's left ear.

"I understand. There is no glove, is there, Izzy?"

Izzy bit down on her lower lip. She still didn't look at Annie.

Annie stood. Carefully taking Izzy by the shoulders, she steered the child toward the bathtub and helped her into the warm water. Izzy hugged the side of the tub, where her left arm hung limply over the edge.

"That's not too hot, is it?" Annie asked. "No, Annie, that's just right. Just exactly the temperature I like."

Izzy stared at her.

Annie grinned. "I can carry on a conversation all by myself. When I was a girl—I was an only child, too—I used to do it all the time."

Annie poured bubble bath into the falling water. Izzy watched, apparently awestruck, as airy white foam bubbled up around her.

Then Annie lighted a trio of votive candles she'd found in the kitchen. The sweet aroma of vanilla rose in the air. "Sometimes a girl needs a romantic bath—just for her. Okay." She reached into her brown bag. "Look at my goodies. I've got Johnson's baby shampoo, Pocahontas soap, a Hunchback of Notre Dame towel, and a Beauty and the Beast comb. And this *darling* play suit. It's lavender with little yellow flowers— just like your mom's garden will be—and a matching yellow hat."

She kept up a steady stream of dialogue, asking questions and answering them herself as she washed Izzy's long hair and lathered and rinsed her body, and finally helped her out of the tub. She wrapped the tiny girl in a huge towel and began combing her hair. "I remember when my daughter, Natalie, was your age. No bigger than a minute. It used to make my heart ache just to look at her." She wove Izzy's hair into a pair of perfect French braids and finished them off with two yellow satin bows.

"Turn around."

Dutifully, Izzy turned.

Annie dressed her in new white cotton underwear and helped her into the lavender blouse and overalls. When she was finished, she guided Izzy to the full-length mirror in the corner.

The little girl stared at herself for a long, long time. Then, very slowly, she lifted her right hand and touched the satin ribbons with her forefinger. Her rosebud mouth wobbled uncertainly. She bit down hard on her lower lip. A single tear trickled down Izzy's flushed pink cheek. Just one.

Annie understood. It was what she'd been hoping for, at least in part. That Izzy would see herself as she used to be. "I bet you always used to look like this, didn't you, Izzy?"

She placed a tender kiss on Izzy's forehead. The child smelled of baby shampoo and new soap. Like little girls everywhere.

Then, Annie sat back on her heels and looked steadily in Izzy's eyes. "You know how you share your toys with a friend, and you have more fun than if you were playing all by yourself? Sometimes that's true of sadness, too. Sometimes if you share it, it goes away."

Izzy didn't respond.

Annie smiled. "Now, I could use some help in the kitchen. I've started dinner, but I can't find the dishes *anywhere*. Maybe you could help me?"

Izzy blinked.

Annie took that as a yes.

Together, they went down to the kitchen. Izzy walked dutifully toward the table and sat down. Her little feet dangled above the floor.

Annie talked the whole time she made dumplings, stirring batter and dropping it into the simmering chicken stew. "Do you know how to set the table?" she asked as she put the lid on the big metal pot.

Izzy didn't answer.

"This isn't going to work, you know, Miss Izzy." Annie picked up a spoon and handed it to the girl. "Here you go—this is for you."

Izzy used her thumb and forefinger to take hold of the spoon. She stared at it, then frowned up at Annie.

"One shake of the spoon is yes. Two shakes is no. That way we can talk . . . sort of in code, without ever having to say something out loud. Now, do you think you could show me where the plates are?"

Izzy stared unblinking at the spoon for a long, long time. Then, very slowly, she shook it once.

"Hey, Nicky, I hear Hank Bourne's daughter is back in town."

Nick glanced up from his drink. There was a headache pounding behind his eyes, and he couldn't quite focus. He'd had it all day, ever since the fiasco at the Weaver place. He'd booked Chuck and thrown him in a cell, but already Sally had been to the station to make sure that no charges were leveled at her husband. Already she'd told the desk sergeant that she'd fallen down the stairs.

Nick thought that if he stopped in at Zoe's for a quick drink—just one to steady his nerves—he'd be okay to face Annie and Izzy at home. But, like always, one drink led to another and another and another . . .

What he'd seen in Sally's eyes opened a wound in his soul, a dark, ugly place that was bubbling with painful memories.

He closed his fingers around the glass and took another long, soothing pull of the scotch. "Whatever you say, Zoe."

Joel Dermot scooted closer to him. "I remember Annie Bourne. Her and my daughter, Suki, used to be in Girl Scouts together."

Nick closed his eyes. He didn't want to think about those days, long ago, when the three of them had been best friends. When he thought of those days, he remembered how much he used to care about Annie, and then he wound up thinking about the previous night, when she'd been in his arms, naked and wild, fulfilling all the fantasies he'd ever had about her. The memory invariably pushed him down a long and treacherous road, a road that made him question all the choices he'd made along the way. How he'd chosen Kathy because she needed him . . . and how he'd let her down, and how loving her had ruined him. Then he'd find himself having dark, dangerous thoughts—like what would his life have been like if he'd chosen Annie, or what it *could* be like if she were the kind of woman who would stay in Mystic.

Another man's wife.

Nick shot unsteadily to his feet, in a hurry to outrun that thought. Tossing a twenty-dollar bill on the bar, he turned and hurried out of the smoky tavern. He jumped into his patrol car and headed for home. By the time he pulled into his driveway, he felt as if he'd driven a thousand miles over a corrugated road. His body ached, his head hurt, and he longed for one more drink to ease the way.

What in the hell would he say to Annie now, after what had happened between them?

Slowly, he got out of the car, walked across the gravel walkway and up the sagging porch steps, and went inside.

Annie was stretched out on the sofa. When the door clicked shut behind him, she sat up and gave him a bleary-eyed smile. "Oh," she said. "I guess I fell asleep."

Her beauty left him momentarily speechless. He backed up a step, keeping as much floor as possible between them. He glanced away. "Sorry I'm late. I . . . meant to show up at Lurlene's, but we had an emergency call, and, well . . ."

She threw the blanket back and got up. Her clothes were wrinkled, and there was a network of tiny pink lines across her right cheek. "It's no problem. Izzy and I had a good time today. I think we're going to get along great."

He wanted to say something that would ease his guilt and make her think well of him. He had a ridiculous urge to talk to her about what had happened today, to share with another human being that he was shaken, that something had spilled out of him today, and he didn't know how to retrieve it, or how to put it back where it belonged. But that kind of intimacy was so alien to him that he couldn't imagine how to begin.

She plucked her purse from the coffee table. She was careful not to look at him for too long. "If you want . . . I could make you and Izzy a nice dinner tomorrow night. I think she'd like that."

"That would be great. I'll be home at six o'clock."

She edged past him but stopped at the door, turning back. "From now on . . . if you're going to be late, I'd appreciate a phone call."

"Yeah. I'm sorry."

She gave him a last smile and left the house.

He stood at the window, watching her drive away. When the tiny red dots of her taillights disappeared around the bend in the road, he slowly climbed the stairs and went into the guest bedroom, the one he'd moved into eight months ago and still used when he didn't fall asleep on the couch. Stripping out of his blue uniform, he slipped into a pair of ragged old sweats and tiredly walked down the hallway. Outside Izzy's door, he paused for a moment, gathering his strength.

A tiny nightlight glowed from the wall next to her bed. It was Winnie the Pooh's face in vibrant yellow. He picked up her favorite book—*Where the Wild Things Are*—and lowered himself slowly to the edge of her bed. As the mattress sagged beneath his weight, he froze. Izzy wiggled in her sleep, but didn't waken.

He opened the book, staring down at the first page. In the old days, when he'd read to her every night before bed, she'd curled her little body so trustingly against his, and cocked her smiling face up. *Daddy, what're yah gonna read me tonight, Daddy?*

He squeezed his eyes shut. It had been a long time since he'd remembered her habit of saying *Daddy* at the beginning and end of every sentence. He leaned down slowly, slowly, and kissed the softness of her forehead. The little-girl scent enveloped him, made him remember giving her bubble baths. . . .

He let out a long, slow breath. Now, all he did was read to her when she was asleep, just a few pages from her favorite book. He hoped the words soaked through her sleeping mind. It was a tiny, stupid way of saying he loved her; he knew that. Still, it was all he seemed to have left.

He read the book in a soft, singsong voice, and then gently placed it back on the bedside table. "Goodnight, Izzy-bear," he whispered, placing a last kiss on her forehead.

Back downstairs, he went to the kitchen and poured himself a stiff drink. He kicked open the front door and slumped onto a chair on the porch.

It came to him then, as he'd known it would. He could recall suddenly how it had smelled at the Weaver house, of bacon and Lysol, and how a thin strip of linoleum had been peeling up from the edge of the kitchen floor. He remembered the bruise on Sally's cheek, how it had been spreading already, seeping like a spot of blood through a bit of tissue paper.

Once, long ago, he had believed he could rescue people like Sally. He'd thought that when he put on his uniform, he would be invincible. God, he'd been such an idiot, believing in the words that meant so little today: honor, respect, justice. He'd actually thought that he could save people who had no desire to be saved.

But life had taught him a lot. Between his job and Kathy, his idealism had been hacked away, bit by bit, until now there was nothing left but rusted scraps. Without it, he didn't know who he was.

He took a long drink and leaned back in the chair, looking up at the night sky. He was startled for a moment to realize that outside, everything was still as it should be. The lake still glittered in the moonlight. Night still fell softly across the mountaintops and through the forests. Soon, dawn would come, chasing darkness to distant corners of the globe.

Once, he'd watched such things with wonder. He'd thought in those days that his needs were simple and easily met. He'd wanted only his family, his job, his home. He'd imagined that he would grow old in this house, sitting in this chair on his porch, watching his children grow up and move on. He'd thought then that age would pull the black from his hair, and that it would take years. He hadn't known then that grief and guilt could age a man and turn his hair silver in the span of a single season.

He drank until his head began to spin, until his vision blurred. The empty bottle slipped through his numb fingers and rolled away, clattering down the steps one by one to land silently in the grass.

The next morning, Izzy woke to the sound of her mommy's voice. She kicked the covers away and sat up, blinking. *Mommy?*

At first, all she could hear was the rain. In the old days—before the bad thing—she'd loved that sound, the way it rattled on the roof. She looked out the window, disappointed to see nothing out there but pink and yellow sunlight. No rain.

Mommy?

There was no answer, just the creaking sound of the house. Izzy slipped on her favorite bunny slippers and crept out of her bedroom. She moved silently down the stairs, hoping not to wake her daddy. He was asleep on the couch, with one arm flung across the coffee table and his bare feet sticking out from the end of his blue blanket.

She tiptoed past him, her heart thudding in her chest as she eased the front door open and closed it silently behind her. She stood on the porch, looking out. A pink mist floated across the lake. *Mommy?*

She walked through the grass, to the edge of the lake. She squeezed her eyes shut and pictured her mommy. When she opened her eyes, her mommy was there, standing in the middle of the water, too far away for Izzy's hands to reach.

Mommy didn't seem to move, but all at once, she was beside Izzy, so close that Izzy could smell her perfume.

It's okay now, Izzy. Her mom's voice mingled with the breeze. Somewhere, a bird squawked and flew up from the brush, flapping its wings as it rose into the sky.

It started to rain for real, a slow pattering shower that kissed Izzy's hair and fell on her lips. She saw that the rain was tinted, a million rainbow-hued flecks landing on the surface of the lake. But on the other side of the water, it wasn't raining.

It's okay now, Mommy said again. *I have to go.*

Izzy panicked. It felt as if she were losing her mommy all over again. *Don't go, Mommy. I'm disappearin' as fast as I can.*

But her mommy was already gone. The multicolored rain stopped falling and the mist went away.

Izzy waited and waited, but nothing happened. Finally, she went back into the house. Crossing the living room, she wandered into the kitchen and started making herself breakfast. She got out the Frosted Flakes and the milk all by herself.

In the other room, she heard her daddy wake up. She'd seen it a bunch of times, and it was always worse when he fell asleep in the living room. First he'd sit up on the sofa, then he'd grab his head and make a little moaning sound. When he stood up, he always hit his shin on the coffee table and yelled a bad word. Today was no different.

"Shit!"

Izzy hurried to put the pink tablecloth on the table—the one her mommy always used for breakfast. She wanted her daddy to notice how smart she was, how grown up. Maybe then he'd finally look at her, touch her . . . maybe he'd even say, *Heya Sunshine, how did you sleep?* That's what he used to say in the mornings, and if he talked to her, maybe she could find her own voice, answer, *I'm fine, Daddy-O,* and make him laugh again. She missed hearing him laugh.

That's all she really wanted. She had given up on lots of the other things that used to matter. She didn't care if he told her he loved her. She didn't care if he kissed her good night on the forehead, or took her on picnics, or twirled her around in his big, strong arms until she squealed. She just wanted him to look at her the way he used to, as if she were the most important person in the world.

Now, he hardly ever looked at her. Sometimes, he looked away so fast, she'd get scared and think she had finally disappeared. But it was never true; she was always there, most of her anyway, except her hand and a few fingers. He just didn't like to look at her anymore.

He stumbled into the kitchen and came to an unsteady stop. "Izzy. What are you doing up?"

She blinked at him in surprise. *You c'n do it,* she thought. *Just answer him. I'm makin' you breakfast, Daddy.* But the words tangled in her throat and disappeared.

"Frosted Flakes," he said with a thin smile. "Annie will love that." He went to the refrigerator and poured himself a glass of orange juice.

He headed toward her. For one heart-stopping moment, she thought he was going to pat her shoulder and tell her she'd set the table real pretty. Or that *she* looked pretty—just like she used to look, with her hair all braided. She even leaned slightly toward him.

But he moved on past, and she had to squeeze back tears.

He looked at the table again. Not at her. "I don't have time for breakfast, Izzy-bear." He touched his forehead and closed his eyes.

She knew he had a headache again—the same one he'd had ever since Mommy went to heaven. It scared her, thinking about that. It always scared her to see how sick her daddy looked in the mornings.

She wanted to tell him that she would try harder to be a good girl, that she'd stop disappearing and start talking, and eat her vegetables and everything.

Her daddy smiled—only it wasn't his real smile. It was the tired, shaky smile that belonged to the silver-haired daddy—the one who never looked at her. "Did you have a good time with Annie yesterday?"

Izzy tried and tried but she couldn't answer. She saw how her daddy looked at her, like he was gonna cry, and it made her ashamed of herself.

Finally, he sighed. "I'm gonna go take a shower. Annie should be here any minute."

He waited a second—as if she were going to answer—but she didn't. She couldn't. Instead, she just stood there, holding two bowls, and watched him walk away.

Later, long after he'd left for work, Izzy sat down on the sofa, her knees pressed together and Miss Jemmie asleep in her lap. Annie came bright and early and started cleaning the house again. All the time Annie was working, she talked to Izzy. She talked so much that sometimes Izzy couldn't listen to it all.

Izzy liked the way her house looked now, after Annie had finished cleaning it up.

It made her feel safe.

She closed her eyes, listening to the soothing sound of the broom. It made her think of her mommy, and all the times she'd sat by herself, looking at a book while her mommy cleaned the house.

Before she knew it, a sound had slipped from her mouth. It was a faint *schk-schk* noise, the same sound that the broom was making on the floor.

Her eyes popped open. It shocked her to hear her own voice after all this time. Even if it wasn't words, it was *Izzy.* She thought that part of her—the talking part—had dried up and disappeared, just like her hand and arm. She hadn't meant to stop talking, but one day after her doctor's appointment, she had opened her mouth to speak and nothing had come out. Nothing.

It had terrified her, especially when she realized that she couldn't change it. After that, everyone treated her like a baby and pretended she couldn't hear, either. It had made her cry, the way they all looked at her, but even her crying had been silent.

Annie was different. Annie didn't look at Izzy like she was a broken doll that belonged in the trash.

Annie looked at her the way her mommy and daddy used to.

Izzy smiled, and the sound kept coming, softly, barely louder than the sound of her own breathing. *Schk-schk-schk.*

CHAPTER 10

The county courthouse had been built a hundred years ago, when Mystic had been a booming log town, when the inlets were swollen with miles of trees waiting to be piled onto locomotives and employment was always high. It was an imposing building of hand-cut gray stone, fronted by dozens of double-hung windows and placed squarely in the middle of a flat green lawn. Precisely trimmed rhododendrons and azaleas outlined the brick walkways. A Washington state flag fluttered in the spring breeze.

Nick stood on the courthouse steps, leaning back against one of the stone pillars that flanked the huge oak doors. He flipped through a slim notebook, reminding himself of the facts of an arrest that had taken place more than a month ago. Testifying was part of his job, but it wasn't something he liked to do—especially not in family court, where everything usually came down to broken families and lost souls.

Today it was Gina Piccolo. He'd known Gina since she was a little girl. He remembered her only a few years back, when she'd had the lead in the junior high production of *Oklahoma!* She was a bright, sunny girl with jet-black hair and shining eyes. But in the past year, she'd gone more than a little wild. At fourteen, she'd fallen in with the wrong crowd, and she wasn't a bright-eyed girl anymore. She was a sullen, nasty, baggy-clothed young woman with a logger's mouth and a penchant for trouble. Her parents were out of their minds with worry—and it didn't help that she'd recently started dating a seventeen-year-old boy. Nothing her parents said seemed to make a difference.

And so Nick was here, preparing to make a statement to the judge about Gina. He checked his watch. Court reconvened in ten minutes. He flipped through his notes again, but he found it difficult to concentrate.

It was a problem that had plagued him for the past four days—really ever since Annie Bourne had shown up in his life again.

Already Izzy was improving. She wasn't talking, of course, and she still believed she was disappearing, but Nick could see the changes. She was interacting, listening, smiling . . . and the reasons were obvious.

Annie was just so damned *easy* to be around. That was the problem—for Nick, anyway. Memories of their lovemaking were everywhere, and Annie fascinated him—the way she squinted when she smiled, the way she kept tucking nonexistent hair behind her ear, the way she shrugged helplessly when she screwed something up.

Most of the time, he couldn't look at her; he was afraid that the wanting would show in his eyes.

With a sigh, he flipped his notebook closed and headed inside the courthouse toward courtroom six.

Gina was waiting by the door, wearing baggy black jeans and an oversized black sweatshirt that hung almost to her knees. Her once-black hair was streaked with pink and purple highlights, and a silver ring pierced her nose.

She saw him, and her eyes narrowed. "Fuck you, Delacroix," she said. "You're here to tell them to put me away."

Where did they get all that anger? He sighed. "I'm here to tell Judge McKinley what happened on February twenty-sixth."

"Like you would know anything about that—or me. I was framed. That wasn't my coke."

"Someone put it in your pocket?"

"That's right."

"If that's the way you want to play it, Gina, fine. But honesty would be a smarter course."

She tapped her thigh nervously. "Yeah, like you would know about honesty. You cops make me sick."

"You're young, Gina—"

"Screw you."

"And like all young people, you think you're a pioneer, the first person ever to find the great undiscovered country. But I know you. I've been where you're going, and believe me, it isn't pretty."

"You don't know shit about the real world. You're a cop . . . in *Mystic*." She pulled out a cigarette and lit up. Her gaze cut to the no-smoking sign behind her and she grinned, daring Nick to do something.

He saw the challenge in her eyes as she exhaled a stream of smoke. He cocked his head toward the open doors. "Follow me."

Without looking back, he crossed the hall and went outside. He was mildly surprised to find that Gina had followed him. He sat down on the top step.

She sat cross-legged a few feet away. "Yeah? What?"

"When I was your age, I lived on the streets."

She snorted. "Uh-huh. And I'm one of the Spice Girls."

"My mom was an alcoholic who used to prostitute herself for booze. It was a lovely life . . . normal for an addict with no formal education and no particular job skills. She dropped out of school at sixteen when she got pregnant with me. My old man dumped her pretty fast—and she didn't have anywhere to go after that."

Gina went very still. The cigarette sagged in her black-painted lips. "No way," she said, but this time there wasn't much conviction in her voice.

"We couldn't afford to pay rent—that's another thing addiction does. It takes your money, fast, then your will and your pride. Pretty soon you don't care that you live in an old Chevy Impala and that your son has no winter coat. All you care about is getting high or drunk. You'll sleep under a sheet of newspaper on a park bench and not even know you're freezing or that some time in the middle of the night you threw up all over yourself."

"You're trying to scare me."

"You're damn right I am. The road you're on leads three places, Gina—to a park bench or a jail cell or a coffin. You think about it."

She slowly lifted her gaze to his. He could see that she was scared. For a split second, he thought she was going to reach out for help.

Come on, Gina, he thought. *You can do it.* He pulled a business card from his pocket and handed it to her. "Call me. Anytime."

"I—"

"Hey, Gino, what're you doin' talkin' to that jerk in blue?"

Gina drew back as if stung and lurched to her feet. The white business card fluttered to the gray stone steps at her feet. She turned and waved at the green-haired boy who was bounding up the courthouse steps. Chains jangled from his ears and pockets, and a thin silver hoop glittered in his eyebrow. He slipped an arm around Gina and pulled her close. Taking the cigarette from her mouth, he took a long drag and exhaled slowly. "You're here to send Gino to lockup, aren't you?"

Nick stared at the boy, Drew Doro. A bad seed who'd first come into contact with the law at age ten, when he'd burned down his family garage. Two years ago, his parents had quietly, and with a broken heart, given up on him. It was only a matter of time before this kid was doing time in Monroe. He was Gina's first boyfriend.

"I'm here to give the family court judge my opinion, Drew. That's all. It's not a trial." He glanced at Gina. "Not yet, anyway."

Gina took a step toward Nick. The uncertainty in her eyes reminded Nick that underneath all that black mascara and attitude, she was still just a kid, scared and trying to find her way in a confusing world. "What are you gonna tell the judge?"

He wished he could lie to her right now, tell her what she wanted to hear. "I'm going to tell her that you present a threat to yourself and others. You left me no choice."

The uncertainty was replaced by a flash of pure hatred. "Screw you, Delacroix. It wasn't my coke."

Slowly, Nick stood. "If you need help, Gina . . . you know where to find me."

"Why in the hell would she need *your* help?" Drew laughed. "She's got tons of friends who really care about her. You're just a low-rent cop in this backwater dump of a town. All you're good for is getting cats outta trees. Come on, Gina."

Nick watched them walk away. He hadn't expected Gina to listen to him. Hoped, perhaps—it was that uncontrollable surge of hope that had chewed viciously through his life. He couldn't seem to completely walk away from it.

He'd had the same talk with a dozen teens over the years and none of them ever listened. None of them ever changed. Most of them died young and violently and far away from the families who loved them.

Just once, he thought dully. It would be nice to actually protect and serve. Just once.

He saw Gina, loitering outside the front door, finishing her cigarette.

"You remember that park bench," he called out.

Gina's answer was an all-too-familiar hand gesture.

By the time Nick finally got home from work—late, as usual—Annie was exhausted. She drove home and stumbled into bed. Almost immediately, she fell into a deep sleep, but sometime in the middle of the night she awoke and reached out for Blake.

Once awake, she couldn't fall back asleep again. It was an unfortunate symptom of her depression that she was tired all the time, but she rarely slept well.

As usual, she spent the hours until dawn trying not to think about the big empty house on the Pacific, and the man who had been a part of her life for so long. The man who'd said, *I love her, Annie.*

She went into the kitchen and ate a bowl of cereal, then she picked up the phone and called Natalie—an unscheduled call. She listened to her daughter's stories about London for several minutes, and then quietly told her about the move to Mystic. *To see Hank and help out an old friend,* she'd said.

Natalie had asked only one question: "What does Daddy say?"

Annie had forced a fluttery laugh that sounded false to her own ears. "You know Dad, he just wants me to be happy."

"Really?"

It made Annie feel inestimably old, that single, simple question that seemed to know too much. After that, they'd talked for almost an hour, until Annie could feel bits and pieces of herself returning. It anchored her to talk to her daughter, reminded her that she hadn't failed at everything in her life.

At the end of the conversation, she made sure Natalie had Hank's phone number in case of an emergency, and then she hung up.

For the next hour, Annie lay in her lonely bed, staring out the window, watching the darkness until, at last, the sun came to brush away the bruising night.

It was thoughts of Izzy that gave Annie the strength to get up, get dressed, and eat something. The child had become her lifeline. Izzy touched something deep and elemental in Annie, and it didn't take a two-hundred-dollar-an-hour psychiatrist to understand why. When Annie looked down into Izzy's frightened brown eyes, she saw a reflection of herself.

She knew the hand Izzy had been dealt. There was nothing harder than losing a mother, no matter what age you were, but to a child, a girl especially, it changed everything about your world. In the years since her mom's death, Annie had learned to talk about the loss almost conversationally, the way you would remark upon the weather. *My mother died when I was young . . . passed away . . . passed on . . . deceased . . . an accident . . . I really don't remember her. . . .* Sometimes, it didn't hurt to say those things—and sometimes the pain stunned her. Sometimes, she smelled a whiff of perfume, or the vanilla-rich scent of baking sugar cookies, or heard the tail end of a Beatles song on the radio, and she would stand in the middle of her living room, a woman full grown, and cry like a little girl.

No mother.

Two small words, and yet within them lay a bottomless well of pain and loss, a ceaseless mourning for touches that were never received and words of wisdom that were never spoken. No single word was big enough to adequately describe the loss of your mother. Not in Annie's vocabulary, and certainly not in Izzy's. No wonder the girl had chosen silence.

Annie wanted to say all of this to Nick, to make him understand all that Izzy must be feeling, but every time she started to speak, she had an overwhelming sense of her own presumptuousness. When she looked into Nick's pale blue eyes, or at his grief-whitened hair, she knew that he understood all too well.

They were still awkward around each other. Uncertain. For Annie, at least, the memory of their passion underscored every look, every movement, and if she spoke to him too intimately, she found that it was difficult to breathe evenly. He seemed equally unnerved around her; and so they circled each other, outfitted more often than not with false smiles and pointless conversations.

But slowly, things had begun to improve. Yesterday, they had spent ten minutes together, standing at the kitchen counter, sipping coffee while Izzy ate breakfast. Their conversation crept along the perimeter of their old friendship, dipping now and then into the shared well of their memories. In the end, they had both smiled.

It had given Annie a new strength, that single moment of renewed friendship, and so, today, she pulled into the driveway a half hour early. Grabbing the bag of croissants she'd picked up from the bakery and the bag of surprises she'd bought for Izzy, she climbed out of her car and went to the front door, knocking loudly.

It took a long time, but finally Nick answered, wearing a pair of ragged gray sweatpants. Swaying slightly, he stared down at her through bloodshot eyes.

She held up the bag. "I thought you might like some breakfast."

He stepped back to let her in, and she noticed that he moved unsteadily. "I don't eat breakfast, but thanks."

She followed him into the house. He disappeared into the bathroom and came out a few minutes later, dressed in his policeman's uniform. He looked sick and shaky, with his silvery hair slicked back from his face. The lines under his eyes were deeply etched, as if they'd been painted on.

Without thinking, she reached for him, touched his forehead. "Maybe you should stay home . . ."

He froze, and she could see that he was startled by the intimacy of her touch. She yanked her hand back, feeling the heat of embarrassment on her cheeks. "I'm sorry. I shouldn't—"

"Don't," he said softly. "I have trouble sleeping, is all."

She almost went to him then, almost started a conversation that wasn't for her to begin. Instead, she changed the subject. That was always the safest thing—to keep it strictly about Izzy. "Will you be home for dinner?"

He turned away, and she knew he was thinking about the last two nights. He'd been too late for dinner both nights. "My schedule—"

"It would mean a lot to Izzy."

"You think I don't know that?" He turned to her, and in his eyes was a bleak desperation that wrapped around her heart. "I'm sorry—"

He shook his head, held a hand up, as if to ward her off. "I'll be home," he said, then he pushed past her and left the house.

Their days together followed a comfortable routine. Annie arrived early and spent the day with Izzy, playing, reading, walking around the forest. In the early evening, she made a hot dinner for the two of them, and afterward, they played board games or watched videos until bedtime.

Every night, Annie tucked Izzy into bed and kissed her good night.

Nick consistently missed dinner, forgot to call, and showed up around nine o'clock, smelling of smoke and booze. Even when he promised to be home, as he did almost every night, he didn't make it.

She was tired of making excuses for him. Once again, it was bedtime and this beautiful child was going to have to go to bed without a kiss from her father.

She glanced at Izzy, who stood now at the big picture window, staring out at the falling night. She'd been stationed there for almost thirty minutes, no doubt listening for the quiet purr of her dad's patrol car.

She went to Izzy and knelt beside her on the hardwood floor. She chose her words with care. "When I was a little girl, my mom died. It made my daddy and me very quiet for a long time. When my dad saw me, all he could think about was my mama, and the hurt made him stop looking at me."

Izzy's brown eyes filled with tears. Her lower lip trembled and she bit down on it.

Annie reached up and caught a single tear on the tip of her finger. "My daddy came back to me, though. It took a while, but he came back because he loved me. Just like your daddy loves you."

Annie waited for Izzy to respond—so long the waiting became noticeable. Then she smiled and pushed to her feet. Her knees popped and cracked at the suddenness of her movement. "Come on, pumpkin. Let's get you to bed." She started to walk toward the stairs.

Izzy fell into step beside her. Annie slowed her steps to match the child's as they climbed the stairs. Halfway up, Izzy inched closer and slid her hand into Annie's. It was the first time Izzy had touched her.

Annie clung to the tiny fingers, squeezing gently. *That's it, Izzy . . . keep reaching out. I won't let you fall.*

Upstairs, after Izzy brushed her teeth, they knelt beside the bed together. Annie recited the "Now-I-lay-me" prayer and then tucked Izzy into bed, kissing her forehead. After a quiet moment, she went to the rocking chair by the window and sat down.

The chair made a soft *ka-thump, ka-thump* on the wooden floor. Her gaze moved from Izzy to the window. She stared out at the glittering moonlit lake, listening to the slow evening-out of the girl's breathing.

As so often happened, the nightly ritual made Annie remember. When her own mother had died, she'd been much too young to handle her grief. All she knew was that one day her world was bright and shining and filled with love, and the next, everything fell into a gloomy, saddened, tear-stained landscape. She could still recall how much it had scared her to see her father cry.

That was when the blueprint of her life had been drawn. She'd become a good little girl who never cried, never complained, never asked uncomfortable questions.

It had taken her years to grieve. Her first year away from home had been incredibly lonely. Stanford was no place for a small-town mill-worker's daughter. It had shown her—for the first time—that she was poor and her family uneducated.

Her love for Hank was the only reason she stayed at that big, unwelcoming school. She knew how much it meant to him that she was the first Bourne to attend college. And so she kept her head down and her shoulders hunched and she did her best to fit in. But the loneliness was often overwhelming.

One day she started her car, and the sound of the engine triggered something. The memory was as unexpected as a snowstorm in July. All at once, she felt her mother beside her in the car, and Annie's Volkswagen "Bug" had become the old station wagon they'd once had, the one with the wood-grain strip along the side. She didn't know where they'd been going, she and her mom, or what they'd talked about, and she realized with a sharp, sudden pain that she couldn't recall the sound of her mother's voice. The more she tried to slip into the moment, to immerse herself in the memory, the more flat and one dimensional it had become.

Until that moment, she had actually—naively—thought she'd overcome the death of her mother, but on that day, more than ten years after they'd placed her mother's coffin in the cold, dark ground, Annie fell apart. She cried for all the missed moments—the nighttime kisses, the spontaneous hugs, the joy that would never be as complete again. She grieved most of all for the loss of her childhood innocence, which had been taken on a rainy day without warning, leaving behind an adult in a child's body, a girl who knew that life was unfair and love could break your heart, and mostly, that nothing was worse than being left behind by the one you loved.

It took her several days to master her grief, and even then control was tissue-thin, a layer of brittle ice on a cold, black body of water. It was not surprising that she fell in love almost immediately after that. She had been a walking wound of loneliness, and caretaking was the only way she knew to fill the void in her soul. When she met Blake, she showered him with all the pent-up longing and love that was inside her.

Annie slowly got out of the rocker and tiptoed to the bed. Izzy was sleeping peacefully. Annie wondered if the child was blessed with dreams in which Kathy appeared; Annie herself was rarely so lucky.

She was halfway down the stairs when the phone rang. She jumped down the last few risers and dove for the phone, answering it on the third ring. "Nick?"

There was a moment of silence, then a woman's voice said, *"Nick?"*

Annie winced. "Hi, Terri."

"Oh, no you don't, don't you dare act like this is a normal conversation. Who in the hell is Nick and where are you? I called Hank and he gave me this number."

Annie sank onto the sofa and tucked her knees up underneath her. "It's nothing, really. I'm baby-sitting for an old friend and he's late getting home."

"I had *hoped* you'd changed. A little bit, at least."

"What do you mean?"

"You just spent twenty years waiting for a man to come home— now you're waiting for another man? That's insane."

It *was* insane. Why hadn't Annie seen that on her own? It made her angry suddenly, both that she'd lost the ability to really get mad, and that she'd allowed herself to take from Nick what she'd spent a lifetime accepting from Blake. Excuses and lies. "Yeah," she muttered more to herself than to Terri. "I only have to take this kind of shit from men I'm in love with."

"Well, that answers my next question. But what—"

"I've got to run, Terri. I'll call you later." Annie could still hear Terri's voice as she hung up the phone. Then she punched in another number.

Lurlene answered on the second ring. "Hello?"

"Lurlene? It's Annie—"

"Is everything all right?"

"Fine, but Nick isn't home yet."

"He's probably down at Zoe's, havin' a drink—or ten."

Annie nodded. That's what she'd suspected as well. "Could you come watch Izzy for a little while? I want to go talk to him."

"He ain't gonna like that."

"Be that as it may, I'm going."

"Give me ten minutes."

After she hung up, Annie went upstairs and checked on Izzy again, then she hurried back downstairs and paced the living room. True to her word, Lurlene showed up in ten minutes, wearing a puffy pink chenille bathrobe and green plastic clogs.

"Heya, honey," she said quietly, stepping into the house.

"Thanks for coming," Annie said, grabbing her purse off the coffee table. "This won't take long."

CHAPTER 11

Annie stood on the sidewalk below a cockeyed pink neon sign that read: *Zoe's Hot Spot Tavern*. It sputtered and gave off a faint buzzing sound.

Clutching her handbag, she went inside. The tavern was bigger than she'd expected, a large rectangular room, with a wooden bar along the right wall. Pale blue light shone from tubes above a long mirror. Dozens of neon beer signs flickered in shades of blue and red and gold. Men and women sat slumped on bar stools, drinking and talking and smoking. Every now and then, she heard the thump of a glass hitting the bar.

Way in the back were two pool tables, resting beneath pyramids of fluorescent lighting, with people bent over them, and others standing alongside, watching. Someone broke up a rack of balls and the sound was a loud *crack* in the darkness.

Keeping her back to the side wall, she edged deeper into the place, until she saw Nick. He was at a table in the back corner. She pushed through the crowd.

"Nick?"

When he saw her, he lurched to his feet. "Is Izzy—"

"She's fine."

"Thank God."

He was unsteady on his feet as he backed away from her. He stumbled and plopped into his chair. Reaching out, he grabbed his drink and downed it in a single swallow. Then he said softly, "Go away, Annie. I don't . . ."

She squatted beside him. "You don't what?"

He spoke so quietly she had to strain to catch the words. "I don't want you to see me here . . . like this."

"Did you know that she listens for you every night, Nick? She sits beside the front door for as long as her little eyes can stay open, waiting to hear your footsteps on the porch."

"Don't do this to me . . ."

Her heart went out to him, but she didn't dare stop, not now when she'd finally found the courage to begin. "Go home to her, Nick. Take care of your little girl. This time you have with her . . . it goes away so quickly, don't you know that? Don't you know that in a heartbeat, you'll be packing her bags and watching her board a plane for somewhere far away from you?"

The look he gave her was sad and hopeless. "I can't take care of her, Annie. Haven't you figured that out? Christ, I can't take care of anyone." In an awkward, jerking motion, he pushed to his feet. "But I'll go home and pretend. It's what I've been doing for the past eight months." Without looking at her, he tossed a twenty-dollar bill on the table and walked out of the bar.

She rushed after him, trying all the way through the crowded bar to figure out what to say to him. At the curb outside, he finally stopped and looked at her. "Will you do me one more favor?"

"Anything."

A quick frown darted across his face, made Annie wonder why he'd expected to be let down. Why was it so hard for him to believe that she wanted to help him?

"Drive me home?"

She smiled. "Of course."

The next morning, Annie arrived at Nick's house an hour early. She slipped through the unlocked door and crept up the stairs. She checked on Izzy, found her sleeping peacefully, then went to Nick's bedroom. It was empty. She went down the hall to a guest room and pushed the door open.

The curtains were drawn, and no sunlight came through the heavy

Navajo-print drapes. Against one wall was an old-fashioned four-poster bed. She could just make out Nick's form beneath a mound of red wool blankets.

She should have known that he didn't sleep in the master bedroom anymore.

Annie knew it was dangerous to enter his room, a place where she didn't belong, but she couldn't help herself. She went to his bed and stood beside him. In sleep, he looked young and innocent; more like the boy she'd known so long ago than the man she'd recently met.

It came to her softly, whispering on the even, quiet sound of his breathing, how much she had once loved him. . . .

Until the night she saw him kiss Kathy.

She needs me, Annie, don't you see that? he'd said afterward. *We fit.*

I can fit with you, Nicky, she'd pleaded softly.

No. He'd touched her cheek, and the gentleness of his touch had made her cry. *You don't need someone like me, Annie Bourne. You're off to Stanford in the fall. You're going to set the world on fire.*

"What are you doing here so early?"

With a start, Annie realized that he was awake, and that he was looking at her. "I . . . I thought you might need me."

Frowning, he sat up. The covers fell away from his body, revealing a chest that was covered with coarse black hair.

She waited for him to say something, but he just sat there, his eyes closed. His skin had a waxy, yellow cast, made even more noticeable by the tangle of silvery-white hair and the blackness of his eyelashes. A fine sheen of sweat had broken out on his forehead and upper lip.

She pulled up a chair and sat beside the bed. "Nick, we've got to talk."

"Not now."

"You've got to make a better effort with Izzy."

He looked at her finally. "I don't know how to help her, Annie. She scares me." The words were spoken softly, and they were steeped in pain. "I mean to have one drink with the boys after work, but then I start thinking about coming home . . . to my empty bedroom and my disappearing daughter, and one drink turns into two. . . ."

"You'd be fine if you'd stop drinking."

"No. I've always been shitty at taking care of the women I love. Ask Kathy about it."

Annie fought an unexpected urge to brush the hair away from his face—anything to let him know that he wasn't as alone as he felt. "You couldn't make her well, Nick."

He seemed to deflate. A low, tired sigh slipped from his lips. "I'd rather not talk about this now. I don't feel good. I need—"

"Izzy loves you, Nick. I understand your broken heart—at least to the extent anyone can understand such a thing—but nursing it is a luxury. You're her father. You simply don't have the right to fall apart. She needs you to be strong. But mostly, she needs you to be *here*."

"I know that," he said softly, and she could hear the heartache in his voice, the hushed admission of his own failure. "I'll be home for a family dinner on Friday night. It'll be a beginning. Okay? Is that what you want from me?"

Annie knew that it was another lie, a promise that would be broken. Nick had lost faith in himself, and without it, he was in a turbulent sea without any sense of direction, waiting to be sucked under the current once again.

"It isn't what I want from you that matters, Nick," she said softly, and in the deep sadness that seeped through his eyes, she knew that he understood.

If Izzy stood very, very still, she could feel her daddy in the house. There was the faintest smell of him, the smoky smell that always made Izzy want to cry.

She hugged Miss Jemmie to her chest and inched out of her bedroom. She heard voices coming from her daddy's new room, and for a split second, it sounded like it used to, before the bad thing.

But it wasn't Mommy who was talking to him.

Mommy was up with the angels, and down in the ground, and once you went to those two places, there was no coming back. Daddy had told her that.

She crept down the darkened hallway and went downstairs. Everything looked so pretty; there were fresh flowers in a vase on the table, and the windows were open. Her mommy would have liked the way it looked now.

She opened the big wooden front door and went out onto the porch.

A pink sun was hanging just above the tops of the trees, and she knew it would soon rise into a blue sky. But it was still too early, and a layer of soft hazy fog clung to the sides of the lake and peeked out from the trees. Her heart started beating faster and she had trouble breathing.

She cast a quick glance back inside to make sure no one was watching, then slipped past the screen door. Birds chirped from the high branches of a big old tree as she made her way across the wet grass.

Ducking into her hiding place in the forest, she stared hard at the fog. *Mommy?*

She listened really, really close. After a few moments, she heard it, the whisper-soft answer of her mother's voice.

Hey Izzy-bear, are yah busy?

Her eyes popped open. In the wavering gray fog, she saw a woman's outline, golden hair and all.

I'm disappearin', Mommy, just like you.

Her mommy's voice was a sigh that sounded like the breeze. She felt her touch, a gentle ruffling of her hair. *Oh, Izzy-bear . . .*

For the first time, her mommy sounded sad, not happy to see her at all. She peered into the mist, saw her mommy's blue, blue eyes through the gray. Red tears fell from her mommy's eyes, like tiny drops of blood. *It's getting harder for me, Izzy, coming to see you.*

Izzy felt a rush of panic. *But I'm comin' as fast as I can!*

She felt it again, the softness of her mother's hand in the coolness of the breeze. *It won't work, Izzy-bear. You can't follow me.*

Tears stung Izzy's eyes, blurred everything until she couldn't see anything anymore. She blinked away the tears.

The fog was moving away from her.

She ran after it, following the pale cloud to the edge of the lake. *Mommy, don't go, Mommy. I'll be good this time . . . I promise I'll be good. I'll*

clean my room and brush my teeth and go to bed without a sound . . . Mommy,
please . . .

But sunlight hit the surface of the water and cut through the fog
until there was nothing left of it.

She knelt down on the cold, gravelly bank and cried.

Nick limped out of his bedroom. It had taken him forever to dress in his
uniform, and buttoning the collar was flat impossible. With one hand
on the wooden wall for support, he made his way down the hallway.
Clutching the slick wooden handrail, he went down the stairs, one
painful step at a time.

His body felt as brittle as a winter leaf. Sweat crawled across his
forehead and slid in cold, wet streaks down his back.

It was a miracle that he reached the bottom of the stairs without
falling or puking. Still holding the banister in a death grip, he paused,
sucking in air, trying to keep the bile from rising in his throat. Tears
stung his eyes from the effort.

He blinked and forced the nausea away.

When he reopened his eyes, he noticed the changes Annie had
made in his home. A fire leaped and danced in the gray river-rock
opening. The two leather chairs had been shined up and now sat opposite the sofa, and between them the rough-hewn wooden coffee table
glowed a beautiful reddish brown. On the table was a polished silver
water pitcher full of fern fronds and white blossoms.

He had often dreamed of a room just like this one, filled with the
sounds of laughter . . . instead of the hushed silences and sudden out-
bursts that had been Kathy's way.

With a heavy sigh, he moved away from the stairway.

That's when he saw his Izzy. She was standing beside the big windows that overlooked the lake; golden sunlight created a halo around
her face. Time drew in a sudden breath and fell away, leaving Izzy as she
once was, a porcelain doll dressed in pretty clothes, with satin ribbons in
her braided hair.

She looked at him from across the room, her eyes wide.

"Hey, Izzy," he said, trying to smile. "You look gorgeous."

She blinked and didn't move.

He wet his dry lips. A bead of sweat slid down his temple.

Just then, Annie came bustling out of the kitchen, carrying a steaming pot of coffee and a covered serving dish. At the sight of him, she stopped dead. "Nick! This is wonderful, you can join us for breakfast."

The thought of breakfast sent his sour stomach into revolt.

"Izzy, go help your daddy into the sunroom. I've got breakfast set up in there. I'd better add another place at the table."

She apparently had no idea he was about to throw up. She just kept on talking—about what, he had no idea—and fluttering between the kitchen and the sunroom. Her chatter buzzed like gnats around his head.

"Annie, I don't—"

"Izzy," she said again. "Go help your daddy. He doesn't feel well." And she was off again, scurrying toward the sunroom.

Izzy looked up at him when they were alone in the room. Her brown eyes were wide with uncertainty.

"I don't need help, Izzy," he said. "I'm just fine, really."

She looked at him a moment longer, then slowly she moved toward him. He thought she was going to walk past him, but at the last second, she stopped and looked up at him.

It killed him to see the fear in her eyes, and that damned black glove almost did him in. Annie was right. He *had* to be a better father. No more drinking to dull the memories and sugarcoat his failures. He had to take care of his baby. Feeling awkward and unsure, he smiled down at her. "Come on, Izzy-Bear. Let's go."

Slowly, he covered her one bare hand with his larger, calloused one. Together, they walked toward the sunroom. His steps matched hers perfectly. It was sadly silent between them, the daughter who no longer spoke and the father who had no idea what to say.

Annie was beaming when they walked in. The sunroom looked like a picture from one of those women's magazines. There was a bright blue tablecloth on the rickety plank table, with a centerpiece of huckleberry and dogwood in a crockery vase. Plates were heaped with scrambled eggs and pancakes. Beside the three empty plates were glasses of milk and orange juice.

"Sit down," she said to both of them. She helped Izzy into a seat and scooted her close to the table.

Nick slowly sat down, trying to ignore the drums beating inside his head.

"Just coffee for me," he croaked. "I feel like shi—" He glanced at Izzy. "I feel bad. A headache, is all."

Izzy's eyes told him that she knew all about daddy's *headaches*. Guilt came at him hard, riding on the crest of shame.

He reached for the pitcher of orange juice, but his aim was off. He whacked the vase with his fist, sent it flying. Water sprayed everywhere, evergreen boughs flopped across the eggs, dripping. The vase hit the floor with a loud *craaack*.

Nick squeezed his eyes shut. "Shit," he moaned, cradling his throbbing head in his hands.

"Now, don't you worry a bit about that. Everyone has accidents—don't they, Izzy?" Annie stood up and dabbed at the puddles with her napkin.

He turned to Annie, ready to tell her that he had to get the hell out of here, but her smile stopped him. She looked so damned . . . hopeful. He couldn't bear to disappoint her. He swallowed the thick lump in his throat and wiped the sheen of sweat from his brow with a weak hand.

Annie gave him a broad smile and began dishing out food. She served herself a man-size portion of eggs and a stack of pancakes a logger couldn't finish.

He tried to concentrate on that, her food—anything beside his headache and the tremors that quaked through his limbs. "Are you going to eat all that?"

She laughed. "I'm from California. I haven't had an egg in fifteen years, and lately I've been eating like a pig. I'm hungry all the time." Still smiling, she poured syrup over the whole god-awful mess and began eating and talking, eating and talking.

Nick curled both shaking hands around a thick porcelain coffee cup. When he thought he was steady enough, he brought the cup to his lips and took a slow, thankful sip. The hot coffee soothed his jittery nerves and took the shine off his headache. Slowly, slowly, he leaned back in the chair and let himself be carried away by the comforting buzz of Annie's voice. After a while, he managed to eat a bit of breakfast. Through it all, Annie talked and laughed and carried on as if they were a family who ate breakfast together every morning, instead of a silent, disappearing child and her hungover father. She acted as if it were normal, what Nick and Izzy had become.

He couldn't take his eyes off Annie. Every time she laughed, the sound moved through Nick in a shiver of longing, until he began at last to wonder how long it had been since *he* had laughed, since his Izzy had laughed . . . how long since they'd had something to laugh about or a moment together in which to find joy. . . .

"I thought we'd go to the Feed Store today and buy some gardening supplies," Annie said brightly. "It's a good day to get that flower garden into shape. Why, if the three of us worked, it would take no time at all."

Gardening. Nick recalled how much he used to love working in the yard, planting bulbs, raking leaves, snipping dead roses from the thorny bushes. He'd loved the triumph of watching something he'd planted and watered and nurtured actually *grow.* He had always loved the first buds of spring, but this year they'd come without his even noticing. All he'd noticed was the spindly, bare cherry tree he'd planted after Kathy's funeral.

"What do you think, Izzy?" Annie said into the thick silence. "Should we let your dad help?"

Izzy picked up her spoon, holding it in two tiny fingers—the only ones his baby thought she had left—and shook it so hard it cracked on the table.

Annie gazed at him across the flowers. "That means your daughter would love to garden with you, Nick Delacroix. Can she count on you?"

Nick wanted to pretend it was that easy, a few spoken words at a breakfast table and everything could be made right again. But it had been a long, long time since he'd been that naive. Even as he nodded, he knew that it could end up being a lie. Another promise made by a man who'd kept too few.

CHAPTER 12

Nick sat in his squad car on the edge of downtown Mystic. Beyond the six short blocks, Mount Olympus rose like something out of a fairy tale, its snow-capped peak brushed up against the swollen gray underbelly of the sky. Leaves scudded across the rough concrete sidewalk, pushed along by a chilly breeze. As always, the town looked beaten and forlorn, tired around the edges. A steady stream of gray white smoke issued from the mill's distant stack, leaving behind the acrid, pulpy scent of wood.

He used to love walking these streets. He'd known everything about the people he was sworn to protect: when their daughters were getting married and their sons were preparing for bar mitzvahs, when their grandparents were moved into nursing homes and when their kids started day care. He'd always taken pride in how well he did his job; he knew that by checking up on these people every day, he contributed to their sense of well-being.

He knew he'd been letting everything that mattered slip away from him, but he was terrified to start caring again. What if he failed Izzy once more? She needed so much from him, his brown-eyed little girl, and Nick had an ugly habit of failing those he loved. Even when he tried his best. It was *his* fault Izzy was disappearing, *his* fault she didn't feel safe or loved; he knew that. If he'd been a stronger man, a better man, he could have helped her through the grief, but he hadn't been able to do a damn thing. Hell, he couldn't even help himself, and he sure as hell hadn't helped Kathy.

It would be difficult, finding his way back, but Annie was right. It was time. For the first time in months, he felt a stirring of hope.

He eased out of the car and took a first cautious step into his old life. He merged quietly into the crowd of late-afternoon shoppers. All around him, people were moving, darting into stores, coming back out with paper bags and parcels. He noticed the sounds of everyday life. Car doors slamming, horns honking, quarters clicking into parking meters.

Every person he saw waved at him, said "Heya, Nick" as he passed, and with each greeting, he felt himself coming back to life. It was almost like the old days, before Kathy's death. Back when his uniform had always been clean and starched, and his hands had never trembled.

He walked past the stores, waving at shopkeepers. At the kids' clothing store, he saw a beautiful little pink dress in the window. It was exactly what Izzy needed. As he opened the door, a bell tinkled overhead.

Susan Frame squealed from her place at the cash register and came at Nick like a charging bull, her pudgy pink hands waving in the air. "Good Lord, I can't believe it's you."

He grinned. "Hi, Susan. Long time no see."

She swatted him on the shoulder and laughed, her triple chins jiggling. "You haven't been in here in ages."

"Yeah, well . . ."

"How are you doing?"

"Better. I saw that little girl's dress in the window—"

She clapped her pudgy hands together. "Ooh-ee, that's a beautiful thing. Perfect for Miss Isabella. How old is she now?"

"Six."

"Ooh, I'll bet she's growing like a weed. I haven't seen her since her mama—" She shut up abruptly and took him by the arm, propelling him through the store. He let himself be carried away by her steady, comforting stream of words. He wasn't listening to her; she knew it and didn't care. She seemed to sense that it was a major event for him to be here.

She plucked the dress off the hanger. It was a pink and white gingham with a white lace underskirt and a pale blue yoke embroidered with tiny pink and white flowers. It reminded him of Kathy's garden—

Come out here, Nicky—the tulips are coming up—

It hit him like a blow, the memory. He winced and squeezed his eyes shut. *Don't think about the flowers . . . don't think about her at all. . . .*

"Nick? Are you feeling well?"

A little unsteadily, he pulled a twenty-dollar bill from his pants pocket and tossed it on the counter. "The dress is perfect, Susan. Can you wrap it up?"

She answered, but he wasn't listening. All he could think about was Zoe's, and how a single drink—just one—would calm the shaking in his hands.

"Here you go, Nick."

It seemed only a second had passed before she was back beside him, waving a big lavender-wrapped package beneath his face. He wet his dry lips and tried to smile.

Susan touched his shoulder. "Nick, are you all right?"

He nodded, though even that simple action seemed to take too long. "I'm fine. Fine. Thanks." Gripping the package, he pushed through the glass door and went outside.

It had started to rain, big nickel-size drops that splashed his face. He glanced longingly toward Zoe's.

No. He wouldn't go that way. He'd finish out his rounds and head home. Izzy and Annie were waiting, and he didn't want to disappoint them. Taking a deep breath, he straightened his shoulders and kept moving down the street, his hand resting lightly on his baton. With each step, he felt better, stronger.

He returned to his patrol car and got inside, ducking out of the hammering rain. He reached for the radio, but before he could say anything, a call came out.

Domestic disturbance on Old Mill Road.

"Shit." He answered the call, flicked on his siren, and headed out of town.

When he reached the Weavers' driveway, he knew it was bad already. Through the falling rain and the curtain of trees, he could see the distant red and yellow blur of lights. He raced up the bumpy road, his heart beating so fast he couldn't draw an even breath.

The mobile home was surrounded by cars—two patrol cars and an ambulance.

Nick slammed the car in park and jumped out. The first person he saw was Captain Joe Nation, the man who had given Nick a place to live all those years ago.

Joe was walking out of the trailer, shaking his head. The long black and gray braids he wore swayed gently at the movement. Across the clearing, he caught sight of Nick, and he stopped.

"Joe?" Nick said, out of breath already.

Joe laid a thick, veiny hand on Nick's forearm. "Don't go in there, Nicholas."

"No . . ."

"There's nothing you can do now. Nothing anyone can do."

Nick shoved past Joe and ran up the muddy driveway, splashing through the puddles. The door fell away beneath his shove and crashed against the wall.

Inside, several people were milling about, searching for clues in the green shag carpeting. Nick pushed past them and went into the bedroom, where Sally lay on the bed, her thin floral dress shoved high on her rail-thin legs, her face bloodied almost beyond recognition. A red-black blotch of blood seeped across her chest and lay in an oozing puddle across the wrinkled gray sheets.

Nick skidded to a stop. It felt as if pieces of him were crumbling away. He knew he was swaying like an old Doug fir in a heavy wind, but he couldn't stop. He was thrown back suddenly to another time, another place, when he had had to identify a similarly beaten body . . .

"Goddamn it, Sally," he whispered in a harsh, fractured voice.

He went to her, knelt beside her bed, and brushed the bloodied, matted hair away from her face. Her skin was still warm to the touch, and he could almost believe that she would wake up suddenly and smile and tell him that it was nothing.

"Don't touch her, sir," said someone. "The evidence . . ."

Nick drew his shaking hand back and got awkwardly to his feet. He wanted to pull her dress down—give her that final dignity at least—but he couldn't. No one could do anything that mattered for Sally anymore. Now it was time for detectives and photographers and pathologists.

He turned blindly away from the bed and stumbled through the cluttered trailer, emerging into the rainy day; everything looked exactly as it had ten minutes ago, but nothing felt the same.

Joe came up to him, pulled him away from the trailer. It felt strangely as if it were years and years ago, back when Joe had met a skinny, freezing fifteen-year-old boy at the bus station in Port Angeles. "There was nothing you could do, Nicholas," he said. "She didn't want our help."

Nick felt as if the life were slowly, inexorably draining out of him. Buried images of another night, not long ago, were oozing to the fore-front of his mind, images that were also stained in blood and violence and tragedy. He'd spent eight months running from the images of that night, burying them deep in his subconscious, but now they were back, killing him. "It's too much," he said, shaking his head. "Too much."

Joe patted his back. "Go home, Nicholas. Go home to the little girl who loves you and your beautiful house on the lake and forget about this."

Unable to move, Nick stood there, gripping the butt of his gun, standing in the rain, knowing there was only one thing that could help him now.

Nick hadn't shown up for dinner again.

Annie had tried to pretend it meant nothing. She'd made a great show of cheeriness for Izzy, but she knew that the child wasn't fooled. No amount of cookie dough or knock-knock jokes could make Izzy stop looking outside. . . .

Annie held the girl in her lap, gently rocking back and forth in a rocking chair on the porch. She hummed a quiet song and stroked Izzy's silky hair.

She could feel a tiny tremble in the child's body, and if she listened very, very carefully, she could hear the unasked questions in Izzy's in-drawn breaths.

"Your daddy will be back soon, Izzy," she said softly, praying it was true. "He loves you very much."

Izzy didn't move, didn't respond.

"Sometimes grown-ups get confused . . . just like kids do. And your dad's confused right now. He doesn't feel like he belongs anywhere, but if we're patient, and we give him time, I think he'll figure it out. It's hard to be patient, though, isn't it? Especially when the waiting hurts."

Annie's voice faded. She closed her eyes and leaned back in the rocker, listening to the rhythmic scraping of wood on wood and the plunking echo of rain on the porch roof.

"He loves you, Izzy," she said at last, perhaps more to herself than to the silent child. "I *know* he loves you."

It took her a moment, but Annie realized there was a sound coming from the child, a tiny, reed-thin whisper that sounded like *png-png-png.*

She was mimicking the sound of the rain hitting the tin roof overhead.

Annie smiled.

Izzy was trying to find her way back.

Izzy felt the scream starting again. It was way down deep inside her, in that dark place where the nightmares lived. Every time she closed her eyes, she saw her mommy, and she remembered what she'd heard. *You can't follow me . . . can't follow me . . . can't follow me . . .*

What if that were true? What if she disappeared into the fog and still couldn't find her mommy? A tiny, whimpering cry escaped her lips.

She was scared. It was one of those nights where nothing good happened in her sleep and she woke up with tears on her cheeks. She kept dreaming about that doctor, the one with the pointy nose and the thick glasses who told her that she had to talk or else she wouldn't get over her mommy. It had scared her so much, those grown-up words that she hardly understood. The last thing she'd ever said was to him. *I don't want to get over my mommy. . . .*

Her whole body was shaking.

She didn't want to scream again.

She threw the covers back and slithered out of bed, walking barefooted to the closed door. There, she stopped. She stared down at her own hand, at all that nothingness around her thumb and forefinger. She wished suddenly that she wasn't disappearing, that she could just reach out and grab that old doorknob and twist it hard.

With a sigh, she used her two fingers to turn the knob. It took a while, but finally, she got the door open.

She poked her head out and saw the dark hallway.

Her daddy's room was to the left, just three doors down, but she knew he wouldn't be there. She'd heard Annie talking to Lurlene. They thought she was gone, but she wasn't. She'd been hiding in the corners, listening.

Her daddy was in the bad place, the place that made him smell like cigarettes even though he didn't smoke, the place that made him come home with that scary look in his eyes and slam his bedroom door shut. The place that made him walk funny.

She crept down the hallway and peeked over the railing, and saw Annie asleep on the sofa.

Annie, who held Izzy's hand and brushed her hair and acted like it didn't matter at all that she didn't talk. Annie, who was going to make her mommy's garden grow again.

Very slowly, she went down the stairs. The steps felt cold beneath her bare feet and made her shiver, but she didn't care. Once she started walking, she felt better. The scream slipped back into the dark place.

She almost wanted to say something, call out Annie's name, maybe, but it had been so long since she'd even wanted to talk, it felt weird. She couldn't even remember what her voice sounded like anymore.

She tiptoed to the sofa. Annie was asleep, with her mouth open. Her short hair was smashed to one side of her head and stuck straight up on the other.

Izzy wasn't sure what to do. When she was little, she used to climb into her mommy and daddy's bed whenever she was scared, and it felt so good, so warm. Mommy would curl Izzy up in her arms and tuck the blanket around them both, and Izzy would go to sleep.

Annie made a quiet snoring sound and stretched out, leaving a big empty space along the edge of the sofa. Just enough space for Izzy.

Izzy cautiously peeled back the scratchy blue blanket and gingerly crawled onto the couch.

She lay stiffly on her side, hardly breathing. She was afraid Annie would wake up and tell her to go back to her room. But she didn't want to be alone in her room. She was scared of the dark in there.

Annie made another quiet sound and rolled toward Izzy.

Izzy clamped down on her breath and went perfectly still.

Annie curled her arm protectively around Izzy's body and pulled her close.

Izzy felt as if she were melting. For the first time in months, she felt as if she could breathe right. She snuggled backward, poking her bottom into the vee of Annie's bent body, so they were like two spoons pressed together.

With a quiet, happy sigh, she closed her eyes.

In the early hours of the morning, Annie woke to the scent of baby shampoo and the feel of a small, warm body tucked against hers. It brought back a flood of memories—days long ago and a child that was now far away and hadn't been a baby in years. She gently stroked Izzy's sweaty hair and kissed her small, pink ear. "Sleep well, princess."

Izzy snuggled closer. A quiet sound answered Annie, so quiet she might have missed it if they'd been outside or if it had been raining or she had been talking.

In her sleep, Izzy laughed.

Annie glanced at the clock on the mantel. It was five-thirty in the morning. Very gently, she peeled back the blanket and climbed over Izzy. Hugging herself against the chill morning air, she walked over to the window and stared out at the lake. Dawn was a pink brush stroke across the serrated black treetops.

"Damn you," she whispered.

This time, Nick hadn't come home all night.

CHAPTER 13

The phone rang at five forty-five in the morning. Annie reached over Izzy and answered softly, "Hello?"

"Hello. Annie Bourne, please."

She frowned, trying to place the male voice. "This is she."

"This is Captain Joseph Nation, of the Mystic police force."

Annie's stomach clenched. She eased away from the sleeping child and sat down on the cold floor. "It's Nick . . ."

"He was in an accident last night."

"Oh, my god. Is he—"

"Fine. Apart from a few bruises and . . . a hell of a hangover, he's going to be fine. He's at Mystic Memorial."

"Was he driving?"

"No. He was smart enough to get a ride home with someone—but not smart enough to pick a sober driver."

"Was anyone else hurt?"

Captain Nation sighed. "No. They hit a tree out on Old Mill Road. The driver walked away without a scratch, and Nick just bonked his head a good one. He has a slight concussion. He was lucky . . . this time. I'm calling because he's going to need a ride home from the hospital."

Annie glanced over at Izzy, sleeping so peacefully on the sofa. She couldn't help remembering the way Izzy had waited and waited for a daddy who didn't come home—because he was getting drunk again.

Enough was enough. Slowly, she answered, "Oh, I'll come get him all right."

Nick moaned and tried to roll over, but the covers were tangled around his legs so tightly he couldn't move. Slowly, so as not to punish his already throbbing head, he pushed to his elbows and looked around. Lights stabbed through his brain, and somewhere a radio was blaring.

He was lying in a narrow, metal-rimmed bed. Fluorescent tube worms crisscrossed the ceiling, sending blinding pyramids of light into the white-walled room. A bright yellow privacy curtain hung in folds from ceiling to floor.

He closed his eyes and thumped back onto the narrow bed, flinging an arm across his face. He felt like shit. His head hurt, his eyes ached, his mouth was dry, and his stomach felt as if it had been scraped clean by a rusty scalpel. His whole body was shaking and weak.

"So, Nicholas? You back among the living?"

All in all, it was not a good sign to wake up in a hospital bed with your boss standing beside you. Even worse when that boss was as close to a father as you'd ever known.

Joe had offered Nick the first real home of his life. Nick had been young and scared and ready to run; his mother had taught him early that policemen were the enemy. But he'd had nowhere else to go. His mother's death and Social Services had given him no options.

You must be Nicholas, Joe had said that day. *I've got a spare bedroom . . . maybe you wouldn't mind hanging out with me for a while. My daughters have all gotten married and Louise—my wife—and I are sorta lonely.* And with those few welcoming words, Joe had shown Nick the first frayed edges of a new life.

Nick pushed up to his elbows again. It hurt to move; hell, it hurt to breathe. "Hey, Joe."

Joe stood quietly beside the bed, staring at Nick through sad, disappointed eyes. Deep wrinkles lined his forehead and bisected his round, dark-skinned cheeks. Long, gray-black hair hung in two skinny braids that curled against the blue checked polyester of his shirt. "You were in a car accident last night. Do you remember it? Joel was driving."

Nick went cold. "Christ. Did we hurt anyone?"

"Only you . . . this time."

Nick sagged in relief. He rubbed a trembling hand over his face, wishing he could take a shower. He smelled like booze and smoke and vomit. The last thing he remembered was taking a drink at Zoe's—his fourth, maybe. He couldn't remember getting into Joel's car at all.

With a high-pitched scraping sound of metal on linoleum that almost deafened Nick, Joe pulled up a chair and sat down next to the bed. "You remember the day we met?"

"Come on, Joe. Not now—"

"*Now.* I offered you everything I had to give. My home, my family, my friendship—and this is what you give me in return? I'm supposed to watch you turn into a drunk? If Louise—God rest her soul—were alive, this would kill her. You blacked out, you know."

Nick winced. That was bad. "Where?" It was a stupid question, but it seemed important.

"At Zoe's."

Nick sank back onto the bed. In public. He'd blacked out in public. "Jesus Christ," he moaned. He could have done it in front of Izzy.

He didn't want to think about that. He threw the covers back and sat up. At the movement, his stomach lurched and his head exploded. He cradled his head in his hands and leaned forward, staring at the floor through burning eyes until he could breathe again.

"Nicholas, are you all right?"

Slowly, he looked up. It came back to him in bits and pieces: Sally Weaver . . . all that blood . . . Chuck's wailing voice, *it's not my fault.* . . . "Remember when you talked me into going into the academy, Joe? You told me I could help people like my mother. . . ."

Joe sighed. "We can't save 'em all, Nicholas."

"I can't do it anymore, Joe. We don't help people. All we do is clean up bloodstains. I can't . . . not anymore. . . ."

"You're a damn fine cop, but you have to learn that you can't save everyone—"

"Are you forgetting what I came home to last year? Hell, Joe, I can't save anyone. And I'm sick to fucking death of trying." He climbed out of bed. He stood there like an idiot, swaying and lurching in a feeble effort to stand still. His stomach coiled in on itself, just waiting for an excuse to purge. He clutched the metal bed frame in boneless, sweaty fingers. "You'll be getting my resignation tomorrow."

Joe stood up. Gently, he placed a hand on Nick's shoulder. "I won't accept it."

"It's killing me, Joe," he said softly.

"I'll agree to a vacation—for as long as you need. I know what you're going through, and you don't have to do it alone. But you do have to stop drinking."

Nick sighed. Everyone said that. *I know what you're going through.* But they didn't know; how could they? None of them had come home to his blood-spattered bedroom. Even Joe, who had been a full-blown alcoholic before his eighteenth birthday, and who had grown up in the blackened, marshy shadow of a drunken father. Even Joe couldn't completely understand. "You're wrong, Joe. In the end, we're all alone."

"It's that kind of thinking that got you into this mess. Believe me, I know the alcoholic-kid's code: don't tell, don't trust. But you've got to trust *someone,* Nicholas. There's a whole town here that cares about you, and you have a little girl who thinks you hung the moon. Stop thinking about what you've lost, and think about what you have left. You want to end up like your mother, half starved on a park bench, waiting to be killed? Or maybe you want to be like me—a man with two beautiful daughters who moved to the East Coast to get away from their drunken father." He pulled a business card out of his pocket and handed it to Nick. "When you're ready to sober up, here's the number for you to call. I'll help you—all of us will—but you have to take the first step by yourself."

"You look like warmed-over shit soup."

Nick didn't even look at Annie. "Nice language. They teach you that at Stanford?"

"No, but they did teach me not to drink and drive."

He glanced around, ran a shaking hand through his dirty, tangled hair. "Where's Izzy?"

"Ah, so you do remember her."

"Goddamn it, Annie—"

"We—your *daughter* and I—were worried about you last night. But you don't care about that, do you?"

Suddenly he was tired, so tired he didn't think he could stand up much longer. He pushed past her and stumbled out of the building. Her Mustang was parked in the loading zone in front of the electronic glass doors. Half falling, he grabbed onto the cold metal door handle and stood there, his eyes closed, concentrating on each breath.

He heard her walk past him. Her tennis shoes made a soft scuffing sound on the cement. She wrenched her car door open, got inside, and slammed the door shut. He wondered dully if she had any idea how loud it sounded to a man whose head was ticking like a bomb ready to go off.

She honked the horn, and the sound sliced painfully through his eardrums. He opened the door and collapsed onto the red vinyl seat with a haggard sigh.

The car lurched onto the rutted road. She sped up at every bump and pothole in the road, Nick was sure of it. He clung to the door handle for dear life, his knuckles white and sweaty.

"I spoke with your police captain, Mr. Nation, while you were getting dressed. He told me you were taking some time off from the force. And he mentioned your blackout."

"Great."

She made a low, whistling sound. "And what's that on your shirt front? Vomit? Yes, yes, what a high time you must have had yourself. God knows, it's better than being at home with your daughter."

He winced and closed his eyes, feeling shame sink deep into his gut. Joe's words came back to him. *You want to end up like your mother? Or maybe you want to be like me?* He thought about Izzy, and how she would remember him, and where she would go when she had the chance . . . he thought about what it would be like if she left him.

He slanted a look at Annie. She was sitting perfectly erect, her hands precisely placed at the ten o'clock and two o'clock positions on the steering wheel, her gaze focused on the empty road in front of them. "Would you do me a favor, Annie?"

"Of course."

"Take me to the Hideaway Motel on Route Seven," he said quietly. "And watch Izzy for a few days."

She frowned. "The Hideaway? It's a dump, and why—"

He felt as if he were treading water in the deep end of a swimming pool full of dark, murky water. He couldn't handle an argument; not now. "Please don't argue with me. I need some . . . time."

She cast a quick, worried look at him, then turned back to the road. "But Izzy—"

"Please?" The word came out soft and swollen, unmanly, but he couldn't help it. "Could you please stay with her while I get my act together? I know it's a lot to ask . . ."

She didn't answer, and for once the silence was uncomfortable. After a mile she flicked on her signal and turned off the highway. Within minutes, she had pulled into the parking lot at the Hideaway Motel. A neon sign flickered in the window. It read: SORRY. VACANCY. That pretty much summed it up.

"Here we are, Nick. I don't know . . ."

"Home sweet home," he said, smiling weakly.

She turned to him then, and there was a softness in her expression that he hadn't expected. She leaned toward him, gently brushed the hair from his eyes. "I'll help you. But you'd better not screw up this time, Nicky. That beautiful child of yours doesn't need to lose her daddy, too."

"Christ, Annie," he whispered in agony.

"I know you love her, Nick." She leaned closer. "Just meet me halfway. Trust me. Or better yet, trust yourself."

Even as he told himself he'd fail again, he didn't care. He wanted the second chance she was offering. He was tired, so tired, of being lonely and afraid. The words *I want to try* weighed heavily on his tongue, but he hadn't the strength to give them a voice. He could remember too many other times he'd wanted a chance . . . and the times his mother had said, *Trust me, Nicky, I mean it this time.* He had long ago gotten out of the habit of trusting people.

He climbed out of the car and stood there, watching her drive away. When she was gone, he jammed his hands into his pockets and turned toward the motel. Fishing his credit card out of his front pocket, he signed the register and got himself a room for the night.

The room was small and dark and smelled of urine. Dirty brown walls ran in a perfect square around a sagging double bed. A gray woven bedspread covered a lumpy mattress. A curtainless window looked out onto the neighboring building's cement brick wall. Gold shag carpet, peeled away in places to reveal the bubbling blue foam pad, lay untacked atop a cement floor.

He could see the closet-size bathroom behind a wood-grain plastic door that hung awkwardly from broken hinges. He didn't have to go inside to know that there was a white plastic shower and beige toilet, and that rust ran in rings around the sink's metal drain.

He sat on the bed with a tired sigh. He had been living less than half a life for so long, and now even the half he'd clung to was slipping through his shaking, numb fingers like crumbled winter leaves. He knew that he'd been wrong to drink, that he'd gone down the wrong road when he first reached for a bottle. The booze was sucking him dry, and when it was finished with him there would be nothing left except a skinny, freezing old man on a park bench. . . .

On the far wall, a cockroach scurried up alongside the brown plastic molding and disappeared beneath a framed picture of Mount Olympus.

Finally, after eight months of drifting, he'd come to the end of the line. There was only one thing that might make a difference. He reached into his pocket and pulled out the card Joe had given him.

Annie kept Izzy busy all day, but as the night began to fall, she couldn't pretend anymore. She read Izzy a bedtime story after dinner, then pulled Izzy into her arms. "I need to tell you something, Izzy," she started softly, trying to find the right words. "Your daddy is going . . . to be away for a while. He's sick. But he'll be back. He loves you more than the world and he'll be back."

Izzy didn't respond. Annie didn't know what to say, what words could soothe this situation. She held Izzy for a long, long time, humming tunes and stroking her hair, and then, finally, she sighed. "Well, it's bedtime." She pulled away from Izzy and got to her feet. She started to head for the stairs, but Izzy grabbed her hand.

Annie looked into the sad, frightened brown eyes, and it broke her heart all over again. "I'm not going anywhere, honey. I'm right here."

Izzy held on to her hand all the way up the stairs and down the hall, and into the bathroom. In the bedroom, she still wouldn't let go.

Annie looked down into the girl's huge brown eyes. "You want me to sleep with you?"

A quick smile darted across Izzy's face. She squeezed harder and nodded.

Annie climbed into Izzy's tiny twin bed, without bothering to brush her teeth or change her clothes. She left the Little Mermaid nightlight glowing next to the bed as Izzy snuggled close.

Annie stroked Izzy's soft cheek, remembering suddenly how much she'd missed talking about her mom when she was young. After the accident, no one ever mentioned her: it was as if she'd never existed in the first place. And so, Annie had begun, day by day, to forget. She wondered if poor, quiet Izzy was facing the same fears.

She pulled up a memory of Kathy, concentrating until she could *see* Kathy, sitting in that old rocking chair on her porch. "Your mom had the prettiest blond hair I ever saw; it was the color of a ripe ear of corn. And it was so soft. When we were little, we used to braid each other's hair for hours. Her eyes were almost black, the deep midnight color of a night sky, and when she smiled, they crinkled up in the corners like a cat's. You remember that?"

Annie smiled. It was funny the things she could recall all these years later. "Yellow was her favorite color. She wore it in every school picture for years. And to her first dance—that was in eighth grade—she wore a yellow cotton dress with a deep blue satin trim that she'd made herself. She was the prettiest girl in the school."

Izzy twisted around to see Annie. There were tears in her eyes, but she was smiling.

"You'll never forget her, Izzy. You remember her laugh? The way it used to spike up at the end, just before she started snorting? And the perfume she liked to wear? And the feel of her hand in yours? You remember how it used to feel to snuggle in her lap and hear her read you a bedtime story? All of that is your mom. My mom's been gone a long, long time, and I still think of her every time I smell vanilla. I still talk to her at night, and I believe she hears me." She brushed a lock of black hair from Izzy's earnest little face. "She hears you, honey. She just can't answer, is all. But that doesn't matter. You snuggle under your blankets with Miss Jemmie and close your eyes and remember one thing about your mom—just one—and the next thing you know, she'll be in bed beside you. You'll feel yourself getting warmer, or you'll see the moonlight get a little brighter, or the wind will moan a little louder, and you'll know. In her own way, she's answering you." Annie took Izzy's cheeks in her hands and smiled down at her. "She's always with you."

She held Izzy close and talked and talked and talked, laughing every now and then, and occasionally wiping a tear from her eye. She talked of girlhood pranks and loves lost and found, and wedding days; she talked of babies being born and growing up, and of Natalie. She talked about Nick, and how strong and handsome he had been and how much he loved Kathy, and how sometimes grief sent a person into a deep, cold darkness from which there seemed to be no escape.

She was still talking when night fell and plunged the room in darkness, when Izzy's breath took on the even wheezing of a deep and peaceful sleep.

Spring chased away the last vestiges of winter, threw its bright colors across the rain forest. Dainty crocuses, hyacinths, and daffodils bloomed in beds, along walkways, and in pockets of sunlight in the damp, needle-strewn forest floor. The birds returned, sat together on telephone wires and dove for bits of string on the road. Jet-black crows hopped across the lawn, cawing loudly to one another, and used the driveway as a landing strip.

Against her father's pointed advice, Annie had packed a small suitcase and moved into Nick's house. It had proved to be a blessing, for although the nights were still long and lonely, she found that she now had someone to help her through it. She was no longer alone. When she woke in the middle of the night, her heart pounding from familiar nightmares, she climbed into bed with Izzy and held her tightly.

They spent all their time together, she and Izzy. They went to town, baked cookies, and made jewelry boxes from egg cartons. They concocted elaborate care packages for Natalie and mailed them every few days. They worked out of kindergarten and first-grade workbooks, to ensure that Izzy was still learning what she needed for school. And every evening, Nick called to say good night.

Today, Annie had special plans. It was time to revive Kathy's garden.

She stood at the wobbly white picket fence that framed the garden, and Izzy was beside her. The earth was a rich brown, soggy to the touch from last night's heavy rain. Here and there, puddles winked with a strange, silvery light.

Annie set down her big cardboard box and began extracting her tools: spades, hand shovels, trowels, scissors.

"I wish I'd paid more attention to the gardeners at home," she said, spying a big lump of brown twigs that looked promising. "That must be something good—or it's the biggest individual pile of weeds I've ever seen. And see how they're growing in clumps—that surely must be a good sign. I think cutting it back will help; at least that's what Hector at the Feed Store said. Come on, Izzy." She led her across the necklace of stepping stones that formed a meandering trail through the large garden. They stopped at the patch of dead stuff.

Annie knelt. She could feel the moisture seeping from the soil into her pants, squishing cold and clammy against her skin. Pulling on a pair of gloves, she attacked the dead plant and yanked a handful out by the roots. "Bulbs," she said with a triumphant smile. "I knew it."

She turned to Izzy, gave her a self-satisfied look. "I knew it was a flower all along. Never questioned it, no sirree."

She separated and replanted the bulbs, then attacked the dead stalks of perennials with her clippers, hacking everything down to ground level. "You know what I love about gardening? Paying someone to do it for me." She laughed at her own joke and kept working. She pulled up everything that looked like a weed and divided and replanted all the bulbs. At last, she turned to the roses, carefully pruning the thorny branches. As she worked, she hummed. She tried to think of a song that Izzy would know, but all she could come up with was the alphabet song, and so she sang it in her wobbly, off-key voice. "A-B-C-D-E-F-G . . . H-I-J-K . . . L-M-N-O-P."

She frowned suddenly and looked down at Izzy, keeping her gaze averted from the tiny black glove. "My goodness, I've forgotten the alphabet. Not that it matters, of course. It's just a song and I'm sure I'll remember it in no time. "L-M-N-O-P. Well, there I go again, getting stuck on P."

Izzy reached slowly for a trowel. It took her a while to pick it up with only two fingers, and after the first fumbling attempts, Annie couldn't watch.

She kept singing. "H-I-J-K . . . L-M-N-O-P . . . darn it. There's that block again. Oh, well. I think we're about done for a while. I'm starving. What do you say we—"

"Q."

The spade fell from Annie's hand and hit the ground with a thunk. She looked at Izzy, who was still kneeling in the dirt, awkwardly pulling up weeds with her two "visible" fingers as if nothing had happened. The moment bloomed, full of beauty and possibilities.

Izzy had spoken.

Annie released her breath in a slow sigh. *Stay calm, Annie.* She decided to act as if speaking were as normal as not speaking. "Why, I do believe you're right. L-M-N-O-P . . . Q-R-S . . ."

"T-U-V."

"W-X-Y . . . and Z." Annie felt as if she would burst with pride and love. She forced herself to keep digging weeds for a few more minutes. She wanted to shriek with happiness and pull Izzy into her arms, but she didn't dare. She didn't want to scare Izzy back into silence.

"There," she said at last. "That's enough for now. My arms feel like they're going to fall off. Jean-Claude—that was my personal trainer in California—he would be so proud of me right now. He always said I didn't sweat. I said if I wanted to sweat, I wouldn't wear color-coordinated clothes that cost a fortune." She wiped a dirty hand across her slick fore-head. "I have lemonade in the fridge, and some leftover chicken from last night. What do you say we have a picnic dinner out here? I could make us milkshakes . . ."

When Izzy looked up at her, there were tears in her eyes.

At last, Annie pulled the little girl into her arms.

CHAPTER 14

Cigarette smoke swirled in a thick blue haze beneath a ceiling of stained acoustical tiles.

Nick stood in the open doorway of a long, narrow room in the windowless basement of the Lutheran church. Two wood-grain Formica tables hugged the back wall, their surfaces covered with coffee-makers and Styrofoam cups and boxes stacked with packaged sugar and instant creamer. There was a crowd of people at the Coke machine, and an even larger crowd at the coffeepot. The smell of burnt coffee mingled with the bitter stench of the cigarettes.

People sat in folding metal chairs, some comfortably stretched out, some perched nervously on the edge of their seats. Nearly all of them were smoking cigarettes.

He didn't know if he could go through with this, if he could stroll into this smoky room and throw his vulnerability on one of those cheap-ass tables and let strangers dissect it. . . .

"It's harder than hell the first time. All the tension of first sex, with none of the fun."

Nick turned and saw Joe standing behind him.

The older man's shoe-leather-brown face was creased into a relieved smile. "I hoped you'd show up. It was sort of a shock to my system after all those years of hoping you'd *never* show up."

"I'm sorry to disappoint you, Joe," Nick said.

Joe laid a hand on Nick's shoulder and squeezed gently. "I'm *proud* of you, Nicholas. Not disappointed. Life's thrown a lot of curves your way—enough to crush a weaker man. I couldn't be prouder of you if you were my own son. If Louise were here, she'd say, 'Give that boy a hug, Joseph,' and I think I will."

It was the first time Joe had ever hugged him, and Nick didn't quite know how to respond. For as long as he could remember, he'd thought there was something wrong with him, something essential missing at his core, and he'd spent a lifetime waiting to be unmasked. He'd shielded himself from the people he loved—Kathy, Izzy, Louise, and Joe—afraid that if they saw the real Nick, they'd turn away. But Joe had seen the truth, seen all of Nick's weaknesses and failures, and still he was here, claiming Nick as his son.

When Joe drew back, his black eyes were moist. "It's going to get tougher before it gets better. You've just jumped into the deep end, and you'll think you're drowning. But I'm here to keep your head above water.

"Thanks, Joe." He didn't say *for everything,* but he could see that Joe understood.

"Come on," Joe said. "Let's sit down."

They headed into the room. Over the next few minutes, more people wandered in, some talking among themselves, others noticeably silent.

Nick shifted in his seat. His feet tapped nervously on the floor. The repetitive sound only increased his anxiety.

"It's okay, Nick," Joe said quietly. "Why don't you get yourself some coffee."

"Right." He surged to his feet and cut across the room. Fishing a few quarters from his pocket, he got a Classic Coke and snapped the tab, drinking greedily.

Feeling a little better, he went back to his seat and the meeting got under way.

A man introduced himself: "Hi, I'm Jim. I'm an alcoholic." The crowd of people answered back like good Catholics on Sunday, "Hi, Jim."

Jim stood in the front of the room and started talking. First there was the "God grant me" prayer, then stuff about meetings and twelve steps and more on serenity.

A young woman stood up suddenly. She was tall and rail-thin, with bleached yellow-white hair and skin the color of candlewax. Obviously shaking, she stepped past the row of chairs and stood in front of everyone.

She looked as if she hadn't eaten in a year, and Nick had been a cop long enough to recognize the signs of long-term drug use. No doubt needlemarks ran like train tracks up the insides of her pale arms. She took an endless drag off her cigarette and exhaled heavily. "I'm Rhonda," she said, nervously eyeing the crowd, "and I'm an alcoholic and an addict."

"Hi, Rhonda," said the crowd on cue.

She sucked in another lungfull. "Today's my seventh sober day."

There was a round of applause; a bunch of people yelled "way to go, Rhonda!"

Rhonda gave a wan smile and stubbed her cigarette out on the ashtray in front of her. "I've tried this before—lots of times. But this time'll be differ'nt. The judge said if I can stay clean for one year, I can see my son again." She paused and wiped her eyes, leaving a black tail of mascara down one white cheek. "I used to be a normal girl, going to junior college, working part-time as a waitress in a ritzy restaurant. Then I met this guy, Chet, and before I knew it, I was guzzling tequila and backing it with mountains of coke."

She sighed, stared dully at the open door. "I got pregnant, and kept drinking. My Sammy was born small and addicted, but he lived. I shoulda been there for him, but all I thought about was getting high and drunk. My son wasn't enough to make me quit drinking and snorting." Her lower lip started to shake, and she bit down on it. "Nooo, I had to drive drunk. I had to hurt someone." She sniffled hard and regained a measure of control. "So, here I am, and this time I mean it. I'm gonna do anything to see my son again. This time I'm gonna get clean and stay clean."

When Rhonda was finished, someone else started talking, then another and another. They all used different words, but the stories were the same, tales of loss and pain and anger. Hard-luck stories and bad-luck stories from people who'd been through hell on earth.

Nick was one of them, he knew it by the close of the meeting, and there was a strange comfort in admitting that, in knowing he wasn't the only one in the world trying to wrestle with a bottle of booze.

Izzy couldn't sleep. She went to her window and stared outside. Everything was dark and scary-looking. The only light was tiny white flecks on the black lake. Annie said those were stars fallen from the sky.

She turned away from the window. All week long, ever since Annie had told her that her daddy wasn't coming home, she'd been scared. Yesterday, she'd stood at the window for a long time, waiting. So long that Annie had come up to her.

I don't know when he'll be coming home, Izzy. That's what Annie had said to her. *You remember I told you that your daddy was sick? The doctors say he needs a little time—*

But Izzy knew the truth about doctors. Her mommy had seen lots and lots of them, and none of them ever made her mommy feel better.

They wouldn't help her daddy, either.

Izzy hadn't been able to stop crying. *I miss him,* was all she said to Annie, but there was a lot more she didn't say. She didn't say that she'd been missing him for a long, long time, and she didn't say that the man with the silver hair wasn't really her daddy—because her daddy never got sick and he laughed all the time. She didn't say that she thought her real daddy had died when her mommy died, and that he wouldn't ever be coming back.

Izzy crept down the stairs and sneaked outside. It was raining gently, and a mist floated on the top of the grass, so thick that she couldn't see her feet.

"Mommy?" she whispered, hugging herself. She closed her eyes and concentrated really, really hard. When she opened her eyes, she saw her mommy, standing alongside the lake. The vision was shimmery and out of focus. Mommy stood with her shoulders rounded and her head cocked at an odd angle, as if she were listening for footsteps, or the sound of a bird's call in the middle of the night. The rain turned all sorts of colors, red and yellow and pink and blue.

You should be sleeping, little girl.

"Daddy's sick again."

Her mom made a quiet sound, or maybe it was a breeze, kicking up along the water. *He'll be okay. I promise.*

"I miss you, Mommy." Izzy reached for her. There was a whisper of something not quite solid against her fingertips, a brushing of heat. She closed her hand around . . . nothing.

The touching days are gone for me, pumpkin.

"Mommy, I love you, Mommy."

I'm sorry, Izzy-bear. God, I'm so sorry . . .

Izzy reached out, but it was too late. Her mom was gone.

An unusual wave of heat rolled across Jefferson County. Flowers unfurled and reached skyward for the precious sunlight. Baby birds squawked from nests in green-budded trees. It still rained each night, but by dawn, the world was a sparkling, gilded jewel.

Annie made sure that Izzy was busy all the time. They colored Easter eggs, baked cookies, and drew pictures for Nick—presents for the day he would return. They shopped on Main Street and bought Natalie hokey presents from the rain forest: pens with ferries in them, slug cookbooks, postcards of Lake Mystic. They doubled their reading efforts, until Annie was certain that Izzy was ready to go back to school. But when she mentioned this hope to Izzy, it scared her. *I don't wanna go back. They'll make fun of me.* Annie had let the issue rest there, knowing that it wasn't her decision anyway. She hoped that when Nick came home, they could convince Izzy to return to school.

But for now, their routines were comforting. Izzy was talking regularly; it no longer seemed hard for her to remember the words. They were gaining strength from each other.

Annie had finally learned to sleep alone. She knew it didn't sound like much, but to her, it was momentous. Sometimes, when she left Izzy and crawled into her empty bed, she didn't even think about the man who used to sleep with her; sometimes she went for whole days without thinking about him. Oh, the ache was still there, and the loneliness, but day by day, she was learning that she could survive without him. She still didn't want to, but she knew now that she could.

Every Monday, like clockwork, she called London and heard about Natalie's week. In her daughter's voice, she heard a burgeoning maturity that filled Annie with pride. Natalie wasn't a child anymore, and when she learned of the divorce, she would be able to handle it.

And Annie finally understood that she could handle it, too. Last night, when Terri had called (after ten minutes of grilling Annie about who this *Nick character* was and why Annie was staying at his house), she had finally settled down and listened to Annie, and when the conversation was over, Terri had said quietly, *Of course you can handle it, Annie. You're the only one who thought you couldn't.*

Easter Sunday arrived wrapped in clouds and drenched in rain, but Annie refused to let the uncooperative weather ruin her plans. She dressed Izzy warmly and drove her to Hank's, where the three of them had a huge brunch and a world-class egg hunt. Then they went to church services in town. Afterward, Annie and Izzy drove back to the house, and Annie gave her a small, wrapped gift. "Happy Easter, Izzy."

Izzy tried to open the package with her two good fingers, and the failing effort pinched at Annie's heart. "Here, I'll do it, sweetheart. It's hard when your fingers are gone."

Annie unwrapped the shiny paper, then placed the box on the coffee table.

Biting back a grin, Izzy flipped open the box top. Inside, on a bed of white tissue paper, was a bronze medallion the size of a quarter, resting on a coil of thin silver chain. At Izzy's frown, Annie took the compass from the box and placed it in Izzy's hand.

"When I was a girl, I thought I was lost all the time. Then my dad gave me this compass, and he told me that if I wore it, I'd always know where I belonged." Annie sighed softly. She hadn't kept wearing the compass. Instead, she'd gone all the way to California and lost her sense of direction again. If only there were some internal mechanism that pointed unerringly to the true north of our selves. It was so damned easy in life to get lost. "So," she said at last, "do you want to learn how it works?"

Izzy nodded.

"I knew you'd say that. Okay, grab your boots and rain gear, and I'll show you."

With a quick smile, Izzy ran to the coat closet and grabbed her still-wet coat and hat. Within moments, they were both dressed in rain gear, with rubber boots and big floppy hats. Annie quickly explained to Izzy how the compass worked, and when she was convinced that Izzy understood, she slipped the compass around the girl's neck. "Let's go exploring."

Outside, the weather was horrible. Stuttering gusts of wind blew across the lake, sending silvery ripples onto the gravel shore. Diamond-drops quivered on the tips of the yellow daffodils and tulips that lined the walkway and grew in clumps in the window boxes.

They veered away from the lake, took their heading, and started down the wide, needle-carpeted trail that led into the rain forest. On either side, the immense wooded sentinels stood guard, catching most of the raindrops on their broad, leafy shoulders. A cool mist swirled along the forest floor, so thick in some places that Annie couldn't see her tennis shoes. At every bend in the trail, Izzy stopped and checked her compass.

By midafternoon, Izzy had a sense for true north, and the quiet confidence that came with knowledge.

They walked down one trail and then another and another. Suddenly, the trees opened up, and they found themselves in an overgrown clearing deep in the oldest part of the rain forest. Tucked in one corner was an old ranger station, obviously abandoned for years. Its shingled roof was furred with moss, and gray fungus peeked out from cracks in the log siding. Scratches from a black bear's claws marked the unhinged door.

Izzy blinked up at her. "Can we go in?"

Annie looked questioningly at the cabin. Unfortunately, there was a lot more mother in her soul than explorer. But when she saw the excitement in Izzy's eyes, she couldn't say no. "Okay, but go slow . . . and don't touch anything icky."

With a shriek, Izzy raced for the cabin. Annie hurried along behind her. Together, they eased through the broken door.

Inside, buried under a gauzy net of spiderwebs and dust, were two twin beds, complete with musty blankets; a flimsy, handmade wooden table and two chairs; and a long-forgotten black iron woodstove.

Annie felt like Daniel Boone. She wandered to the old stove and picked up a dusty coffee can, turning it over.

Izzy let out a squeal and pulled something out from under the bed. "Look!" She thrust her hand at Annie.

It was a silver coin, dated 1899.

"Oh, my," Annie said, touching the metal. "That's a treasure indeed. You'd best put that in a safe place."

Izzy frowned, then very solemnly looked up at Annie. Wordlessly, she shoved the coin toward her.

"It's yours, Izzy. Don't give it to me."

"Annie? You'll always be here, won'tcha, Annie? That makes you a safe place."

Annie knew she should force the coin gently back into Izzy's small hand. She should give the child the gift of honesty. *I'm not safe, Izzy. Not really. This isn't my life at all. . . .*

But then she looked into Izzy's liquid brown eyes and she was lost. "Always is a lot longer than you'll need me, Izzy, but I'll keep the coin until you're ready to give it to your daddy, okay?"

"'Kay. Don't lose it." Izzy grinned and nodded and started to run for the door. Halfway there, she skidded to a stop and turned around. She was staring at her right hand.

"Izzy, what is it?"

Slowly, Izzy turned. Frowning, she stuck her right hand up in the air. "I can see all my fingers on this hand again."

"Oh, Izzy . . ." Annie went to Izzy and knelt beside her, pulling the child into her arms. But Izzy was stiff and awkward, and she couldn't seem to take her eyes away from her hand.

Izzy started to cry. "She said I couldn't follow her."

Annie stroked the child's soft, soft cheek and smiled. "Who said that?"

"Mommy. I . . ." She bit her quavering lower lip and looked away.

"Tell me, Izzy," Annie said softly. "I can keep a secret."

"Promise?"

"Promise."

Izzy stared at Annie for a long, silent moment, then said quietly, "I . . . I see her sometimes . . . in the fog. I was disappearin' to be with her . . . but last time I saw her . . ." Huge tears welled in Izzy's eyes and spilled over, streaking down her pink cheeks. "Last time she said I couldn't follow her."

Annie's heart squeezed into a tight little fist. She took Izzy's hand and led her outdoors. Side by side they sat on the rickety, moss-haired porch of the cabin.

"You can't follow your mom, Izzy, and you know why?"

Izzy turned to her. "Why?"

"Because it would break your mommy's heart. She's up in Heaven now, and she wants to watch you grow up. She wants you to have fun and make friends and go to school—to do all the things she did when she was a little girl. She wants to see you wear a pretty white dress on your wedding day and hold your own baby in your arms." Annie sighed. "She wants so much for you, Izzy."

"How do you know she's watchin' me?"

Annie smiled at her. "*You* know. In your heart. That's why you see her in the fog. You know she's watching over you, and when it rains . . . that's when she's missing you. The rain is her tears, and the sunshine is her smile."

Izzy stared out at the trees a long, long time. "I miss her, too."

Annie curled an arm around Izzy's narrow shoulders and drew her close. "I know, baby."

They sat that way for a long time. The rain softened the world into the muted blues and greens of a Monet painting. Then, finally, Annie smiled brightly and tapped on Izzy's right hand. "Why, I do believe you're right, Miss Izzy. I can see those fingers just as clear as a bell. I say we drink a toast."

"I like my toast with jam."

Annie laughed. "I don't have toast, but I have lemonade. And if we don't eat soon, I'm going to start chewing on your coin. I think it's time to head home."

Izzy laughed, and it was such a high, clear, heartbreakingly beautiful sound that Annie let herself forget the tiny strand of worry.

If nothing else, she'd given Izzy back her voice and her smile . . . and now one hand was visible again. Maybe tomorrow, that glove would come off the left.

For now, that was enough.

CHAPTER 15

It was raining on the day Nick came home.

He paid the cabdriver and got out of the car, watching the town's only taxi drive away.

He flipped up the collar of his Levi's jacket and hunched his shoulders against the driving rain. Tucked under one arm was the ragged, wrinkled bag of clothes and toiletries he'd purchased to get him through his time away from home. Rain thwopped the sack, but it couldn't be helped. Day had just rounded the bend into a lavender evening, and there was a slight chill in the air. The gravel road that led to the house went straight for about a quarter of a mile, then turned sharply around a triangular patch of Douglas fir trees. Beyond that, it disappeared into the misty mauve shadows along the lake.

He could have had the cab drive him to the front door, but he needed the time to approach slowly.

Blinking against the rain, he began the long walk home. To his left, the lake reflected the twilight sky. Glossy green leaves, rhododendron, azalea, trillium, and salal hemmed the road on either side, creating a shadowy tunnel that led him ever closer to the house.

At last, he turned the corner. Soft, golden light poured through the windows of his home. The chimney puffed smoke into the purple sky. It was how he'd always imagined it. . . .

This house had seized his imagination from the start. He could still recall the night Annie had brought him here. Kathy had the flu, so Nick and Annie had gone to the carnival alone, and afterward, she'd brought him here, to the "haunted" house by the lake.

He'd first seen this house through her dreamer's eyes. She'd lit a fire inside his soul that night, and this old house had become the physical embodiment of that dream. Perfect for a boy who'd lived in a car for two years and eaten breakfast from Dumpsters.

It had taken him years, but he'd finally saved enough money to buy the place. It had been summer then, August, when he'd signed the papers and written the down-payment check. Yet even on that hottest day of the year, this road had been cool and shaded, and a breeze had swept along the banks of the lake. He had gazed into the distance at Mount Olympus, which stood as an immense granite triangle thrust high, high into the robin's-egg-blue sky, with only the barest hint of snow left to dust its jagged crown.

The memory was as sharp as broken glass. He'd raced to bring Izzy and Kathy here, but it was night by then and shadows lay thick and dark along the porch rails.

He'd grabbed Kathy's hand and dragged her through the murky, musty interior.

Can't you just see it, Kath? This'll be the sunroom—where we'll have breakfast . . . and that's the kitchen, they don't make stoves like that any-more . . . and check out that fireplace—I bet it's one hundred years old. . . .

He smelled hope and home and possibilities.

She smelled must and dirt and work.

How had he failed to notice? And why hadn't he stopped talking long enough to ask her opinion? Why had he just thought, *she's having one of her bad days,* and let it go at that?

With a tired sigh, he straightened his shoulders, crossed the grass, climbed the porch steps, and knocked on the front door. The wet sack of his useless new belongings hit the floor beside his feet, forgotten.

There was a flurry of footsteps behind the door, and a muffled "just a minute," then the door opened and Annie stood before him.

The silence between them was deafening; every sound seemed amplified, the rhythmic thunking of the rain on oversized leaves, the quiet licking of waves on gravel.

He wished he could smile, but he was afraid. He looked away, before she could see the sudden longing in his eyes.

"Nick." It was just a whisper of sound; he imagined he could feel the moist heat of her breath on his neck. Slowly, slowly, he looked at her.

She was standing so close he could see the smattering of freckles that lay along her hairline, and a tiny white scar that bisected one eyebrow. "I've been going to AA twice a day," he said quickly, without even adding a mumbled hello. "I haven't had a drink since you dropped me off at the motel."

"Oh, Nick, that's wonderful. I—"

It was as if she suddenly realized how close they were standing. In the pale glow of the porch light, he saw a sweet blush color her cheeks.

She broke eye contact and cleared her throat, moving back a respectable few feet. "Izzy is in the family room. We were painting. Come on in."

"Painting. Sounds fun. I wouldn't want to—"

"You can do this, Nick." She took hold of his hand—her grasp was solid and comforting—and pulled him into the house. The door banged shut behind him.

The house smelled clean, and somewhere a radio was playing, but he didn't have time to really notice the changes she had made. She was pulling him down the hallway.

Her "family room" was what Nick used to think of as the shit room. Years ago, probably in the fifties, somebody had tried to remodel this room on a skimpy budget. Pressboard wood paneling hid the log walls underneath, and mustard-colored carpet covered the hardwood floor. The only nice thing in the room was a big old brick fireplace, in which Annie had a fire going.

The French doors that led onto the back porch were open. A cool, early evening breeze ruffled their gauzy white curtains, and the rain was a silvery veil between the house and the falling night. Multicolored jars and paintbrushes cluttered a portable card table. Spilled paint lay in bright blemishes on the newspaper that protected the carpet.

Izzy stood with her back to them, one gloved hand hung limply at her left side. There was a huge easel in front of her, with a piece of white paper pinned in place. He could see splashes of color on the paper, but her body blocked the picture.

He realized suddenly that Annie was gone. His hand felt cold and empty. Turning slightly, he saw her in the hallway. She gave him a quick thumbs-up and disappeared.

He sighed. Turning back toward the room, he took a cautious step inside. He expected Izzy to spin around and stare at him, but the carpet muffled the sound of his steps, and she kept on painting.

"Izzy," he said her name softly, as if a quiet voice could somehow soften the surprise.

She dropped a baby-food jar full of blue paint. The colorful liquid splashed across the newspaper. Slowly, clutching her paintbrush, she turned around.

She looked like an angel. She was wearing a paint-stained pair of yellow overalls, but there were no streaks of color on her hair or face. Her jet-black hair lay in two evenly plaited braids, tied at the ends with bits of yellow ribbon.

She looked like she used to.

It was that thought, more than anything, that brought him fully into the room. His knees felt weak, and fear was a cold knot in his stomach, but he kept moving, going toward his little girl, who stood so silently beside the easel, her big brown eyes fixed on his.

Beside her, he knelt. His knees squished in the puddle of blue paint.

She looked down at him, her eyes unblinking, her pink lips drawn in a serious line.

Only a few years ago, she would have leapt into his arms and smothered him with kisses. Even when he'd had a hangover, or after a fight with Kathy, Izzy had always adored him. She'd never looked at him like she did right now—with the wary, worried expression of an animal that was ready to flee at the first hint of danger.

He realized with a sudden tightening in his chest how much he'd missed her kisses . . . the sweet smell of her hair . . . the gentle softness of her hand as she slipped it into his.

"Hey, Sunshine," he said, his eyes avoiding the tiny black glove that evidenced his failure and her heartbreak.

It was his pet name for her—given on the first day she'd smiled and he'd said it was like sunshine after a rain. He hadn't called her Sunshine in a long time. Since Kathy's death, and probably even before that.

She remembered. A little jumping smile tugged one side of her mouth.

There were so many things he could say to her right now, promises he could make, but in the end, he knew it would only be words. Promises made by a man who'd broken too many to be trusted.

One day at a time; that was one thing AA definitely had right.

That was how he'd lost his daughter—one moment at a time—and that was the only way to get her back. He couldn't ask for her trust; even though she'd probably give it to him freely, he had to *earn* it. One day at a time.

In the end, he made no promises. Instead, he said only, "What are you painting?"

She cocked her head toward the paper and stepped back. It was a colorful smearing of squiggly lines and globs of falling paint. Because he'd seen her artwork before, he could make out Izzy's self-portrait: she was the tiny, big-headed stick figure in the corner with the floor-length cascade of black hair. Someone—probably Annie, judging by the spiked brown hair—stood beside her, wearing a broad brush stroke of a smile. Above the two stick figures was a bright yellow sun bracketed by writhing red rays.

Nick grabbed a clean paintbrush from the card table and dipped it into a jar of brown paint. Trying not to spill—although he had no idea why he bothered—he carefully maneuvered the paintbrush to the paper. "Can I add something?"

She stared up at him. Then slowly she nodded.

He drew a quick, misshapen circle alongside Annie. Another four strokes and he had a body of sorts. "This is daddy," he said, without looking at her. Then he added eyes, a nose, and a flat line of a mouth. "I don't need to paint the hair—it's almost the same color as the paper. We'll just imagine it." Lowering the brush, he looked at her.

Her gaze was level and steady. Two oversized front teeth—her only grown-up teeth—nipped nervously at her lower lip.

"Is it okay if I come home, Izzy?" He waited a lifetime for her answer, a nod, a blink, anything, but she just stood there, staring at him through those sad, grown-up eyes in her little-girl's face.

He touched her velvet-soft cheek. "I understand, Sunshine."

He started to get to his feet.

She grabbed his hand.

Slowly, he lowered himself back to his knees. He stared at her, losing himself in the chocolate-brown eyes that had once been his world. In that instant, he remembered it all—walking down the docks with her, looking at boats, dreaming about sailing around the world someday. . . . He remembered how it had felt to hold her hand and laugh with her and swing her in his arms on a beautiful, sunny spring day.

"I love you, Izzy," he said, remembering then how simple it used to be.

Nick stood on the porch, his legs braced apart, his arms crossed. He was hanging onto his world by a fraying thread. Dinner had been a tense affair, with Annie's cheerful chatter punctuated by awkward silences. He'd noticed that Izzy was using her right hand again—and not in that pathetic two-fingered way.

Every time he looked at his daughter, he felt a hot rush of shame, and it took all his self-control not to turn away. But he hadn't taken the coward's road tonight, and that was something of a triumph. He'd looked Izzy square in the eye, and if he flinched at the wariness in her gaze, he did it inwardly, so she couldn't see.

Behind him, the screen door screeched open and banged shut.

It took him a second to find the courage to turn around. When he did, Annie was standing there, alongside the old rocking chair that had been Nick's gift to Kathy when Izzy was born.

Annie's fingers trailed lightly across the top rail, and her wedding ring glittered in the orange glow of the outdoor bulb. The size of the diamond reminded Nick once again of how different her world was from his. As if he needed reminding.

She was holding a small designer suitcase.

"Izzy has brushed her teeth. She's waiting for you to tuck her in."
Her voice was as soft and cool as a spring rain, and it soothed the ragged
edges of his anxiety.

She was standing close to him, her arms at her sides. Even with that
Marine-issue haircut, she was beautiful. A tired gray UW sweatshirt
bagged over a pair of oversized jeans, but it didn't camouflage her body.
Suddenly he could remember her naked, recall vividly how she'd lifted
her arms and pulled off her shirt . . . the moonlight kissing her breasts. . . .

"Nick?" She took a step toward him. "Are you all right?"

He forced a weak laugh. "As well as a drunk who has stopped
drinking can be, I suppose."

"You're going to make it." She started to reach for him, and he
leaned slightly toward her, needing that touch more than air, but at the
last minute, she drew back. "It's not easy to start over. I know . . ."

He saw the haunted look in her eyes and wondered what he'd done
to her, the man who'd put that egg-size diamond on her left hand. He
wanted to ask, but it felt wrong, presumptuous, to probe her wounds.
"You saved my life, Annie. I don't know how to thank you."

She smiled. "I always knew you'd be back for her, you know. It
wasn't much of a risk. I could see how much you loved Izzy."

"Such optimism." He glanced out at the darkened lake. "I loved
Kathy, too, and look what happened." He sighed and leaned back
against the porch rail, staring out at the yard. "You know what haunts
me? I never really understood my wife. The sad thing is—I do now. I
know what hopelessness feels like; before, I thought I did, but I was
skimming the surface. She used to tell me that she couldn't feel the sunlight anymore, not even when she was standing in it, not even when it
was hot on her cheeks." It surprised Nick that he could talk about his
wife so easily. For the first time, he remembered *her,* not the illness or
the crumbling of their marriage over the last few years, but Kathy, his
Kathy, the bright-eyed, big-hearted girl he'd fallen in love with. "She
didn't want to live in the darkness anymore. . . ."

When he turned back to Annie, she was crying. He felt awkward and
selfish in the wake of her grief. "I'm sorry . . . I didn't mean to upset you."

She gazed up at him. "You're so lucky."

"What?"

"It doesn't matter how you felt about Kathy by the end, or since the end. You obviously loved her. No matter what she did, or why she did it, she must have known." Her voice fell to a throaty whisper. "Most people are never loved like that in their whole lives."

He knew he was going to ask the question, though he shouldn't. He stepped toward her, a heartbeat closer than was safe. "How about you? Have you known that kind of love?"

She gave him a fleeting, sad little smile and looked away. "No. I have loved that way . . . but been loved . . . I don't think so."

"You deserve better than that."

She nodded and nonchalantly wiped her eyes. "Don't we all."

Silence fell between them, awkward and uncomfortable. "Annie—"

She stopped and turned to him. "Yes?"

"Maybe you'd like to come over tomorrow—spend the day with us."

"I'd like that," she answered quickly, then she looked away.

"Thank you." His voice was soft, and came as close to a kiss as he dared.

"You're welcome, Nicky." There was another moment of awkwardness as she stared up at him. "You should know that Izzy started talking while you were gone."

Nick frowned. "She didn't talk to me."

Annie touched his arm in a brief, fleeting caress. "She will. Give her time."

He couldn't meet Annie's gaze. Instead, he stared out at the lake.

She moved nervously from foot to foot, then said, "Well, I should be getting home. . . ."

"See you tomorrow."

She nodded and hurried past him. With a quick wave, she climbed into her Mustang and drove away.

Nick watched her taillights, two bright red dots in the darkness of the forest, until she turned the corner and was gone. Reluctantly, he went back into the house and climbed the stairs. Outside Izzy's room, he paused, then knocked.

Answer, baby . . . you can do it.

But there was no response. Slowly, he turned the knob and opened the door.

She was sitting up in bed, her right arm curled around Miss Jemmie. The black glove on her left hand was a tiny blotch against the white and lavender lace comforter.

He went to the bed and sat down beside her.

Silence spilled between them, and every heartbeat plucked at the fragile strands of Nick's self-confidence. "I thought I'd read you a story."

She let go of Miss Jemmie and pulled a book out from under the covers, handing it to him.

"Ah, *Where the Wild Things Are.* I wonder how Max has been doing lately. He probably turned into a warthog."

Izzy made a small, hiccuping sound, like a hacked-off laugh.

Curling an arm around her tiny shoulders, he drew her close. With the book open on his lap, he began to read. He used his best storyteller voice, the one Izzy had always loved.

And as he slipped into the familiar story, he felt for the first time as if he might have a chance.

But it was not so easy. For the first week, Nick was shaky and short-tempered and afraid that if he made one wrong move, he'd end up back on a bar stool at Zoe's. Every moment of every day was an agonizing test of his will.

He rose early, needing a drink, and went outside to chop wood, where, still needing a drink, he stood for hours, chopping, sweating, wondering if today was the day he'd fail.

Annie arrived every day with a smile on her face and an activity planned. By sheer force of will, she was turning the three of them into a patchwork family, and it was that connection that kept Nick going to his AA meetings every day. He'd be damned if he'd let Annie and Izzy down.

Now, he was driving to the four o'clock meeting. He slowed the car to a crawl at Main Street, his hands curled tightly around the steering wheel. It had started to rain about five minutes ago, and the suddenness of the storm had forced the pedestrians inside, left the town rainy-day quiet. Only a few scattered cars filled the row of empty stalls.

Except at Zoe's. In front of the tavern, there was a steady line of cars. He knew from experience that every bar stool would be occupied. He stared at the tavern's murky windows, hearing in his head the quiet clinking of the glasses and the sloshing of scotch over ice cubes.

He licked his dry lips and swallowed thickly, trying not to imagine how sweet a shot of scotch would taste right now. He still couldn't imagine the rest of his life without booze, but he could manage this one day.

He eased his foot down on the accelerator and sped up. He felt every inch of road as he drove past Zoe's, and by the time he reached the Lutheran church, the shaking had receded a bit and the sweat was a cold, drying trail on his skin.

He pulled into the paved lot behind the church and parked beneath a Rainier Beer billboard. Taking a second to collect himself, he pocketed his keys and went inside.

By now, the room was full of familiar faces, and it was oddly comforting to step through the open door.

Joe grinned at him, waved him over to a seat.

Nodding, Nick quickly got himself a can of Coke, then took the empty seat beside Joe.

"Nicholas, are you okay? You look pale."

"I don't know," he answered, thankful in a small way that AA had given him that—the ability for the first time in his life to be honest. This room, among these strangers-who-would-be-friends, was the one place where he could haul his vulnerability and his failings out of the pocket of his soul and throw them under the glaring light of scrutiny. There was some comfort in that, he knew now. Honesty helped. Admitting that the addiction was stronger than he was helped even more.

He was hanging on by a thread at home. Wherever he went, whatever he said, he felt Izzy's eyes on him. She was waiting for the inevitable screw-up.

She hadn't spoken a word to him yet, and this time, the silences were worse than before, because she was talking to Annie—though he'd never heard it. Not once had he heard the sweetness of his little girl's voice.

Mealtimes were bad, too. Sometimes, when he reached for the fork, his hand was shaking so badly that he had to plead a headache and run for the dark isolation of his bedroom.

He gave Joe a weak smile. "Trying is a hell of a lot harder than not trying, you know?"

"It always is, Nicholas. You know I'm here for you. We all are."

Nick took the statement at face value and was thankful for it. "I know."

The meeting got under way. One by one, the people around him spoke up—those who wanted to share their burden—revealing their anniversaries and their failures and their hopes and dreams. As always, they came around, finally, to Nick.

He thought about saying something. *Hi, I'm Nick. I'm an alcoholic. I haven't had a drink in twenty-three days.*

But, in the end, like all the other times, he couldn't quite manage it.

CHAPTER 16

Their days followed a familiar pattern. Monday through Friday, Annie showed up at Nick's house bright and early. He made pancakes and eggs for breakfast, and then the three of them spent the day together. Rain or shine, they were outside, fishing along the crumbling rock banks of the river, riding bikes on the trails around the lake, or window-shopping on Main Street. Today they had hiked deep into Enchanted Valley, and now, several hours and even more miles later, each of them was exhausted. Poor Izzy had fallen asleep almost before her head hit the pillow.

Annie leaned down and kissed Izzy's forehead, murmuring a quiet good night.

"'Night, Annie," Izzy mumbled back, her eyes closed.

Annie drew back. This was the time of the week she hated most. Friday night. She wouldn't see Nick and Izzy again until Monday, and though she enjoyed the time she spent with Hank, she couldn't wait to get back here Monday morning. She didn't often let herself think about how much she liked Nick and Izzy, or how *right* it felt to be with them. Those thoughts led her down a dark and twisting road that frightened her, and so she pushed them away, buried them in the dark corner that had always housed her uncertainties. She had come to the sad realization that Blake wasn't going to change his mind, that she wasn't going to receive the apologetic phone call she'd fantasized about for weeks. Without even that slim fantasy to cling to, she was left feeling adrift. Sometimes, in the midst of a lovely spring day, she would stumble across her fear and the suddenness of it shocked and frightened her.

Those were the times when she turned to Hank—but his comforting words *he'll be back, honey, don't you worry, he'll be back* didn't soothe Annie anymore. She couldn't believe in them, and somehow the not believing hurt more than the believing ever had. Terri was the only one who understood, and a phone call to her best friend, often made late at night, was the only thing that helped.

She started to turn away, when she noticed something through the window, a movement. She pushed the patterned lace curtains aside.

Nick was standing down alongside the lake, his shadow a long streak across the rippling silver waves. As usual, he'd helped with the dinner dishes, read Izzy a story, and then bolted outside to stand alone.

He was as lonely as she was. She saw it in his eyes all the time, a sadness that clung even when he smiled.

He was trying so hard. Yesterday, he'd spent almost two hours playing Candy Land with Izzy, his long body crouched uncomfortably across the multicolored board. Every time Izzy smiled, Nick looked like he was going to cry.

Annie had never been as proud of anyone as she was of him. He was trying to do everything right—no drinking, no swearing, no broken promises. Nothing but soft, sad smiles and time spent with the little girl who still studied him warily and didn't speak to him.

So often, during the day, she was reminded of Blake, and the kind of father he'd been. Never there, physically or emotionally, for his daughter, taking so much of his life for granted. It was partially Annie's fault; she saw that now. She'd been part of what their marriage had become. She had blindly done everything he'd asked of her. Everything. She'd given up so much—everything of herself and her dreams; she'd given it up without a whimper of protest . . . and all because she loved him so much.

Her life, her soul, had faded into his, one day, one decision at a time. Little things . . . nothing by themselves . . .

A haircut she didn't have because Blake liked her hair long, a dress she didn't buy because he thought red was a tramp's color.

She'd done what they "agreed" she should do. She'd stayed home and become the perfect suburban wife and mother, and in her quest for quiet perfection, she'd let Blake become a bad husband and bad father.

And all the while, she'd thought she was the perfect wife. Only now she saw how wrong she'd been: she'd made all those sacrifices not out of strength and love, but out of weakness. Because it was safer and easier to follow. She had become what she'd set out to be, and now she was ashamed of her choices. But still she had no true understanding of where she would go from here.

Alone. That was all she knew. Wherever she went from here, it would be as a middle-aged woman alone.

She wished she had Nick's strength, his willingness to shove past his fear and *try*.

She touched the glass softly, feeling the cool smoothness beneath her fingertips. "You're going to make it, Nick."

And she believed it.

She closed the bedroom door behind her and went downstairs. Plucking her purse from the sofa, she headed for the door. Outside, the cool night air breezed across her cheeks.

She stared across the blackened lawn at Nick. It was at times like these, at the quiet end of the day, that memories of their lovemaking floated to the surface of her mind.

She closed her eyes for a moment and remembered the feel of his hands on her naked skin . . . the softness of his lips . . .

"Annie?"

Her eyes popped open. He was in front of her, and when she looked at him, she was certain that it was all in her eyes: the naked, desperate need for companionship and caring. She was afraid that if she spoke to him, if she said anything, and heard the soft tenor of his voice in response, she would be lost. She was vulnerable now, longing to be held and touched by a man . . . even if it was the wrong man . . . even if she wasn't truly the woman he wanted.

She forced a quick, nervous smile. "Hi, Nick . . . 'bye Nick. I've got to run."

Before he could answer, she ran to her car.

But a mile later, all alone in her car, listening to Rod Stewart's scratchy-voiced song about his heart and soul, and an attraction that was purely physical, she was still remembering . . .

Saturday morning, Izzy stood on the porch in her bright new overalls and rain boots, watching her daddy. He was kneeling in the yard, beside that tree they'd planted on the day of her mommy's funeral. The skinny cherry tree that wouldn't turn green, not even now when everything around it was blooming. It was dead, just like her mommy.

Her daddy was all hunched over, like a character from one of her books, wearing dirty gloves that made his hands look like bear claws. He was yanking up weeds from around the baby tree, and he was humming a song, one Izzy hadn't heard in a long time.

All of a sudden, her daddy looked up and saw her. He gave her a big smile and pushed the silvery hair away from his face. The glove left a big streak of brown mud across his forehead. "Heya, Izzy-bear," he said. "Wanna help me pull up weeds?"

Slowly, she moved toward him, past the row of primroses Annie had planted last week. He was still smiling when she came up beside him.

All she could think was that her daddy was back and she wanted a hug more than anything in the world, but she was afraid. What if he didn't stay again? She almost said something to him, she even opened her mouth and tried.

"What is it, Izzy?"

The words wouldn't fall out. They were jammed in her throat behind a big old lump. *Come on, Izzy,* she told herself, *just say, "Hi, Daddy, I missed you."*

But she couldn't. Instead, she reached out her hand and pointed to the trowel that lay on the ground. He bent down and picked up the big fork, handing it to her slowly. "It's okay, Sunshine," he said softly. "I understand."

I love you, Daddy. Tears stung her eyes; she was sad and embarrassed that she couldn't force herself to say the words. She squeezed her eyes shut before he could see the stupid, babyish tears. Then she took the trowel and moved in beside him.

He started talking, about the weather and flowers and the beautiful day. He talked so long she forgot she was embarrassed and sad and that she was a stupid little girl who couldn't talk to her daddy anymore.

Sunday was the kind of day that tricked people into moving into this damp, soggy corner of the world. The kind of day when hapless tourists who stumbled into the rain forest tended to draw in deep breaths of awe and then find themselves driving their rental cars slowly past real estate offices. Almost involuntarily, they reached for pamphlets about cabins for sale, and called their faraway families with stories of the most gorgeous land they'd ever seen.

When Nick flung back the living room curtains and looked outside, he was as awestruck as any foreigner. A bright yellow sun had just crested the trees; lemony streamers of light backlit the forest and gave it a translucent, otherworldly glow. Lake Mystic swallowed the surrounding images and held them against its blue mirrored surface. On the far bank, a single gray heron stood on one leg, proudly surveying his domain.

It was a perfect day for a father-daughter outing. He hurried up the stairs and woke his sleeping child. He helped her brush her teeth and get dressed in warm woolen clothes. While she was sleepily making her bed, he went downstairs and packed a picnic lunch—smoked salmon bought fresh from the Quinault tribe at the local roadside stand, cream cheese and crackers for him, and peanut butter and jelly sandwiches and string cheese for Izzy. Annie had left a quart of homemade lemonade, and he poured it into a thermos, then crammed everything into a picnic basket.

Within the hour, they were driving down the winding coastal road that seemed to bisect the world. On one side stood the darkest, densest of all American woodlands, and on the other, the crashing wildness of the Pacific Ocean. Along the coastal side, the evergreen trees had been sculpted by a hundred years of gale winds; their limbs bent backward in an unnatural arc.

Nick parked in one of the turnouts that were designed to showcase the view to tourists. Taking Izzy's hand, he led her down the trail toward the beach.

Below them, huge, white-tipped waves crashed against the rocks. When they finally dropped onto the hard-packed sand, Izzy grinned up at him.

The silver-blue ocean stretched out for a thousand miles away from the land. Sometimes, the wind along this stretch of the Pacific howled so hard no man could draw a breath, but today it was almost preternaturally quiet. The air was as crisp and delicious as a sun-ripened apple. Cormorants and kingfishers and seagulls cawed and wheeled overhead, landing every now and then on one of the wind-sculpted trees that grew atop house-size rocks in the surf.

Nick set the basket down on a gray boulder near the land's end. "Come on, Izzy."

They ran across the sand, laughing, creating the only footprints for miles, searching for hidden treasures: sand dollars, translucent quartz stones, and tiny black crabs. Around a bend in the coastline, they stumbled into a knee-deep mass of tiny blue jellyfish, blown ashore by the wind—a sure sign to old-timers that tuna would appear off the coast this summer.

When the sun reached its peak in the sky and sent its warmth through their layers of wool and Gortex, Nick led Izzy back to where they'd begun. He threw a huge red and white blanket over the hard sand and unpacked the basket. They sat cross-legged on the blanket and ate their lunch.

All the while, Nick told stories—about the Native Americans who had first combed this beach, hundreds of years before the first white settlers appeared; about the wild parties he had attended in high school on this very same stretch of sand; about the time he'd brought Kathy here when she was pregnant.

Once, he'd thought that Izzy was going to say something. She'd leaned forward, her brown eyes sparkling, her lips trembling.

He'd put down his glass of lemonade. *Come on, Izzy-bear.* But in the end, she'd held back. Whatever had made it to the tip of her tongue was lost.

That silence was worse than the others, somehow. It lodged in his heart like a steel splinter; he felt it with every in-drawn breath afterward. But he forced a smile and went on with another story, this time about a night long ago when he and Annie had climbed to the top of the town's water tower and painted GO PANTHERS on the metal sides.

At the end of their picnic, they loaded up the basket with their leftovers and made their slow, silent way back up to the car. They drove home in the last fading rays of the setting sun. Nick found it difficult to keep talking, to keep spilling his soul into the stony silence that surrounded them, but he forced himself to do it. When they passed Zoe's, the need for a drink rose in him, relentless as the surf. He hit the gas harder and they sped beyond the tavern.

When they pulled into the driveway, day had given way to a pink and gold evening. He held Izzy's hand as they quietly made their way back into the house.

"What do you say we play a game?" he said, shutting the door behind him.

Izzy didn't answer, but scampered away. In a few moments, she appeared again, with the big, multicolored Candy Land box mashed to her tiny chest.

He groaned dramatically. "Not that—anything but that. How about Pick-up Sticks?"

A tiny smile tilted her mouth. She shook her head.

"You think I don't want to play that because I never win, but that's not true. It's because I fall into a coma. Come on—Pick-up Sticks. Please?"

She gave him a grin that bunched her cheeks. Her index finger thumped on the Candy Land box.

"Okay. One game of Candy Land, then Pick-up Sticks."

She released a giggle, and the simple sound of that soothed the ragged edges of his nerves. He quickly made a fire, then they set up the board in the middle of the living room floor.

One game turned into another and another. When Nick had finally lost his fine motor skills, he tossed the tiny blue and yellow board pieces into the oblong box. "I give up. You're the queen of Candy Land. No one can beat you. Come on, Izzy-bear, it's dinnertime. Even *cooking* is better than this game." He got slowly to his feet—he'd lost half the bloodflow into his legs—and staggered to a stand.

She lurched up and grabbed his hand. Worry furrowed her brow.

He smiled down at her. "It's okay, honey. I'm just old, and old people wobble a bit. Remember Grandma Myrtle? She used to totter around like a broken toy."

Izzy giggled.

In the kitchen, they sat at the big plank table and ate store-bought macaroni and cheese until their skin took on the orange glow of whatever passed for cheese in that little white packet. Izzy helped Nick wash and dry the dishes and put them away, and then they went upstairs. He helped her into her nightgown, brushed those incredibly tiny white teeth of hers, and together they climbed into her narrow twin bed.

He pulled the tattered copy of *Alice in Wonderland* off the bedside table. Curling an arm around Izzy's tiny shoulders, he drew his daughter close and began to read.

When he closed the book, her eyes were heavy and she was more than half asleep. "Good night, Sunshine," he said softly, kissing her forehead. Slowly, he drew back and stood up.

She reached out suddenly and grabbed his hand. He turned back, stared down at her. "Izzy?"

"Daddy?"

For a second, he couldn't breathe. It was the first time he'd heard her sweet child's voice in almost a year. Slowly, slowly, he sat down beside her. Tears stung his eyes, turned his precious baby into a blur. "Oh, Izzy," he whispered, unable to find any other words.

"I love you, Daddy," she said, and now she was crying, too.

He pulled her into a bear hug, hiding his face in the crook of her neck so she wouldn't see him crying. "Oh, Izzy-bear, I love you, too," he whispered over and over again, stroking her hair, feeling her tears mingle with his on the softness of her cheek. He held her tightly, wondering if he'd ever have the strength to let her go.

She fell asleep in his arms, and still he held her. Finally, he laid her head gently on the pillow and tucked the covers up to her small, pointed chin. When he looked down at his sleeping child, he felt a rush of emotion so pure and sweet and all-consuming that no single word—not even *love*—could possibly be big enough.

Triumph was a trembling, high-pitched aria in his bloodstream. And all because of something as simple, and as infinitely complex, as a child's *I love you*. Three little words he'd never take for granted again.

He couldn't contain the enormity of his emotions; they were spilling over, breaking one after another in waves. He felt the most incredible urge to laugh out loud. He wanted to share this moment with someone he cared for.

Annie.

He knew it was dangerous, this sudden desire to talk to her, be with her, tell her what he was feeling. Knew it, and didn't care. Couldn't care.

He went into his room and picked up the phone.

Monday was a magical day, filled with laughter. Once again the sun banished the clouds from the sky. Nick and Annie and Izzy rode bicycles and collected wildflowers and made crowns from the dainty purple and white flowers that had opened during the night.

Annie couldn't remember when she'd had so much fun. Blake had never spent a day like this with his girls, just the three of them; even when he'd had a rare day at home, he'd spent it on the phone or the fax or the computer. Annie was only now beginning to realize how lonely her life had been.

As she pedaled her bike down the National Park trail, she found herself recalling bits and pieces of her phone conversation with Nick last night. *She talked to me, Annie. She told me she loved me.* The awe in his voice had brought tears to Annie's eyes, and when he went on, telling her about their day at the beach, she'd envied them the easy perfection of it all.

Though neither one of them had mentioned the conversation today, it hung in the air between them, like dust motes that were occasionally thickened by a flash of sunlight. They'd woven a new strand of intimacy during their conversation. The distance of the telephone had made it easier somehow.

In the middle of it all, Annie had begun to remember the old Nick—the young Nick—and how she'd loved him. And when she closed her eyes while he was talking, she saw the boy who'd first kissed her beneath a starry night sky. The boy whose gentle, tentative kiss had made her cry.

She could feel herself drifting into dangerous waters. So many things about Nick touched her, but it was the depth of his love for Izzy that tangled her up inside and left her aching. No matter how hard she tried to forget the life she'd lived in California and the choices she'd made, Nick brought it all up again. Annie had raised a daughter who would never truly know the comforting embrace of a father's adoration.

And she had been a wife in love alone for too many years.

She had felt pathetic and small as she crossed the rickety bridge to that realization. For years, she'd mistaken habit and affection for true love. She had assumed that the love she gave her husband was a reflection of the love he felt for her, and now, because of her blindness, she was alone, a thirty-nine-year-old woman who faced her "golden" years without a child at home or a husband in her bed.

At that moment, she and Nick were separated by miles, and she was glad because if he'd been beside her, she would have reached for him, would have begged him to hold her and kiss her and tell her she was beautiful . . . even if the words were a lie.

Now, as they drove home after their bike ride, Annie prayed that Nick hadn't heard all that loneliness and pain in her voice. Every time he looked at her today, she'd looked away, fast.

By the time they returned to the house, she was a wreck. She sat quietly at the table, her eyes focused on her food, her right foot tapping nervously on the floor.

As soon as dinner was over, she bolted from the table and hustled Izzy up to bed, leaving Nick to wash and dry the dishes.

"Good night, Izzy," she said, tucking the child into bed. "Your daddy will be up in a minute."

"'Night, Annie," Izzy muttered, rolling onto her side.

Annie closed the bedroom door and headed downstairs. She found Nick in the living room, staring out at the lake. Even from this distance, she could see that his hands were shaking. There was a damp dishrag lying at his feet.

The last step creaked beneath her foot and she froze.

He spun toward her. His skin was pale in the lamplight, and sweat sheened his forehead.

"You want a drink," she said.

"Want?" His laugh was low and rough. "That doesn't even begin to cover it."

Annie didn't know what to do. It was dangerous to touch him, but she couldn't turn away. Cautiously, she moved toward him. He reached for her hand, his sweaty fingers coiling around hers with a desperate squeeze.

After a long minute, she said, "How 'bout a bowl of Chocolate Chip Mint instead?"

"Great. I'll just go say good night to Izzy, then . . . I'll meet you by the fire." He gave her a relieved smile before turning and bolting up the stairs.

Annie went to the kitchen and scooped out two bowls of ice cream. The whole time she told herself that it was nothing, just a bowl of ice cream between friends. By the time she was finished, Nick was back downstairs. Together, they sat on the sofa.

In silence, they ate. The tinny clang of spoons on porcelain seemed absurdly loud. She was sharply aware of everything about him, the uneven way he tapped his foot anxiously on the floor, the way he kept tucking a flyaway lock of hair behind his right ear.

All at once, he turned to her. "How long will you be here?"

So that was it. She sighed. "About another month and a half. Natalie gets home on the fifteenth of June."

His gaze caught hers, and she felt as if she were falling into his blue eyes.

Annie's breath caught in her chest. She found herself waiting to hear what he would say next, though she couldn't imagine what it would be.

"What do you think of Mystic?" he asked slowly, watching her. "You sure couldn't wait to leave after high school."

"It wasn't Mystic that sent me running."

It was a long minute before he answered softly, "I never meant to hurt you."

"I know."

"You scared me."

She felt it blossom again at his words, that delicate bud of intimacy that had drawn them together last night. It scared her, especially now when she was so close to him. She tried to brush it away with a laugh. "You're kidding, right?"

He leaned forward and set the bowl down on the coffee table. Then, slowly, he turned toward her. One arm snaked down the back of the sofa toward her, and she had to fight the urge to lean back into it. "I think our lives are mapped out long before we know enough to ask the right questions. Mine was cast in stone the day my dad abandoned my mom. She had . . . trouble handling life. Before I even knew what was happening, I was her caretaker. I learned what every child of a drunk learns: don't talk, don't trust, don't care. Hell, I was an adult before I was ten years old. I shopped, I cooked, I cleaned . . . wherever we lived. I loved her, so I took care of her, and when she turned on me or became violent, I believed what she said—that I was worthless and stupid and lucky she stayed with me." He leaned back into the sofa.

Annie felt his fingertips brush her shoulders. She gazed at him, remembering how handsome he had been, how when she'd looked at him for the first time, she hadn't been able to breathe.

"Living here with Joe was like a dream for me. Clean sheets, clean clothes, lots to eat. I got to go to school every day and no one ever hit me." He smiled at her, and the heat of it sent shivers through her blood. "Then I met you and Kath. Remember?"

"At the A and W, after a football game. We invited you to sit with us. There was a K-Tel album playing in the background."

"*You* invited me. I couldn't believe it when you did that . . . and then, when we all became friends, it stunned me. Everything about that year was a first." He smiled, but his smile was sad and tired around the edges and didn't reach his eyes. "You were the first girl I ever kissed. Did you know that?"

Annie's throat felt dangerously tight. "I cried."

He nodded. "I thought it was because you *knew.* Like you could taste it in me somehow, that I wasn't good enough."

She wanted to touch him so badly her fingers tingled. She forced her hand into a fist. "I never knew why I cried. Still don't."

He smiled at her. "See? The paths are set before we're aware. Kathy was so much simpler. I *understood* her. She needed me, even then she needed me, and to me that was the same as love. I just plopped into the role I knew. I mean, what was I supposed to do? Ask you to give up Stanford? Or wait for you, even though you hadn't asked me to?"

Annie had never once considered being bold enough to talk to Nick about how she felt. Like him, she'd fallen easily—tumbled—into the role she knew. She did what was expected of her; Annie the good girl. She went away to college and married a nice boy with a bright future . . . and lost herself along the way.

"I always figured you'd be famous," he said at last, "you were so damned smart. The only kid from Mystic ever to get an academic schol- arship to Stanford."

She snorted. "Me, famous? Doing what?"

"Don't do that, Annie." His voice was as soft as a touch, and she couldn't help looking at him. The sadness in his eyes coiled around her throat and squeezed. "That's a bad road to go down. Believe me, I know. You could succeed at anything you tried. And screw anyone who tells you different."

His encouragement was a draught of water to her parched, thirsty soul. "I *did* think of something the other day. . . ."

"What?"

She drew back. "You'll laugh."

"Never."

Dangerously, she believed him. "I'd like to run a small bookstore. You know the kind, with overstuffed chairs and latte machines and employees who actually *read.*"

He touched her cheekbone, a fleeting caress that made her shiver. It was the first time he'd deliberately touched her since that night by the lake. "You should see yourself right now, Annie."

Heat climbed up her cheeks. "You probably think I'm being ridiculous."

"No. Never. I was just noticing how your eyes lit up when you said 'bookstore.' I think it's a great idea. In fact, there's an old Victorian house on Main Street. It used to be a gift shop until a few months ago. When the owner died, they closed it up. They've been trying to find a renter. With a little elbow grease, it could make a great location." He paused and looked at her. "If you wanted to open that bookstore in Mystic."

The fantasy broke apart. They both knew that her life wasn't in Mystic. She belonged in another state, beneath another sun, in a white house by the sea. She stared down at her diamond ring, trying to think of something to say, a way to brush off the silly daydream and pretend she'd never voiced it.

He said suddenly, "Have you seen *Same Time, Next Year?*"

She frowned. "The Alan Alda movie—the one about the couple who have an affair for one weekend every year?"

"Yeah."

She found it difficult to breathe evenly. The air seemed electrified by the simple word: affair. "I-I always loved it."

"It's starting in ten minutes. You want to watch?"

Her breath expelled in a rush. She felt like a fool for reading something into a simple little question about a movie.

"Sure."

They settled onto the sofa and watched the movie, but all the while, Annie had the strangest sensation that she was falling. She kept glancing at Nick, whom she often caught staring at her in return. She didn't want to consider how much he had begun to matter, but there was no way to avoid the obvious.

Last night, she'd learned that he liked chocolate chip ice cream and hated beets . . . that blue was his favorite color and professional sports bored him to tears . . . that he liked his baked potatoes with butter and bacon bits, but no salt or pepper, and that sometimes a kiss from Izzy, given as she snuggled close to him, had the power to make him cry.

She knew that often the need for a drink rose in him with such sudden ferocity that it left him winded and glassy-eyed. In those moments, he would push away from Annie and Izzy and run into the forest alone. Later, he would return, his hair dampened by sweat, his skin pale and his hands trembling, but he would smile at her, a sad, desperate smile that didn't reach his eyes, and she would know that he had beaten it again. And sometimes, in that moment, when their gazes locked across the clearing, she could feel the danger, simmering beneath the surface.

She didn't want to care too deeply about Nick Delacroix, and yet she could feel each day bringing them closer and closer.

When the movie ended, she couldn't look at him, afraid of what she'd see in his eyes . . . afraid of what he'd see in hers. So, she grabbed her box of tissues and her purse and ran for the door. She hardly even mumbled a good-bye.

CHAPTER 17

Izzy woke up scared. She'd been dreaming about her mommy . . . that was all she could remember. Her mommy had been down by the lake, calling out to her . . . crying.

She threw back the covers and climbed out of bed. Without bothering to put on her robe and slippers, she crept out of her bedroom and hurried down the hall. She paused at her daddy's bedroom, then moved past. Down the stairs and out the front doors, into the darkest part of the night.

She stared at the lake. At first it was nothing but a charcoal-gray shadow in the vee of the mountains, but after a while, she could see the glistening waves and hear the murmuring voice of the water against the gravelly shore. The mist had thickened into a gray fog spiked with black toothpick trees.

Izzy-bear, is that you?

She flinched. The screen door jumped out of her hand and banged back into place. "Mommy?"

Something white flashed beside the shore.

She glanced back at the house and saw that her daddy's bedroom was dark. She knew she should tell her daddy where she was going, but then she saw the flash of white again and heard the sound of a woman crying, and she forgot all about it. She picked up the hem of her nightgown and hurried across the wet grass, her toes squishing in muddy ground.

There were sounds everywhere—the cawing of crows, the hooting of a lonely owl, the ribbiting of bullfrogs—and though the sounds scared her, she didn't stop until she reached the lake.

"Mommy?" she whispered.

A fine mist rose from the water. It was in the mist that she saw her mommy. Clear as day, she was standing on the water, her hands clasped at her waist, her golden-blond hair a halo around her face. Izzy got a flashing glimpse of white wings, and she heard a rhythmic sound, like the blurring start of a lawn mower, but she couldn't be sure of what she was seeing. There was a brightness to her mommy that hurt Izzy's eyes, like looking right at the sun. She blinked and tried to focus, but she kept seeing a spray of black dots and stars and her mommy went in and out of focus.

Izzy-bear, why did you call me?

Izzy blinked and tried to see her mommy's pretty blue eyes. "I didn't call you this time."

I heard you calling in your sleep.

Izzy tried to remember her dream, but it was just pictures and feelings and panic and it didn't seem to mean anything at all right now. "I don't know what I wanted."

She felt her mother's touch, a breeze on her forehead, brushing the hair away, a kiss that smelled of mist and rain and her mommy's favorite perfume. "I miss you, Mommy."

Your daddy's back now.

"What if he goes away again?"

Another touch, softer. *He won't, Izzy-bear.*

This time, when Izzy looked up, her mother was closer, and she was certain she saw dove-white wings. "I can't follow you, can I?"

For a split second, the mist was gone, and Izzy saw her mom. There were no wings, no white brightness, no mist. There was just a sad-eyed, blond-haired woman in a pink-flowered flannel nightgown, looking down at her little girl. *I'll always be inside you, Izzy. You don't have to disappear or follow me or reach for me. All you have to do is close your eyes and think of me and I'll be there. You think about the time we went to the circus and I was laughing so hard at the clowns that I fell off the bench. And when you smile at that, you'll find me.*

Tears streaked down Izzy's face, plopped on her hands. She stared, blinking, into her mommy's blue, blue eyes. "I love you, Mommy . . ."

And then suddenly her mommy was gone.

"Izzy!"

Her father's panicked voice sliced through Izzy's thoughts. She twisted around and saw him running toward her. "Daddy?"

He pulled her into his arms and held her tightly. "Izzy," he said her name in a weird way, as if he'd been running for miles. "Oh, Izzy . . . you scared me. I didn't know where you were. . . ."

"I di'n't go anywhere bad, Daddy."

He gave her a wobbly smile. "I know, honey."

He carried her back into the house and put her gently in bed. She scooted under the covers, but she wasn't ready to be by herself yet. She grabbed a book off the table by the bed. It was her treasured copy of *Cinderella,* the one that had been handed down from Grandma Myrtle, to Mommy, to Izzy. "Could you read me a story, Daddy?"

He climbed into bed beside her. Very gently, he opened the book to the first page. He read as he'd always read to her, with vigor and gusto and lots of funny voices.

Only Izzy didn't laugh. She couldn't; instead, she sat propped against the bright yellow Big Bird pillow, staring at the vibrant paintings on the page. When he finished the story, she was very quiet. "What happened to Cinderella's mommy?"

It was a minute before he said softly, "I think Cinderella's mommy went to Heaven."

"Oh."

"And you know what I think?"

She shook her head. "No."

"I think she and mommy are friends now, and they're looking down on us, making sure we're okay."

Izzy thought about that. It was sort of what she thought, too. "Annie says that when it rains, it's mommy and the angels crying."

He brushed the tangle of hair from her face. "Annie knows an awful lot."

She turned away from him, trying to hide the tears that burned her eyes. "I'm startin' to forget her, Daddy."

He slipped an arm around her and drew her close, gently stroking her moist cheek. "Mommy had the prettiest eyes in the world, and when she looked at you, it felt as if the rain had stopped and the sunlight was on your face. And she had a crooked front tooth—it sort of slanted sideways, and a tiny mole right next to her ear. She loved you, Izzy . . . she loved you more than her own life."

"She loved both of us, Daddy."

He didn't say anything. He just kissed her, right on the tip of her nose, and it reminded her of when she was a baby; he used to do that all the time. For the first time since her mommy died, Izzy wasn't scared. The scream that had been inside her for months shriveled up like an old raisin and rolled away. She knew, finally, that everything was going to be okay.

Her daddy loved her again.

She squeezed her eyes shut, really hard so she wouldn't cry like a baby. When she could breathe again, she slowly opened her eyes.

She couldn't believe what she saw. "Daddy?" she said softly.

"Yeah, Sunshine?"

She slowly lifted her left hand. Clear as day, she could see the little black glove that grew out of her sleeve. She bit down on her trembling lower lip, afraid it was a mistake. Slowly, she took off the glove, and there was her hand. "Do you see it, Daddy?"

He looked right at her hand—she was sure he saw it—but he didn't smile. Instead, he looked at her. "What *should* I see?"

She swallowed thickly. "I see my hand . . . and my arm. Do you see 'em?"

Her Daddy made a raggedy sound. "Yeah. I see your hand." Very slowly, like he was afraid she was going to stop him, he took the glove from her.

She giggled, wriggling her fingers. "I guess I'm stayin' here with you, Daddy."

"Yeah, Izzy-bear. I guess you are."

He made a sniffing sound. Izzy looked up and saw the strangest thing: her big, strong daddy was crying.

She loved both of us.

Much later, when Nick was in bed, with his arms wishboned behind his head, he finally allowed himself to think about what Izzy had said to him.

She loved both of us.

It was the sentence he'd been unable to believe in for so long, spoken with such certainty in the voice of a child.

The tears he'd hidden away for over a year came spilling down his cheeks. He had loved his wife, loved her from the time he first saw her, and somehow in the last few years he'd forgotten; he'd seen all that darkness and forgotten the light. She had loved him, too, with all her broken heart; she had loved him.

"I loved you, Kath," he whispered into the quiet solitude of his bedroom. "I loved you . . ."

The Mystic Rain Festival started on schedule, on the first Saturday in May, just as it had for each of the last hundred years. A low-slung gray sky hung over downtown. Rain fell in a stuttering curtain on the storefront awnings. Fresh green leaves floated in murky gutter water, swirling alongside the sidewalks.

Annie wore a slick yellow raincoat, with her Levi's tucked into high-topped black rubber boots, and a Seattle Mariners' baseball cap. Hank stood beside her, munching on a homemade scone he'd purchased at the Rotary Club booth.

The parade moved slowly down Main Street, splashing on the wet pavement. There were fire trucks, police cars, Boy Scout troops, and six little girls in pink tutus from Esmeralda's Dance Barn.

Annie was enchanted by the schmaltzy, small-town production. She knew from experience that the parade would clatter down the six blocks and then turn around and come back.

She had missed this. How was it that she hadn't known that? She'd gone to California and raised her daughter behind iron gates and in

CDAgARgC

air-conditioned rooms, in a city where hometown parades had celebrity marshals and corporate sponsors.

She didn't want to go back there.

It surprised her, the sudden certainty of her decision. It was the first time in her life she'd come to a conclusion without thinking of other people's feelings, and it felt good.

She didn't want to live in California anymore, and she didn't have to. After the divorce, when Natalie went away to college, Annie could return to Mystic, maybe even open that bookstore. . . .

Dreams. They were such precious commodities, and she'd given so many of hers away without a fight. Never again.

She turned to her dad. "Let me ask you something, Dad. Do you think this town could use a bookstore?"

He smiled. "Hell, yes. We've needed one for years. Your mom used to dream of opening one."

Annie shivered. For a strange, disorienting second, she felt as if her mom were beside her. "Really? I was thinking the same thing."

He turned to her, looked at her long and hard. "You're hurting right now, Annie, and you're running, but don't forget where your real life is. You're never going to live in Mystic again, and besides, you're not a businessperson. You're a housewife." He slipped an arm around her, drawing her close.

His lack of faith stung. For the first time, she wondered how long her father had been spoon-feeding her a diet of self-doubt. When had it begun? When she was a child? The first time he told her not to worry her pretty head about something? Or all the times he'd told her that Blake would take care of her?

If she were a different kind of woman, Annie might feel angry right now, but as it was, all she felt was the vague residue of sadness. Her father was from another generation, and he'd done the best he could with his only child. If his wife had lived, everything would have been different. . . .

But she hadn't, and with her death, Hank had been thrown into a role he couldn't handle. All he knew of womanhood came from his own mother, a tired, washed-out woman who died at forty-seven, driven to an early grave by hard work. Like his father, Hank had grown up in Mystic, and never seen much of the world beyond. He'd thought the best he could do for Annie was to get her educated, so that she could find a husband who could give her a better life than the one to which she'd been raised.

Unfortunately, Annie had followed his lead. She'd gone all the way to Stanford—where the world had been open to her if only she'd known where to look—and she'd kept her gaze on the straight and narrow. She'd asked too little of herself . . . and gotten exactly what she'd sought. It was funny how that worked in life.

It wasn't her father's fault, any more than it was Blake's or Annie's fault. It simply was. She was lucky to have seen the truth at all, she supposed. If not for Blake, she would have walked down the road of the ordinary for the whole of her life, a middle-aged woman, and then at last an old woman, wearing the blinders that had been passed down from generation to generation.

She slipped her hand into her dad's and gave him a gentle squeeze. The last entry in the parade, the Bits and Spurs 4-H club, clattered past on horseback, and as it rounded the corner and disappeared, everyone clapped and cheered. When the applause died down, the crowd began to disperse, slipping off the sidewalk and onto the street.

Annie and Hank strolled arm in arm down the sidewalk, past the artisans' booths and hot-dog stands, past the Victorian house with a FOR RENT sign in the window.

Hank stopped at the Lutheran church stand and bought two mocha lattes, handing one to Annie. The pungent aroma of the coffee swirled between them, and the heat of it soothed her scratchy throat. Neither of them noticed the gentle patter of the rain; it had never bothered Annie. It was funny how she'd forgotten that. In California, she used to race for an umbrella at the first hint of precipitation. Here, the only people who used umbrellas were tourists.

"So, Natalie gets home in six weeks."

Annie took a sip of coffee, then nodded. "June fifteenth. I can't wait."

"What will you say to Blake when you see him?"

The question surprised Annie. It wasn't something she wanted to think about, and it was unlike her father to ask. She shrugged. "I don't know. For weeks, all I wanted was to see him again, to make him remember what we had together, but now I can't seem to grab hold of what we had."

"Is it because of him?"

She started to ask what he meant, but when she looked up, she saw Nick. He was standing across the street, with Izzy on his shoulders. They were both eating ice cream cones. He turned, and across the crowded street, their eyes met and held for a heartbeat. He flashed her a smile, waved, then moved on. She tried to frame an answer for her dad, but she honestly didn't know how Nick fit into the picture. "Who knows what causes anything? All I know is that I'm not the same woman I was before."

"You be careful, Annie."

She glanced across the street again, but Nick was gone. She felt a pang of disappointment. "You know what, Dad? I'm tired of being careful."

"When you play with fire, you get burned."

She laughed. "More bumper stickers, Dad?"

He laughed with her. "How do you think people come up with bumper stickers? Some things are just plain true."

CHAPTER 18

On Monday Annie, Nick, and Izzy drove to Sol Duc Hot Springs and hiked deep into the Olympic National Forest. Afterward, they swam in the lodge's huge swimming pool and relaxed in the steaming, sulphuric hot springs. When dusk started to fall, they piled back into the car and headed home.

By the time they unpacked the car and got everything put away, it was almost midnight. Nick offered Annie his room, and she took him up on the offer. She called her dad, who was waiting up for her again, and told him that she'd be home first thing in the morning.

Is that wise, Annie Virginia? he asked in a quiet voice.

She told him not to worry, and hung up the phone. Afterward, she wasn't so sure she'd made a smart decision, but the truth was that she didn't feel well. She wanted to collapse in a convenient bed and sleep for ten hours. Her back hurt, her head hurt, and she'd felt nauseous for most of the drive home. She was definitely not cut out for hiking.

She was careful to avoid Nick as she hurried upstairs, brushed her teeth, and fell into a deep sleep.

The next morning, she woke up feeling even worse. A headache pounded behind her eyes, and she had to lie very still in bed, concentrating on each breath, or she was certain she was going to throw up.

She counted slowly to ten, then angled up to her elbows. Sunlight slanted through her bedroom window. The glare hurt her eyes and intensified her headache. A beautiful morning in May, and she couldn't enjoy it.

Swallowing thickly, she threw back the comforter and stumbled into the small adjoining bathroom. She didn't bother turning on the light—she could see the shadowy pockets under her eyes perfectly well. She moved like a hundred-year-old woman, taking forever to brush her teeth and wash her face. When she was finished, she felt even worse.

She went back to bed and snuggled under the covers. A chill racked her body, and she closed her eyes.

Some time later—an hour? a minute?—a knock sounded at her door. Annie forced herself to sit up. "Come in."

Izzy poked her head through the open door. "Annie? I'm hungry."

Annie manufactured a wan smile. "Hi, honey. Come on in—but don't get too close, I think I have the flu."

Izzy slipped into the room, closing the door behind her. "I was waitin' for you to show up. I thought maybe you'd left us . . . but then Daddy tole me you'd spent the night."

Annie's heart went out to the girl, whose brown eyes looked so big and worried. "I wouldn't do that, Izzy. I wouldn't disappear without saying good-bye."

"Grown-ups do that sometimes."

"Oh, Izzy . . ." Annie shifted her position, trying to ignore a sudden wave of dizziness. "I know they do." She started to say something else, preferably something blindingly insightful, when she sneezed hard. She barely had time to get her hand in front of her mouth before she sneezed again. She sagged in bed, trying to remember when she'd felt this rotten.

Izzy's eyes widened. "Are you sick?"

Annie gave her a weak smile of understanding. "Not *really* sick," she answered quietly. "It's just a cold. I bet you get them all the time."

Izzy visibly relaxed. "Yeah. That's when green snot comes out of your nose."

"A lovely image, to be sure. I think I'm going to go to sleep for a while, but we'll talk later. Okay?"

Izzy nodded slowly. "Okay. See yah."

Annie smiled weakly. "See you, pumpkin." When Izzy was gone, she leaned toward the bedside table and picked up the phone. After asking for the number from directory assistance, she called Dr. Burton's office.

The receptionist answered on the first ring. "Mystic Family Clinic. This is Madge, how can I help you?"

"Hi, Madge. This is Annie Colwater. I'd like to make an appointment to see Dr. Burton."

"Is it an emergency, sweetie?"

Only if green snot constituted an emergency. "No."

"Well, the doctor's out of town right now, on vacation at Orcas Island. He was afraid you might call. He wanted me to refer you to Dr. Hawkins in Port Angeles." Her voice lowered to a stage whisper. "He's a *psychiatrist.*"

Even in her weakened state, Annie smiled. "Oh, that's not necessary."

"Oh, good. Now, you're still booked for June first. Is that appointment okay?"

Annie had forgotten all about it. The depression she'd felt in March had faded into a dull, sepia-toned memory. She probably didn't need the appointment, but it would reassure Doc Burton. He'd be proud of how well she'd recovered. "Yeah, that appointment's fine. Thanks, Madge."

"Okay. Ten-thirty in the morning. Don't forget."

Before she even hung up the phone, Annie had closed her eyes.

Annie dreamed she was in a cool, dark place. She could hear the cascading fall of water and the buzzing drone of a dragonfly. There was someone waiting for her in the forest's darkness. She could hear the even cant of his breathing in the shadows. She wanted to reach for him, but she was afraid. Where she was felt familiar, safe, and he was waiting for her in a strange world where she didn't know the rules. She was afraid that if she followed, she'd lose her way.

"Annie?"

She woke up suddenly and found Nick sitting on the end of her bed. Trying to smile, she struggled to sit up half way. "Hi."

"Izzy tells me you're sick." He leaned toward her, touched her forehead. "You're warm."

"I am?"

He slid closer to her and produced a thermometer. "Open up."

Like an obedient child, she opened her mouth. The slick, cool thermometer slid under her tongue and settled in place. She closed her lips, but she couldn't take her eyes away from Nick.

"I've brought you some orange juice and a couple of scrambled eggs. Oh, and Tylenol and a pitcher of ice water."

Annie watched in surprise as he went into the bathroom. Then he came back to her, carefully folding a wet cloth in thirds as he walked. He sat back on the chair beside the bed and placed the cool rag on her forehead. Then he handed her two Tylenols. "Here."

She stared down at the two little pills in his hand.

He frowned. "Annie? You're crying."

She blinked hard. *Damn.* "Am I? Don't worry about me. It's probably allergies. Or menopause. I've been feeling hormonal all week. And I think I'm gearing up for a howler of a—" She bit back the word *period.* This wasn't her husband she was talking to, and her periods weren't exactly an acceptable topic for conversation. The realization isolated her. With that one tiny word she couldn't say, she understood how adrift she was, how unconnected. It was something she'd always taken for granted in her marriage, the way you could say anything at any time, reveal any secret thing about yourself. There was no one now with whom she could be so free.

"What is it, Annie?"

The gentleness in his voice only made her cry harder, and though it was humiliating to sit here crying for no reason, she couldn't seem to stop herself.

"Annie?"

She couldn't meet his eyes. "You'll think I'm an idiot."

He laughed, a quiet, tender sound. "You're worried about what the town drunk thinks?"

She sniffed hard. "Don't talk about yourself that way."

"Is that how the rich people in California do it—am I just supposed to pretend you're not crying? Now, tell me what's the matter."

Annie closed her eyes. It seemed to take forever to find her voice. "No one has ever given me an aspirin before—I mean, without me asking for it." God, it sounded as pathetic as she'd thought it would. She felt ashamed and horribly exposed. She tried to tack an explanation on, so it sounded better. "I've been a wife and mother for so long. I've always been the one who took care of people when they were sick."

"But no one took care of you." He said it as a simple statement, and though she wanted to reject it as being silly, she couldn't.

It was all there, in that simple, simple sentence, everything that had been wrong with her marriage. She'd done everything to make Blake's life safe and perfect; she'd loved him and cared for him and protected him. All those years she'd made excuses for his selfishness: he was tired, or busy, or distracted by business. They were just layers of pretty wrapping paper on a dark and ugly truth.

No one took care of you.

Suddenly she was crying for all of it, every missed moment, every dream she'd ever had. The marriage she'd had wasn't good enough. She'd never really, truly been loved . . . not the way she deserved to be loved.

With a deep, ragged sigh, she wiped her eyes and smiled up at Nick. "I'm sorry for being such a baby."

She glanced at the things he'd placed on her nightstand. Orange juice, water, cold tablets, Tylenol, a plate of scrambled eggs, and a piece of cinnamon toast. And it made her want to cry all over again. She didn't know what to say to him, this man who'd accidentally opened a door on her old life and shown her the truth.

"You should drink something."

She wiped her runny nose and gave him a crooked grin. "Well, you should know."

He looked stunned for a second, then he burst out laughing.

The cold hung on for two days, and when it was over, Annie was left feeling tired and weak. Her stomach stayed queasy afterward, but she refused to pay any attention to it.

On Friday, she and Nick and Izzy drove to Kalaloch and spent the day beachcombing. Izzy squealed with delight every time she found a sand dollar or a crab. They raced down the beach together, all three of them, turning over rocks and sticks in their search for hidden treasures, and when the sun was high in the sky, they had a picnic lunch in a secret cave. Afterward, they waded and splashed in the icy cold water until their cheeks and hands and feet turned a stinging red. Finally, when the sun began its slow descent, they returned to the car and headed home.

Annie sat in the passenger seat of her Mustang, with a plastic bucket of shells and rocks in her lap.

"Daddy, can we stop and get ice cream, Daddy?"

Nick answered easily, laughing. "Sure, Izzy-bear."

Annie glanced at him, mesmerized. In the past few weeks, he'd become a new man entirely. He smiled all the time, and laughed easily, and spent hours playing with his little girl. Sometimes, like now, when the sunlight hit his profile and cast him in golden light, he was so handsome, he took Annie's breath away.

But there was more to Nick; his vulnerability and his strength moved her, and the tenderness of his care had almost undone her. She'd never known anyone who loved as deeply, as completely as Nick. That was why life had been able to pummel him so brutally. Nothing was easier to shatter than the fragile shield of an idealist.

She was still watching him hours later, after she'd put away the last dinner dish and picked up the last of Izzy's crayons. He was standing down at the lake again, his body a shadow within shadows, but Annie was well aware of the subtle differences of light and dark, the pale outline of his hair, the broad shelf of his shoulders, the moonlight that glimmered every now and then off the metal rivets on his jeans.

She threw the damp dishrag on the kitchen counter and headed outside. She wanted to be with him, and though the realization frightened her, it also set her heart racing with anticipation. When she was with Nick, she was a different woman. Some of his glitter fell onto her and made her feel beautiful and sparkly and more alive.

There were stars everywhere. Frogs and crickets sang in a staccato chorus that died at her approach. The grass was cold and wet on her bare feet.

Nick stood motionless, his shoulders rounded, his head dropped forward.

"Hi, Nick," she said softly.

He spun around, and she saw the pain in his eyes.

"Hi, Annie." His voice was low, and as rough as old bricks. A cool night breeze caressed her face and slid between the buttons of her cotton shirt, like a man's cold fingers, inching tenderly along her flesh. She had come to know him so well in the past weeks that his longings were obvious to her. "You want a drink."

He laughed, but it was a sharp, bitter sound, not his laugh at all. He reached out and held her hand, squeezing hard.

She knew from experience that he needed the sound of her voice now. It didn't matter what she said, anything would do; he simply needed an anchor to hold him steady. "Remember the senior party, when Kath disappeared for a half hour or so?" she said quietly. "We were at Lake Crescent. You and I sat by the lake, right in front of the lodge, and talked and talked. You said you wanted to be a cop."

"You said you wanted to be a writer."

She was surprised that he remembered, and though she didn't want to, she found herself remembering the girl who'd wanted to be a writer. The old dream was heavy now. "That was before I'd learned . . ." Her voice faded into the breeze and fell silent.

He turned, gazed down at her. "Learned what?"

She shrugged, unable suddenly to meet his gaze. "I don't know. How life slips away from you while you're standing in a grocery line, waiting to pay for a quart of milk . . . how time passes and takes everything in its path—youth, hopes, dreams. Dreams—it takes those most of all."

She felt his gaze on her again, and she was afraid to meet it, afraid of what she'd see in his eyes.

"Sometimes I don't even recognize you," he said, gently tilting her chin up. "You say things like that and I don't know the woman who is speaking at all."

She released a laugh that fluttered like a moth into the darkness. "You're not alone."

"What happened to you, Annie?"

The question was startling in its intimacy. The night fell silent, awaiting her answer, so quiet that she could hear her own rapid intake of breath. She pushed the poisonous words out in a rush. "My husband is in love with another woman. He wants a divorce."

"Annie—"

"I'm fine, really." She tried to think of something to say that would make them both laugh, but when she looked in his eyes, she saw a terrible, harrowing compassion, and it was her undoing. The strength she'd been gathering and hoarding for the past weeks fell away from her. A single tear streaked down her cheek. "How does it happen? I loved Blake with all my heart and soul and it wasn't enough. . . ."

He sighed, and the sadness of the sound bound them together. She watched as he tried to find the words to answer her, saw his frustration when he came up empty.

"The worst thing is you don't see it coming," she said. "You don't even suspect that Monday will be the last time you'll ever come up behind him and kiss the back of his neck . . . or the last time you'll sit watching television and rub the soft skin just below his ankle. And you think you'd remember something like the last time you made love, but you can't. It's gone."

She gazed up at him, surprised at how easily the words had come to her. In the weeks since Blake's confession, she'd trapped the pain inside her heart and kept it there, fanning the hot coal with dreams and nightmares and memories. But now, all at once, the fire of it was gone. In its place was a dull, thudding ache.

She still had the hurt; probably that would never completely heal. Like a broken bone that was badly reset, the wound would always be a place of weakness within her. When the cold weather hit, or she remembered a special time, she would recall the love she had had for Blake, and she would ache. But the raging fire of it had burned down to a cold, gray ember.

Nick didn't know when it happened exactly, or who moved first. All he knew was that he needed Annie. He reached for her. His hand slipped underneath her flannel collar and curled around the back of her neck, anchoring her in place. Slowly, watching her, he bent down and kissed her. It was gentle at first, a soft mingling of lips and breath. But then she moved toward him, settled into his embrace. He felt her hands, so small and pliant, moving across his back in a soothing, circular motion.

He deepened the kiss. His tongue explored her mouth, tasting, caressing. He kissed her until he was light-headed with longing, and then slowly he drew back.

She stared up at him. He saw sadness in her eyes, but something else, perhaps the same quiet wonder he had felt. "I'm sorry," he said softly, even though it wasn't true. "I had no right—"

"Don't be," she whispered. "Please . . . don't be sorry. I wanted you to kiss me. I . . . I've wanted it for a long time, I think."

She opened the door to intimacy and he couldn't walk away. He didn't care if he was being stupid or careless or asking for trouble. He only knew that he wanted her, heart, body, and soul. He curled a hand around her neck and urged her closer, so close he could feel her rapid breathing against his mouth. "I want you, Annie Bourne. It feels like I've wanted you all my life."

A tear slipped down her cheek, and in that glittering bead of moisture, he saw reflections of all the distance that separated them. She still looked amazingly like the sixteen-year-old girl he'd first fallen in love with, but like him, the life she'd led and the choices she'd made lay collected in the tiny network of lines around her beautiful face.

"I know," was all she said in answer, but in the two simple, sadly softened words, he heard the truth: that sometimes, the wanting wasn't enough.

He reached down and took hold of her hand, lifting it. In the glittering silver moonlight, the diamond ring seemed to be made of cold fire. He stared at the ring a long time, saying nothing. Then he turned from her. "Good night, Annie," he said softly, walking away from her before he made a fool of himself.

Back in his room, Nick peeled out of his clothes and crawled into his unmade bed. He was surprised to realize that he was shaking. And for once, it wasn't an absence of alcohol that was playing hell with his body. It was a woman.

Don't think about her . . . think about AA and their advice. No new relationships when you're getting sober. . . .

Thinking about the Twelve Steps didn't help. He closed his eyes and pictured Annie. She was probably to town by now. He wondered what song was playing on the Mustang's radio, what she was thinking.

It had taken every bit of strength and honor he possessed to walk away after that kiss. He'd wanted to pull her into his arms and ravish her on the spot. Lose himself and his past in the sweet darkness of her body. But it wasn't right, and he didn't dare . . . for so many reasons. And so here he lay, alone.

It occurred to Annie that if she were smart, she would leave right then. But all she could think about was Nick, and the way he'd kissed her. The way he'd touched and held her had swept her away. And when it was over, when he'd said, *I want you, Annie Bourne,* she'd known that she was lost.

She glanced up at his bedroom. A shadow passed in front of the glass, then disappeared. He thought she'd gone home—and she knew that she should.

Instead, she glanced down at the wedding ring on her left hand. The diamond glittered with color in the lamp's glow. The ring she'd worn for years. Blake had placed it on her hand beneath a shower of romantic words on their tenth anniversary.

Gently, she pulled the ring from her finger. "Good-bye, Blake." It hurt to say the words, even to think them, but there was a surprising freedom in it, too. She felt unfettered, on her own for perhaps the first time in her life. There was no one to guide her choices or determine her path. No one but her.

Before she could talk herself out of it, she hurried back into the house and up the stairs. Outside Nick's door, she paused. In the time it took to draw a breath, she lost her nerve. All the reasons for being here scurried away, cowards leaving a sinking ship. Suddenly she didn't feel sexy; she felt vulnerable and alone. A middle-aged woman begging for sex from an old friend . . .

She was just about to turn away when she heard the music. Beyond the door, a radio was playing, a scratchy old rendition of Nat King Cole's "Unforgettable."

It soothed her ragged nerves, that song, and even more the fact that he was listening to it. Nick wasn't some inexperienced teenager; he was a man, her age, and as ravaged by life and love as she was. He would understand why she was here. He would ask nothing of her except the simple, uncomplicated act of sharing.

She rapped sharply on the door.

There was a pause. The music snapped off. "Come on in, Izzy."

Annie cleared her throat. "It's me . . . Annie."

Another pause, a scuffling sound. "Come in."

She pushed on the door; it opened with a slow, creaking noise.

Nick was in bed.

She swallowed hard and moved toward him. Anxiety was a rattling jangle inside her; she felt as gawky and awkward as a teenager. She thought about the weight she'd gained in the past weeks, and wondered if he'd find her attractive. Blake had always made such cutting remarks when Annie gained a pound. . . .

He looked at her and the intensity of his gaze caused a heat to flutter through her. She shivered.

"Are you sure?" He asked it simply, the only question that mattered.

And she was. Utterly, absolutely, positively sure. She felt herself moving toward him, reaching out. Later, she would never be able to remember who had touched first, or how they had come to be naked together on that massive, four-postered bed . . . but she would never forget the soft, singsongy way he whispered her name while he kissed her . . . or the way his arms wrapped around her body, holding her so close that sometimes she couldn't breathe . . . or the shattering intensity of their lovemaking. All she could remember was that at the jagged peak of her pleasure, it was *his* name she cried out. Not Blake's.

CHAPTER 19

Beside the bed, an oil lamp flickered gently; a ribbon of black smoke curled lazily up from the glass mouth.

Annie lay cuddled alongside Nick, her naked leg thrown across his thigh. They had been together for hours now, talking softly and laughing, and making love. About midnight, she'd reluctantly called her father and told him that she wouldn't be home tonight—that Izzy was fighting a cold and needed Annie; but her father hadn't been fooled. He'd listened to her rambling excuse, then asked the now familiar question: "Are you sure that's wise, Annie Virginia?"

She'd brushed him off with a schoolgirl's giggle and told him not to worry. She didn't want to think about whether this was wise. For the first time in her life, she felt wicked and wild, and wonderfully alive. She'd been a good girl for so damned long. . . .

So much had changed for her tonight. The simple act of removing her wedding ring had transformed her. She'd become younger, braver, more adventurous. She had never known that sex could be so . . . fun. Tonight, in the hours she'd spent in Nick's arms, she'd discovered a whole new woman.

When it was over—the first time—she'd expected to feel guilty and ashamed. She'd tensed herself for it, quickly devising rationalizations for her wanton behavior; but all it had taken was a word from Nick, a smile, a kiss, and all her explanations had taken flight.

Don't pull away, he'd said, and that was all it took.

Now, they were tangled in the sheets together. About an hour ago, they'd gone scouting in the kitchen and come up with a plate of cheese and crackers and fruit, which they'd taken back into bed with them. Neither of them wanted to leave the bed and reenter the world that lurked outside this room.

Nick slid an arm around Annie and drew her close. For the first time, there was sadness in his blue eyes. "June fifteenth, huh?"

Annie caught her breath. Their gazes locked, and she felt her smile weaken.

In less than a month, Annie would be going home—such as it was. She would be leaving Nick and Izzy and Mystic, and returning to the brown world of her real life . . . or whatever was left of it.

He touched her face with a tenderness that made her heart ache. "I shouldn't have said that."

"We have what we have, Nicky. Let's not ruin it by looking ahead. The future isn't something I like to think about."

His hand slid down her bare arm and settled possessively on her left hand. She knew that he was thinking about the ring she no longer wore—and about the tiny white tan line that remained to mark its place. When he finally looked at her, he was smiling again. "I'll take whatever you have to give, and . . ."

"And what?"

It took him a long time to answer, so long that she thought he'd changed his mind. Then, in a quiet voice, he said, "And hope it's enough."

Every day brought them closer together. In the last week of May, summer threw its multicolored net across the rain forest. Entire days passed without a drop of rain. Temperatures hovered around the low seventies. It was an unseasonal heat wave, and everyone in Mystic treasured the newfound warmth. Kids dug out last year's cutoffs and pulled their bicycles out of storage. Birds clustered on telephone wires and swooped down, chattering and cawing, in search of plump, juicy worms.

Annie spent less and less time at her father's house, and more and more in Nick's bed. She knew she was playing with fire, but she couldn't help herself. She was like a teenager again, consumed by her

first lover. Every time she looked at Nick—which was about every fifteen seconds—she remembered their lovemaking. She couldn't believe
how uninhibited she'd become.

During the day, they were careful not to touch each other, but the
forced abstinence only increased their desire. All day, Annie waited for
the night to begin, so that she could creep into his bed again.

Today they'd had a wonderful time at Lake Crescent. They'd played
volleyball on the beach, and rented paddleboats, and on the long ride
home, they had sung along with the radio. At home, Annie made a big
pot of spaghetti, and after dinner, they sat around the big kitchen table
and worked on Izzy's reading skills.

Later, when they went upstairs, they all climbed into Izzy's bed for
story time.

Annie refused to think about how *right* all of this felt, how much
she was beginning to belong here. She reached behind Izzy's head and
touched Nick's shoulder, squeezing so hard for a moment that he
looked up at her. At first he smiled, then slowly, that smile fell, and she
knew he was seeing it in her eyes, the sudden fear, the desire that was
going to hurt them all.

She turned away, focused instead on the open book.

Nick had read only the first page when the sound of a ringing telephone interrupted them. "I'd better go answer that," he said.

"We'll wait for you, Daddy," Izzy said, snuggling up to Annie.

Nick pressed the book into Izzy's hands and hurried out of the
room. He came back a few minutes later, looking solemn.

Annie felt a prickling of fear. She sat up straighter, leaning forward.
"Nick?"

He eased back into the bed, on the other side of Izzy. "That was
your teacher, Izzy-bear. She said they're having a class party on Friday—
and all the kids want you to come."

Izzy looked scared. "Oh."

Nick smiled at her, a soft, gentle smile that seemed to reach right
into Annie's heart. "She said something about cupcakes."

Izzy frowned. "I *do* like cupcakes."

"I know you do, Sunshine." He pulled her against him with one strong arm. "There's nothing wrong with being scared, Izzy. It happens to all of us. What's wrong is if we don't try things because we're afraid. We can't hide away from the things that scare us."

Annie heard so much in his voice, all the remnants of the lessons he'd learned the hard way. She felt a warm rush of pride for him, and she wondered again how she was going to leave this man, how she was going to return to her cold, sterile life, where she would end up searching in mirrors once again for evidence of her own existence.

Izzy sighed. "I guess a party would be okay. Will you'n Annie take me?"

"Of course we will."

"Okay." She looked up, gave Nick a tentative smile. "Daddy, will you read me another story, Daddy?"

He grinned. Reaching down to the floor beside the bed, he produced another book. "I thought you might ask that."

He read like an actor, using deep, bass monster voices and high-pitched little-boy roars. Izzy sat perfectly still, her adoring eyes focused on her daddy's face. When he smiled, she smiled; when he frowned, she frowned.

As he turned a page, he glanced at Annie. Over the child's dark head, their gazes locked. There was nothing sexual in his eyes at all; there was just the simple pleasure of a man reading his daughter a bedtime story. The way he looked, as if this moment were the culmination of his every hope and dream, tore a ragged bite from Annie's heart and left her with the strangest urge to cry.

After story time was over, Nick went back to his room and waited. Twice, he poked his head out and looked down the hallway. Twice it was empty, save for the feeble glow of a few poorly placed wall lights.

He paced the tiny room, bumping his head on the slanted roof almost every time he turned to the right.

Then he heard a knock.

He surged to the door and yanked it open. Annie stood in the doorway, wearing an oversized T-shirt and a pair of navy-blue kneesocks.

They barely made it to the bed. Kissing, groping, laughing, they fell onto the pile of wrinkled sheets. The tired old mattress creaked and groaned beneath them.

Nick had never wanted a woman so badly in his life, and Annie seemed to share his urgency. He held her, stroked and fondled and caressed her. She rolled with him, kissing him with a greediness that left him breathless, pulling his tongue deep into her mouth. They did anything and everything, made love and slept and made love again.

When it was over, Nick lay exhausted on his bed, one arm flung out against the wall, the other curled protectively around Annie's naked hip. She lay tucked against him, her bare leg thrown casually over his, her nipple pressed against his rib cage.

He could feel the aftermath of their lovemaking in the fine sheen of sweat that clung to her skin, smell it in the sweetness of the air. Her head was resting on the ball of his shoulder, her breath caressed his skin.

He was afraid suddenly that she would pull away now, draw out of his arms and scurry back to her father's house, and that he'd be left with nothing but her lingering scent and the cold chill of her absence along his side. "Talk to me, Annie," he said softly, stroking the velvety skin in the small of her back.

"That's always dangerous," she said with a laugh. "Most people who know me want me to shut up."

"I'm not Blake."

"Sorry." She snuggled closer to him. One pale finger coiled in his chest hair, then absently caressed his skin. "You . . . bring out something in me. Something I wouldn't have believed was there."

"Oh yeah? What is it?"

She rolled half on top of him, her crotch settled intimately against his thigh. Her beautiful breasts swung enticingly in front of his face, and it was damned hard to keep his concentration on her words. "I used to be . . . organized. Efficient. I fed everyone and dressed everyone and went shopping and made lists and kept appointments. Blake and I had sex, if we were lucky, on Friday nights at eleven forty-five, between Jay Leno's first and second guests. It was always . . . nice sex, comfortable. It felt good and I had orgasms. But it wasn't like it is with you. I never felt as if I were going to leap out of my skin." She laughed, that broad, infectious laugh that seemed to come from someplace deep inside her. Kathy had never made him feel this way, as if the whole world was open to him and all he had to do was reach for his dreams.

Dreams. He closed his eyes. They came to him so often now, the dreams he'd long ago put aside. He remembered again how important a family had always been to him, how he'd imagined his life would chug along on a bright and easy road, crowded with laughing children all around him.

If he'd chosen Annie, all those years ago, maybe everything would have been different. . . .

"How come you and Kathy never had more children?" Annie asked suddenly.

Her question disconcerted Nick for a second, made him wonder if she could read his mind. "I always wanted to. Hell, I wanted six kids, but after Izzy, it was obvious that Kathy couldn't handle any more. When Izzy was about two, I had a vasectomy." He glanced down at her, cuddled so close to him. "How about you? You're such a wonderful mother."

It was a long time before she answered. "Adrian would have been fourteen this year. He was my son."

"Annie . . ."

She didn't look at him. "He came prematurely and only lived for four days. After that, we tried everything, but I couldn't get pregnant again. Usually he's just a little smile I get, or a tear that stings my eyes, but sometimes . . . it's harder. I always wanted more children."

He didn't want to say he was sorry; he knew firsthand how plastic the words could sound, a Band-Aid on an arterial wound. Instead, he pulled her into his arms and held her as close as he could, so close he could feel her heartbeat against his skin.

He knew he was losing himself in the moment, in Annie, but right now he didn't care. It was too late to be safe, too late to keep from loving her.

Jefferson R. Smithwood Elementary School sat on a grassy hill surrounded by hundred-year-old fir trees. A long cement walkway started at the double black doors and slid down to the parking lot, where cars were lined along a tall chain-link fence.

Nick stood close to the curb, with Izzy beside him. Annie stood on Izzy's other side.

His little girl was scared, and it was up to him to make her feel confident; but he had no idea how to do that. Over Izzy's dark head, he gave Annie a helpless look.

You can do it, she mouthed with a smile.

Swallowing hard, he bent to his knees and looked at Izzy. She tried to smile, but it was a quick, jerking little tilt of the mouth that didn't reach her eyes. He reached out and plucked up the satiny yellow ribbon that hung at the bottom of her braid.

Her lower lip quivered. "They'll make fun o' me."

"Then I'll beat the sh—"

Annie squeezed his shoulder and Nick bit back the words. "They won't make fun of you," he said instead.

"I'm . . . different."

He shook his head. "No. You've had some . . . sadness. And sometimes that makes a person go a little . . . crazy. But you're going to be okay this time. I promise."

"Will you be here to pick me up after the party?"

"Yep."

"*Right* after?"

"Right after."

"Okay," she said at last.

He smiled. "That's my girl."

Slowly, knees popping, he got back to his feet. He glanced at Annie, who was grinning at him, although her eyes were suspiciously moist.

Together, the three of them started up the cement sidewalk toward the school.

"Lions and tigers and bears, oh my!" Annie said suddenly.

Nick almost burst out laughing. It was a ridiculous thing to do, but at that moment it felt exactly right. He joined in. "Lions and tigers and bears, oh, my!"

At first, Izzy's voice was hesitant, but with each chorus it gained strength, until all three of them were singing at the top of their lungs as they strode up the sidewalk, up the steps, and right to the front door.

Nick pushed through the double black doors, and the three of them entered the quiet hallways of the elementary school. To the left there was a long Formica table, piled high with all the jackets and lunch boxes and sweaters that the children left behind.

Izzy stopped. "I wanna go in by myself," she said quietly. "That way they won't think I'm a baby." She gave Nick and Annie one last, frightened look, then started down the hallway.

Nick fought the urge to run after her.

Annie slipped her hand in his. Nick sighed, watching his little girl walk down the hallway. He saw the hesitation in each of her footsteps and knew how hard she was trying to be brave. He knew how that felt, going forward when all you wanted to do was crawl into a warm darkness and hide. Finally, he had to look away. He'd never known it would be so damned hard to watch your child face fear.

"She'll be fine," Annie said. "Trust me."

He looked at her, and at the soft certainty in her gaze, something in his chest felt swollen and tender. "I do, Annie," he said softly. "I do."

At the end of the hall, a door opened. A feminine voice said, "Izzy! We've missed you." A bubble of applause floated through the open door. Izzy glanced back, gave Nick and Izzy a huge grin, then raced into the classroom.

CHAPTER 20

"Well, that certainly took my mind off Izzy," Nick said, panting, when finally he could speak. He rolled off of Annie but kept an arm around her. Gathering her against him, he settled comfortably with his back against the wall and propped his sweaty cheek in his hand, gazing down at her.

She looked incredibly beautiful, with the sunlight from the half-open window on her face and her hair all spiky in a dozen different directions. Her breathing was shallow, and it reminded him with every tiny, wheezing sound that, for now at least, she was his. Beneath the flimsy cotton blanket, his hand found her breast and held it.

He wanted to lie with her for hours, talking about nothing and everything, sharing more than just their bodies. It was a dangerous desire, he knew, wanting more from Annie than the body she shared so willingly. No matter how hard he tried to forget it, he remembered that she was leaving June fifteenth—now less than three weeks away. She was going back to her real life.

He held her tightly, knowing he should just keep his mouth shut. But he couldn't. "What was your marriage like?"

"From whose perspective? I thought it was nineteen great years with the only man I ever loved. Then one day he pulled our car into the driveway and said, 'I love another woman; please don't make me say it again.'" She released a laugh that was short and bitter. "Like I wanted to hear it twice."

"Are you still in love with him?"

"*In* love? How would that be possible?" She sighed, and he felt the gentle swell and fall of her chest. "But love . . . ah, now that's a harder thing. He is . . . was my best friend, my lover, my *family* for almost twenty years. How do you stop loving your family?"

"What . . . what if he wanted you back?"

"Blake's not that kind of man. It would mean admitting that he'd been wrong in the first place. In all our years together, I've never once heard him say he was sorry. To anyone."

He heard sorrow in the quietly spoken words.

She smiled weakly and looked away from him, staring beyond his shoulder to a spot on the wall.

He gathered her into his arms, turning her so that he could lose himself in the green of her eyes. "I remember a story you wrote in Senior English. It was about a dog who helped a lost boy find his home. I always thought you'd be a famous writer."

"That was 'Finding Joey.' I can't believe you remembered it."

"It was a good story."

She was silent for a long time, and when finally she spoke, her voice was thick. "I should have trusted myself, but Blake . . . he thought writing was a silly little hobby, and so I put it away. It's not his fault, it's mine. I gave in too easily. After that I tried everything—calligraphy, judo, painting, sculpting, floral arranging, interior design." She snorted derisively. "No wonder Blake made fun of me. I was a poster child for a missing soul."

"I can't imagine that."

"It's true. I wrapped up my two unfinished novels in pretty pink boxes and tucked them under my lingerie chest. I let Blake's acid comments about 'Mom's current hobby' derail me. After a few years, I forgot I'd even had a dream in the first place. I became Mrs. Blake Colwater, and without him, I felt like nobody. Until now. You and Izzy gave me my self back."

He touched her face. "No, Annie. You took it back yourself. Hell, you *fought* for it."

She stared at him. "I lost myself once, Nick. I'm terrified of doing it again."

There was no point in asking what she meant. He knew. Somehow, she'd seen the secret he was trying so hard to keep from her. He'd fallen in love with her, and they didn't have much time together; that was the truth he'd understood at the outset, the truth that came from sleeping with a married woman, even if she were headed for divorce. She still had Natalie, and a whole life that didn't include Nick. "Okay, Annie," he said quietly. "Okay for now."

But it wasn't okay. He knew it, and now she was beginning to know it as well.

Annie stood on the porch of her father's house, staring out at the sinuous silver ribbon of the salmon stream. Bright blue harebells danced nimbly through the high grass at the river's edge. Somewhere, a woodpecker was drilling through a tree trunk; the ra-ta-ta-tat echoed through the forest.

She heard the door squeak open behind her, then the banging of the screen door.

"Okay, what's going on, Annie Virginia?"

She knew by the quiet tone of his voice that it was the question he'd followed her out here to ask. "What do you mean?" She played dumb.

"You know what I mean. You blush like a teenager every time you say Nick's name, and I've hardly seen you in the past two weeks. You're doing a hell of a lot more than baby-sitting up there. Last night I heard you talking on the phone. You were telling Terri that Nick was just a friend. So, I guess I'm not the only one who has noticed."

"It isn't love," she answered quietly, but even as she spoke the words, she wondered. When she was with Nick, she felt young, full to bursting with adrenaline. Dreams seemed tangible to her again, as close as tomorrow; it wasn't how she'd felt in her marriage. Then, she'd thought dreams were the toys of childhood, to be put away when real life came to call.

"Are you doing it to get back at Blake?"

"No. For once, I'm not thinking about Blake or Natalie. I'm doing this for me."

"Is that fair?"

She turned to him. "Why is it that only women have to be fair?"

"It's Nick I'm thinking of. I've known that boy for a long time. Even as a kid, he had eyes that had seen a dozen miles of bad road. When he started dating Kathy, I thanked God it wasn't you. But then he settled down and became the best cop this town has ever had. We all saw how he loved Kathy; and that little daughter of his was the apple of his eye. Then, that . . . thing happened with Kathy, and he . . . disintegrated. His hair turned that weird color, and every time I saw him, I remembered what had happened. It was like a physical badge of sorrow. No one blamed him, of course; but he blamed himself, you could tell. It was damned hard to watch."

"Why are you telling me this?"

"You're a fighter, Annie, and—"

"Ha! Come on, Dad, I'm a doormat of the first order."

"No. You never have seen yourself clearly. You've got a steel core inside you, Annie—you always did. And you see the world in positive terms. Your glass is always half full."

"When Blake left me, I fell apart," she reminded him.

"For what—a month?" He made a tsking sound. "That's nothing. When your mom died, I didn't hide out for a couple of weeks and then emerge stronger than I'd started." He paused, shaking his head. "I'm not good at saying what I mean. What I'm trying to say, honey, is that you don't understand despair or weakness, not really. You can't get your mind wrapped around hopelessness."

She stared out at the river. "I guess that's true."

"You're still a married woman, and if you think Blake is really going to leave you for a bimbo, you're crazy. He'll be back. When he comes to his senses, Blake will come home to you."

"I don't feel married."

"Yes, you do."

She had no answer to that; it was true and it wasn't. As much as she'd grown and changed in the last months, Hank was right: Annie *did* still feel married to Blake. She'd been his wife for almost twenty years . . . that kind of emotional commitment didn't evaporate on account of a few hastily thrown words, even if those words were *I want a divorce.*

Hank came up beside her, touched her cheek. "You're going to hurt Nick. And he's not a man who rolls easily with life's punches. I don't mean to tell you what to do. I never have and I'm sure as hell not going to start now. But . . . this thing . . . it's going to end badly, Annie. For all of you."

The next night, long after the dinner dishes were washed and put away and Izzy had gone to bed, Annie sat in the rocker on the front porch. She watched a tiny black spider spin an iridescent web on a rhododendron bush. The scratchy creak-creak-creak of the rocker kept her company in the quiet. She knew she should go inside; Nick would be waiting for her upstairs. But it was so quiet and peaceful out here, and the lingering echo of her father's words seemed softer and more distant when she was alone. When she actually went inside and looked into Nick's blue, blue eyes, she knew her dad's advice would return, louder and too insistent to ignore.

Nick and Izzy had already been hurt so badly. She didn't want to do anything that would cause them more pain, and yet she knew, as certainly as she was sitting here, that she was going to do just that. She had another life in another town, another child that was going to need a mother as desperately as Izzy had only a few months ago. Her real life was out there, waiting for Annie, circling in the hot, smoggy air of Southern California, readying itself for the confrontation that was only a few short weeks away. It would test Annie, that reunion; test everything that she was and everything she'd decided up here that she wanted to be.

Behind her, the screen door creaked open. "Annie?

She closed her eyes for a second, gathering strength. "Hey, Nick," she said softly, staring down at the hands clasped in her lap.

The door banged shut and he came up beside her. Placing a hand gently on her shoulder, he crouched down. "What are you doing out here all by yourself?"

She looked at him and, for a second, felt a flash of panic. The thought of giving him up was terrifying.

But it was Nick she had to think of, not herself. She gazed at him. "I don't want to hurt you, Nick."

He took hold of her left hand, tracing the white tan line with the tip of his finger. "Give me some credit, Annie. I know it's not as simple as taking off a ring."

She stared at him for a long time. The urge rose in her to make impossible promises, to tell him she loved him, but she couldn't be that cruel. She would be leaving in two weeks. It would be infinitely better to take the words with her.

"We don't have forever, Annie. I know that."

She heard something in his voice, a little crack in the word *forever*, but he was smiling at her, and she didn't want to think about what he was feeling. "Yes," she whispered.

He swept her into his arms and carried her up to his bed. And as always, once she was in his arms, she stopped thinking about the future and let the present consume her.

On Tuesday morning, they planned a trip to the beach. Annie glanced down at the picnic basket beside her, checking the food supplies for the tenth time, then she checked her watch. It was already ten-thirty. She went to the bottom of the stairs and yelled up at Nick and Izzy to get a move on. Then, humming to herself, she headed back toward the kitchen.

The phone rang as she walked past it. She bent down and picked it up on the second ring. "Hello?"

"Hold for Blake Colwater, please."

For a disorienting moment, Annie couldn't connect the name to her own life. Nick came down the stairs. She threw him a confused look. "It's Blake."

Nick froze in mid-step. "I'll . . . leave you your privacy."

"No. Come here. Please."

Nick crossed the room and came up beside her. Turning slightly, she took hold of his hand.

Blake's authoritative voice came on at last. "Annie—is that you?"

At the sound of his voice, it all came rushing back. She stood perfectly still. "Hello, Blake."

"How are you, Annalise?"

"I'm fine." She paused, trolling for what came next. "And you?"

"I'm . . . okay. I got your number from Hank. You know Natalie will be getting home soon."

"The fifteenth of June. She wants us to meet her at the airport." She put the slightest emphasis on *us*.

"Of course. Her plane lands at . . ."

She hated that he didn't know. "Five-ten in the afternoon."

"I knew that."

An uncomfortable silence followed the apparent lie. Blake laughed easily, as if it had been three hours since they'd spoken instead of almost three months. "We need to talk, obviously, before we meet Natalie. I want you to come down to Los Angeles this weekend."

"Do you?" It was so like Blake. He wanted to talk, so she had to get on an airplane.

"I'll FedEx a ticket."

She drew in a sharp breath. "I'm not ready to see you yet."

"*What?* I thought—"

"I doubt it. We don't have anything to talk about now."

"I do."

"Funny words, coming from you."

"Annalise." He sighed. "I want you to come home this weekend. We need to talk."

"I'm sorry, Blake. I have no intention of coming home this weekend. I know we agreed to discuss our separation in June. Let's leave it at that, okay? I'll come home on the thirteenth."

"Goddamn it, Annalise. I want—"

"Good-bye, Blake. See you in two weeks." She hung up the phone and stared down at it.

"Are you okay, Annie?"

Nick's voice pulled her back from the dark edge gathering on her horizon. Forcing a smile, she turned into his arms. "I'm fine."

He stared down at her a long, long time. For a second, she thought he was going to kiss her, and she pushed onto her toes to meet his lips. But he just stood there, gazing down at her face as if he were memorizing everything about this moment. "It's not going to be long enough."

CHAPTER 21

As Blake drove down the rutted pavement of Mystic's main street, he remembered how much he'd always disliked this shabby little logging town. It reminded him of the town he'd grown up in, a dingy, forgotten farming community in Iowa—a place he'd worked hard to forget.

He pulled the rented Cadillac into a gas station and parked. Flipping up the collar of his overcoat—who in the hell wanted to live in a place where you needed an overcoat in late May?—he strode through the pouring rain toward the phone booth. Rain thumped overhead, so loud he could barely hear himself think.

It took him a minute to remember Hank's number. He hadn't dialed his own calls in years. Dropping a quarter in the slot, he punched out the number and listened to the ring.

On the third ring, Hank answered. "Hello?"

"Hi, Hank. It's me, Blake . . . again. I wanted to speak to my wi— to Annie."

"Did you? That wasn't my understanding."

Blake sighed. "Just put her on the line, Hank."

"She isn't here. She's *never* here during the day."

"What do you mean?"

"I gave you a number the other day. You can reach her there."

"Where is she, Hank?"

"She's out visiting . . . friends at the old Beauregard place."

"The old Beauregard place. Now, that certainly pinpoints it for me."

"You remember the old house at the end of the lake road? An old friend of hers lives out there now."

Blake got a strange feeling in the pit of his stomach. "What's going on, Hank?"

There was a pause, then Hank said. "You'll have to figure things out for yourself, Blake. Good luck."

Good luck. What the hell did that mean?

By the time Blake had asked directions to the lake road and got back in his car, he was irritated as hell. Something was not right here.

But then, things hadn't been right in a long time.

He'd first realized that something was wrong about a month ago; he'd stopped being able to concentrate. His work had begun to suffer.

And it was little things, nothing really. Like the tie he was wearing today. It was wrong,

It was a stupid, nonsensical thing, and certainly no one would notice, but *he* knew. When Annie had bought him the two-thousand-dollar black Armani suit, she'd chosen a monogrammed white shirt and a silk tie of tiny gray and white and red stripes to go with it. It was a set, and he always wore them together. He'd realized a few weeks ago that he couldn't find the tie. He'd torn the bedroom apart looking for it.

"I hope you're going to pick all that shit up," was what Suzannah had said when she'd seen the mess.

"I can't find the tie that goes with this suit."

She'd eyed him over the rim of her coffee cup. "I'll alert the press corps."

She thought it was funny that the tie was missing, and that he needed it so much. It had occurred to him that maybe it was at the cleaner's somewhere, his favorite tie, his *necessary* tie.

Annie would know where it is.

That had been the beginning.

He flicked the car's Bose stereo on, wincing as some hick country song blasted through the speakers. He flipped through the channels, but nothing else came through clearly. Disgusted, he turned off the radio.

The road unfurled in front of him, steeped in shadows in the middle of the day and battered by silver rain. After a few miles, he began to see flashes of the lake through the trees. The pavement gave out to a gravel road that turned and twisted and finally led him to a huge clearing. A bright yellow house sat primly amid a front yard awash in brightly colored flowers. A red Mustang and a police car were parked beneath an old maple tree.

He parked the car and got out. Flipping his collar up again, he strode across the yard and bounded up the stairs, knocking hard on the front door. It opened almost instantly, and a little girl stood in the opening. She was wearing a pair of Gortex overalls and a baseball cap. In her arms, she held a raggedy old doll.

Blake smiled down at her. "Hello. I'm—"

A man appeared suddenly behind the child. His hands rested protectively on the girl's shoulders and drew her back slightly into the house. "Hello?"

Blake stared at the tall, silver-haired man, then craned his neck to look inside the house. "Hi. I'm sorry to bother you, but I'm looking for Annalise Colwater. Her father, Hank, told me she'd be here."

The man tensed visibly. His eerie blue eyes narrowed and swept Blake from head to toe in a single glance. Blake was somehow certain that the man's eyes missed nothing, not the expense of his Armani suit nor even the oddness of his tie. "You're Blake."

Blake frowned. "Yes, and you are . . ."

From somewhere inside the house, Blake heard the clattering of someone running down stairs. "I'm ready, you guys."

Blake recognized Annie's voice. He sidled past the silent man and child and slipped into the house.

Annie saw him and skidded to a stop.

He almost didn't recognize her. She was wearing yellow rain gear and a big floppy hat that covered most of her face. The boots on her feet had to be four sizes too big. He forced a big smile and opened his arms. "Surprise."

She threw an odd glance at the silver-haired man, then slowly her gaze returned to Blake. "What are you doing here?"

He looked at the two strangers; both were watching him. Slowly, he let his arms fall to his sides. "I'd rather not discuss it in public."

Annie bit on her lower lip, then sighed heavily. "Okay, Blake. We can talk. But not here."

The girl whined and stomped her foot. "But Annie—we were gonna get ice cream."

Annie smiled at the child. "I'm sorry, Izzy. I need to talk to this man for a while. I'll make it up to you, okay?"

This man. Blake's stomach tightened. What in the hell was going on here?

"Don't make this hard on Annie, okay, Sunshine? She has to go for a minute." It was the man's voice.

"But she'll be comin' back . . . won't she, Daddy?"

The question fell into an awkward silence. No one answered

Annie moved past the little girl and came up beside Blake. "I'll meet you at Ted's Diner and Barber shop in about ten minutes. It's right downtown. You can't miss it."

Blake felt as if the world had tilted. He looked down at her, this woman he barely recognized. "Okay. See you in ten minutes."

He stood there for an interminable moment, feeling awkward and ill at ease. Then he forced a smile. All they needed was a few minutes alone, and everything would be fine. That's what he told himself as he turned and left the house. He was still telling himself that ten minutes later as he parked in front of the cheesiest, sleaziest diner he'd ever seen. Inside, he slipped into a yellow Naugahyde booth and ordered a cup of coffee. When it came, he checked his Rolex: 11:15.

He was actually nervous. Beneath the Formica wood-grain table, he surreptitiously wiped his damp palms on his pants

He glanced at his watch again—11:25—and wondered if Annie was going to show. It was a crazy thought and he dismissed it almost instantly. Annie was the most dependable person he'd ever known. If Annie said she'd be someplace, she'd be there. Late, maybe; harried, often. But she'd be there.

"Hello, Blake."

He snapped his head away from the window at the sound of her voice. She was standing beside the table with one hip cocked out and her arms crossed. She was wearing a pair of faded blue jeans and a sleeveless white turtleneck, and her hair . . . it looked as if someone had hacked it off with a weed-eater.

"What did you do to your hair?"

"I think the answer is obvious."

"Oh." He frowned, disconcerted by the sight of her and by her answer. It was flip and unlike her. He'd imagined this moment—dreaded and looked forward to it in equal measure—for weeks. But whenever he'd imagined their meeting, it was with the old Annie, impeccably dressed, smiling wanly, a little nervous. This woman standing in front of him was someone he didn't recognize. "Well, it'll grow back." Belatedly, he got to his feet. "It's good to see you, Annie."

The smile she gave him was reserved and didn't reach her eyes. She sidled into the booth and sat across from him.

With a quick wave of his hand, he signaled a polyester-clad waitress, who hurried to the table. Blake looked at Annie. "Coffee?"

"No." She drummed her fingernails on the table, and he noticed that she was wearing no polish and that her nails were blunt, almost bitten-off short. And on her left hand, in the place where his ring belonged, there was only a thin band of pale, untanned skin. She smiled up at the waitress. "I'll have a Budweiser."

He stared at her in shock. "You don't drink beer." It was a stupid thing to say, but he couldn't think of anything else. All he could focus on was the ring she wasn't wearing.

Another false smile. "Don't I?"

The waitress nodded and left.

Annie turned her attention back to Blake. Her gaze swept him in a second, and he wondered what this new woman saw when she looked at the old Blake. He waited for her to say something, but she just sat there with her new haircut and her no makeup and her terrifyingly ringless finger and stared at him.

"I thought we should talk . . ." he said—rather stupidly, he thought afterward.

"Uh-huh."

Another silence fell, and into the quiet, the waitress came to the table. She placed a frosted mug of beer on a small, square napkin, and Annie gave her a bright smile. "Thanks, Sophie."

"You bet, Miss Bourne."

Miss Bourne? The address left him winded.

"So," she said at last, sipping her beer. "How's Suzannah?"

Blake winced at the coldness in her voice. He knew he had it coming, but still he hadn't expected anger. Annie never got angry. "I'm not living with her anymore."

"Really?"

"Yes. That's what I wanted to talk to you about."

She stared at him across the rim of her glass. "Really?"

He wished he'd rehearsed this more, but he hadn't expected her to make it so difficult. In his mind, it always went the same way: He swept into a room and she hesitated, then smiled and cried and told him how much she missed him. He opened his arms and she hurled herself at him . . . and that was that. They were back together.

He tried to gauge her emotions, but the eyes he knew so well were shuttered and unwelcoming. He tripped through the words uncharacteristically. "I made a mistake." He slid his hand across the table.

"A mistake." She drew her hand back.

He heard the censure in her voice and knew what she meant. It was a mistake to be late on your Visa payment; what he'd done was something else entirely. The way she looked at him, the soft, reserved sound of her voice—not Annie at all—punched a hole in his confidence, and he began to feel as if something vital were leaking away from him. "I want to come home, Annie," he said softly, pleading with her in a way he'd never pleaded in his life. "I love you, Annalise. I know that now. I was a stupid, stupid fool. Can you forgive me?"

She sat there, staring at him, her mouth drawn in a tight, hard line.

In the silence, he felt a spark of hope ignite. He scooted around the vinyl booth and came up beside her, staring at her, knowing that all his heart and soul was in his eyes and hoping to hell that she still cared. Memories of their life together swelled inside him, refueled his confidence. He remembered a dozen times he'd hurt her, birthdays he'd missed, nights he hadn't come home, dinners that had been ruined by his absence. She had always forgiven him; it was who she was. She couldn't have changed that much.

She stared straight ahead, her eyes wary and filled with a pain he knew he'd put there. He gazed at her profile, willing her to look at him. If she did, if she looked at him for even a second, he'd see the answer in her eyes. "Annie?" He took her hand in his, and it was cold. "I love you, Annie," he said again, his voice choked. "Look at me."

Slowly, slowly, she turned, and he saw then that her eyes were flooded with tears. "You think you can say you're sorry and it's all over, Blake? Like it never happened?"

He clutched her hand, feeling the delicacy of her bones and the softness of her skin. "I'll spend the rest of my life making it up to you."

She closed her eyes for a second, and a tear streaked down her cheek. Then she opened her eyes and looked at him. "You did me a favor, Blake. The woman I was . . ." She drew her hand away from his and swiped the moisture from her cheek. "I let myself become a nothing. I'm not that woman anymore."

"You're still my Annie."

"No. I'm *my* Annie."

"Come back to me, Annie. Please. Give us another chance. You can't throw it all—"

"Don't you *dare* finish that sentence. *I* didn't throw anything away. You did, with your selfishness and your lies and your wandering dick. And now you've figured out that little Suzannah wants to be your lover, not your wife and your mother and your doormat and you come running back to me. The woman who'll take your shit with a smile and give you a safe place where nothing is expected of you and everything goes your way."

He was stunned by her language and her vehemence. "Annie—"

"I've met someone."

His mouth dropped open. "A man?"

"Yes, Blake. A man."

He slid back over to his seat. He took a long gulp of his lukewarm coffee, trying to get over the shock of her statement. A *man? Annie with another man?*

The silver-haired man with the sad blue eyes.

Why was it that in the months they'd been apart, he had never considered such a thing? He'd always pictured her as quiet, dependable Annie, mothering everyone, smiling and laughing and trying her hand at some god-awful craft or another. He'd pictured her sewing and decorating and pining. God damn it—mostly, he'd pictured her pining away for him, inconsolable. He looked up at her. "Did you . . . sleep with him?"

"Oh, for God's sake, Blake."

She had. Annie—his Annie, his *wife*—had slept with another man. Blake felt a surge of raw, animal anger, a fury he'd never known before in his life. He wanted to throw his head back and scream out his rage, but instead, he sat very still, his hands fisted in tight, painful blocks beneath the table. Now things were different, very different, and he had to proceed with the greatest caution.

"An affair," he said quietly, wincing at the sound of the word and the images it brought to mind. Annie, writhing in pleasure, kissing another pair of lips, touching another man's body. He pushed the horrible thoughts away. "I guess you did it to get back at me."

She laughed. "Not everything revolves around you."

"So . . ." What in the hell did you say at a time like this? He wanted to put his fist through a plate-glass window, and instead he had to sit here like a gentleman, pretending it didn't hurt like hell, pretending she hadn't just ripped his heart out and stomped on it. "I guess . . ." He shrugged. "I guess we can forgive each other."

"I don't want your forgiveness."

He flinched. They were the same words he'd thrown at her a few months ago, and they hurt. Sweet Jesus, they hurt. "I'm sorry, Annie," he said quietly, looking up at her. For the first time, he truly understood what he'd done to her. In his arrogant selfishness, he hadn't really thought about what he'd put her through. He'd sugar-coated his behavior in the vocabulary of the nineties: *I need my space; there's no reason to stay together if you're not happy; you'll be better off without me; we've grown apart.* And he'd believed all of it. Now, he saw his mistake. The words were meaningless excuses for a man who didn't think the rules applied to him. He'd acted as if their marriage were an inconvenient encumbrance, an irritating lien on property you wanted to develop. The words that truly mattered—*love, honor, and cherish, till death do us part*—he'd slapped aside as if they meant nothing.

He felt the first wave of honest-to-God shame he'd ever experienced. "I never knew how it could hurt. But Annie, I love you—you can believe that. And I'm going to go on loving you for the rest of my life. No matter what you do or where you go or what you say, I'll always be here, waiting for your forgiveness. Loving you."

He saw a flash of pain in her eyes, and saw the way her mouth relaxed. For a heartbeat, she weakened, and like any great lawyer, he knew how to pounce on opportunity. He touched her cheek gently, forcing her to look at him. "You think I don't really love you, that I'm just the same selfish prick I always was, and that I want you because you make my life easier . . . but that's not it, Annie. You make my life complete."

"Blake—"

"Remember the old days? When we lived in that beach house in Laguna Niguel? I couldn't wait to get home from work to see you. And you always met me at the door—remember that?—you'd yank the door open and throw yourself into my arms. And how about when Natalie was born, when I crawled into that narrow hospital bed with you and spent the night—until that bony old nurse came and threw me out? And how about that time on the beach, when you and I made sand castles at midnight and drank champagne and dreamed of the house we would someday own. You said you wanted a blue and white bedroom, and I said you could paint it purple if you wanted, as long as you promised to be in my bed forever. . . ."

She was crying now. "Don't, Blake, please . . ."

"Don't what? Don't remind you of who we are and how long we've been together?" He pulled a handkerchief from his breast pocket and wiped the tears from her face. "We're a *family*. I should have seen that before, but I was blind and stupid and selfish, and I took so much for granted." His voice fell to a throaty whisper and he stared at her through a blur of his own tears. "I love you, Annie. You have to believe me."

She rubbed her eyes and looked away from him, sniffling quietly. "I believed you for twenty years, Blake. It's not so easy anymore."

"I never thought it would be."

"Yes, you did."

He smiled ruefully. "You're right. I thought you'd hear my apology and launch yourself into my arms and we'd ride off into the sunset together." He sighed. "So, where do we go from here?"

"I don't know."

It was an opening, something at least. "You have to give me—give *us* another chance. When you asked for one, I agreed, and I thought about where we'd gone wrong and here I am. You owe me the same consideration, Annie. You owe it to our family."

"Oh, good. A lecture on family values from *you*." She pulled a compact from her purse and flipped the mirror open. "Perfect. I look like the Pillsbury Dough Girl."

"You look beautiful."

She looked up at him sharply. "But my hair will grow out."

"I shouldn't have said that."

She clicked the compact shut. "No, you shouldn't have."

Her gaze was uncomfortably direct, and he was reminded that in some ways, after almost twenty years of marriage, he didn't know the woman sitting across from him at all. "On June fourteenth, I'll meet you at the house. We can discuss . . . this . . . then." She got to her feet, and he saw that she was a little unsteady. She was obviously holding herself together with incredible effort.

He took hope from that. "I won't give up, Annie. I'll do whatever it takes to get you back."

She sighed. "Winning was always very important to you, Blake." On that final, cutting remark, she turned and walked out of the diner.

CHAPTER 22

Nick waited for Annie to return. For the first hour, he told himself he was being an idiot. He knew she couldn't possibly meet with her husband and be back here in less than two hours.

But then two hours had stretched into three, and then four, and then five.

Forcing a smile, he'd made a big production out of dinner, for Izzy's sake. He'd stumbled through one of Annie's recipes: chicken breasts breaded with cornflakes and potato chips. He'd forgotten to start the rice in time, and so he served the oven-fried chicken with sliced bananas and chunks of cheese. He'd tried his best to keep a conversation going, but he and Izzy were both keenly aware of the empty chair at the table.

Everything had gone well enough until Izzy had looked at him, her upper lip mustachioed with a thin band of milk. "Daddy, she's comin' back, isn't she, Daddy?"

Nick's fork had hit the edge of his plate with a *ping*. He hadn't known how in the hell to answer, and so he'd fallen back on standard parenting. Avoidance. "Don't talk with your mouth full," he'd said, looking quickly away.

By the time they'd done the dishes and he'd given Izzy her bath and put her to bed, he was as jittery as a bird. He couldn't even concentrate enough to read her a bedtime story. Instead, he'd kissed her forehead and run from the room.

Blake had been exactly what Nick had expected—and precisely what he'd feared. When he'd seen the handsome, confident, obviously successful man in his expensive black suit, Nick had felt as if he were nothing. He saw his own flaws in sharp relief: the cheap, small-town jeans that needed hemming, the T-shirt that had once been blue but after countless washings had been rendered a dull and lifeless gray, the ripped belt loop he'd never bothered to sew. And he didn't even want to *think* about his looks—the deeply etched lines around his eyes that were Kathy's legacy, and the unnatural color of his hair.

Blake was everything that Nick could never be.

He wished he could push his worry aside, think about something else—anything else. But the more he tried to clear his thoughts, the more she was there, inside him. Annie held his heart and soul in the palm of her hand, and she didn't even know it.

He'd never felt as much a part of a family as he did now.

With another man's wife.

Annie saw him standing out at the lake. She got out of her Mustang and eased the door shut quietly, walking slowly across the grass.

Wordlessly, she came up beside him. She waited for him to touch her, move close enough that she could feel the comforting heat of his presence, but he didn't. Instead, he stood stiffly in place. "How did it go?"

There was no point in lying to him. "He made a terrible mistake and he loves me."

"He *did* make a terrible mistake."

There was a crack in his voice, and in it, she heard his pain.

"What are you going to do?" he asked softly.

"I don't know. I spent two and a half months trying to fall out of love with him, and now when I've almost succeeded, he wants to take it all back. I can't adapt this quickly."

He fell silent, and she realized what she'd said. *Almost succeeded.* Almost fallen out of love with her husband. She wanted to place a Band-Aid on the wound of her words, but *almost* was the sad truth of her feelings for Blake. Anything else would be a lie.

On the shore, the water lapped quietly against the gravel. Breezes whispered through the leaves of a huge old maple tree.

The thought of leaving here terrified her. She thought of her big, empty house in California, and all the time she'd have alone. "What if—"

He turned to her. "What if what?"

She took a deep breath. "What if I . . . came back here? After . . . everything is settled? I've been thinking more and more about a bookstore. You were right, that house on Main Street would be perfect. And God knows, this town needs one . . ."

He went very still. "What are you saying?"

"After the divorce . . . and after Natalie leaves for college, I'll be down in Southern California all by myself—"

"Don't do that to me, Annie. Don't throw me hope like it was a bone to bury in my backyard. I can't spend the rest of my life waiting for you, watching the driveway, thinking *today, maybe today.* It'd break what's left of my heart. Don't make me any promises if you can't keep them. It's . . . easier for me that way."

The wind seemed to leak out of her lungs. She sagged. He was right; she knew he was right. Her future was a mystery, impenetrable and uncertain. She had no idea what would happen when she returned home. She wasn't even sure what she wanted to happen. "I'm sorry," she whispered. She wanted to tack on some kind of excuse, to remind him that she'd known Blake forever, that Natalie was her daughter, that she had always been a married woman, but none of the words mattered.

He didn't say anything. He just stood there, swaying slightly, gazing down at her as if he had already lost her.

The next morning, Annie was so depressed she didn't even go to Nick's. Instead, she lay in bed and alternately cried and stared.

Her mind was too full; it was making her crazy, all the things she had to think about. Her husband—the man she'd loved since she was nineteen years old—wanted another chance to make their marriage work. He was sorry. He'd made a mistake.

Hadn't she *begged* him to give their marriage a chance just a few months ago?

Beside her bed, the phone rang. She leaned over and picked it up. "Hello?"

"Annie Colwater? This is Madge at Dr. Burton's office. I'm calling to remind you of your ten-thirty appointment this morning."

She'd forgotten all about it. "Oh, I don't know—"

"Doc Burton told me not to take no for an answer."

Annie sighed. Last week she'd thought she'd beaten the depression, but now she was there again, slogging through the bleak confusion, unable to break through to the surface. Maybe it would be good to talk to the doctor. If nothing else, it gave her somewhere to go and something to do. She would probably feel better just getting out of bed. "Thanks, Madge," she said softly. "I'll be there."

With a tired sigh, she rolled out of bed and headed for the shower. By ten-fifteen, she was dressed in a pair of jeans and a worn sweatshirt. Without bothering to comb her hair—what was the point?—she grabbed her handbag and car keys and left her room.

Hank was on the porch, sitting in his rocker, reading a book. At her hurried exit, he looked up. "You're running late this morning."

"I have a doctor's appointment."

His smile faded. "Are you okay?"

"Other than the fact that I'm depressed and retaining more water than a Sea World seal tank, I'm fine. Doc Burton made the appointment when I saw him. He wanted to make sure I wasn't still feeling blue before I . . . went home."

Blue. Such a nothing little word for the emptiness seeping through her bloodstream.

Forcing a smile, she leaned down and kissed his forehead. "'Bye, Dad."

"'Bye."

She hurried down the steps and jumped into her Mustang.

Downtown, she parked in the shade of an elm tree and left her car without bothering to lock the door. She hurried up the concrete steps and into the brick building she'd visited so often in her youth.

Madge grinned up at her. "Hello, sweetie. The doctor's waiting for you. Go on back to exam room two."

Annie nodded and headed down the white-walled hallway. She found a door with a huge black *2* stenciled on it, and she went inside. Taking a seat on the paper-covered table, she flipped through the current issue of *Fishing News.*

About five minutes later, Dr. Burton knocked on the door and pushed it open. "Hi, Annie. Are you still feeling blue?"

How in the hell could she answer that? One minute she was pink, and the next—especially since Blake's call—the blue was so bad it was a dark, violent purple. She tossed the magazine onto the vacant chair. "Sometimes," she answered.

"Marge tells me you tried to make an appointment while I was gone. What was that about?"

"A bout with the flu. I won, but . . . in the last day or two, the nausea has come back a bit."

"I told you that this was a time to take extra good care of yourself. When the depression bites, your system has a hard time with bugs. How about if we draw a little blood and see what's what. Then, if everything's okay, we can talk about how you really feel."

Three hours later, Annie stood in front of her father's house. Shivering, she moved forward. Her legs didn't seem to work; it felt as if she were walking through a dense gray fog that resisted her movements.

Slowly, she climbed the steps and went inside.

Hank was sitting by the fireplace, doing a crossword puzzle. At her entrance, he looked up. "I didn't expect you until—"

She burst into tears. He was beside her in an instant. He scooped her into his big arms and held her, stroking her hair. Holding her close, he guided her onto the sofa, sitting beside her. Behind her, the door slammed shut, closing out the world.

"What is it, Annie?"

She sniffed hard and wiped her runny nose on her sleeve. She turned to him, but the words wouldn't come.

"Annie?"

"I'm pregnant," she whispered, and at the words, she started to cry again. She wanted to be filled with joy over the news; she was three months pregnant. After endless years of taking her temperature, religiously charting her ovulation cycles, and standing on her head after sex, she had effortlessly conceived a child.

Blake's child.

She'd never been so confused and shaken in her whole life, not even when Blake had asked for a divorce. At first when Dr. Burton had given her the results of the blood test, she'd assumed it was a mistake. When she realized it was no mistake, she'd had a moment of paralyzing, gut-wrenching fear. She wondered whose baby it was.

Then she remembered what Nick had told her. He'd had a vasectomy when Izzy was two. And then there'd been the pelvic exam, which showed that Annie was three months along.

It was definitely Blake's child.

Hank touched her cheek, gently turned her to face him. "It's a miracle," he said, and she knew it was true. She *felt* it, the small seed of a baby growing inside her. She placed her hand on her stomach. It thrilled her and terrified her.

"It changes everything," she said softly.

That's what scared her most. She didn't want to step back into the cold, sterile life she'd had in California. She wanted to stay here, in Mystic, to let the cool green darkness become her world. She wanted to keep on loving Nick. She wanted suddenly, ferociously to watch Izzy get braces and cut her hair and learn to dance. She wanted to open her own bookstore and live in her own house and be accountable to no one but herself.

But mostly, she wanted to be in love for the rest of her life, to wake up every morning with Nick beside her and go to sleep each night in his arms. But she couldn't do that. There wasn't a good enough perinatalogist within a hundred miles of Mystic, and no hospital with a neonatal ICU. She'd called her obstetrician in Beverly Hills and been told to get home. Bed rest was the order of the day. Just like it had been with Adrian. Only this time Annie was almost forty years old; they weren't going to take any chances. The doctor was expecting Annie in three days—and not one day more, she'd said sternly.

"Have you told Blake?"

This time, she wanted to cry, but she couldn't. She stared at her dad, feeling already as if everything she wanted was moving away, receding just beyond her touch. "Oh, Dad, Blake will want—"

"What do *you* want?"

"Nick," she whispered.

Hank gave her a sad smile. "So, you think you're in love with him now. Annie, you've been with him for a few months. You've loved Blake since you were a teenager. Just a couple of months ago, you were so devastated by the breakup of your marriage that you couldn't get out of bed. Now you're willing to toss it out like yesterday's garbage?"

She knew her father was right. What she had with Nick was special and magical, but it didn't have the foundation that was her marriage. "Blake and I tried for so long to have more children. After Adrian, I was desperate to conceive again, but years went by and . . . nothing. When he finds out about the baby . . ."

"You'll go back to him," Hank said, and the quiet certainty in his voice tore her apart.

It was the right thing to do, the only thing to do, and Annie knew it. She couldn't take Blake's child from him and move up here on her own. A baby deserved its father.

There it was, the truth that stripped her soul and left her with nothing but a handful of broken dreams and soon-to-be-broken promises.

She was crying again; she couldn't help herself. She kept picturing what was to come—the moment when she would tell Nick about the baby—and it hurt so badly she couldn't breathe. She didn't want to be strong, didn't want to be honorable, didn't want to do the right thing.

She thought about all their time together, all the moments he'd held her and touched her and kissed her lips with a gentleness she'd never imagined. She thought about Izzy, and how much she'd lost, and then she thought about going back to California, to Blake's bed, to a place where the air was brown and the earth was dry. But most of all, she thought about how desperately lonely her world would be without Nick. . . .

Annie drove and drove, until she couldn't drive anymore. Finally, she made her way back to Nick's house. When she got there, he was in the garden with Izzy.

It would all go on without her, this place, this family. Izzy would grow up and learn to dance and go on her first date, but Annie wouldn't be there to see it.

She looked at Nick and was horrified to realize that tears were blurring her vision.

"Annie?"

She took a deep, shaking breath. More than anything, she wanted to throw herself into his big, strong arms. She ached suddenly to say the precious words, *I love you,* but she didn't dare. She knew that if Nick could, he'd promise that the sun would shine on them forever. But neither of them was so naive anymore; both had learned that everything could change in an instant, and that the heartfelt vows of people in love were fragile words that, once shattered, could cut so deeply you'd bleed forever.

He stood up, moved toward her. With one dirty finger, he touched her chin, so gently it was like the brush of a butterfly's wing. "Honey, what is it?"

She forced a bright smile, too bright, she knew, but there was no help for that. "I got something in my eye. It's nothing. Let me change my clothes, then I'll come out and help you guys."

Before he could answer—or ask another painful, loving question—she ran into the house.

Nick and Annie lay in bed, barely touching, the sheets thrown back from their naked legs. A big old oak fan turned lazily overhead, swooshing through the air, stirring it with a quiet *thwop-thwop-thwop.*

After Izzy had been put to bed, they'd circled each other, he and Annie, saying none of the things that seemed to be collecting in the air between them. Now, he held her tightly, stroking the soft, damp flesh of her breast. She'd been quiet all evening, and every so often he'd looked at her and seen a faraway sadness in her eyes. It scared him, her sudden and unexpected quiet. He kept starting to ask her what was wrong, but every time the words floated up to his tongue, he bit them back. He was afraid of whatever it was that lay curled in all that silence.

"We need to talk," she said softly, rolling toward him.

"God, if those aren't the worst four words a woman can say." He waited for her to laugh with him.

"It's serious."

He sighed. "I know it is."

She angled her body until she was almost lying on top of him. Her eyes looked huge in the pale oval of her face, huge and filled with sadness. "I went to see a doctor today."

His heart stopped. "Are you okay?"

The smile she gave him was worn and ragged at the edges. "I'm healthy."

His breath expelled in a rush. "Thank God."

"I'm also three months pregnant."

"Oh, Christ . . ." He couldn't seem to breathe right.

"We tried for years and years to get pregnant."

Blake's baby. Her husband's baby, the man who'd said he'd made a terrible mistake and wanted her back. Nick felt as if he were melting into the hot, rumpled sheets that smelled of her perfume and their spent passion.

I always wanted more children. Those had been her exact words, and in them, he'd heard the residue of a lifetime's pain. He'd known then it was the one thing he couldn't give her. Now it didn't matter.

He knew Annie too well; she was a loving, honorable person, and a ferocious mother. It was one of the things he loved about her, her unwavering sense of honor. She would know that Blake deserved a chance to know his child.

There would be no future for them now, no years that slid one into the next as they sat on those big rockers on the porch.

He wanted to say something that would magically transform this moment into something it wasn't, to forge a memory that wouldn't hurt for the rest of his life. But he couldn't.

Before their love song had really begun, it was coming to an end.

CHAPTER 23

Nick knew that Annie was making her arrangements to return home, but she was careful around him. She hung up the phone when he came into the room.

He tried to erect a shield between them, something that would soften his fall when she left, but it was impossible. Yesterday, he and Annie had driven to Seattle to see a specialist in high-risk pregnancies. He couldn't stay detached. He was there for her every minute, encouraging her to keep drinking water when she thought she couldn't take another sip, holding her hand during the ultrasound. When he saw the baby—that tiny, squiggly gray line in a sea of fuzzy black, he'd had to turn quickly away and mumble something about having to go to the bathroom.

Each day, he tried not to think about what was to come, but he felt the silent, insistent march of every hour, ticking away what he wanted most in his life.

Sometimes, in the middle of the day, when a strand of sunlight slid through an open window and highlighted Annie's cropped hair, he was stunned by her beauty; and then she'd smile at him, that soft, sad, knowing smile, and it would all come crashing back. He'd hear that ticking in his head again.

She had changed him so much, his Annie. She'd given him a family and made him believe that love was a heavy winter coat that kept you warm all year. She'd shown him that he could pull himself out of the destructive patterns of his life; he could quit drinking and take care of his daughter. She'd given him everything he'd dreamed of.

Except a future.

When they were together, they didn't talk about the baby or the future.

Now she was standing in the living room, staring at the pictures on the fireplace mantel. Absently, she stroked her still-flat abdomen.

As he walked down the stairs, he wondered what she was thinking. The steps creaked beneath his weight, and at the sound, she looked up, giving him a tired smile. "Hey ya, Nicky," she said.

He went to her, slipped his arms around her, and pulled her against him. She leaned her head back against his shoulder. Tentatively, he reached a hand out, let it settle on her stomach. For a single heartbeat, he allowed himself to dream that the child was his, that *she* was his, and this moment was the beginning instead of the end.

"What are you thinking?" he asked quietly, hating the fear that came with the simple question of lovers everywhere.

"I was thinking about your job." She twisted in his arms and looked up at him. "I . . . want to know that you'll be going back to it."

It hurt, that quiet statement of caring. He knew what she needed from him right now, a smile, a joke, a gesture that reassured her that he would be all right without her. But he didn't have that kind of strength; he wished he did. "I don't know, Annie . . ."

"I know you were a good cop, Nick. I've never known anyone with such a capacity for caring."

"It almost broke me . . . the caring." The words held two meanings, and he knew that she understood.

"But would you give it all up . . . the caring and the love and try-ing . . . would you give it up because in the end there is pain?"

He touched her face gently. "You're not asking about my job. . . ."

"It's all the same, Nick. All we have is the time, the effort. The end . . . the pain . . . that's out of our control."

"Is it?"

A single tear streaked down her face, and though he longed to wipe it away, he was afraid that the tiny bead of moisture would scald his flesh. He knew that this moment would stay with him forever, even after he wanted to forget. "I'll never forget us, Annie."

This time he didn't care how much it hurt; he let himself dream that the baby she carried was his.

Annie showed up at her dad's house bright and early. For a moment after she got out of the car, she simply stood there, staring at her childhood home as if she'd never seen it before. The windows glowed with golden light, and a riot of colorful flowers hugged the latticework below the wraparound porch. She wouldn't be here to see the chrysanthemums bloom this year, and though she hadn't seen them flower for many, many years, now it saddened her.

She would miss seeing her dad. It was funny; in California she had gone for long stretches of time without seeing him—sometimes as much as a whole year would slip by without a visit—and she hadn't had the ache of longing that now sat on her chest like a stone. She felt almost like a girl again, afraid to leave home for the first time.

With a sigh, she slammed her car door shut and walked up to the house.

She hadn't even reached the porch when Hank flung the door open. "Well, it's about time, I haven't seen you in days. I was—"

"It's time, Dad."

"Already?"

She nodded. "I'm leaving tomorrow morning."

"Oh." He slipped through the door, closing it behind him. He sidestepped around her and sat down on the wicker love seat. Then he motioned for her to sit beside him.

She sat down in her mom's rocking chair and leaned back. Memories of her childhood were close out here; they came encoded in the sound of the rocker on the wooden porch. She could almost *hear* her mother's voice, calling Annie to come into the house.

Hank stared out at the green darkness of the forest. "I'm sorry, Annie. About all of it."

Annie felt her throat tighten. "I know, Dad."

Hank turned to her at last. "I made you something." He went into the house and came out a moment later, carrying a present.

She took the thin box, wrapped in beautiful blue foil, and opened it. Inside was a thick, leatherbound photograph album. She flipped the cover open. The first page held a small black and white Kodak print that had seen better days; the edges were dog-eared, and tiny white creases covered the print in maplike patterns.

It was a rare photo of Annie and her mom, one she'd never seen before. Her mother was wearing a pair of white pedal pushers and a sleeveless shirt, with her hair pulled back into a ponytail. She was smiling. Beside her, a spindly Annie was standing next to a brand-new bike.

Annie remembered that bicycle. She'd gotten it for her birthday, amid a shower of balloons and cake and laughter. She remembered how proud her mother had been when she first rode it. *There you go, Annie, honey, you're on your way now.*

Slowly, she turned the pages, savoring each and every photograph. Here she was at last, Annie . . . from the early, toothless days of kindergarten through the midriff-baring teenage years.

It was her life spread out before her, one frozen moment at a time, and each one brought a bittersweet remembrance. Lady, the puppy they'd brought home from the grocery store . . . the Christmas tree ornament she'd made in Mr. Quisdorff's woodshop class . . . the white satin sleeveless dress she'd worn to the junior prom.

The memories crowded in on her, clamoring to be held and savored, and she wondered how it was that she'd forgotten so much. In every photograph, she saw herself, saw the woman emerging through the freckled, gap-toothed features of the girl in these pictures. The final page of the book was reserved for the family photograph she and Blake and Natalie had posed for only two years ago.

There I am, she thought, gazing at the smiling, bright-eyed woman in the black St. John sweater . . . *and there I'm not.*

"I couldn't find very many pictures of your mom," Hank said softly. "I went through a dozen boxes up in the attic. That's pretty much what there is. I'm sorry."

Annie was surprised to hear his voice. She'd fallen so deeply into her own thoughts, she'd forgotten that her dad was beside her. She gave him a small smile. "We're like that, we moms. We take the pictures, but we don't record our own lives very well. It's a mistake we never realize until it's too late. . . ."

She flipped back to the beginning of the album, to a five-by-seven black and white copy of her mom's graduation picture. She looked so heartbreakingly young. Though you couldn't tell, Annie could recall perfectly the hazel hue of her mother's eyes. She caressed the photograph. *Did you ever look for yourself in mirrors, Mom? Were you like the rest of us? Is that why you dreamed of opening a bookstore?*

She wondered now, for the first time in years, what her mom would be like today. Would she be dying her hair, or would she have allowed her beautiful blond to fade into gray? Would she still be wearing that electric-blue eye shadow from the seventies, and those fuzzy hot-pink bits of yarn to tie up her layered ponytails? Or would she have gracefully turned to a conservative shoulder-length cut by now?

"She was beautiful," Hank said quietly, "and she loved you very much." He touched Annie's cheek with his papery, old man's hand. "I should have told you that—and given you these pictures—a long time ago. But I was young and stupid and I didn't know. . . ."

There was an emotional thickness in Hank's voice. It surprised Annie, his unexpected journey into intimacy. "What didn't you know?"

He shrugged. "I thought you grieved for a few respectable months and then got on with your life. I didn't know how . . . *deep* love ran, how it was in your blood, not your heart, and how that same blood pumped through your veins your whole life. I thought you'd be better off if you could forget her. I should have known that wasn't possible."

Annie's heart constricted painfully. Never had her father shown his grief and his love in such sharp relief. It moved her to touch his velvety cheek. "She was lucky to be so loved, Dad. By both of us."

"She's still loved and still missed. No one can ever take her place for me, except you, Annie. You're the best of Sarah and me, and sometimes, when you smile, I see your mama sitting right beside me."

She knew then that she would remember this day forever. She would buy a wicker love seat for her deck, and she would sit there with her new baby and remember what she had once allowed herself to forget.

"I'll visit more often this time," she said. "I promise. And I want you to come down for Thanksgiving or Christmas this year. No excuses. I'll send a ticket."

"It better be coach."

She smiled. It was exactly what she would have expected him to say. "Hell, Dad, I'll put you on a bus if it'll get you down there."

"Are you going to be okay, Annie Virginia?"

"Don't worry about me, Dad. That's the one thing I learned up here in Mystic. I'm stronger than I thought. I'm always going to be okay."

It rained on the day Annie left. All the night before, she and Nick had lain awake in bed, talking, touching, trying in every way they could to mark the memory on their souls. They had watched in silence as the sun crept over the dome of Mount Olympus, turning the glaciers into spun pink glass on the jagged granite peaks; they'd watched as the clouds rolled in and wiped the sunlight away, and as the rain tiptoed along the surface of the lake, turning from a gentle patter to a roaring onslaught, and then back to a patter again. They'd stared at each other, their gazes full of pent-up longing and fear, and still they'd said nothing.

When finally Annie rose from the passion-scented warmth of his bed, he reached out and clasped her hand. She waited for him to speak, but he didn't. Slowly, hating every motion, she slipped out of her T-shirt and dressed in a pair of leggings and a long sweatshirt.

"My bags are in the car," she said at last. "I'll . . . say good-bye to Izzy and then . . . go."

"I guess we've said our good-byes," he said softly. Then he smiled, a tender, poignant smile that crinkled his eyes and made her want to cry. "Hell, I guess we've been saying them from the moment we met."

"I know . . ."

They stood for a long time, gazing at each other. If it were possible, she fell in love with him even more. Finally, she couldn't stand how much it hurt to look at him.

She pulled away from his hand and went to the window. He came up behind her. She wanted him to take her in his arms, but he just stood there, distant and apart.

"I've been married for almost twenty years," she said quietly, watching her own reflection in the glass. She saw her mouth move, heard the words come out of her lips, but it felt as if it were another woman talking.

And it was. Annalise Colwater.

Slowly, slowly, she turned to face him.

"I love you, Annie." He said it like he said everything, with a quiet seriousness. "It feels like I've loved you forever." His voice was gravelly and low. "I never knew it could be this way . . . that love could catch you when you fell. . . ."

The words made her feel fragile, as if she were crafted of hundred-year-old glass and could be shattered by the touch of the wind. "Oh, Nick . . ."

He moved closer, close enough to kiss, but he didn't touch her. He just stared down at her through those sad blue eyes and gave her a smile that contained all his joy and sadness, his hope and fear.

And his knowing. His knowing that love wasn't everything it was cracked up to be. That sometimes it could break your heart. "I need to know, Annie . . . am I in love alone?"

Annie closed her eyes. "I don't want to say it, Nick. Please . . ."

"I'm going to be alone, Annie, we both know that. As the months pass, I'm going to start forgetting you—the way your eyes crinkle in the corner when you smile, the way you bite down on your lower lip when you're nervous, the way you chew on your thumbnail when you watch the news."

He touched her face with a tenderness that broke her heart. "I don't want to make you cry. I just want to know that I'm not crazy. I love you. And if I have to let you go to make you happy, I'll do it, and you'll never hear from me again. But, God, Annie, I have to know how you feel—"

"I love you, Nick." She smiled sadly. "I'm crazy in love with you. Over the moon in love with you. But it doesn't matter. We both know that."

"You're wrong, Annie. Love matters. Maybe it's the only thing that does."

Without waiting for her to answer, he leaned down and gave her one last tender kiss—a kiss that tasted of tears and regret, a last kiss that said good-bye.

As Annie walked through the house, it occurred to her that she should have left something behind, a sweater hanging in the closet or a pair of shoes tucked under the bed. There was nothing of her here now, no token that recalled the times she'd laughed in this room or the nights she'd slept in Nick's arms.

Biting down on her lower lip, she went to Izzy's room and found the little girl sitting on the end of her bed, her feet swinging just above the floor. She was wearing Annie's white sweater, the cashmere cardigan with the pearl buttons. A pretty lacquered box lay open on her lap.

"Hey, Izzy-bear," Annie said softly, "can I come in?"

Izzy looked up. She tried to smile, but already her brown eyes held a sheen of tears. "You wanna look through my collection again?"

Annie went to the bed and sat down beside Izzy. She pointed to a pretty purple ring. "That one is awfully pretty."

"It was my grandma Myrtle's . . . and these buttons were my mommy's." Izzy picked out a big cream-colored one with four holes in the middle. She handed it to Annie. "Smell it."

Annie took the button and lifted it to her nose.

"That one smells like my mommy's bedroom."

Slowly, Annie put the button down. Then she reached into her pocket and pulled out a folded-up handkerchief. It was a pretty pink thing with a big red *AVC* sewn across the bottom. "Why don't you put this in your collection?"

Izzy pressed it to her nose. "It smells like you."

Annie was afraid she was going to cry. "Does it?"

Izzy pulled a faded pink ribbon from her box. "Here. This is one o' my hair ribbons. You can have it."

Annie took the satin ribbon. "Thanks, pumpkin."

Izzy closed her box and clambered into Annie's lap. Annie held her tightly, savoring the feel of her, the smell of her hair.

Finally, Izzy drew back, and her brown eyes were huge in her pale face. Annie could tell that she was doing her best not to cry. "Today's the day, isn't it? You're leavin' us."

"Yes, Izzy, today's the day."

Izzy swallowed hard. "But Annie, who's gonna braid my hair now? Who's gonna paint my toenails and make me look pretty?"

Annie couldn't meet Izzy's earnest, overbright eyes. Forcing a wan smile, she took the child's hand. "Come with me." She led Izzy outside. They walked through the soggy grass, and Annie eased open the new white gate to the garden. They picked their way down the stone path toward the park bench that sat in the midst of the flowers.

They stared in silence at the blooming flowers, and Annie knew that, like her, Izzy was remembering the day they'd planted them. Afterward, when the first flower had bloomed, she and Izzy and Nick had sat in the garden in a darkening night and shared their memories of Kathy. They'd laughed and cried and talked. And since then, Izzy said that every new blossom reminded her of her mommy.

Izzy scooted closer. Annie tried to shore up her courage for what was to come. With a sigh, she reached into her pocket and pulled out the antique coin. Closing her damp fingers around the slim metal disk, she stared blindly at the colorful wash of blooming flowers. "I'm going to miss you something fierce, Izzy."

"I know, but you gotta go be with your daughter now."

It was a heartbeat before Annie could find her voice. "Yes."

"I wish . . . I wish I was your daughter."

"Oh, Izzy . . . your mommy loved you very, very much. And your daddy loves you with all his heart and soul."

Izzy turned to her. "Natalie could come here, couldn't she? I'd let her have my room. And when the baby comes, he could sleep with me. I'd . . . I'd share Miss Jemmie with him. Honest, I would. I'll be a good girl, I promise. I'll brush my teeth and make my bed and eat my vegetables."

"You already are a good girl, Izzy." She touched the child's small, tear-streaked face. "Natalie and I have a home in California. And the baby has a daddy who misses me."

Izzy sighed. "I know. By Disneyland."

"Um-hmm." She squeezed Izzy's tiny hand. "But it doesn't mean I don't love you, Izzy. I'll be thinking about you, and I'll call you lots and lots . . ." Her voice cracked, and for a minute the pain was so intense, Annie was afraid she was going to spoil everything by bursting into tears. "I'll always love you, Izzy-bear."

"Yeah." It was a quiet sigh, barely audible.

She twisted around to face Izzy. "I need you to do something for me while I'm gone."

"What's that?"

"You have to take care of your daddy for me. He's big and strong, but he's going to need you sometimes."

"He's gonna be sad."

The words stung. "Yes." She handed Izzy the coin they'd found at the abandoned ranger's station, the one Izzy had asked Annie to protect. "You'd better give this to your daddy. He's a safe place now, Izzy. You can trust him with everything."

Izzy stared at the coin in Annie's hand; then, slowly, she looked up. Tears magnified her brown eyes. "You keep it."

"I can't."

Izzy's tears started to fall. "You keep it, Annie. Then I know you'll be back."

The next thing she knew, Annie was crying. She pulled Izzy into her lap and hugged her. It started to rain softly; droplets slid down the white pickets and hit the marshy grass, their fall as quiet as the sound of a woman's tears or of a soul breaking softly in two.

"I love you, Izzy," she whispered, stroking the child's hair. Then, very softly, she said, "Good-bye."

Nick left Izzy with Lurlene and followed Annie out of town, keeping the squad car a safe distance behind. He felt like one of those crazy stalkers, but he couldn't help himself. He followed her all the way to the Hood Canal Bridge.

There, he pulled over and got out, watching her red Mustang speed across the bridge, becoming smaller and smaller and smaller.

And finally, just as suddenly as she'd come into his life, she was gone.

Out of the corner of his eye, he saw a bank of beautiful delicate yellow flowers along the edge of the road.

Look Annie, the glacier lilies are blooming. The thought came out of nowhere, cutting deep. He could no longer turn to her and say whatever came to mind. Besides, she was going to a place where flowers bloomed all year.

The urge for a drink came on him, hard and fast.

He closed his eyes. *Please God, help me hold on . . .*

But the prayer was useless. He felt himself starting to fall, and there was no one to catch him. He lurched for his car and jumped in. The car spun away from the bridge turnout, fishtailing back onto the highway, speeding back toward Mystic.

At Zoe's, he found his favorite chair empty, waiting for him in the darkened corner. It was middle-of-the-day quiet, with just the occasional clinking of a heavy glass on the bar and the low buzz of a television.

It looked like it always had, and for no good reason, that surprised him. The same oak bar, flanked by empty stools. The same cheap fans, circling tiredly overhead, barely disturbing the smoky air. There weren't more than a handful of people in the place, the old faithfuls who'd staked out their usual spots and sat, glassy-eyed and smoking, clutching drinks.

"Jesus, Nick, where yah been?"

Nick looked up and saw Zoe standing by him. She plunked a drink down in front of him. Then, with a slow nod, she turned and headed back to her place at the bar.

Nick took the glass in his hand. It felt cool and smooth and comforting. He swirled it around, watching the booze shimmer in the dull
light from an overhead fixture.

He brought the drink to his lips, inhaling the sweet, familiar fragrance of the scotch. *Drink . . . drink,* said a tiny voice deep inside. *You
know it will take the pain away. . . .*

It was seductive, that voice, luring him into the fragrance of the
scotch, promising a solution to the pain in his heart, a blurring filter
through which to remember Annie.

He wanted to guzzle this drink and then order another and another
and another, until he could barely remember that he'd loved her in the
first place.

But then he thought of Izzy.

Can I come home, Izzy? When he'd said those words to her, he'd
wanted her trust more than anything else in the world. And he wanted
it still.

The booze wouldn't help; the rational part of his brain knew that.
He'd get drunk—be a drunk again—and then what? Annie wouldn't be
any closer to coming back to him, and he would have failed his little girl
again.

He slammed the drink down, threw a ten-dollar bill onto the table,
and lurched to his feet, backing away. At the bar, he waved at Zoe. "I'm
outta here."

She grabbed a wet towel from underneath the bar and wiped the
wood down, eyeing him. "You okay, Nick?"

He tried to smile, but couldn't quite manage it. "Good as
always, Zoe."

He raced out of the bar. His hands were shaking and his throat felt
uncomfortably dry, but he was glad to be out of there.

He ran until his side ached and his breathing was ragged, until the
need for a drink didn't consume him. Then he sat for two hours on a
park bench, watching the sun slowly set on Main Street. Breath by
breath, the panic and fear passed. The pain was still there, throbbing on
his heart like an open wound, and he recognized that it would be there

for a long, long time, but Annie had changed him, helped him to see himself in a different and kinder light. That's what he had to focus on now. He had a life that mattered, a daughter who loved and needed him. Falling apart was a luxury he couldn't afford.

By the time the AA meeting started, Nick had pushed the need for a drink to a small, dark corner of his soul. He filed into the smoke-filled room behind a string of friends.

Joe was right behind him. He felt Joe's hand on his shoulder, heard his rough, sandpapery voice, "How are you doing, Nicholas?"

Nick was able to smile. "I'm doing okay, Joe. Thanks." He took a seat on a folding metal chair, and Joe sat down beside him.

Joe eyed him. "Are you sure you're all right?"

Nick knew he must look pale and tired. "I'm okay, Joe," he said, settling onto the hard plastic seat.

Joe grinned and clapped him gently on the shoulder. "I'm proud of you, Nicholas."

Nick closed his eyes and leaned back, sighing deeply. At first, he didn't notice the tap on his back. When he did, he snapped upright. His heart pounded with anticipation. Annie had changed her mind, she had turned around and come back. He spun around in his metal chair—

And saw Gina Piccolo standing behind him. Her unmade-up eyes looked tired against the chalky pallor of her face. He noticed that the nose ring was gone, as was the black lipstick. She looked as young and innocent as when he'd first seen her, riding her bike to the World-of-Wonders putt-putt golf course all those years ago.

He got slowly to his feet. "Gina," he said. "What are you doing here?"

"Drew died this week. O.D." Her voice was quiet and shaky. Tears washed her eyes, slid slowly down her gaunt cheeks. "You said if I ever needed help . . . I mean . . . I couldn't think of anybody else . . . at the station they told me you might be here. . . ."

"It's okay, Gina. . . ."

"I don't want to die, Mr. Delacroix."

Before this spring, Nick would have been afraid of this moment; he would have seen another tragedy in the making, another failure nipping at his heels. But now, he felt Annie beside him, as strong and warm as sunlight. He heard her voice whispering inside him: *Would you give it all up, Nick . . . the caring . . . would you give it all up because at the end there is pain?*

Maybe he would fail—probably he would fail—but he wouldn't let that stop him now. It was in the trying that he could save himself, and possibly this one desperate girl beside him.

He took her hand. "You've come to the right place, Gina. It's scary and hard to give up the crutches, but I'll be here for you. I won't give up on you if you won't."

A smile broke across her face, making her look impossibly innocent and hopeful. "I'll just get a Coke, and then I'll sit with you."

"Okay." He watched her walk through the crowded room, and then he sat down.

"So, Nicholas," said Joe. "What's that all about?"

Nick turned to his mentor, smiling broadly. "I guess it's just another cop trying to save another kid from ruin."

Joe grinned. "Welcome back, Nicholas. We missed you."

The words settled through Nick, sifting gently, finding a comfortable perch. "I missed me, too," he said quietly. "I guess you can put me back on the schedule. Say, Monday morning?"

"Ah, Nicholas. I never took you off."

Smiling, Nick leaned back in his seat. In a moment, Gina sat in the chair beside him.

The meeting got under way. Nick listened to the stories, and with each one, each tale that was so like his own, he felt himself grow stronger. When at last the meeting was coming to a close, he motioned to the chairman. "I'd like to speak," he said quietly.

There was a flutter of surprise around the room. Chairs squeaked as people turned in their seats to look at Nick.

"My name is Nick," he said into the quiet. The next part stuck in his throat, so he tried again. "My name is Nick, and I'm an alcoholic."

"Hi, Nick," they answered in unison, smiling proudly at him.

He saw the understanding in their eyes, in the way they nodded or looked at him or leaned forward. *It's okay*, they said wordlessly, *we know.* "I think I was an alcoholic long before I took my first drink. But everything started getting out of control about a year ago, when my wife died. . . ."

Word by tender word, he relived it all, picked through the rubble of his life and exposed all his vulnerabilities and failures and triumphs and heartbreaks. He gave everything inside him to the nodding, understanding faces in this cheap, smoke-filled room, knowing that they would hold his pain in careful hands and transform it into something else, a new awareness that would get him through the long, lonely nights without Annie. As he spoke, he felt the weight of the past year begin to lift. It wasn't until he spoke of Izzy, sweet Izzy, and the memory of the day she'd said, *I love you, Daddy,* that he finally broke down.

PART THREE

*God gave us memories
so that we might have
roses in December.*

JAMES M. BARRIE

CHAPTER 24

Heat rose in shimmering waves from the black ribbon of asphalt and melted into the brown, smog-filled air. Annie leaned deeper into the smelly velour upholstery of the taxicab and sighed, resting her hand on her stomach.

Already, she couldn't stand being away from Nick and Izzy; it felt as if a vital part of her had been hacked off and left to wither in some other place.

This concrete-encrusted land didn't hold her life anymore. It seemed to her to be an apocalyptic vision of the future in which green trees and blue skies and white clouds had been replaced by a million shades of man-made gray.

The cab veered off the Pacific Coast Highway and turned onto her road—funny, she still thought of it as her road. Beyond the Colony's guarded gate, they drove past the carefully hidden beach houses, each cut from the same contemporary designer's cloth; huge, multilayered homes built practically on top of each other, most with less than eight feet of ground between them. Each one a tiny kingdom that wanted to keep the rest of the world at bay.

They turned into her driveway, and the white angles of the house soared toward the blue sky. The yard was in full bloom, a riot of pink and red hibiscus and glossy green leaves. Its beauty was so . . . false. If they stopped watering, this contrived garden would shrivel and die.

The cab pulled up to the garage and stopped. The driver got out of the car and went to the trunk, popping it open.

Slowly, Annie got out. She stared down at the driveway, remembering how she had watched over the placement of the bricks, each and every one. *That one's not right, it's crooked. Could you please do it again before the cement hardens?*

"Ma'am? Is that everything?" The cabdriver was standing beside her Louis Vuitton luggage.

"Yes, thank you." She flipped her purse open and retrieved the fare from her wallet, plus a healthy tip. "Here you go."

He snatched the money and pocketed it. "You call me if you need to go to the airport again," he said.

The airport.

"Thanks. I will."

When he was gone, she turned back to the house. For a second, she thought she couldn't do it, couldn't walk down to the hand-carved mahogany door, push it open, and go inside. But then, she was moving, walking beneath the arched entrance that smelled of jasmine, pulling the jangle of keys from her pocketbook.

The key slid in; what had she expected? That it would no longer fit here because she didn't? The door whooshed open, and the smell of stale air greeted her.

She walked through the house, room by room, waiting to feel something . . . sad, happy, depressed . . . something. The floor-to-ceiling windows framed the brilliant blues of the sea and sky.

She felt as if she were walking through a stranger's house. Thoughts of Nick and Izzy crowded in on her, begging to be replayed and picked over, but she didn't dare. Instead she focused on the little things: the grand piano she'd purchased at a Sotheby's auction, the chandelier she'd rescued from an old San Francisco hotel, the Lladró statue collection she'd begun when Natalie started junior high.

Things.

She went up to her bedroom. Their bedroom.

There, certainly she would feel *something*. But again, there was only that odd sensation that she was viewing the remains of a long-dead civilization. This was Annie *Colwater's* room, and it was all that remained of her.

Her closet was full of expensive silks and woolens and cashmeres, skirts in every color and length, shoes in boxes still marked with exorbitant price tags.

At the bedside table, she picked up the phone and listened for a long time to the dial tone. She wanted to call Nick and Izzy, but she didn't. Instead, she carefully dialed Blake's office number. Without waiting to speak to him, she left a message that she was home.

Then she replaced the receiver and sat heavily on the end of her bed.

Soon, she'd see Blake again. In the old days, she would have obsessed over what to wear, but now, she couldn't have cared less. There was nothing in that vast, expensive closet that mattered to her anymore, nothing that felt like hers. It was nothing but acres and acres of another woman's clothes.

The office was like the man, understated, expensive, and seething with power. Years before Blake could afford this corner office in Century City, with its expansive views of glass and concrete skyscrapers, he'd imagined it. He always knew it would be stark and unrelieved, that there would be nothing in the room that said, *Come on in, sit down, tell me your troubles.* He'd never wanted to be that kind of lawyer, and he wasn't. It was the kind of office that made a client squirm and reminded him with every silent tick of the desk clock how much it was costing to sit here.

In truth, of course, it was Annie who'd given him this office. She'd spent hours choosing the drapes and the upholstery. She had designed and commissioned the ornate African mahogany desk and each hand-stained leather accessory.

Everywhere he looked now, he saw her.

He sighed and leaned back in his chair. The pile of paperwork on his desk blurred in front of him. He shoved the papers aside, watched as the Beaman deposition fluttered to the marble floor.

He felt odd and out of sorts, and he'd felt this way since his impromptu trip to that shithole diner in Mystic.

He'd thought he could apologize to Annie and step back into the comfortable shoes of his old life. Except that Annie wasn't Annie any-more, and he didn't know what to say or do to get her back.

On his desk, the intercom buzzed. He flicked the button impa-tiently. "Yes, Mildred?"

"Your wife called—"

"Put her through."

"She left a message, sir. She wanted you to know that she was home."

Blake couldn't believe it. "Clear my schedule, Mildred. I'm gone for the rest of the day."

He sprinted out of the building and jumped into his Ferrari, speed-ing out of the parking lot and onto the freeway.

At home, he raced up the front steps and jammed the key in the lock, swinging the door open. There was a pile of luggage at the base of the stairs. "Annie?"

She was standing at the edge of the archway that separated the liv-ing room from the formal dining room.

She was home again. *Now,* at last, everything would be all right.

He moved cautiously toward her. "Annie?"

She turned away from him and walked into the living room, stand-ing alone at the windows. "I have something to tell you, Blake."

It unnerved him, the way she wouldn't look at him. The sight of her, so stiff and unyielding, was a sharp reminder that she was not the same woman he'd left only a few months before. His throat was dry. "What is it?"

"I'm pregnant."

His first thought was *no,* not again. He couldn't go through that again. Then he remembered the other man, the man Annie had slept with, and he could hardly breathe. It was as if someone had just run an ice cube down his spine. "Is it mine?"

She sighed, and it was a sad little sound that didn't reassure him. "Yes. I'm three months along."

He couldn't seem to think straight. He shook his head, sighing. "A baby . . . Christ, after all these years."

She turned and gave him a quirking smile, and there she was at last.

His Annie. He realized then what he hadn't before. It was the baby that had brought her back to him. "A baby." This time he could smile. "*Our* baby . . ."

"All those years I thought God wasn't listening. It turns out He's got a mean sense of humor. He obviously wanted me to go through menopause and potty training at the same time."

"We'll make it work this time," he said softly.

She flinched at the words, and he wondered if he should have phrased it as a question. "Blake—"

He didn't want to hear what she was going to say. "Whatever happened in Mystic is over, Annie. This is our child you're carrying. *Our* child. We have to become a family again. Please give me another chance."

She didn't answer, just stared for a long time at his hand on her stomach. Then, unsmiling, she looked away.

Please give me another chance.

Annie closed her eyes. God, how many nights had she lain in her lonely bed, aching to hear those words from him? Yet now they fell against her heart like stones down an empty well. Clattering, bouncing, signifying nothing.

And what had she said to him, all those months ago? *I can't believe you'd throw it all away. We're a family, Blake, a family.*

"Annie—"

"Not now, Blake," she said in a fragile voice. "Not now."

She heard him sigh, a tired, disappointed sound that she knew well. He was confused and more than a little angry; he didn't know how to lose or how to be patient or how to hold his tongue.

"I'll have to be bedridden, just like with . . . Adrian." She gazed up at him. "It's going to take some work on your part. I won't be able to be good old Annie, taking care of everyone else. For once, you'll have to put me first."

"I can do that."

She wished she could believe it.

"I know it won't be easy for you to trust me again. I screwed up. . . ."

"A mammoth understatement."

His voice dropped to a plaintive whisper. "I can't believe you don't love me anymore. . . ."

"Neither can I," she said softly, and it was true. Somewhere, deep inside of her, a shadow of their love had to remain. She'd loved him for twenty years. Certainly that kind of emotion didn't simply disappear. "I'm trying to believe in what we had, and I pray we can find our way back to love, but I'm not in love with you now. Hell, I don't even *like* you much."

"You will," he answered with a confidence that set her teeth on edge. He leaned toward her. "Let's go to bed."

"Hel-*lo* Blake. Have you been listening to me? I'm not ready to sleep with you yet . . . besides, Dr. North said it was risky. Remember? Early contractions."

He looked ridiculously deflated. "Oh, yeah. I just thought, if this is a reconciliation, you should—"

"No more telling me what I should and shouldn't do, Blake. I'm not the same woman I was before. And I'm scared to death you're the same damn man."

"I'm not. Really, I'm not. I've grown, too. I know how precious our life was. I won't make the same mistakes again."

"I hope not."

He moved toward her. "You always used to say that the longest journey begins with a single step."

He was right; it used to be one of her favorite sayings. Now, that kind of optimism felt far, far away.

He was obviously waiting for her to respond, and when she didn't, he glanced around. "Well, do you want to watch television for a while? I could make some popcorn and hot chocolate—like the old days."

The old days.

With those simple words, she saw her whole life flash before her eyes. This spring she'd worked to unearth the real Annie, and now Blake wanted to bury her once again beneath the sand of their old patterns. Tomorrow, she knew she would have to make an effort, an *honest* effort to find her way back to Blake, but tonight, she was too damned tired to start. "No, thanks," she said quietly. "I think I'll just go to bed. It's been a long day. You can sleep in the green guest room. I put fresh sheets on the bed today."

"Oh. I thought—"

"I know what you thought. It isn't going to happen."

She might have laughed at his expression—so confused and crest-fallen—but it wasn't funny. He was her husband, the father of her children, the man she'd vowed to love, honor, and cherish until death parted them, and right now, standing in the living room of the house they'd shared for so many years, she couldn't think of a single thing to say to him.

Blake met Natalie at Customs.

She gave him a big hug, then drew back, looking around. "Where's Mom?"

"She couldn't make it. I'll tell you all about it in the car on the way home."

"Do you have the Ferrari?"

"What else?"

"Can I drive?"

Blake frowned. "Did someone tell you I'd suffered recent brain damage? I never let—"

"Oh, *please,* Dad. I haven't driven in months."

"This is hardly an argument that helps your cause."

"Come on, Dad. *Pleeeeease.*"

He imagined the look on Annie's face if she heard he'd let Natalie drive. Slowly, he pulled the keys out of his pocket and tossed them in the air. Natalie snagged them in one hand. "Come on, Dad!" She grabbed his hand and dragged him through the terminal. Within moments, they were strapped into the sportscar and heading down the freeway for home.

As always, Blake was uneasy around his daughter. He tried to think of something to say to her now, something to break the uncomfortable silence that always stood between them.

She changed his radio station. A hard-edged rock-and-roll song blasted through the speakers.

"Turn that thing down," he said automatically.

She clicked the music off, then signaled for a turn and jerked into the fast lane, sucking up behind a black Mercedes convertible. Before he had time to tell her what to do, she slowed down and backed off.

"So, Dad, how's Grandpa Hank?"

"How should I know?"

She glanced at him. "You *did* go up to Mystic?"

He shifted uncomfortably, thankful when her gaze turned back to the road. He wasn't good at handling this stuff. It was Annie's job to put the right spin on their separation. "I . . . was really busy. There was this big case between a rock star and—"

"So, you were really busy," she said quietly, her hands curled tightly around the wheel, her eyes staring straight ahead.

"Consumed."

"That must be why you never called me."

He heard the hurt in her voice and he didn't know what to say. He'd never heard that tone before, but he wondered suddenly if it had been there all along. "I sent flowers to you every Friday."

"Yeah. You thought of me long enough to ask your secretary to send flowers every week."

Blake sighed. He was way out in left field with this one. How could he tell his teenage daughter he'd thrown their family away—and all for a few months of hot sex with a woman who hadn't been alive when Kennedy was shot.

What was he supposed to tell her? The truth, a lie, or something in between?

Annie would know what to do and say. She'd always guided his relationship with Natalie. She told him subtly, with a look or a touch or a whisper, when to reach out to Natalie and when to pull back.

But he had to say *something*. Natalie was obviously waiting to hear his explanation. "Your mother's . . . angry with me. I made a few mistakes, and . . . well . . ."

"You two were separated this summer." She said it in a dull, monotonous voice, without looking at him.

He winced. "Just a little break, is all. Everything will be fine now."

"Really? Did you have surgery while I was gone—a personality transplant maybe? Or did you retire? Come on, Dad, how is everything going to get better? You hate being at home."

He frowned, staring at her stern profile. It was an odd thing for her to say. "That's not true."

"Yeah, right. That's why I have no memories of you until high school."

He sank deeper into his seat. Maybe this was *why* he stayed away so much. Annie and Natalie were masters at piling on the guilt. "Everything will be fine, Natalie. You'll see. Your mom's . . . going to have a baby."

"A *baby*? Oh, my God, how could she not tell me that?" She laughed. "I can't believe it . . ."

"It's true. She's back in bed with this one—just like with Adrian. And she's going to need our help."

"*Our* help?" It was all she said, and he was glad she'd dropped the subject of the separation, but after a while, the silence began to gnaw at him. He kept thinking about that ridiculous little sentence, *I have no memories of you*. It kept coming back even as he tried to push it away.

He stared out the window at his whole life. Years ago, when Natalie was a pudgy-faced child who talked incessantly, it hadn't been like this between them. She'd looked at him through adoring eyes.

But somewhere along the way, she'd stopped thinking he'd hung the moon, and for no reason that he could remember now, he'd let it go. He was always so damned busy.

He'd never had much time for her; that was certainly true. But that was Annie's job, motherhood, and she'd done it so effortlessly that Blake had told himself he wasn't necessary. His job was to bring home money.

And by the time he realized that his daughter had stopped coming to him with her problems—a wiggly tooth, a lost teddy bear—it was too late. By then he barely knew her. One day she was a toothless toddler, and the next, she was off to the mall with a group of girls he didn't recognize.

Sadly, when he thought about it, he had damn few memories of her, either. Moments, yes; pictures in his mind, certainly. But memories, recollections of time spent together, were almost totally absent.

Annie heard the scream first. *Mommmm!*

She sat up in bed, fluffing the pillows behind her. "I'm in here, Nana!"

Natalie burst into Annie's bedroom. Grinning, laughing, she dove onto the big king-size bed and threw her arms around Annie. Blake came in a few moments later and stood beside the bed.

Finally, Natalie drew back. Her beautiful blue eyes were filled with tears, but she was smiling from ear to ear.

Annie drank in the sight of her daughter. "I missed you, Nana," she whispered.

Natalie cocked her head, eyeing Annie critically. "What happened to your hair?"

"I got it cut."

"It looks *great*. We could be sisters." A look of mock horror crossed her face. "I hope this doesn't mean you're going to college with me. . . ."

Annie feigned a hurt look. "I didn't think you'd mind. I signed up to be your dorm mother."

Natalie rolled her eyes. "From anyone else's mother it would be a joke." She looked at Blake. "You're not letting her go, are you, Dad?"

Annie looked up at Blake, who was staring down at her. He moved in closer and laid a possessive hand on her shoulder. "I'm trying like hell to keep her at home," he said evenly.

"Dad tells me you're pregnant." A tiny bit of hurt flashed through Natalie's blue eyes and then was gone. "I can't believe you didn't tell me."

Annie gently touched her daughter's cheek. "I just found out, honey."

Natalie grinned. "I ask for a sister for sixteen years, and you get pregnant just before I leave for college. Thanks a lot."

"This definitely falls into the 'accident' category. Believe me, I always wanted to fill this house with children—but not just before I cashed my first Social Security check."

"You're not that old. I read about a sixty-year-old woman who had a kid."

"How comforting. You understand, of course, that the rules have changed now. You aren't allowed to have a child until your sister or brother graduates from high school. And you will have to introduce me as your stepmother."

Natalie laughed. "I've been lying about you for years, Mom. Ever since you sobbed at my dance recital and had to be escorted from the building."

"That was an allergy attack."

"Yeah, right." She laughed. "Hey, guess what, Mom. Dad let me drive the Ferrari home."

"You're kidding."

"It's a good thing you weren't there. You'd have made me wear a crash helmet and drive on the side of the road—preferably with my emergency blinkers flashing."

Annie laughed, and she couldn't escape how *right* this all felt—the teasing, the joking, the familiarity. How natural.

They were a family. A *family.*

Blake bent closer to Annie. He whispered in a voice so soft that only she could hear, "People change, Annalise."

It scared her, that deceptively simple sentence that seemed to promise the sun and the moon and the stars.

That's when she knew she was at risk. This man she'd loved for so long knew what to say, always, what to do. He could push her onto the edge again. If she wasn't careful, she'd slide without a ripple into the gently flowing stream of her old life, pulled back under the current without a whimper of protest. Another housewife lost in the flow.

CHAPTER 25

The shattered pieces of their family fell back together with a surprising ease. Like a glass vase that had been broken and carefully mended, the tiny fissures could be seen only on close examination, when Blake and Annie were alone. They were soldiers, the two of them, warily circling each other, negotiating an awkward and unfelt peace.

But Annie had spent twenty years wearing a groove into her life, and she now slipped smoothly back into it. She awakened early, dressed in an expensive silk robe with a pretty bow tied at her expanding waist. She carefully accentuated her features with makeup, layering putty color beneath her eyes to erase the dark circles that came from restless nights.

On Mondays, she made out the weekly grocery lists and sent Natalie to the gourmet shop on the corner. On Tuesdays, she paid the household bills. On Wednesdays, she conferred with the housekeeper and gardener, and on Thursdays she sent Natalie on errands, using her daughter to collect all the various and sundry pieces of their lives. Once again, the house was a well-run unit.

She helped Blake choose his suits and ties, and reminded him when to pick up his dry cleaning. Every morning, she kissed him good-bye—a chaste, dry little kiss planted on his cheek—and every night she welcomed him home from work with a smile. He sat on her bed and talked stiltedly about his day.

In truth, she was glad to spend her days in bed, hidden away from the reality of the marriage. Most days, while Blake was at work, she and Natalie spent long hours talking and laughing and sharing memories.

Annie learned that Blake hadn't called Natalie in London. She heard the hurt and disappointment in her daughter's voice when she spoke, but there wasn't a damn thing Annie could do to fix it. "I'm sorry" was all she could say. Again and again.

Increasingly, Annie noticed changes in Natalie, a new maturity that hadn't been there before. Every now and then, she zinged Annie with an unexpected observation. Like yesterday.

All you think about is making us happy. What makes you happy, Mom?

Or: *This spring . . . you sounded so different. So happy.*

And the most surprising of all: *Do you love Dad?*

Annie had meant to respond reflexively, to say, *Yes, of course I love your dad.* But then she'd looked in Natalie's eyes and seen a grown-up understanding. And so, Annie had spoken to the woman her daughter had become.

I've loved your dad since I was a teenager. We're just going through a hard time, that's all.

He loves you, Natalie had said. *Just like he loves me, but . . . his love . . . it isn't very warm . . . I mean . . . it's not like being loved by you, Mom.*

It had brought tears to Annie's eyes, that quiet observation. She was saddened to realize that Natalie would never really understand what a father's love could be. It would be a loss in Natalie's life forever. . . .

Unlike Izzy.

She closed her eyes and leaned back in bed, remembering Nick and Izzy when they'd played Candy Land, Nick hunched over the board . . . or when the two of them had played Barbies on the living room floor, Nick saying in a falsetto voice, *Have you seen my blue dancing shoes?*

Yesterday, when she and Natalie had gone into the doctor's, Annie had been unable to stave off the memories. It was simply too painful. There had been no husband there to hold her hand and laugh at how badly she had to pee. No husband to watch the fuzzy black screen and marvel at the miracle.

No Nick.

How long would it be this way? she wondered. Would she spend the rest of her life feeling that she'd left an essential part of herself in another place and time?

269

The first letter, when it arrived, was small and crinkled. A blue, faded postmark read *Mystic, WA*.

Annie stared down at the pink envelope. Very gently, she eased the back open and pulled out the paper. It was a pen-and-ink drawing of Mount Olympus. Inside was a letter from Izzy.

Dear Annie:
How are you? I am fin.
The flwrs are pritty. Today I learnd to ride a bike.
It was fun.
I miss you. When are you cuming home?
Love, Izzy.
P.s. My Dadde helped me rite this lettr.

Annie clutched the note in her hand. Everything about it, every misspelled word, tugged at her heartstrings. She sat stiffly in bed, staring out at the blue, blue sky beyond her room, wishing it would rain. She knew she would write back to Izzy, but what would she say? A few hopeless words that held no promises? Or a string of pointless banalities that pretended they'd all be friends. Nothing but friends, and sometimes friends moved on. . . .

There were only a few words that mattered, and they were the truest of them all. "I miss you, too, Izzy. . . ."

She opened the nightstand drawer and pulled out Izzy's hair ribbon, stroking the satin strip. She knew that tomorrow she would answer the letter, and she would fill a sheet of paper with words and more words, but it wouldn't say what mattered. It wouldn't say what Izzy wanted to hear.

She picked up the cordless phone from the table and listened to the dial tone for a long time, then slowly she hung up. It was unfair to call Nick and Izzy, unfair to let the sound of their voices soothe her loneliness. *Don't do that to me, Annie,* Nick had said, *don't throw me hope like it was a bone to be buried in my backyard. . . .*

"Mom?" Natalie poked her head into the bedroom. "Are you all right?"

Annie sniffled and turned away.

Natalie hurried over to the bed and crawled up beside Annie. "Mom? Are you okay?"

No, she wanted to say, *no, I'm not okay.* I miss the man I love and his daughter, and I miss a place where rainfall is measured in feet and your hair is never dry and where grown-ups play Chutes and Ladders in the middle of the afternoon with a six-year-old girl. . . .

But none of that was the sort of thing you said to your teenage daughter, no matter how grown up she looked. "I'm fine, honey. Just fine."

No matter how hard she tried to be her old self, Annie couldn't quite manage it. No matter how many of the old routines she pushed herself through, she felt herself slipping away. With each day, she saw the future approaching in a low-rolling fog of lost chances and missed opportunities.

Summer blasted through Southern California on a tide of unseasonable heat. The Malibu hills dried up and turned brown. Leaves began, one by one, to curl up and die, dropping like bits of charred paper on artificially green lawns.

Blake stood on the deck outside his room, sipping a scotch and soda. The wood was warm beneath his bare feet, the last reminder of a surprisingly hot day.

He hadn't slept well last night. Hadn't, in fact, slept well in weeks. Not since he'd apologized to Annie and discovered that she didn't care.

She was trying to make their marriage work. He could see the effort, in the way she put on makeup every morning and wore the colors she knew he liked. She even touched him occasionally—brief, flitting gestures that were designed to make him feel better, but that had the opposite effect. Every time she touched him, he felt a tiny, niggling ache in his chest, and he remembered the way it used to be, the way she used to touch him all the time and smile at his jokes and brush the hair away from his face, and when he remembered he hurt.

She wasn't herself anymore, that was obvious. She lay in their big bed like a silent, pregnant ghost, and when she smiled, it was a brittle, fleeting thing, and not Annie at all.

She was . . . disappearing, for lack of a better word.

She used to talk and laugh all the time. She used to find joy in the craziness of life, but nothing intrigued her anymore. Her moods were a flat line, even and smooth. So smooth, there was no hint of Annie inside the quiet woman who sat with him in the evening, watching television.

Last week, when it rained, she had sat up in bed, staring through the silver-streaked window. When he called out to her, she'd turned, and he hadn't missed the tears in her eyes. She'd been holding some ragged scrap of a hair ribbon as if it were the Holy Grail.

He couldn't stand this much longer. He wasn't the kind of man who liked to work this hard for what he wanted. Enough was enough.

He set down his drink on the table and strode back into the house. He knocked on Annie's door—quickly, before he lost his nerve.

"Come in," she called out.

He opened the door and went inside. The room was as comforting as ever, with its sea-blue walls and carpet and white bedding.

Annie was in bed, reading a book called *How to Run Your Own Small Business.* Beside her, there was a pile of similarly titled self-help books.

Jesus, was she thinking of getting a *job*?

It would humiliate him if she sought employment; she knew how he felt about his wife working. Especially with her lack of skills. What would she do—pour lattes and pick croissants from a glass case?

He had no idea who this woman was, who sat in bed and read how-to books. He felt unconnected to Annie; he had to do something to get them back together.

She looked up, and he noticed the dark circles under her eyes and gray cast to her skin. In the past month, she'd gained a lot of weight, but somehow her face looked thinner. Her hair had grown out some, and the tips were beginning to curl wildly. Again, she looked like a woman he didn't know. "Hi, Blake," she said softly, closing the book. "Is it time for the movie to start? I thought—"

He went to the bed and sat beside her, gazing down into her beautiful green eyes. "I love you, Annie. I know we can work all this out if we're . . . together."

"We are together."

"Where's your wedding ring?"

She cocked her head toward the mahogany highboy. "In my jewelry box."

He got up and went to the highboy, carefully opening the hand-painted box that held all the treasures he'd given her over the years. There, among the black velvet rolls, was the three-carat diamond he'd given her on their tenth wedding anniversary. Beside it was the plain gold band they'd originally bought. He picked up the two rings and returned to the bed, sitting down beside his wife.

He stared down at the fiery diamond. "Remember that vacation we took, years ago, at the Del Coronado Hotel? Natalie wasn't more than a year old—"

"Six months," she said softly.

He looked at her. "We brought that big old blue and red blanket— the one I had on my bed in college—and laid it out on the beach. We were the only people out there, just the three of us."

Annie almost smiled. "We went swimming, even though it was freezing cold."

"You were holding Natalie, with the waves splashing across your thighs. Your lips were practically blue and your skin was nothing but goose bumps, but you were laughing, and I remember how much I loved you. My heart hurt every time I looked at you."

She looked down at her hands, folded on her lap. "That was a long time ago."

"I found a sand dollar, remember? I handed it to you with our baby wobbling on the blanket between us, rocking her little butt back and forth. I think she was trying to learn to crawl."

Annie closed her eyes, and he wondered what she was thinking. Could she remember the rest of that day? How often he'd touched her . . . or when he'd leaned over and grazed the back of her neck with a kiss. *Hey Godiva,* he'd whispered. *They rent horses down the road. . . .*

And her laughing answer, *Babies can't ride.*

"When did we stop having fun together, Annie? When?" He was seducing her with their memories, and he could see that it was working;

he could see it in the way she stared at her hands intently, in the sheen of moisture that filled her eyes.

Slowly, he reached down and placed the two rings back on her finger. "Forgive me, Annie," he said quietly.

She looked up. A tear streaked down her cheek and dropped onto her nightgown, leaving a gray-wet blotch. "I want to."

"Let me sleep with you tonight. . . ."

She sighed. It was a long time before she answered, time enough for him to feel hope sliding away. "Yes," she said at last.

He told himself that nothing mattered but the answer. He ignored the uncertainty in her voice and the tears in her eyes and the way she wouldn't quite look at him. It would all be okay again after they slept together. Finally, the bits of their broken lives would fuse together again.

He wanted to crush her against him, but he forced himself to move slowly. He got up, went into the closet, and changed into his pajamas. Then, very slowly, he went to the bed and peeled back the coverlet, slipping beneath the cool, white cotton sheets.

It was soothing to hold her again, like easing into a favorite pair of slippers after a long day at the office. He kissed her lightly, and as always, she was quiet and undemanding in her response. Finally, he turned over—the regular beginning of their nightly ritual. After a long moment, she snuggled up behind him.

Her body spooned against his, her belly pressed into his back. It was the way they'd always slept, only this time she didn't curl her arms around him.

They lay there, touching but not touching in the bed that had held their passion for so many years. She didn't speak, other than to say good night, and he couldn't think of anything else.

It was a long time before he fell asleep.

Natalie set a big metal bowl full of popcorn at the foot of Annie's bed, then she climbed up and snuggled close to her mom. It was Friday afternoon: girls' day. Annie and Natalie and Terri had spent every Friday together since Annie returned home. They laughed and talked and played cribbage and watched movies.

"I left the front door open for Terri," Natalie said, pulling the bowl of popcorn onto her lap.

Annie grinned. "You know what your dad would say. He thinks criminals spend all day in the rosebushes, just *waiting* for us to leave the door open."

Natalie laughed. They talked about this and that and everything. Their conversation followed the river of their years, flowing from one topic to the next. They laughed about antics that were as old as Natalie and as new as yesterday. Through it all, Annie was amazed at Natalie's maturity; the teenager who had gone off to London had come home a young woman. It seemed light years ago that Natalie had rebelled, that she'd shorn her hair and dyed it platinum and pierced her earlobes with three holes.

"How come Dad never talks about the baby?"

The question came out of the blue, smacking Annie hard. She tried not to compare Nick and Blake, but it was impossible at a moment like this. Nick would have been with Annie every step of the way, sharing in the miracle, watching her belly swell. She would have clung to his hand during the amniocentesis, letting his jokes distract her from the needle . . . and she would have laughed with him later, when they found out it was a girl, skipping through name books and spinning dreams. . . .

She sighed. "Your dad is uncomfortable with pregnancy; he always has been. Lots of men are like that. He'll be better after the baby is born."

"Get real, Mom. Dad's good at doing his own thing. I mean, you guys are supposedly getting over your 'bad patch,' but he's never here. He still works seventy hours a week, he still plays basketball on Tuesday nights, and he still goes out for drinks with *the boys* every Friday night. When are you guys working out your problems? During Letterman?"

Annie gave her a sad smile. "When you get older, you'll understand. There's a certain . . . comfort in the familiar."

Natalie stared at her. "I have almost no memories of Dad—did you know that? All I remember about him are a few hurried good-bye kisses and the sound of a slamming door. When I hear a car engine start or a garage door close, I think of my dad." She turned to Annie. "What about after this summer . . . when I'm gone?"

Annie shivered, though the room was warm. She looked away from Natalie, unable to bear the sad certainty in her daughter's eyes. "When you're gone, I'll be worried about potty training and what to do with the Baccarat on the living room table. I'll consider plastic surgery to pull my breasts back up from my navel. You know, the usual stuff."

"And you'll be lonely."

Annie wanted to deny it. She wanted to be grown up and a good parent and say just the right thing that would alleviate Natalie's worry. But for once, no parental lies came to her. "Maybe a little. Life can be like that, Nana. We don't always get what we want."

Natalie glanced down at her own hands. "When I was little, you told me that life *did* give you what you wanted, if you were willing to fight for it and believe in it. You told me that every cloud had a silver lining."

"Those were a mother's words to a little girl. These are a mother's words to a nearly grown woman."

Natalie looked at her, long and hard. Then she turned away.

Annie felt suddenly distant from her daughter. She was reminded of four years ago, when Natalie had turned into someone else. It had seemed that overnight, their tastes had diverged: whatever Annie liked, Natalie hated. Christmas that year had been a tense, horrible affair, with Natalie dully opening each carefully wrapped package and then muttering a caustic *gee thanks.* "Nana? What is it?"

Slowly, Natalie turned to face Annie. "You don't have to be this way, you know."

"What do you mean?"

Natalie shook her head and looked away. "Never mind."

Understanding dawned slowly, and with it, pain. It all fell into place: Natalie's desire to study biochemisty at Stanford, her sudden trip to London, her unwillingness to date the same boy for more than a few months. Behind it all was a sad message: I don't want to be like you, Mom. I don't want to be dependent on a man for everything.

"I see," Annie said.

Natalie turned to her at last, and this time there were tears in her eyes. "What do you see?"

"It doesn't matter."

"It *does*. What are you thinking?"

"I'm thinking you don't want to grow up to be like your old Mom, and . . . as much as that hurts, it makes me proud. I want you to count on yourself in life. I guess, in the end, it's all we have."

Natalie sighed. "You never would have said that before he broke your heart."

"I think I've grown up a little bit lately. Life isn't all sunny days and blue skies."

"But you always taught me to look for the silver lining to every cloud. Are you doing that, Mom? Are you looking to be happy?"

"Of course I am," she answered quickly, but they both knew it was a lie. Annie couldn't meet her daughter's penetrating gaze. "I'm glad you don't want to be like me, Nana."

Sadness suffused Natalie's face. "I don't want to have a marriage like yours, and I don't understand why you stay with him—I never have. That doesn't mean I don't want to be like you. There are only two people in the world who don't respect you . . . as far as I know, anyway."

She looked at Natalie, shaking her head slightly, as if she could stop her daughter's words.

"Just two," Natalie said. A single tear streaked down her cheek and she impatiently brushed it away. "Dad . . . and you."

You. Annie felt a sudden urge to disappear, to simply melt into the expensive bed linens and vanish. She knew that Natalie was waiting for her to say something, but she didn't know what was the right answer. She felt as if she were the child, and Natalie the mother, and as the child, she'd let her parent down.

She opened her mouth to say something—she had no idea what—when suddenly Terri charged into the bedroom like a multicolored bull, her body draped in layers of red and gold lamé.

She came to a breathless stop beside the bed. Planting her fists on her meaty hips, she surveyed the bowl of popcorn. "So, where's *my* popcorn? I mean, that's enough for two skinny chicks like you, but we real women like our popcorn to come in bowls that could double as lifeboats. And I certainly want it coated in butter."

Natalie grinned. "Hey, Terri."

Terri smiled back, her heavily mascaraed lashes almost obscured her twinkling eyes. "Hiya princess."

"I'll go make another batch of popcorn."

"You do that, sweetie," Terri said, uncoiling the gold turban from her head.

When Natalie scurried from the room, Terri sat down on the end of the bed and leaned back against the footboard, sighing. "Christ, what a day. Sorry I'm late."

Annie smiled wanly at the theatrics. "What happened?"

"My character is running from the law—again—only this time they put her on a plane." Terri shook her head. "Bad news."

"What's wrong with that?"

"In the soaps, there's only one thing worse than getting on a plane, and that's getting in a car. The next thing you hear is sirens . . . and funeral music. If they actually *name* the flight tomorrow, I'm dead meat."

"You'll bounce back."

"Oh, perfect, make fat jokes." Terri scooted up the bed and twisted around to sit beside Annie. "So, kiddo, how's the ever-growing Good-year blimp?"

Annie glanced down at her stomach. "We're doing okay."

"Well, I've been coming every Friday for weeks now, and we talk on the phone constantly. I think I've been patient as hell."

"About what?"

Terri looked at her, hard. "About *what*? Come on."

Annie sighed. "Nick."

"What else? I've been waiting patiently—and we both know that patience is not one of my virtues—for you to bring his name up, but obviously, you're not going to. I'm sick of respecting your privacy. Now, spill the beans. Have you called him?"

"Of course not."

"Why not?"

Annie turned to her best friend. "Come on, Terr."

"Ah . . . that honor thing. I've read about it. We don't see much of it in Southern California. And *none* on the soaps. But you *are* in love with him?"

"I don't think I want to talk about this."

"There's no point lying to an old slut like me. Hell, Annie, I've been in love more times than Liz Taylor and I've slept with enough men to protect this country in time of war. Now, do you love him?"

"Yes," she whispered, crossing her arms. It hurt to say the words aloud, and instantly she regretted it. "But I'll get over it. I *have* to. Blake is doing his best to put our family back together. Things are . . . rough right now, but they'll get better."

Terri gave her a sad smile. "I hope it works that way for you, Annie. But for most of us, when love is gone, it's gone, and all the pretending and wishing in the world can't bring it back."

"Can't bring what back?" It was Natalie, standing in the doorway with another bowl of popcorn and a bottle of spring water.

"Nothing, honey," Annie said softly.

Natalie produced a videotape from behind her back. "I rented us a movie." She popped it in the VCR, then climbed up onto the bed beside Terri.

Terri grabbed a handful of popcorn. "What's the movie?"

"Same Time, Next Year."

"That Alan Alda movie?" Terri gave Annie a sharp, knowing look. "I always thought that was a hell of an idea. An affair once a year, I mean. Ellen Burstyn's husband is probably a real shithead—a workaholic with the moral integrity of an alley cat. He probably fucked around on Ellen and then came crawling back like the worm he is. And because Ellen's a grade-A sweetie pie, she took him back and tried to pretend that everything was okay. Still, she meets her secret lover for one weekend a year on the wild Oregon coast. Yep, sounds like heaven to me."

"Shhh," Natalie said. "It's starting."

Annie looked away from Terri. She tried not to feel anything at all, but when the music came on and the credits began to roll, she sank deeper and deeper into the pillows, as if distance could soften the sharp edges of her memories.

CHAPTER 26

Nick made it through the summer one day at a time. The last thing he did every night was stand by the lake, where Annie's memory was strongest. Sometimes, the missing of her was so acute, he felt it as a pain in his chest. Those were the nights when he heard the call of the booze, the soothing purr of his own weakness.

But he was making it. For the first time in years, he was actually living life on his own terms. Annie had been right in so many of the things she said to him. He'd gone back to work, and the job had given him a purpose. He was the best policeman he'd ever been. He gave everything to the people under his protection, but when his shift was over, he left the worries behind. He had learned, finally, to accept that there would be failures, and that it was okay. All he could do was try.

Like with Gina. She was still fighting the pull of old patterns and comforting, self-destructive routines. The other kids were often blatantly cruel to her. The "good" kids didn't want to hang around with a loser, and the "bad" kids spent all their time trying to lure her back into their circle of drugs and truancy, but, like Nick, Gina was holding her own. She'd moved back into her old bedroom and was reforging the bonds of the family she'd so carelessly torn apart. Last month she'd registered for school.

And there was always Izzy, waiting for Nick at the end of the day with a smile and a picture she'd drawn or a song she had learned. They'd become inseparable. Best buddies. He never took a moment or a word for granted.

During the week, he worked from nine to five; the second his shift was over, he picked up Izzy from the Raintree Day Care, and they were off. They spent all their free time together.

Today, he'd gotten off work three hours ago and their nightly ritual had begun. First, dinner on the porch (lasagna and green salads from Vittorio's), then they quickly washed the dishes together.

Now, Nick sat cross-legged on the cold plank floor, staring down at the multicolored Candy Land game board. There were three little pieces at the starting box, a red, a green, and a blue.

But there are only two of us, Izzy, he'd said when Izzy put the third man down.

That's Annie, Daddy.

Nick watched with a growing sadness as Izzy stoically rolled for Annie and moved her tiny blue piece from square to square.

"Come here, Izzy," he said at last, pushing the game away. She crawled across the floor and settled into his lap, hooking her spindly legs around him. He stared down at her. The words congealed in his throat; how could you tell a little girl to stop believing?

"She's comin' back, Daddy," Izzy said in the high-pitched, certain voice of an innocent.

He stroked her hair. "It's okay to miss her, Sunshine, but you can't keep thinking that she's going to come back. She has another life . . . she always did. We were lucky to have her for as long as we did."

Izzy leaned back into his laced fingers. "You're wrong, Daddy. She's comin' back. So, don't be so sad."

Sad. Such a little word, no more than a breath; it didn't begin to describe the ocean of loss he felt at Annie's absence.

"I love you, Izzy-bear," he whispered.

She planted a kiss on his cheek. "I love you, too, Daddy."

He stared down at her, lying in his arms in her pink flannel jammies with the bunny feet, with her black hair still damp and squiggly around her face, and her big brown eyes blinking up at him with expectation.

He knew then, as he'd known so many times before, that no matter what, he'd always love Annie for what she'd given him.

The air was crisp the next morning, chilly with the promise of fall. The flowers were fading now at the end of summer, and autumn colors— orange and green and scarlet—had replaced the bright hues of August. A cloudy sky cast shadows across the cemetery, where acres of grass rolled gently toward a curtain of evergreen trees. It was well cared for, this final resting place for most of Mystic's citizens.

Nick walked slowly toward the easternmost corner of the cemetery. Izzy was beside him, holding his hand. With each step, he felt his insides tighten, and by the time he reached his destination, his throat was dry and he needed a drink desperately.

He gazed down at the headstone. *Kathleen Marie Delacroix. Beloved Wife and Mother.*

He sighed. Four words to sum up her life. They were the wrong four words; he'd known it at the time, but then he'd been so twisted with grief that he'd let the small, round-faced funeral director handle everything. And in truth, Nick didn't know what other words he would have chosen, even now. How could you possibly express the sum of a person's life in a few words cut into smooth gray stone?

He glanced down at Izzy. "I should have brought you here a long time ago."

Izzy let go of his hand. She reached into her pocket and pulled out a wrinkled sheet of paper. Last night, when he'd told her they were going to come here, Izzy had picked up a piece of paper and her crayons, then she'd gone into her room alone. When she emerged, she held a picture of her mom's favorite flower. *Daddy, I'll give her this. That way she'll know I was visitin' her.*

He had nodded solemnly.

She walked over to the wrought-iron bench and sat down. Smoothing the paper on her lap, she stared at the headstone. "Daddy said I could talk to you, Mommy. Can you hear me?" She drew in a ragged breath. "I miss you, Mommy."

Nick bowed his head, thinking of a dozen things at once, and thinking nothing at all. "Heya, Kath." He waited for her to answer, but, of course, there was nothing except the swaying of the evergreen boughs and the trilling call of a bird.

This place had so little to do with his Kathy. It was why he hadn't come here before, not since the day they placed her gleaming mahogany casket in a gaping hole in the earth. He couldn't stand to look at the evenly clipped carpet of grass and know that she was below it, his wife who'd always been afraid of the dark and afraid of being alone. . . .

He reached out, touched the cold headstone with the tip of a finger, tracing the etched canal of her name.

"I came to say good-bye, Kath," he said softly, closing his eyes against the sudden sting of tears. His voice broke, and he couldn't speak out loud. *I loved you for most of my life, and I know you loved me, too. What . . . what you did was about something else, something I never could understand. I wanted you to know that I forgive us. We did the best we could. . . .*

He touched the stone again, felt it warm beneath his fingertips, and for a moment—a heartbeat that winged into eternity—he imagined her beside him, her golden hair streaming in the sunlight, her black eyes crinkled in a smile. It was the day Izzy was born, that was the memory that came to him. Kathy sitting up in the hospital bed, her hair all askew, her skin left pale by exhaustion, her pink flannel nightgown buttoned improperly. She had never looked so lovely, and when she looked down at the sleeping infant in her arms, she'd begun softly to cry. "Isabella," she'd said, trying the name on her tongue before she looked up at Nick. "Can we call her Isabella?"

As if Nick could deny her anything. "It's perfect."

Kathy had continued to look at him, while tears streaked down her cheeks. "You'll always take care of her, won't you, Nicky?"

She had known even then the darkness that was coming for her.

But did she know that he loved her, that he had always loved her, and that he always would? She was a part of him, perhaps the biggest part, and sometimes even now, he heard her laughter in the whisper of the wind. Last week, when he'd seen those beautiful white swans across the lake, he stopped and stared and thought, *there they are, Kath . . . they've come back again. . . .*

Izzy slipped her hand in his. "It's okay, Daddy. She knows."

He pulled her into his arms and held her, looking up at the sky through hot, stinging tears. *I have her, Kath—the best part of us—and I'll always be here for her.*

They placed a wicker basket full of blooming chrysanthemums on the grass, then drove home.

"I'm gonna check the garden," Izzy said when they pulled into the driveway.

"Don't be long. It looks like it's going to rain."

Nodding, she got out of the car and made a beeline to the white picket fence. Nick slammed the door shut and headed for the house. Sure enough, it started to rain before he reached the porch.

"Daddy, Daddy, come here, Daddy!"

He turned. She was standing in front of the cherry tree they'd planted last year. She was hopping up and down like an agitated bird, flapping her arms.

He raced across the yard. When he reached her, she looked up at him, grinning, her face washed by rain. "Look, Daddy."

Nick saw what she was pointing at, and slowly he dropped to his knees in the already moist grass.

The cherry tree had produced a single, perfect pink bud.

Autumn brought color back to Southern California. Brown grass began to turn green. The gray air, swept clean by September breezes, regained its springtime blue. The local radio stations started an endless stream of football chatter. The distant whine of leaf blowers filled the air.

It was the season of sharp, sudden changes: days of bright lemon heat followed by cold, starlit nights. Sleeveless summer shirts were packed away in boxes and replaced by crew-neck sweaters. The birds began one by one to disappear, leaving their nests untended. To the Californians, who spent most of their days in clothes as thin as tissue and smaller than washrags, it began to feel cold. They shivered as the wind kicked up, plucking the last dying red leaves from the trees along the road. Sometimes whole minutes went by without a single car turning toward the beach. The crossroads were empty of tourists, and only the stoutest of spirit ventured into the cool Pacific Ocean at this time of year. The stream of surfers at the state beach had dwindled to a few hardy souls a day.

It was time now to let go. But how did you do that, really? Annie had spent seventeen years trying to protect her daughter from the world, and now all of that protection lay in the love she'd given Natalie, in the words she'd used on their talks, and in the examples she'd provided.

The examples.

Annie sighed, remembering the talk she'd had with Natalie and the disappointment she'd felt in realizing that she hadn't been a good role model. Now it was too late to change all that she'd been and done as a mother. Annie's time was over.

"Mom?" Natalie poked her head into Annie's bedroom.

"Hey, Nana," she answered, trying to inject cheerfulness into her voice. "Come on in."

Natalie climbed onto the bed and stretched out alongside Annie. "I can't believe I'm really going."

Annie put an arm around her daughter. Surely this beautiful creature couldn't be the child who'd once licked the metal ski-chair pole at Mammoth Mountain . . . or the girl who'd climbed into her parents' bed after a nightmare when she was only a year away from being a teenager.

Seventeen years had passed in the blink of an eye. It was too fast. Not long enough . . .

Idly, Annie finger-combed her daughter's long blond hair. She'd been preparing for this day for ages, almost since she'd first dropped Nana off at kindergarten, and still she wasn't ready. "Have I told you today how proud I am of you?"

"Only a billion times."

"Make it a billion and one."

Natalie snuggled closer and pressed a hand to Annie's stomach. "How were the latest stress tests and ultrasounds?"

"Everything shows a healthy baby girl. There's nothing for you to worry about."

"She's lucky to have you for a mom."

Annie laid her hand on Natalie's. There were so many things she wanted to say, on this day when her daughter was embarking on the adventure of her own life, but she knew that she had had her time. Everything of magnitude that was hers to say had been said, and if it hadn't, it was too late now. Still, she wished she could think of one single, flawless bit of advice to hand down like an heirloom to her child.

Natalie leaned against her. "What are you going to do while I'm gone?"

Gone. Such a hard, cold, uncompromising word. It was like *death,* or *divorce.* Annie swallowed. "Miss you?"

Natalie turned to her. "Remember when I was little . . . you always used to ask me what I wanted to be when I grew up?"

"I remember."

"What about you, Mom? What did you used to tell Grandpa Hank when he asked you the same question?"

Annie sighed. How could she make Natalie understand what Annie herself had only figured out this year, after almost forty years of living? Hank had never asked his only daughter that question. He'd been a lonely, lost single father, caught between the decades of Donna Reed and Gloria Steinem, and he had taught his daughter that a woman was defined by the men around her. He had been taught, and so he believed, that girls didn't need dreams for the future—those were for little boys, who would grow up to run businesses and make money.

Annie had made so many mistakes, and most of them had been because she'd planted herself firmly in the middle of the road. But now she knew that life without risk was impossible, and if by chance you stumbled across a safe, serene existence, it was because you'd never really reached for anything in the first place.

At last, Annie had something she wanted to reach for, a risk she wanted to take. She turned to her daughter. "When I was in Mystic, I started thinking about opening my own bookstore. There was a wonderful old Victorian house at the end of Main Street, and the downstairs was vacant."

"That's why you've been reading all those business books."

Annie bit down on her smile and nodded. She felt like a child again, who'd just shown a friend her most precious possession and found that it was as beautiful as she'd imagined. "Yes."

Natalie gave her a slow-building grin. "Way to go, Mom. You'd be *excellent* at that. You could give the Malibu bookstore a run for its money. Maybe I could even work for you in the summers."

Annie looked away. That wasn't part of her dream at all, doing it here, under the watchful, critical eye of her husband. She could just *hear* his comments . . .

Not like Nick's response.

There was a knock at the door.

Annie tensed. *It's time.* "Come in," she called out.

Blake strode into the room, wearing a black silk suit and a bright smile. "Hey guys. Is Natalie ready? Mrs. Peterson and Sally are here to pick her up."

Annie manufactured a brittle laugh. "I always pictured myself lugging your suitcases up the dorm stairs and unpacking your clothes for you. I wanted you to at least *start* school with your things organized."

"I would have had to call security to get rid of you." Natalie started out laughing and ended up crying.

Annie pulled Natalie into her arms. "I'll miss you, baby."

Natalie clung to her, whispering, "Don't you forget that bookstore while I'm gone."

Annie was the first to draw back, knowing she had to be the one to do it. She touched Natalie's soft cheek, gazed into her precious blue eyes, remembering for the first time in years how they used to be the color of slate. So long ago . . .

"Good-bye, Nana-banana," she whispered.

"I love you, Mom." It wasn't a child's wobbly voice that said the words. It was a young woman, ready at last to be on her own. Sniffling, her smile trembling, Natalie pulled away.

She gave her dad a weak grin. "Okay, Dad. Walk me out."

After they'd turned and walked away, Annie kept watching, as the door slowly clicked shut. She surprised herself by not crying.

Oh, she knew that later, in the long darkness of the night, and in the many days that lay ahead, a new kind of loneliness would creep toward her, loose its silent voice in the echo of this emptier house, but she knew, too, that she would survive. She was stronger than she'd been in March. She was ready to let her eldest daughter go into the world.

"Good-bye, Nana," she whispered.

Annie went into labor in the first week of November. She woke in the middle of the night, with her stomach on fire. The second cramp hit so hard, she couldn't breathe.

She doubled forward. "Oh . . . God . . ." She focused on her own hands, until the pain released her. Clutching her belly, she flung the covers back and clambered out of bed. She started to scream, but another cramp sliced her voice into a pathetic hiss. "Blake—"

He sat upright in bed. "Annie?"

"It's too . . . early," she wheezed, clutching his pajama sleeve. She thought of Adrian and panicked. "Oh, God, it's too early. . . ."

"Jesus." He lurched out of bed and raced for the clothes that lay heaped over a chair. In a matter of minutes, he had Annie in the car and they were speeding toward the hospital.

"Hang on, Annie. I'll get you to the hospital." He shot her a nervous look. "Just hang on."

She squeezed her eyes shut. *Imagine you're on a white sand beach.*

Another cramp.

"Shit," she hissed. It was impossible. All she could think about was the pain, the red-hot pain that was chewing across her belly, and the life inside her. *Her baby.* She clutched her stomach. "Hold on, baby girl . . . hold on."

But all she saw was Adrian, tiny Adrian, hooked up to a dozen machines, being lowered into the ground in a casket the size of a bread box. . . .

Not again, she prayed silently over and over. *Please God . . . not again.*

The sterile white walls of the hospital's waiting room pressed in on Blake. He paced back and forth, one minute watching the clock, then skimming through some idiotic magazine about celebrities and their infantile problems.

He kept reliving it in his mind. Annie being rushed into the delivery room, her eyes wide with fear, and her voice, broken and braying, saying over and over again, *it's too early*.

Everything had flashed before his eyes in that single, horrifying moment when they'd put her on a gurney and wheeled her away from him. He'd seen his whole marriage in an instant, all the good times and the bad times and the in-between times; he'd seen Annie go from a fresh-faced college sophomore to a pregnant thirty-nine-year-old.

"Mr. Colwater?"

He spun away from the window and saw Annie's obstetrician, Dr. North, standing in the doorway. She wore a crisp white coat and a tired smile. "The baby—"

"How's Annie?"

Dr. North frowned for a second, then said, "Your wife is sleeping peacefully. You may see her now."

He sagged in relief. "Thank God. Let's go." He followed Dr. North down the quiet white hallway to a private room.

Inside, the curtains were drawn and the room lay steeped in bluish shadows. The bed was a narrow, steel-railed thing tucked neatly inside an L-shaped privacy curtain. A bedside table held a telephone and a blue plastic water pitcher with the room number scrawled across the side—as if someone would steal it. Metal IV racks stood alongside the bed like tall, thin vultures, their plastic bags and see-through veins connected to Annie's pale wrists.

She looked young and frail in the strange bed. It brought back a dozen painful memories of his son.

"When will she wake up?" he asked the doctor.

"It shouldn't be long."

Blake couldn't seem to move. He stood in the center of the room, staring at his wife. He'd almost lost her. It was the thought that kept spinning through his head. He'd almost lost her.

He went to the bed and pulled up a chair. He sat there, staring at the woman who'd been his wife for almost twenty years. Dr. North said something—he didn't know what—and then left the room.

After forever—he'd lost track of time—she opened her eyes. "Blake?"

His head snapped up. He saw her sitting up, looking at him. She looked scared and broken. "Annie," he whispered, reaching for her hand.

"My baby," she said. "How's our little girl?"

Shit. He hadn't even asked. "I'll go find out." He rushed away from her and hurried down the hall. He found Dr. North at the nurses' station, and he dragged her back to Annie's room.

At the doctor's entrance, Annie straightened. She was trying desperately not to cry; Blake could see the effort she was making. "Hi, doctor," she said, swallowing hard.

Dr. North went to Annie, touched her hand. "Your daughter is alive, Annie. She's in neonatal intensive care. There were some complications; she was barely five pounds and developmentally that's a problem. We're worried about—"

"She's alive?"

Dr. North nodded. "She still has a lot of hurdles to overcome, Annie, but she's alive. Would you like to see her?"

Annie clamped a hand over her mouth and nodded. She was crying too hard to answer any other way.

Blake stood aside as the doctor helped Annie into the wheelchair stationed in the corner. Then, feeling left out, he followed them down the hallway and into the neonatal ICU.

Annie sat huddled beside the incubator. Inside the clear plastic sides, the baby lay as still as death, a dozen tubes and needles connected to her thin red arms.

Blake came up beside her and laid a hand on her shoulder.

She looked up at him. "I'd like to call her Kathleen Sarah. Is that okay?"

"Sure." He glanced around—up, down, sideways, anywhere except at the incubator. "I'm going to get us something to eat."

"Don't you want to sit with us?"

He didn't look at the baby. "I . . . can't."

Annie didn't know why she was surprised, or why it hurt so deeply. Blake was no good with tragedy or fear; he never had been. If the emotions couldn't fit in a neat little box, he pretended they didn't exist. She would have to handle this in the way she'd handled every upset in her life: alone. Dully, she nodded. "Fine. Get yourself something. I'm not hungry. Oh, and call Natalie. She'll want to know what's happening."

"Okay."

After he left, she reached through the bagged opening in the incubator's side and held her baby's hand. Though she couldn't feel the skin, she could still remember the velvety softness. She tried not to think about Adrian, and the four futile days she'd sat beside him in a room exactly like this one, mouthing the same useless prayers, crying the same wasted tears.

Katie's hand was so damned small and fragile. Annie tucked her fingers around the minuscule wrist. For the next hour, she talked, hoping that the familiar sound of her voice would soothe her daughter, make her know that even in this brightly lit new world full of needles and breathing machines and strangers, she wasn't alone.

She couldn't have said later what she talked about, what she dredged up from her frightened soul to spill onto that austere, frightening plastic box.

But it didn't take long for the words to dry up, taking the false optimism with them.

Finally, the nurses came and took her away. They reminded Annie that she needed to keep her strength up, that she needed to sleep and eat. Annie had tried to argue with them—didn't they know that she couldn't? Not while her precious newborn was struggling for every breath of life.

But of course, she went back to her room, climbed back into her narrow, uncomfortable bed, and stared at the blank walls. She called Stanford and talked to Natalie, who had booked a flight for Friday evening—right after her big Oceanography test. Then she'd called both Hank and Terri.

When the calls were done, Annie lost her strength. She kept thinking about those tiny red fists and the legs that looked like strands of spaghetti, and she closed her eyes. The pain in her chest was so great, she wondered if she could withstand it, or if this old heart of hers would simply seize up and die.

Somewhere, a phone rang. The sudden, blaring sound jarred her from her thoughts. Blinking, she glanced around, realized it was the phone beside her bed.

She picked up the phone and answered dully. "Hello?"

"Annie? It's Nick. Your friend Terri called me . . ."

"Nick?" That's all she said—just his name—and the floodgates opened. She couldn't hold it in anymore. "Duh-did Terri tell you about the baby? My beautiful little girl . . . oh, Nick . . ." She sobbed into the telephone. "She only weighs five pounds. Her lungs aren't fully developed. You should see all the needles and . . ." She cried until there were no more tears inside her, until she felt exhausted and drained and inexpressibly old.

"Where are you?"

"Beverly Hills Memorial, but—"

"I'll come right down."

She closed her eyes. "You don't have to do that. I'll be fine, really . . . Blake's here."

There was a long, scratchy silence between them, then finally, Nick said, "You're stronger than you think you are. You can get through this, whatever happens, you can get through it. Just don't forget."

She wiped her eyes. "Forget what?"

"The rain," he said softly. "It's an angel's tears. And every glass you've ever seen is half full. Don't let yourself forget that. I know what it does to a person . . . forgetting that hope is out there."

She almost said, *I love you, Nick,* but she held the words back just in time. "Thanks."

"I love you, Annie Bourne."

It made her want to cry all over again, that soft, quiet reminder of something that was already leaking away. *Colwater,* she wanted to say. I'm Annie Colwater, and you love a woman who is fading every second. Instead, she forced a wan, tired smile, thankful that he couldn't see it. "Thank you, Nick," she whispered. "Thank you so much. Tell Izzy I'll call her in a few days, when . . . when I know what's happening."

"We'll be praying for . . . all of you," he said finally.

She sighed, feeling the useless tears start all over again. "Good-bye, Nick."

CHAPTER 27

It was the middle of the night, but Annie couldn't sleep. Though she was no longer technically a patient, the hospital had given her a room so she could be near Katie. She'd tried reading and eating and writing, anything to take her mind off of Katie, but nothing worked.

She'd spent hours hunched alongside the incubator, reading, singing, praying. She'd expressed milk into a bottle, but when she looked at the creamy-colored liquid, she wondered if her baby would ever get a chance to drink it. Or a chance to grow strong and move out of this sterile world, a chance to grow and start school and snuggle with her mommy. . . .

We'll get through this, she said to herself, straightening her spine, but every time a machine buzzed, Annie thought *this is it, she's stopped breathing.*

Blake had tried to help, in his own way, but it hadn't worked. He'd said, *She'll be okay,* in a quiet voice, over and over again, but when he spoke, his eyes were blank and afraid.

In truth, Annie had been glad when he left the hospital.

I just can't stay here, he'd said.

Okay. That was her answer, and even then, in the quiet darkness, the single word seemed coiled in sorrow and regret.

He'd tried to laugh it off. *I don't have to sleep in a chair to prove my love—do I?*

Of course not, she'd answered, knowing that it was a lie. *Go get Natalie. Her plane lands at nine o'clock.*

He'd jumped on the opportunity, just as she'd known he would. He'd rather be anywhere than in this cold, unfamiliar world where his wife cried all day.

She climbed out of bed and moved slowly to the window. Her stitches hurt, but she welcomed the pain. She leaned forward and pressed her forehead against the window's cold glass. Below, the parking lot was a huge gray square, dotted with a few shadowy black cars.

Finally, she turned away. She'd just gotten back into bed when the phone rang. She picked it up. "Hello?"

"Annie? It's me, Nick."

"Nick," his name came out on a whisper of longing.

"I thought you might need me."

It sounded so simple, those few little words, but they wound around her heart and squeezed. She'd spent a lifetime going through crises alone, always being the strong one, always being in control, and she hadn't realized until just now how much she yearned to be comforted.

"How is she doing?" he asked.

She ran a shaking hand through her short hair. "She's holding on. The neonatologist says she'll be okay if she can just . . . hold on another few weeks. . . ." Quietly, she began to cry again. "I'm sorry, Nick. I'm tired and scared. All I seem to do is cry."

"You want to hear a story?"

She wanted desperately to be whisked away from reality on the wings of his voice. "Yes, please . . ."

"It's about a man who started life as poor white trash, a kid who ate out of Dumpsters and lived in the backseat of an old Impala. After his mom died, the world gave this young boy a singular chance, and he moved to a soggy little town he'd never heard of, where they didn't know about his ugly past. He went to high school there, and he fell in love with two girls. One was the sun and the other was the moon. He was young, and he reached for the moon, figuring it was a safe, quiet place—and he knew that if you reached for the sun it could burn you away to nothing. When his wife died, he lost his soul. He turned his back on his child and his dreams and he crawled into a bottle of booze. All he wanted was to die, but he didn't have the guts."

"Nick, don't . . ."

"So this drunk waited for someone to end his life for him. He waited for someone to take his child away. *Then,* he thought, then he'd have the guts to kill himself. Only none of that happened, because a fairy princess came into his life. He still remembers what it was like that day, the way the rain was just starting to fall and the lake was as still as glass. He remembers everything about the day she came into his life."

"Nick, please . . ." She wanted him to stop, now, before the story spun its gossamer strands around her heart and romanced her beyond repair.

"She changed his world, this woman who wandered uninvited into his life and demanded the very best of him. Before he knew it, he had stopped drinking and he'd taken the first steps toward becoming a parent again, and he'd fallen in love—for the second and last time in his life."

"You're drowning me, Nick," she whispered brokenly.

"I don't mean to. I just wanted to let you know that you aren't alone. Love can rise above tragedy and give us a way home. You taught me that, and now you need me to remind you."

Annie's days bled one into the next in a monotonous flow of hours spent huddled alongside the incubator in a helpless, hopeless confusion. The hospital had given her a new room, so she was always close to Katie, but at night, when she lay alone on her narrow bed, she felt miles away from the people she loved.

She counted the passing of time in little things: Natalie was here on the weekends and at school during the week; Hank showed up unannounced and came daily to the hospital. Terri and Blake both visited each day after work. The clock ticked. Every day, Rosie O'Donnell showed up on the television screen in the corner of the room, and with each new segment, Annie knew that a day had passed. Thanksgiving came and went; they ate pressed turkey and canned gravy off yellow plastic trays in the frighteningly empty cafeteria.

But Annie barely noticed any of it. Sometimes, when she sat beside the incubator, Natalie became Adrian and Adrian became Katie, and in those moments, when Annie closed her eyes, she couldn't see anything except that tiny coffin draped in flowers. But then an alarm would go off, or a nurse would come in, and Annie would remember. With Katie, there was hope.

She talked to her baby constantly. *(I am sitting beside you now. Can you feel me? Can you hear my breathing? Can you feel me touching you?)*

"Mom?"

Annie wiped her eyes and glanced at the door. Natalie and Hank stood there. Her dad looked ten years older than he was.

"We brought Yahtzee," he said.

Annie smiled tiredly. It must be another week gone by; Natalie was home again. "Hey guys. How did the Psych test go, Nana?"

Natalie pulled up a chair. "That was two weeks ago, Mom, and I already told you I aced it. Remember?"

Annie sighed. She had no memory of that conversation at all. "Oh. Sorry."

Natalie and Hank sat beside the bed and started unpacking the game. They kept up a steady stream of chatter, but Annie couldn't concentrate.

All she could do was stare at the side of her bed. It was where the bassinet belonged, where they put it when the tiny, pink-swaddled baby inside of it was healthy. She remembered that the bassinet had been there with Natalie—and never with Adrian.

Hank leaned toward her, touched her cheek. "She's going to be fine, Annie. You've got to believe that."

"She's gaining weight steadily, Mom. I talked to Mona—you know, the ICU night charge nurse—and she said Katie's a champ."

Annie didn't look at either of them. "She hasn't been held yet . . . does anyone realize that but me?" It plagued her, that thought, kept her up at night. Her baby, stuck full of needles and tubes, had never felt the comfort of her mommy's arms, had never been soothed to sleep by a lullaby. . . .

"She will, Mom," Natalie said, squeezing her wrist. "She's going to be fine. Maybe—"

There was a knock at the door, and Dr. North pushed through the opening. Dr. Overton, the neonatologist, was standing beside her, wearing green surgical scrubs.

Annie's heart stopped at the sight of them. Blindly, she reached out for Natalie's hand, squeezing the slim fingers until she could feel the birdlike bones shift. Hank shot to his feet and squeezed Annie's shoulder.

"Oh, God," she whispered.

The door opened again and a stout, white-clad nurse named Helena swept into the room on a tide of rustling polyester. In her arms she held a small pink-swaddled bundle.

Dr. North came to the end of the bed. "Would you like to hold your daughter?"

"Would I—" Annie couldn't seem to draw a solid breath. She hadn't believed in this moment; hoped, yes, but she hadn't really believed. She'd been afraid to believe; afraid that if she believed and lost, she would never find the surface again.

Unable to say anything, she reached out.

The nurse moved toward her and placed her daughter in Annie's arms.

The newborn smell filled her nostrils, at once familiar and exotic. She peeled back the pink blanket and stroked her daughter's forehead, marveling at the softness of the skin.

Katie's rosebud mouth puckered and yawned, and a little pink fist shot out from the blanket. Smiling, cooing, Annie peeled back the cotton fabric and stared down at her little girl, dressed in a tiny doll's diaper. A network of blue veins crisscrossed her pale chest and dappled her thin arms and legs.

Katie opened her mouth and made an angry squeaking sound.

Annie's breasts tingled; moisture seeped through her nightgown. Quickly, she untied her gown and eased Katie toward the nipple. There was a moment of fumbling around, a few repositionings, and then Katie latched on.

"Oh, Katie," she whispered, stroking her daughter's soft, soft head, laughing quietly at the miracle of it all. "Welcome home."

The first days home were crazy. Hank and Terri hovered beside Annie, demanding to help, refusing to take no for an answer. They decorated the house for Christmas, dragging box after box from the attic and squealing as each new treasure was found. They put up a ten-foot tree in the living room and proceeded to add an obsessive number of gifts beneath it. Natalie called home between every class and asked how Katie was doing. Annie couldn't handle it all, not when all she wanted to do was stare at the miracle of her child. At last, Hank went home—but only after he vowed to return at Christmas.

Alone again, Blake and Annie tried to find their way back to the familiar routine, but it wasn't as easy as before. Annie spent all her time huddled on the sofa with Katie, and Blake spent more and more time at the office.

In the third week of December, Hank met Natalie at the San Francisco airport, and they flew down to LAX together. The family shared a tense, quiet holiday dinner that only reminded Annie of how shredded their relationships had become. Even opening the presents on Christmas morning had been a subdued affair.

Hank watched Blake every minute. Annie had heard the questions he jabbed at her husband: *Where are you going? Why won't you be home tonight? Have you spoken to Annie about that?*

Annie had known that Blake felt like a stranger in his own home. Natalie watched him warily, waiting for him to pick up Katie, but he never did. Annie understood; she'd been through it before. Blake simply wasn't one who fell head-over-heels in love with newborns. They frightened and confused him, and he was not a man who liked either emotion. But Natalie didn't understand that, and Annie saw her daughter's disappointment again and again as she handed her baby sister to their father, only to watch Blake shake his head and turn away.

Now, Annie lay huddled along the mattress's edge. Beside her, Blake was stretched out, one arm flung her way, one knee cocked against her hip, hogging the bed in his characteristic fashion. She could hear his breathing; the rhythmic score had accompanied her own sleep for so many years.

She gently peeled out of the bed and went to the French doors, opening them. Sheer white silk curtains billowed with night's breath along her bare leg.

She woke so often, alone, desperate to reach out for comfort in the darkness, but there was no comfort in her marriage. Oh, they'd tried, each of them in their own way. Him, with gifts and promises and quiet conversations about things that mattered to Annie; her, with brittle smiles and rented movies and elegant dinners for two. But it wasn't working. They were like butterflies caught on separate sides of a window, each trying with fluttered desperation to break through the glass.

With a tired sigh, Blake pushed the Dictaphone aside and shoved the depositions back into their folder. He was having trouble concentrating lately, and his work was beginning to suffer. Katie only slept a few hours at a time, and whenever she woke up, crying or whimpering, Blake couldn't get back to sleep.

He got to his feet and poured himself a scotch. Swirling the amber liquid around in the Waterford tumbler, he walked to the window and stared outside. The city was a blurry wash of January gray. A few ragged New Year's decorations swung forgotten from the streetlights.

He didn't want to go home to his strangely unfamiliar wife and his squalling newborn daughter. As he'd expected, Annie's whole existence revolved around the baby's needs. There was no time left for Blake, and when she did finally get the child to sleep, Annie stumbled blindly to bed, too exhausted for anything beyond a quick peck on the cheek and a mumbled *good night*.

He was too damned old to be a father again. He'd been no good at it when he was young, and he had even less interest now.

There was a knock at the door.

Blake set the glass down. "Come in."

The door swung open and Tom Abramson and Ted Swain, two of Blake's partners, stood in the opening. "Hey, bud—it's six-thirty," Ted said with a wicked grin. "What do you say we head on down to the bar and celebrate the Martinson decision?"

Blake knew he should say no. In the back of his mind was the thought that he had something to do at home, but he couldn't for the life of him remember what it was.

"Sure," he said, reaching for his coat. "But just one. I have to get home."

"No problem," Tommy said. "We've all got families."

It was true, of course. All three of them had wives and children at home, waiting for them. But somehow they were still at the bar at eleven o'clock that night, laughing and shouting and clanking toasts.

Ted went home at eleven-thirty, and Tom followed him out. That left Blake, sitting alone on the bar stool. He'd told his friends that he wanted to finish his drink, but the truth was, he'd been nursing the same cocktail for about an hour. He kept looking at the door, thinking, *I should go;* then he'd think of that big bed at home, and the way his wife slept huddled along the mattress's edge, and he stayed where he was.

Annie had set the table beautifully. Candlelight flickered above the Battenberg lace cloth, casting slippery shadows on the sterling silver dishes that held all of Natalie's favorite dishes: homemade macaroni and cheese, hot crescent rolls with honey and butter, and corn on the cob. There was a small stack of multicolored, foil-wrapped presents at one end of the table, and bright, helium-filled balloons were tied above each chair.

Tonight was Natalie's eighteenth birthday party, and they were all coming together to celebrate. Annie was determined to fit this family back into its groove, at least for these few hours.

Annie glanced once again at the table, her critical eye missing no detail. Hank came up beside her, put an arm around her shoulder and drew her close. Through the open archway to the kitchen, they could hear Natalie and Terri laughing. Annie leaned against her dad. "I'm glad you could come down for the holidays, Dad. It means a lot to Natalie and me."

"I wouldn't miss it for the world." He glanced around. "So, where's that busy husband of yours? We're ready to party."

"He's only fifteen minutes late. For Blake, that's nothing. I told him six-thirty so he'd be here by seven."

Slowly, Hank withdrew his arm. Turning slightly, he went to the window that overlooked the driveway.

She followed him. "Dad?"

It was a full minute before he spoke, and then his voice was softer than she'd ever heard it. "When you first brought Blake home, I was impressed. Sure, he was young and skinny and poor, but I could see the man emerging inside him. He was what every father dreams of for his daughter, intelligent and ambitious. Not like the boys I knew in Mystic. I thought to myself, now here's a boy who will take care of my little girl—"

"I know the story, Dad. . . ."

He turned to her. "I was wrong, wasn't I?"

She frowned. "What do you mean?"

"What you'd brought home was just someone else for you to take care of." He frowned. "I should have worried about your heart instead of your financial comfort. If your mother had been alive . . . she would have known what to look for. It's just that I wanted you to have better than I could give you."

"I know, Dad."

"It . . ." His voice trembled and he wouldn't meet her gaze. "It hurts me to see how you are now. Last spring you were so happy. I miss hearing you laugh. I think . . . when you were in Mystic, I gave you some bad advice. Hell, I gave you bad advice your whole life. I should have told you that you'd make a wonderful bookseller. I should have been telling you that kind of thing for years." He turned to her at last. "I should have told you that you were the smartest, most talented, most incredibly gifted person I've ever known . . . and that I was proud of you. That's what your mama would have said."

"Oh, Daddy . . ." Annie knew that if she tried to say anything more, she'd start to cry.

"A dad . . . he teaches responsibility and accountability, but a mom . . . ah, a mom teaches her child to dream, to reach for the stars and to believe in fairy tales. At least, that's what Sarah would have given you. But me? What does an uneducated old millworker like me know about fairy tales and possibilities and dreams?" He sighed, and when he looked at her there were tears in his eyes. "I wish I had it to do over again, Annie Virginia. . . ."

She stepped into her father's big, strong arms and clung to him. "I love you, Dad," she whispered against his warm neck.

When she finally drew back, her mascara was running down her face. She grinned. "I must look like something out of the *Rocky Horror Picture Show.* I'd better run to the bathroom and freshen up."

She spun away and hurried through the kitchen. She passed Terri and Natalie, who were busy arranging candles on the cake.

Natalie looked up. "Are you okay?"

Annie nodded. "Fine. My mascara is bothering me."

"Is Dad home yet?"

"I'm going to try his car phone right now. He's probably pulling up the driveway."

Above Natalie's head, Terri shot Annie an irritated look. Annie shrugged helplessly and went to the phone, punching in Blake's cellular number. It didn't even ring; it just patched her through to his voice mail.

Annie turned, faced their expectant looks. "He's not in the car."

They waited another forty minutes for Blake, and then by tacit consent, they started the party without him. They came together at the table, the adults talking furiously to cover the awkwardness and disappointment. Still, the empty chair at the head of the table couldn't be ignored.

Annie forced a bright smile all through the meal. Terri regaled them with funny anecdotes about life on the soaps—and death in the air—

until everyone was laughing. After dinner, they sat around the fireplace and opened gifts.

At ten o'clock, Terri reluctantly went home. She hugged Natalie tightly, then held Annie's hand as they walked to the front door. "He's a real shithead," she whispered furiously.

There was no point in answering. Annie hugged her friend and said good-bye, and then walked slowly back to the living room.

Hank rose immediately. "I think I'll go to bed. Us old guys need our beauty sleep." He squeezed Natalie's shoulder and bent to kiss her cheek. "Happy birthday, honey." Straightening, he threw Annie a frustrated look and strode from the room.

Silence fell.

Natalie went to the window. Annie came up beside her. "I'm sorry, Nana. I wish I could change it."

"I don't know why I keep expecting him to be different. . . ."

"He loves you. It's just . . ." Words failed Annie. She'd said the same tired thing too many times and she couldn't even pretend tonight that it made a difference.

She turned to Annie. "What good does his love do me?"

The softly spoken question raised a red, stinging welt on Annie's heart. "It's his loss, Natalie."

Natalie's eyes filled slowly, heartbreakingly, with tears. "When I was a little girl, I used to pretend that he wasn't my real dad. Did you know that?"

"Oh, Nana . . ."

"Why do you stay with him?"

Annie sighed. She wasn't up to this conversation. Not tonight. "You're young and passionate, honey. Some day you'll understand. Obligations and commitments build up around you—sort of like plaque. You have to do the right thing. I have other people to think about."

Natalie snorted. "I may be young and passionate, but you're naive, Mom. You always have been. Sometimes *I* feel like the grown-up around you. You always think everything will work out for the best."

"I used to think that. Not so much anymore."

Natalie's gaze was solemn. "You should have heard yourself last spring, Mom. You sounded so . . . happy. Now, I know why. He wasn't around, making you jump every time he came into the room and scurry around to do his bidding."

It took Annie a second to find her voice, and when she did it was soft and hurting. "Is that how you see me?"

"I see you for who you are, Mom. Someone who loves with all her heart and will do anything to make us happy. But last spring, something made *you* happy."

Annie swallowed past the lump in her throat. She turned away, before Natalie could see the moisture gathering in her eyes.

"Tell me about Izzy. I bet you fixed her right up."

"Izzy." Although Annie knew it was opening the door on her pain, she let herself remember. Her thoughts scrolled back to the garden, to a handful of straggling shasta daisies, and a small, black-gloved hand. "She was something, Natalie. You would have loved her."

"And what about him?"

Annie turned slowly back to Natalie. "Who?"

"Izzy's dad."

"He's an old friend of mine from high school." Annie could hear the way her voice softened, and though she knew it was dangerous, she couldn't change it. She smiled at a memory. "He was the first boy I ever kissed."

"There it is again, Mom."

Annie frowned. "There's what?"

"That voice. It's the way you sounded while I was in London. Is he part of what made you happy, Mom?"

Annie felt vulnerable and exposed, a woman walking out a thin, rickety bridge. She couldn't tell her daughter the truth. Perhaps some-day, when the bridge of their years had brought Natalie to full woman-hood, when she'd seen something more of life and love. When she could understand. "A lot of things made me happy in Mystic."

It was a long minute before Natalie spoke. "Maybe he and Izzy can come down here some time. Or maybe you and I can visit them."

"No," Annie said softly. She wanted to say something more, tack an excuse onto the simple word that seemed to make no sense. But she couldn't manage it. Instead, she pulled Natalie into her arms and squeezed tightly. "I'm sorry your dad forgot your birthday."

Natalie sniffled. "You're the one I feel sorry for."

"How come?"

"In eighteen years you'll be saying the same thing to Katie."

CHAPTER 28

Some time around midnight, a woman walked up to Blake. She was wearing a skin-tight black catsuit with a huge silver belt and black stiletto heels. With an easy smile, she sat down next to him. She tapped a long fingernail on the bar. "Vodka martini—two olives," she said to the bartender.

In the background, a throaty Dwight Yoakam song came on, something about the pocket of a clown.

The woman turned to him. Nibbling on her olive, she asked him to dance.

Blake pushed off the bar stool and stumbled back from her, putting as much distance as he could between them. "Sorry," he mumbled. "I'm married."

But he didn't turn away; he couldn't. He stood there like a man possessed, staring at the woman. He couldn't help wondering how those breasts would feel in his hands—the young, solid breasts of a woman who'd never had children, the small, pink nipples that had never nursed a baby.

At that, Blake felt something inside him shift and give way. He realized the truth, the one he'd been denying for months. He loved Annie, but it wasn't enough. He'd cheat on her. Maybe not tonight, maybe not even this year; but sooner or later, he'd slide back into his old routine. It was only a matter of time.

And when he did, he would be lost again. There was nothing on earth lonelier than a man who betrayed his wife on a regular basis. Blake knew how seductive it was—the temptation to possess a stranger, make love in the middle of the night with a nameless woman. But afterward, it left him broken somehow, ashamed of himself and unable to meet his wife's gaze.

Shaken, he turned away from the woman in the catsuit and left the bar. He drove home and parked in the garage. Tiredly, he went into the dark, cool house. Without bothering to flick on any lights, he headed through the kitchen.

He found Annie waiting for him in the living room. She was sitting on the sofa, with her feet tucked up underneath her. "Hello, Blake," she said in a soft, tired voice that seemed to cut through his heart.

He stopped dead. For no reason at all, he thought she'd seen him tonight, that she knew what he'd almost done. "Hey, Annie," he said, forcing a smile.

"You're late."

"A bunch of us went to the sports bar on Fourth. We won a big settle—"

"It was Natalie's birthday party tonight."

Blake winced. "Oh. *Shit.* I forgot to mark it on my office calendar."

"I'm sure she'll love that answer."

"You should have called to remind me."

"Don't turn it on me, Blake. You're the one who screwed up. You can remember when a client owes an alimony check, but you forget your daughter's eighteenth birthday." She sighed. "You should go see her now—I'll bet she's still awake."

"She's probably tired . . ."

"She deserves an explanation."

He turned and moved to the elegant stone table that hugged the wall, staring at his own reflection in a gilt-framed mirror. "Natalie's angry with me," he said softly. "When she was in London, I didn't call her. I sent flowers every week. A girl loves to get flowers, that's what Suz . . ." he realized what he was going to say and clamped his mouth shut.

"Suzannah was wrong," Annie said tiredly, reading his thoughts. "A seventeen-year-old girl needs a lot more than flowers from her father's secretary every Friday."

He ran a hand through his hair. "Without you, I was . . . lost with Natalie. I kept thinking I should call, and then a deposition or a court date would come up, and I'd forget. I'll make it all up to her, though, even tonight."

He turned back to Annie. Now she was on her feet. She stood a few feet away, her arms crossed. In a pair of ratty sweats and a UW sweatshirt that had seen better days, she looked more like a runaway teen than his wife. "I'll get her a laptop."

"She'll be leaving for school on Sunday. We won't see her again until spring break, and soon . . . we won't be seeing much of her at all. She'll find her own place in the world and she won't be coming home to us as much."

Us. He tried to take courage from that single, simple word, but he couldn't quite manage it. "So, what do I say to her?"

"I don't know."

"Of course you do. You always—"

"No more. If you're going to forge a relationship with your daughter, it's up to you. No more Cliffs Notes on the situation from me."

"Come on—"

"Who's her boyfriend, Blake?"

"She doesn't have one."

"Really? That will come as something of a surprise to Brian. And what does she want to study in school?"

It was hard to think with her looking at him that way. "Law, like me. She wants to be a partner in the firm some day."

"Really? When did you last discuss it?"

"Last year?" It came out as a question, and at her look, he knew it was wrong. "Two years ago?"

"Really?"

She kept throwing that word at him like a dart. He felt like a man reaching for a lifeline that was just beyond his grasp. At last he gave up trying to lie and told the truth. "I don't know."

Annie's face softened at the admission. "You have to talk to her, Blake. But mostly you have to listen." She gave him a smile that was as sad as it was familiar. "And we both know you're listening-impaired."

"Okay. I'll go talk to her."

He said the words, softly and in exactly the right tone of voice, but they both knew the truth. They'd had this same discussion a hundred times before, with Annie begging him to spend time with Natalie.

They both knew he'd never quite get around to doing it.

On the last day of January, Terri showed up bright and early, holding a bottle of Moët & Chandon and a bag of croissants. "When a woman turns forty," she said brightly, "she should begin drinking early in the day. And before you start whining about nursing and alcohol in the breast milk, let me reassure you that the champagne is for me and the croissants are for you."

They sat together on the big wooden deck. The hot tub bubbled gently beside them.

"So," Terri said, sipping her champagne. "You look like shit, you know."

"Thanks a lot. I hope you'll come by to celebrate my fiftieth birthday—when I *really* need cheering up."

"You're not sleeping."

Annie winced. It was true. She hadn't slept well in weeks. "Katie's been fighting a cold."

"Ah," Terri said knowingly, "so Katie's the problem."

"No . . . not really, Dr. Freud." Annie glanced out at the glittering surface of the sea, watching the white-tipped waves lick gently at the sand. She didn't have to close her eyes to see another place, a place where winters were real. There, nature would have reclaimed its rain forest. The tourists would be long gone, driven away by the swift and sudden darkness that came with winter. There would be alpine mountainsides where the snow was five feet deep, where tiny purple flowers would still bloom amid the whiteness, against all the laws of nature. Deep in the woods, where the land had never been damaged by human hands, the trees would seem to draw closer together, creating a curtain of black tinged only occasionally with the faintest hint of green. In the middle of the day, it would be dark, and not even the brightest winter sun would make it to the cold, frosted forest floor. Anyone crazy enough, or desperate enough, to venture into that gray and black wilderness this time of year would be lost forever.

Annie longed to see it now, to feel the crisp winter air on her cheeks. She wanted to bundle up in layers and layers of clothing and lie in the snow, to make angels with her arms and legs while she watched her breath puff into the silver air.

"Why do you stay with him?"

Annie sighed. She had known the question was coming; she'd expected it every day since the fiasco of Natalie's birthday party. It was the same thing she asked herself at night, as she lay in her bed, beside her husband, unable to sleep.

She thought so often about Natalie, grown now and on her own, and Katie, with so many years before her. At those times, achingly lonely, she would stare into the darkness of her own life, searching for some dim reflection of herself. And when she looked back, she saw a skinny, brown-haired girl who'd done what was expected of her, always.

She missed the woman she'd become on the shores of Mystic Lake, the one who dared to dream of her own bookstore, and learned to wager her heart on a game as risky as love. She missed Nick and Izzy and the family they'd quilted together from the scraps of their separate lives.

It was the kind of family Annie had always dreamed of . . . the kind of family Katie deserved. . . .

Did you know I have no memories of Dad?

Terri touched her shoulder. "Annie? You're crying. . . ."

She'd been holding it in for too long, pretending that everything was okay, pretending that everyone mattered but her. She couldn't hold it in anymore.

"I matter," she said quietly.

"Well, praise God," Terri whispered and pulled Annie into her arms. Annie let herself be held and rocked by her best friend.

"I can't live this way anymore."

"Of course you can't."

Annie eased back, shakily pushing the grown-out hair away from her eyes. "I don't want some day to hear Katie tell me that she has no memories of her dad, either."

"And what about *you, Annie?*"

"I deserve more than this . . . Blake and I don't share anything anymore. Not even the miracle of our two children."

It was the truth she'd been avoiding all these months. Their love was gone, simply gone, extinguished as cleanly as candlelight, with the sooty scent of smoke the only reminder that it had ever burned at all. She couldn't even remember those days, long ago, when they had been in love.

She couldn't help grieving for the loss of that fire, and she was as much to blame as he. She'd spent a lifetime in the shadows, too afraid of failure or abandonment to reach for even the light of a single candle. Their marriage was what they together had created—and that was the saddest truth of all.

Blake wasn't happy, either. Of that she had no doubt. He wasn't ready to let go of Annie quite yet, but the Annie he wanted was Annalise Bourne Colwater, the woman she'd become after years and years of living in a rut of their combined creation.

He wanted back what couldn't be had.

Faint strains of music came from the bedroom speakers. Blake stood in front of the baby's bassinet, staring down at the tiny infant swaddled in pink.

He reached into his pocket and withdrew a slim black velvet box. His finger traced the soft fabric as he remembered a dozen gifts he'd given Annie in the past, presents on Christmas mornings, on anniversaries, on birthdays.

Always, he'd given her what he thought she should have. Like her wedding ring. On their tenth anniversary he'd bought her the three-carat diamond solitaire, not because she wanted it—Annie was perfectly happy with the gold band they'd bought when it was all they could afford—but because it made Blake look good. Everyone who saw his wife's ring knew that Blake was a successful, wealthy man.

He'd never given her what she needed, what she wanted. He'd never given her himself.

"Blake?"

At the sound of her voice, soft and tentative, he turned around. She stood in the open archway, wearing a beautiful blue silk robe he'd given her years ago, and she looked incredibly lovely.

"We need to talk," she said.

Steeling himself, he moved toward her. "I know."

She stared up at him, and for a second, all he wanted to do was hold her so tightly that she could never leave him again. But he'd learned that holding too tightly was as harmful as never reaching out at all. "I have something for you. A birthday present." He held the box out to her. It lay in his palm like a black wound.

Tentatively, still staring up at him, she took the box and opened it. On a bed of ice-blue silk lay a glittering gold bracelet. The name *Annie* was engraved across the top.

"Oh, Blake," she whispered, biting down on her lower lip.

"Turn it over," he said.

She eased the bracelet from the box, and he saw that her hands were trembling as she turned it over and read the inscription on the underside.

I will always love you.

She looked up at him, her eyes moist. "It's not going to work, Blake. It's too late."

"I know," he whispered, hearing the unmanly catch in his voice and not caring. Maybe if he'd cared less about things like that in the past, he wouldn't be standing here, saying good-bye to the only woman who'd ever truly loved him. "I wish . . ." He didn't even know what he wished for. That she had been different? That he had? That they'd seen this truth a long time ago?

"Me, too," she answered.

"Will you . . . remember the words on that bracelet?"

"Oh, Blake, I don't need a bracelet to remember how much I loved you. You were my life for more than twenty years. Whenever I look back, I'll think of you." Tears streaked in silvery lines down her cheeks. "What about Katie?"

"I'll support her, of course. . . ."

He could tell that she was hurt by his answer. "I don't mean money."

He moved toward her, touched her cheek. He knew what she wanted from him right now, but it wasn't really in his power to give. It never had been, that was part of their problem. He wouldn't be there for Katie, any more than he'd been there for Natalie. Suddenly, he grieved for all of it. For the good times and the bad, for the roads not taken and the lives that had carelessly grown apart. Sadly, he gazed down at her. "Do you want me to lie to you?"

She shook her head. "No."

Slowly, he pulled her into his arms. He held her close, knowing he'd carry this image in his heart for as long as he lived. "I guess it's really over," he whispered into her sweet-smelling hair. After a long moment, he heard her answer, a quiet, shuddering little, "Yes."

Natalie's dorm room was cluttered with memorabilia from London. Pictures of new friends dotted her desk, mingled with family photos and piles of homework. The metal-framed twin bed was heaped with expensive Laura Ashley bedding, and at the center was the pink pillow Annie had embroidered a lifetime ago, the one that read: A PRINCESS SLEEPS HERE.

Natalie sat cross-legged on the bed, her long, unbound hair flowing around her shoulders. Already she looked nervous and worried—a normal teenage response to *both* parents flying up to see you at college.

Annie wished there were some way to break the news of their divorce without words, a way to silently communicate the sad and wrenching truth.

Blake stood in the corner of the room. He looked calm and at ease—his courtroom face—but Annie could see nervousness in the jittery way he kept glancing at his watch.

Annie knew this was up to her; there was no use putting it off any longer. She went to the bed and sat down beside Natalie. Blake took a few hesitant steps toward them and then stopped in the middle of the room.

Natalie looked at Annie. "What is it, Mom?"

"Your dad and I have something to tell you." She took Natalie's hand in hers, stared down at the slender fingers, at the tiny red birthstone ring they'd given her on her sixteenth birthday. It took an effort to sit straight-backed and still. She took a deep breath and plunged ahead. "Your dad and I are getting a divorce."

Natalie went very still. "I guess I'm not surprised." Her voice was tender, and in it, Annie heard the echo of both the child Natalie had once been and the woman she was becoming.

Annie stroked her daughter's hair, untangling it with her fingers like she used to when Natalie was little. "I'm sorry, honey."

When Natalie looked up, there were tears in her eyes. "Are you okay, Mom?"

Annie felt a warm rush of pride for her daughter. "I'm fine, and I don't want you to worry about anything. We haven't worked out all the details yet. We don't know where we'll each be living. Things like addresses and vacations and holidays are all up in the air. But I know one thing. We'll always be a family—just a different kind. I guess now you'll have two places in the world where you belong, instead of only one."

Natalie nodded slowly, then turned to her father.

Blake moved closer, kneeling in front of Natalie. For once, he didn't look like a three-hundred-fifty-dollar-an-hour lawyer. He looked like a scared, vulnerable man. "I've made some mistakes. . . ." He glanced at Annie and gave her a hesitant smile, then turned back to Natalie. "With your mom and with you. I'm sorry, Sweet Pea." He touched her cheek.

Tears leaked from Natalie's eyes. "You haven't called me that since I fell off the jungle gym in third grade."

"There are a lot of things I haven't said—or done—in years. But I want to make up for lost time. I want to do things together—if that's okay with you."

"*Phantom of the Opera* is coming to town in May. Maybe we could go?"

He smiled. "I'd love to."

"You mean it this time? I should buy two tickets?"

"I mean it," he said, and the way he said it, Annie believed him. Of course, she always believed him.

Slowly, Blake got to his feet and drew back.

"We're still going to be a family," Annie said, tucking a flyaway strand of hair behind Natalie's ear. "We'll always be a family." She looked at Blake and smiled.

It was true. Blake would always be a part of her, always be her youth. They'd grown up together, fallen in love and built a family together; nothing would ever erase that connection. A piece of paper and a court of law couldn't take it all away—it could only take what they were willing to give up, and Annie was going to hold on to all of it, the good, the bad, the in-between. It was part of them. It made them who they were.

She reached out. He took her hand in his, and together they drew around Natalie, enfolding her in their arms. When Natalie was little, they'd called this a "family hug," and Annie couldn't help wondering why they'd ever stopped.

She heard the soft, muffled sound of her daughter's crying and knew it was one of the regrets that would be with her always.

It was like going back in time. Once again, Annie and Blake were strolling through the Stanford campus. Of course, this time Annie was forty years old and as much of her life lay behind her as lay ahead . . . and she was pushing a stroller.

"It's weird to be back here," Blake said.

"Yeah," she said softly.

They'd spent the whole day with Natalie, being more of a family in one afternoon than they'd been in many of the previous years, but now it was time to go their separate ways. Annie had driven the

Cadillac up here, and Blake had flown in, renting a car to get to the campus.

At Annie's car, they stopped. Annie bent down and unstrapped Katie from the stroller.

"What will you do now?" he asked.

Annie paused. It was the same question he'd asked her when Natalie had left home last spring. Then, it had terrified her. Now, these many months later, the same words opened a door, through which Annie glimpsed a world of possibilities. "I don't know. I still have tons to do at the house. Twenty years has to be sorted and catalogued and packed away. I know I want to sell the house. It's not . . . me anymore." She straightened, looking at him. "Unless you want it?"

"Without you? No."

Annie glanced around, a little uncertain as to what to say. This was the fork in the road of their lives; after all these years, he would go one way and she another. She had no idea when she would see him again. Probably at the lawyer's office, where they'd become a cliché—a cordial, once-married couple coming in as separate individuals to sign papers. . . .

Blake stared down at her. There was a faraway sadness in his eyes that made her move closer to him. In a soft voice, he asked, "What will you tell Katie about me?"

Annie heard the pain in his voice, and it moved her to touch his cheek. "I don't know. The old me would have fabricated an elaborate fiction to avoid hurting her feelings." She laughed. "Maybe I'd have told her you were a spy for the government and contacting us would endanger your life. But now . . . I don't know. I guess I'll cross that bridge when I come to it. But I won't lie to her."

He turned his head and looked away. She wondered what he was thinking, whether it was about lying, and how much it had cost him over the years. Or if it was about the daughter he had lived with for eighteen years and didn't know, or the daughter he'd hardly lived with at all, and now would never know. Or if it was the future, all the days that lay ahead for a man alone, the quiet of a life that included no child's laughter. She wondered if he'd realized yet that when he was an old, old man, when his hair had turned white and his eyes had grown coated with cataracts, that he would have no grandchildren to bounce on his knee, no daughter to kneel in the grass beside his wheelchair and reminisce about the time-worn antics of the past. Unless he reached out now, in the days that mattered, he would learn that some roads could not be refound and that true love took time and effort . . . that a life lived in the glare of summer sunlight never produced a rainbow.

"Will you miss me?" he asked, finally looking at her again.

Annie gave him a sad smile. "I'll miss who we used to be—I already do. And I'll miss who we could have been."

His eyes filled slowly with tears. "I love you, Annie."

"I'll always love the boy I fell in love with, Blake. Always . . ."

She moved toward him, pressing up on her toes to kiss him. It was the kind of kiss they hadn't shared in years; slow, and tender, and heartfelt. There was no undercurrent of sexuality in it. It was everything a kiss was supposed to be, an expression of pure emotion—and they had let it go so easily in their life together. She couldn't remember when kisses had become something perfunctory and meaningless. Maybe if they had kissed this way every day, they wouldn't be here now, standing together in the middle of the Stanford campus, saying good-bye to a commitment that had been designed to last forever.

When Blake drew back, he looked sad and tired. "I guess I screwed up pretty badly."

"You'll get another chance, Blake. Men like you always do. You're handsome and rich; women will stand in line to give you another chance. What you do with that chance is up to you."

He ran a hand through his hair and looked away. "Hell, Annie. We both know I'll screw that up, too."

She laughed. "Probably."

They stared at each other for a long minute, and in that time, Annie saw the arc of their love; the bright and shining beginning of it, all those years ago, and the way it had eroded, one lonely night at a time for years.

Finally, Blake checked his watch. "I have to go. My plane leaves at six o'clock." He bent down to the stroller and gave Katie a last, fleeting kiss. When he drew back up, he gave Annie a weak smile. "This is hard. . . ."

She hugged him, one last time, then slowly she drew back. "Have a safe flight."

He nodded and turned away from her. He got into his rented car and drove away.

She stood there watching him until the car disappeared. She had expected to feel weighed down by sadness at this moment, but instead she felt almost buoyant. Last week she had done what she'd never thought she could do: she'd traveled alone. Just for fun. She'd given Katie to Terri for the day—complete with two sheets of instructions and a shelf full of expressed milk—and then Annie had just started to drive. Before she'd even realized where she was going, she'd arrived at the Mexican border. A flash of fear had almost stopped her as the rickety red bus pulled up to the curb, but she hadn't let it own her. She'd boarded the bus with all the other tourists and ridden into Mexico. All by herself.

The day had been wonderful, magical. She'd walked down the dingy, overcrowded streets, eating *churros* from the stands along the way. At lunchtime, she'd found a seat at a restaurant and eaten unrecognizable food and loved every bite, and as night had begun to fall and the neon sputtered to life, she'd understood why she'd always been afraid of traveling alone. It changed a person somehow—wasn't that the point, after all? To go to a wildly different place and learn that you could negotiate for a silly trinket in a foreign language, and then to hold that item a little closer to your heart because it represented something of your self. Each peso she'd saved had somehow become an expression of how far she'd come. And when she finally had returned home that night, dragging her tired body up the stairs, snuggling up with her cranky daughter in her big king-size bed, she'd known that finally, at forty years of age, she had begun.

"Come on, Katie Sarah. Let's go." She picked up her almost-sleeping daughter and strapped her into the car seat in the back of the Cadillac.

Then, throwing her clunky diaper bag onto the passenger seat, she climbed into the car and started the engine. Before she even pulled out, she flicked on the radio and found a station she liked. Humming along with Mick Jagger, she maneuvered onto the highway and nudged the engine to seventy miles per hour.

What will you do now?

She still had months of responsibilities in Southern California. Closing and selling the house, packing everything up, deciding where she wanted to live and what she wanted to do. She didn't have to work, of course, but she didn't want to fall into that life-of-leisure trap again. She *needed* to work.

She thought again about the bookstore in Mystic. She certainly had the capital to give it a try—and that Victorian house on Main Street had plenty of room for living upstairs. She and Katie could be very comfortable up there, just the two of them.

Mystic.

Nick. Izzy.

The love she felt for them was as sharp as broken glass. Sometimes, when she woke in the middle of the night, she reached out for Nick— only he wasn't there, and in those quiet moments the missing of him was an actual pain in her chest.

She knew she would go to him again when her life was in order; she had planned it endlessly in the past few weeks.

She would buy herself a convertible and drive up Highway 101 along the wild beaches, with her hair whipping about her face. She would play show tunes and sing at the top of her lungs, free at last to do as she pleased. She would drive when the sun was high in the sky and keep going as the stars began to shimmer overhead. She would show up without warning and hope it was not too late.

It would be springtime when she went to him, in that magical week when change was in the air, when everything smelled fresh and new.

She would show up on his porch one day, wearing a bright yellow rain slicker that covered most of her face. It would take her a minute to reach for the doorbell; the memories would be so strong, she'd want to wallow in them. In her arms would be Katie, almost crawling by now, wearing a fuzzy blue snowsuit—one they'd bought just for Mystic.

And when he opened the door, she would tell him that in all the long months they'd been apart, she'd found herself falling, and falling, and there'd been no one there to catch her. . . .

Ahead, the road merged onto the interstate. Two green highway signs slashed against the steel-gray sky. There were two choices: I-5 South. I-5 North.

No.

It was crazy, what she was thinking. She wasn't ready. She had oceans of commitments in California, and not even a toothbrush in her diaper bag. It was winter in Mystic, cold and gray and wet, and she was wearing silk. . . .

South was Los Angeles—and a beautiful white house by the sea that held the stale leftovers of her old life.

North was Mystic—and in Mystic was a man and a child who loved her. Once, she had taken love for granted. Never again. Love was the sun and the moon and the stars in a world that was otherwise cold and dark.

Nick had known that. It was one of the last things he'd said to her: *You're wrong, Annie. Love matters. Maybe it's the only thing that does.*

She glanced in the rearview mirror at her daughter, who was almost asleep. "Listen to me, Kathleen Sarah. I'm going to give you lesson number one in the Annalise Bourne Colwater book of life. I may not know everything, but I'm forty years old and I know plenty, so pay attention. Sometimes you have to do everything right and follow the rules. You have to wait until all your ducks are in a row before you make a move." She grinned. "And other times . . . like now . . . you have to say 'what the hell' and go for it."

Laughing out loud, Annie flicked on her turn signal, changed lanes—

And headed north.

ABOUT THE AUTHOR

Kristin Hannah practiced entertainment and antitrust law before becoming a full-time writer. She is the award-winning, best-selling author of eight novels. Her 1996 novel, *Home Again,* was named a Best Book of the Year by both *Publishers Weekly* and *Library Journal.* She lives in a small town in the Pacific Northwest with her husband and son.

FIC
HAN

Hannah, Kristin.

On mystic lake.

$19.95

		DATE	